THE DEMON HUNTER SAGA

Cynthia Vespia

"Every legend begins with a story...
Every great story starts with a hero."

Acknowledgements:

Authors always say their novels are a labor of love. And at the risk of sounding cliché I have to say the same. Since the initial idea stuck in my head Demon Hunter grew out of passion. I love this story as one of my very favorites.

Ironically, given the theme, getting it into print form literally took going through hell and back. In the midst of that some people stood by me to help and encourage the vision that you finally see before you. So a big hug and thank you goes out to my supporters.

A lot of the training depicted within Demon Hunter was inspired by my boys Ray and Blaze, my mentors and brothers. I learned much from you both and I know you always have my back. My family who drives me crazy sometimes but I can always turn to and bounce ideas off them. And my true friends who have stood by me (some for years) and kept the fun in my life grounded me with sanity in rough tides, and reminded me I had a gift worth sharing. And to my fellow writers who have inspired me since I was eight years old. Keep painting pictures with your words!

Much love and respect to all.

Reviews for the Demon Hunter Saga

“Vespia's DEMON HUNTER: THE CHOSEN ONE turned out to be more like a classic re-telling of Conan with a bit of Doug Clegg's "Priest of Blood" series thrown in. Vespia's tale of a 16 year-old hunter named Costa Calabrese is chock-full of action, demons, shapeshifters, and vampires (who are thankfully vicious bloodsuckers, NOT "Twilight-ish" crybabies). What follows is standard sword & sorcery fare, although Vespia's fine writing keeps the pages flipping.”- NICK CATO, Author of “Don of the Dead”

“This novel had a unique taste, a mixture between The Odyssey and Gulliver’s Travels. I thoroughly enjoyed reading each word, each blow, and each reaction. Costa and the people he meets during his journey help him to grow and balance the demons inside him and outside. It’s a great fantasy novel for anyone who wanted to be a hero, who knew there was something inside them, and who never knew they needed help all along.” - BITTEN BY BOOKS

“For fans of dark fantasy, this book is a must read. It has all the qualities dark fiction readers could want: adventure; mystery; demons; werewolves; vampires and more. A truly good, old fashioned legend and lore adventure novel that leaves readers thirsting for the sequel.” - WRITING TO BE READ

"Loved it! Your writing reminded me of Stephen King's last book. From Chapter Five on, the fast pace had me totally mesmerized. High adventure, steamy love affair, deception, demons, vampires, werewolves, zombies and even Satan himself. Thanks for the exciting ride!" -Lynne Tierney, Author of Going to Extremes

"SEEK & DESTROY is a wonderful adventure that will satisfy those who enjoy vampires, demons and human foibles on center stage. Ms. Vespia is a masterful storyteller and she weaves a magical spell around you as you read her stories." - Love Romances and More

A fast paced, thriller with surprises at every turn, I found this book difficult to put down once I started reading. If you enjoy an action adventure story with a dark edge and lots of supernatural creatures you will certainly enjoy Demon Hunter: Seek and Destroy." – FICTION VIXEN

Demon Hunter: Saga

ISBN: 978-0-578-12841-2

Released in the United States of America

Original Editor: Pat Sager

Cover Photos: Dmitrijs Bindemanis via Shutterstock.com

Additional Cover Manipulation: Original Cyn Advertising

The Chosen One

Beware

"There are things in this world filled with such evil that the earth turns black upon their footsteps. They would hollow out your eyes and eat you alive. I hunt these creatures not for bounty but to destroy them, rid the scourge from the earth before the unsuspecting lot are murdered in their beds and slaughtered like sheep in the night. I did not choose this path, it chose me, but I embrace it. The beings I hunt are more dangerous than any man that lives...I am a hunter of demons."

Prologue

It was morning as pitch black as a moonless night. Ravenwood had succumbed to many storms over the past week. The sun had retreated behind silver-black clouds leaving the world below in a perpetual state of twilight.

A cloaked figure was moving with much effort over the paved cobblestone paths linking each of Ravenwood's quarters. A heavy rain took him by surprise, dampening his robes and pressing them to his skin. He pressed on with haste, making his way safely inside.

With a wave of his hand the room came alive with illumination. Four lighted candles hovered over two cushions upon the floor. The figure relinquished his hooded robes to reveal a mane of white hair and crystal eyes stricken with blindness.

He settled upon the cushion farthest from the door, legs crossed beneath his body, and waited. Moments later the rusted hinges of the door announced the arrival of a guest. A young man entered. He was tall and broad shouldered. Dirty-blonde hair fell loose across his shoulders.

A dark cloak hugged his body, moist patches showing where the rain had come upon him. He settled on the cushion across from the older man and bowed his head.

"Are you ready to begin?" the older man asked, his voice a soft whisper on the air.

"Yes, mentor," the younger man replied.

"So where is the lesson in all of this?"

"Must there be a lesson in all things?"

"You've journeyed a long way, my young apprentice...physically, mentally, emotionally, spiritually. Surely there was something of significance which presented itself to you along the way."

A long, heavy silence crept over the room. It was full of quiet thought. Finally, having prepared his answer the young man spoke:

"It was a lesson of growth, mentor."

The older man leaned forward resting his chin atop fisted hands. His sightless eyes were brought alive by the flicker of candle-light. He saw more of what was in front of him than if he had his actual sight. He offered up his request in a dry rasp of a whisper:

"Tell me your tale, Costa."

There was a moment's hesitation as Costa sought his words, then he began:

"I'd been living a bleak life with a blackened soul tormenting a troubled mind. I cursed the Gods daily because of my fate, longing for someone or something to silence the cry of my restless heart. Often in life people cross our paths to help us on our journey. It was a hunter of demons who would answer my plea...."

Chapter One
Life Lessons

A hard swallow gulping down my throat is about as much noise as I could make at the moment, and even that proved too disturbing to my ears. The still of the morning air had been marred by the presence of another but the distinctive snap of dry twigs under weighted feet told me nail-down boots or sandals were coming in my direction. I dared not give him any advantage.

Life had always been a strange dichotomy of choice – peril or pleasure? I'd known the choices well before setting out into the depths of Muir Woods. These kinds of thoughts were an ingrained part of my being. Light and dark, good and evil, Heaven and Hell, I'd always merged both sides as one. So, in my mind, peril was my pleasure.

Squatting on my haunches, knee-deep in the flat of a blackberry bush, I'd come to realize an important fact: I hunted danger – anything making me feel alive. So, while my tense body gave rise to slick palms and a racing heart, I secretly embraced it. I longed for danger to face me and stare me down with its cold inkling of death.

I had reached my 16th year. I already embodied a lifetime's worth of adventure and excitement. Though the merits of those lives largely belonged to other men, recited through scriptures and barroom tales, I nonetheless soaked up every word and carried it as part of my own identity. So even if on the outside the world saw Costa Calabrese as a mere boy, I held within me the furtive knowledge of a man double my years.

Staying low, I crept through the thick of the bush, with my lucky sling in one hand, a good size stone in the other. I didn't chamber the stone in the stirrup band until making certain where the faceless intruder would come from.

His clumsy footwork gave him away immediately as being dead North from me. I knocked the stone and drew back on the band. My arms were steady and I dimmed one eye before letting the stone fly on its own. It whizzed and whistled through the thicket in front of me and I waited until I heard the satisfying hollow "plink" as it found its mark. My satisfaction did not arrive. Instead, a mess of activity came from my direct right and before I knew what happened I hit the soft earth with my shoulder.

The fall momentarily knocked the wind out of me. My recovery was quick but before I could scramble to my feet my assailant mounted me at the waist and pinned my arms to the ground by both wrists.

I struggled and twitched under the weight. As I heard laughter it prompted more struggle until I came to recognize the nasal-filled whine of my close friend Tuck Goodall.

"Settle down, Costa. You're turning all red in the face."

"Then by the Gods get your fat arse off me!" I demanded.

As soon as Tuck moved I hurried to my feet, dusted the soil from my tunic, and then did my best to insist the moment hadn't fazed me.

"Nice tackle, Goodall. I wonder if you'd be able to do it again if my back wasn't to you."

"Of course I could." Tuck insisted on showcasing his full girth with a cinch of his belt. He shared my age but his stature was such, stalky and round in the belly, that he'd been mistaken for his own father many times over.

Unfortunately, his mind still held wit only half a step up from a child.

Sometimes I wondered why I continued to remain as his companion, except that no others in the town of Gryphant held my interest – or rather I theirs. So as outcasts Tuck and I traveled together making daily jaunts into Muir Woods to flush out our own brand of trouble. Still, his jovial taunting grew tiresome and drew a red hue to my cheeks time and time again.

"Half the fun is surprising you," Tuck continued, his round cheeks lighting up in his excitement as he mocked me with his words. "Some deadly tracker you are."

He knew just what to say to entice me. I rounded my fists and moved forward causing his full retreat and surrender. For all his size and status Tuck was a gentle soul. Watching as he knocked both elbows up over his head and turned his back to me, I breathed a heavy sigh into the morning air and allowed him his small victory.

"Alright," I told him. "You had me, but it won't happen again."

The words proved difficult to say. Competitive by nature, I hated giving an inch. To me it showcased weakness. Early on in life I learned weakness would not be acceptable to indulge, in any manner.

Still, as Tuck uncovered his head and flashed a warm smile at me I couldn't help but return the favor. His smiles were infectious and reminded me there was a time and place to be serious and a time to laugh at myself.

"I nearly wet my shorts just then, Costa," he told me. "You had that look of rage in your eyes again – like a man gone mad."

The rage he spoke of had held close to me ever since the loss of my mother. Anger is what I've become. For the longest time that anger and dark fire has been my only companion. I embrace it, curl up with it, and allow the pain and depression to envelope me, threatening to swallow me whole if I let it. I hold the beast at bay most times, but I'd be a fool to think that I had control over my emotions.

"If you want to see a madman then watch what happens if I'm late returning to town." As I spoke a chill ran up over my spine and its tingling spell lingered at the base of my skull.

"Right," Tuck agreed with a nod knowing full well what, or rather whom, I was referring to. "Old man Benton."

"Let's make haste," I told him, shaking off the discomfort that had suddenly clenched my shoulders up. "The day is already at our backs."

I pointed past the large Birchwood trees towards the setting sun. A pool of its golden light broke over the tree tops touching the ground inviting us to stay and explore further into Muir Woods. As much as my heart begged me to do just that I knew where my responsibilities lay.

"We best go."

Collecting my lucky sling from the ground Tuck and I started out towards our home of Gryphant Village, all the while making plans for what adventures we would seek out on the next morning's travels.

"We could take the fork at El Sentro next time," Tuck suggested. "I hear there is a year round spring."

"That's kids' stuff," I protested. "We should seek out Lake Chippewa. My guess is it's frozen solid about now."

"I don't know, Costa, Lake Chippewa is pretty far north. What if we get lost?"

"Are you kidding? I know this area better than anyone in the village.."

In the middle of my convincing argument my words were bitten off when I heard a low howl stopping us in our tracks. My ears perked up to catch the sound again. When it did my blood ran cold.

Tuck's voice was quaking. "If you know the area so well, my brother, then tell me what it is we heard just then."

"Quiet!" I demanded. My own voice held steady but not without effort. "Let me listen."

The sound called out again. It carried with it a great wailing that grew more guttural with each call.

"Maybe it's a wolf," Tuck suggested, speaking in a shallow whisper now at my insistence.

"That was no simple wolf. It held human qualities to it."

"Are you saying it was some sort of half-breed? Such things do not exist, you know that."

I arched my eyebrow and crooked my mouth up to a half-smile. "One way to find out."

Moving forward through the thick underbrush I paused only long enough to prod Tuck into following at my heels before shooting deeper into the foliage.

"What about old man Benton?" Tuck asked as he struggled to keep his stout body in pace with my lithe, quick frame.

"We'll be quick," I told him. "Besides, what if we find a carcass or something? Imagine the stories to tell."

"I should know better than to argue with you when you get that look on your face. It's a maniacal little smirk but it tells a thousand tales. You're genuinely having fun aren't you?"

"Of course, aren't you?" I replied. "I mean how can you stand to toil in the self-same mundane activities day-in and day-out?"

Tuck didn't have an answer for me and I didn't bother waiting for one. I knew a part of him sometimes preferred staying in the village and helping his mother bake, which was something else I couldn't understand about him, but something I accepted regardless. For all the faults he accepted about me I owed him at least that one.

We moved swift and steady into the deep underbrush. I kept low in a crouched position and was careful not to disturb the forest floor with my sandaled feet for fear the sound would carry to the ears of whatever was in the trees.

Through my readings I had always envisioned developing into a great hunter, a man of the land, one who lived off the earth and answered to no one. That is why the call to venture into Muir Woods day after day drew so strong. Until that day came when I held my fate in my own hands I would settle for seeking adventure wherever I could find it.

We'd moved only half a stone's throw from the forest path when the sound cried out again. It echoed off the everlasting sky and came back down with a sharp jolt to our ears once again stopping us cold in our tracks. The cry was much closer than before. This time it held a mix of hatred and anguish that suddenly ceased as quickly as it had rung out.

I stood as still as a statue and strained my ears to mark the sound once more, but the only thing audible was the whine of Tuck Goodall.

"I don't like this," he said. "I'm going to go back."

Before Tuck made it two paces away, I caught the meaty part of his forearm and forced him still.

"Quiet!" I insisted in a dark whisper. "Something is coming."

We waited for what seemed like an eternity. Sweat pasted my leather jerkin to my chest and dampened my hair. My heart was pounding and filling my ear with the pulsing sound of my own blood. No sound pierced the sky; no monster fled the thick of the trees.

Finally Tuck withdrew his arm and rounded about. "I'm turning back."

I shook my head in disappointment. If only there had been something more. I lingered on for a moment before reluctantly turning to join Tuck on the trail back to town.

"Maybe next time," I said, my voice had deflated and no longer held a spark of expectancy.

"You get yourself too worked up about such things, Costa," Tuck told me. "And what have we ever come across except some broken arrow heads?"

"No one is forcing you to come. Next time I'll journey alone and you'll be sorry when I tell you what I found."

We scampered around a dense corner of forest and for the third time that day fear stood us in our tracks. A hulking shape loomed just paces ahead. From the short span of distance that separated us I could make out that it was a man of considerable stature.

He was adorned in the color of night from his tall leather boots to the dark hood fitting closely to his head. A heavy cloak about his shoulders was stained with a fresh, thick liquid undistinguishable in nature. But it was the manner in which he moved, striding with purpose and heavy feet that held no fear of capturing attention, that had me duck for cover in the thicket and pull Tuck down with me.

The stranger's body was alive with movement in every fiber of his being. Ears perked, eyes roaming, his senses were lifted to the extreme. Finally he took a position of defense just behind one of the larger Birchwood trees. His back lay flat against the trunk. He withdrew a small hunting knife from a leather belt looped double about his waist and waited. Tuck and I waited as well, watching with baited breath as the stranger marked something unknown in the distance.

A shuffle-scrape of leaves signified the presence of another. A man looking worn and bedraggled, wearing nothing but coarse patches of hair up along his back and legs, staggered out of the thicket just west of us. His face seemed contorted in a snarl of unbearable anguish.

I wondered if this poor fellow had been the one we had heard shouting before, perhaps calling for help before one of the forest animals scented him and tore him down. But the four-footed inhabitants of Muir would be the least of this man's worries.

As he stumbled, still trying to keep his balance on shaky legs, the stranger in black made his move. I marveled at his inhuman speed as he left his cover and confronted his hapless prey.

The drifter could not mount a defense. His best effort was an attempt to bite the man in black before the silver tipped blade plunged deep into his chest, severing his heart. Blue-black blood rushed out in torrential rivers signifying a gruesome end, but that didn't stop the stranger in black from delivering several more sloping stabs down into the man's throat, belly, and even his face. The shine of the blade was tarnished with blood as he fell to the forest floor, dead.

Using quick, hard strokes the man in black cut a swatch of fabric from the tattered jerkin. This he wadded in his left hand and began polishing the knife. It required much effort from the stranger and I could make out the sinew of muscle bulging from the man's forearm with each hard stroke. He ran the cloth over the fine blade several times managing to transfer the dark stain from the knife to the cloth with little leaving the blade itself.

Whether from discomfort or just blind and foolish curiosity, Tuck shifted forwards from his position in the bushes. The leaves and twigs crunching under his weight sounded out like an alarm. The noise seemed to reverberate against the hard bark of the trees and return magnified tenfold against the forest floor where the three of us occupied space.

The stranger immediately halted. His eyes scanned across the forest on either side of him. He had heard.

I reached forward too late and grasped Tuck high upon the shoulder. We met eyes briefly and in that silent exchange I implored Tuck to cease any further movement. Even the breath in my body and the beat of my heart seemed to halt in my pursuit of unlimited silence.

When I looked back towards our dark suited friend I almost gasped. I saw nothing but an empty forest. In a blink the man, with blade in hand, had vanished.

The grip I held on Tuck's shoulder increased in pressure until I could feel the tense muscle tissue deep beneath the meat. I knew from experience that my skittish friend would run like a scared rabbit if he believed he had even half a chance of escape.

Truth be told, I would lament that I had endured enough excursions for one day. I was just as eager to race home as Tuck was. I'd read enough adventures written of pen on parchment, and had heard enough tales told from many exotic travelers, to realize the stranger in black could be upon us within the first moment we lifted from the cover of the thicket.

It was now a waiting game—who would show themselves first? Unfortunately, Tuck saw matters his own way. He began squirming under my grip until he finally shook free.

"We need to go now!" His voice remained low but held enough emotion to carry on the still of the morning air.

I shook my head vigorously, setting a finger to my lips in demand of silence. Tuck persisted with his usual stubborn grimace until I mouthed the words "We'll be killed."

The proclamation of death was enough to halt Tuck in his decision. Only the Gods knew what our fate would've been had he proceeded forward at the last second. For in the next instance the stranger dropped from the open sky above and came down directly in front of the two of us.

His heavy boots made a sick-wet sound as they slapped the soft earth. Debris and chunks of dirt blew into our faces taunting us with the desire to cough aloud but we remained as still as statues. Our eyes kept trained on the man's every move.

The knife was outstretched in his hands. Almost all of the blood had dried, giving its color a dark crimson masking rather than the brighter sheen of a fresh kill. The remaining liquid congealed at the tip pulling one solitary, fat droplet down off the knife. It plummeted fast and found its landing direct upon the back of my hand.

Warmth and cold both blanketed me in the same sensation as the blood sat soaking upon my skin. Both Tuck and I sat staring at the droplet in stark terror, daring not to move one single inch. That one small drop of blood marked what true danger we were exposed to.

Finally I managed to pull my gaze away and regard the stranger before us. My blood ran cold as the man's eyes rained down upon me, locked against my own. They were dark orbs, almost as dark as night, and they held within them just a touch of madness staring out from under his full brimmed hat.

Every ounce of my being wanted to turn and run away, but fear gripped me still until my joints ached and my muscles throbbed. I didn't move, didn't utter a sound, didn't withdraw my gaze nor make a motion towards Tuck who remained transfixed with the blood spot on my hand.

The stare down lasted but a moment longer and then the man simply stepped away. Just as swiftly as he had appeared he now disappeared from sight through the thick of the trees.

When he was no longer visible both Tuck and I leapt to our feet and made a mad scramble for the edge of the forest. With the last of the trees behind us, and the path back to town firmly under our feet once more, we stopped to catch our breath.

My heart pounded with rapid force, but it wasn't the sprint to safety that caused such a rhythm. It was the firm realization that for the second time in my life I had narrowly escaped death.

Tuck and I spoke not a word on our return to the village. We merely walked in silence, every so often glancing over a shoulder to shake the indomitable feeling that we were being stalked like prey.

Stepping through the splintered wooden gates housing the perimeter of Gryphant Village the danger presented itself directly in front of me.

Mace Benton, tall and brooding with hard plumes of angered breath flaring out his flat nose, met me upon our return. He wasted no time in letting his big, leathery hands fly. His meaty hooks struck me alone, but they struck again and again with such force that I had no choice but to topple to my knees, arms raised in a feeble attempt to deflect the blows.

Tuck was spared the lashings merely through his position in life. He was the son of the blacksmith, a well-to-do and loving family. Benton held no claims to him as he did myself, which Benton reminded me of as each hard strike came thundering down.

"You vile miscreant, I should tan your hide for such disobedience! What lame ignorance would prompt you to return at your discretion rather than when I told you to be here?"

My arms grew weaker with each heavy strike until I could no longer hold them up to protect myself. They slid down just past my ears to expose the top of my head. Seizing the opening, Benton reeled back and dropped a clubbing blow downwards with the flat of his fist.

A loud, dull popping rang in my head and sparks of darkness filled my sight line. Before I knew it I was nose first in the dry dirt listening to the hate-filled tongue lashing from Benton, which had grown indistinguishable through the ringing in my ears.

I looked up with tear-filled eyes towards Benton only to see the man in black standing before me instead. The blood-stained knife pointed down towards my exposed throat and the dark eyes seemed to absorb my very soul. The situation seemed surreal and for a moment I wondered if it could possibly be that I had not yet left Muir Woods.

Somewhere in the distance Tuck's voice called out for the beating to cease. In that self-same moment I blinked back my growing haze to realize the form in front of me remained that of my domineering master, Benton. The stranger in black was nowhere in sight.

"You rise to your feet like a man and get to work," Benton demanded, "lest I drag you through town by your filthy long locks."

As I lay on the ground, breathing in coarse dirt, I watched with a heavy heart as Benton took out his frustrations on my prize possession. He brought his heavy nail-down boot up to knee level and laid it down with full force upon my lucky sling. The snap-crackle resounded in my ears like a thunderclap in such a way that I felt as though my head were splitting.

Be it for exclamation on his statement or mere fun Benton lodged a single, swift kick to my side before he turned and went on his way. The blow brought a hacking cough up from deep within my throat and lungs and forced me to double over to absorb the pain.

Tuck dipped a knee and tended to me with all the care of a nursemaid rather than with the hands of a blacksmith's son.

"I should've stopped him," he said drawing me to my feet and dusting the crusted earth from my jerkin. "Maybe if you explained to him what had happened y'know, with the madman in the woods?"

I brushed him aside and had to make considerable effort to remain standing on my own volition. "It doesn't matter, Tuck."

"You don't deserve to be treated like that, Costa."

"I was late," I repeated. On shaky legs, and still doubled over from the wailing pain in my gut, I started in the path left by Benton's large boots. My head still swam with clutter making the world seem to spin before my eyes.

I managed to lean over and collect the remains of my sling. It was broken in two, shattered and destroyed. I'd never been able to afford any real kind of weaponry so I had fashioned the sling myself out of a large chunk of cedar wood. It had taken days of toiling work but the end result had made me hold my head a little higher with the pride of accomplishment. Now I held in my hands nothing but bent and twisted wood. I discarded it into the dirt without a second thought.

One final thought rang true and I wasted no time dispelling it to Tuck. "As far as the man in the woods goes...we never saw him."

"But shouldn't we tell someone what happened?" Tuck argued. "A man was murdered out there. Perhaps someone is looking for him."

I shook my head. "No one would believe us."

Tuck nodded agreement watching as his good friend staggered back towards a dwelling and a home life as broken and diminished as my pain inflicted body.

It had never been revealed to me why the marauders had swept over the village I'd called home for six years. Everyone had their ideas about it. Some of the more prominent reasons seemed to center on ritualistic acts of sacrifice. I myself held no real memories of my past. All I knew were facts that had been mentioned over the years. When the stench of dark smoke and death had cleared on that fateful morn, my birth town of Rhone had been subjected to ruin. I wound up wandering the streets half-starved and alone. My mother had been killed in the raid; my father was a stranger to me since birth. A small child at the time I'd no idea where to go or what to do.

When I came upon Gryphant the people there accepted me. I roomed with a kindly old woman who would tell me tales of her sea faring husband, Crassis, and the many adventures he'd recalled to her upon his return. One day he did not come back. The sea had claimed him. I remember envying Crassis. Even in death he'd been a man of adventure.

It was a good life for me, but short lived. After the old woman herself passed on, her foolish, drunken son bartered my services in a game of cards and lost. My fate wound up in the grisly hands of the local tavern owner, Mace Benton who'd won me. He'd weakened my spirit, breaking me down through a regimen of punishing physical work, inadequate food and clothing. It had been the same manner of torturous living spanning eight year's time with no end in sight.

My only reprieve came from the curiosity and imagination of my mind. I sought out excitement close to home wherever I could find it, longing for the day when I would be a man of my own choosing who could travel the land in search of high adventure never to look back. Those thoughts seemed like distant dreams now. The jaunt through Muir Woods had brought nothing but trouble. A dull ache at the back of my skull and the stinging scrapes upon my cheek and lips reminding me as I returned home.

I could barely remain standing. Several times I had to bend over and stabilize myself as I felt I might retch. Just paces from the stables where my sleeping quarters were, I fell to my knees and had to crawl my way inside like a mongrel dog.

Every movement spread agony over my torso and limbs. In my days on the farm I had received worse beatings for less, but this time my throbbing head and the swelling of my lips reminded me that I was alive. Had fate carried any other message that afternoon I may not have left Muir Woods with my young life intact.

I could still feel the dark eyes of the stranger looking down upon me, could still make out the cold, dark orbs in my memory. There was no mistake...I knew he had seen me, but for whatever reason he had let Tuck and I go. There was something else behind the madness; a strong sense of power that shined through those eyes like a beacon in the night. The dark clad stranger would never have lain down at the foot of a swine like Benton. He would've risen up and taken back his control.

Something in that summation delivered strength to me, forcing me to get to my feet. I demanded that I lift myself up off the floor. I willed it. I did it. At first my legs were shaky beneath me as if I were relearning how to use them. Then they grew to strong supports; I knew that I would not fall...not now, not ever again.

Mace Benton's tavern thrived with business from its regular patrons as well as a troop of traveling performers who had been passing through town. They were a lively bunch of minstrels, jugglers, jesters and the like. All manner of entertainers, whom Benton despised, but as long as they paid their fare he tolerated them.

For me the gentle chimes of the flute, combined with the steady rhythm of the drum were a fine distraction from my woes. I felt misplaced, used up. There was a hole inside me, some void needing to be filled. Living a life of servitude was certainly not going to fill it.

I looked out over the tavern dwellers all laughing, dancing, and enjoying their lives with carefree zest. The traveling performers especially caught my attention. They held no responsibility but their own, wandering from place to place on their own volition, answering to no one but themselves. I envied them.

As I let my mind linger on daydreams of a life far more fulfilling than that which I presently lived, Benton's meaty paw crimped the back of my neck. His thick fingers bit into my tender flesh until he gripped the cords just underneath the surface and he moved me out from behind the bar.

"Make use of yourself and go service the stranger who just came in."

With that Benton shoved me out into the thick of the crowd directed towards the small group of tables sitting at the back of the tavern. The tavern dwellers were up dancing, or more accurately staggering about on drunken legs. Some of the more inebriated tried in vain to get me to join them in their frolicking. I would've been happy to accept their invitation if it were not for the hard stare of Mace Benton holding heavy to the back of my head watching my every move. Instead, I carried on with business as usual, proceeding towards the new stranger who had entered the tavern.

The man sat deep in the corner, far from the crowd where the shadows cast over him like a cloak. His heavy boots were stacked one atop the other upon the table and a dark brimmed hat was cast down over his eyes.

As I moved closer, I felt the strangest sensation of danger all around me. It was as if my mind and body were setting off an internal alarm. My world seemed to move in slow motion. The dancing guests, the traveling performers, all of them flailed their arms and moved in simplistic rhythm like puppets on a string. Everyone of them grew dim, drawn away from the light as I focused only on the man in front of me.

The man in black. The boots, the hat, the bloody dagger that rested at his side. But how was it that I saw blood upon a blade that was clearly sheathed? My mind was not playing tricks, my memory was with me now. It was the memory of a blood stained dagger unleashing its fat drops down upon my hand while I crouched in the forest like a frightened doe while before me I surveyed a monster—a monster dressed in black. When his head tilted back, his eyes, still holding madness at the forefront, looked up at me, the nightmare memory and reality joined together as one in a loud thunderclap.

Not a word was spoken, the stranger's eyes alone told the story. This was no mistaken meeting. The stranger in black had followed me from Muir Woods back into town, back to the place I called home. Though checkered with pain and discontent, Gryphant remained a sanctuary from the far greater evils of the world. But somewhere, somehow the gates of Hell had opened and allowed one of their demons to slip out and find its way into the tavern that very night.

Several thoughts entered my mind at that exact moment. All of them ended very poorly and disgracefully. Rather than chance an attack, a distraction, or all out begging, I instead made move to run but I turned too swiftly and caught my heel on the bottom edge of the chair the stranger sat upon. Both ankles felt the strain of the wood cut deep into the tender flesh. Before I knew what had happened I bounced my chin off the polished wood of the tavern floor.

I lay there going in and out of consciousness, taking in the lingering scent of soap from the floorboards that I had scrubbed earlier in the day. There was laughter ringing in my ears. The tavern dwellers in their drunken stupor were mocking me in my anguish. Their voices seemed a million miles away.

Benton's voice boomed out demanding me to get to my feet. Try as I might none of my limbs seemed to be working at that moment. The last thing I saw as I tried in vain to force my way up was the cold, hard stare from the dark clad stranger.

For a moment I was back in Muir Woods, Tuck at my side, the drop of blood from the stained dagger pooling over my hand. The stranger's eyes were set upon me as they had been that morning, only this time he did not vanish. He stayed to finish the job. Tuck was the first to fall victim as I looked on in horror. My body remained frozen, unwilling to move forward even as the stranger lifted Tuck from the underbrush and tore open his throat with the sharpest part of the blade.

Blood curled from Tuck's lips running down his beefy jowls back into the hole which had once been his throat. The stranger discarded Tuck to the wayside like so much rotten meat, then he turned his attention on me. Fear gripped me still. I opened my mouth to scream but no sound would come out. Soon my fate would mirror that of my friend.

The madman reached out a blood soaked hand towards me. His fingertips came within inches of grasping my sand-colored locks. The eyes burned me to the core. The rough barking of Mace Benton echoing with stern demand brought me awake from this nightmare.

"Up boy pack your things. You're no longer in my care."

Benton's face was nothing but shadows as it hovered over my own. I couldn't remember how I'd returned home but there I was laying upon my sleeping roll with a massive headache. The words Benton spoke were those that I had only ever hoped to hear in the past. As Benton gave me such news this morning I imagined I must still be dreaming.

As I came awake my reply was jumbled, a mix of sleep and surprise. "What're you talking about?"

"You've been sold for the season," Benton said grabbing my sleeping roll and shaking it until I rolled out on the floor with a hard thud. "Now pack up and get moving. Your new lord expects you promptly."

As soon as Benton left I wasted no time in procuring the meager provisions I called my own. I tucked my tattered clothing, old scrolls, and grooming brushes in my sleeping roll, binding it tight with a braided cord. Once settled I hefted the pack over my shoulder and hurried to the front.

The memory of the past night still held in my mind, but it was faint now. At first I thought it a dream, a horrible torturous dream, only it felt like reality, until I noted the small bruising on my chin from where I'd struck the bar floor.

I shifted my focus away from the blurred images of the previous evening focusing instead on the change at hand.

Whomever my new keeper was mattered little, for anyone in town would be better suited than Mace Benton.

My heart felt like soaring for a moment as I dared to hope it would be Tuck's own father who had come calling for me. Tuck was a solid friend, best as they came. He had been trying in vain to convince his father, the blacksmith, to take me on as an apprentice of sorts, but he had always been turned away with rejections. Perhaps now Tuck had finally been able to sway his father in my favor.

My improbable joy came crashing down around me the moment I laid eyes on the man holding court with Benton. Despite the warmth of the day he wore the same fitted leather boots and the dark, tattered cloak that fell loosely about his shoulders.

The brim of his hat was tipped down over his brow casting a shadow over his face but the gleam from his wild eyes could still be seen as he noticed my hesitant entrance.

The weight of that stare felt far from comfortable. Instinctively I turned to run as I had the night before. I would run, and run until my legs gave out and my lungs could no longer sustain the pounding air being driven through them. But the moment I back-stepped Benton caught me under the arm in his heavy grip positioning me almost at the feet of the man in black.

"Show some respect to Cain Coleridge, your new keeper," Benton told him. "Unless you want a stiff backhand for your troubles."

Benton motioned back his thick, calloused hand and I cowered from the intent of the blow, but the strike was held off by words spoken from Coleridge himself.

"Leave the boy be," he said. His voice was a dark whisper. Up until that moment I had only imagined what the man must sound like if indeed he could speak at all. I'd had it in my head that Coleridge's voice held the same qualities of a hissing snake, forked tongue and all. "He is under my care now." he continued. "I shall deal out his punishments accordingly."

The low pitch in Coleridge's voice made my skin crawl. It was as dark and sinister as the manner of wardrobe he was clad in or the spark of madness creeping over his eyes.

I'd heard Coleridge's name mentioned before around town. He was something of a legend though none had ever really seen him. They'd spoken tales of a bounty hunter who wandered from town to town collecting wrong doers for profit. I'd always been enamored of such feats. He sounded like such a noble and courageous man.

Watching him butcher that wounded traveler out in Muir Woods like a fallen animal proved to me my original assessment had been wrong. Everyone's assessment had been wrong. It seemed Coleridge was nothing more than a cold-blooded killer. Now I was in his care.

In the eight years I'd been under Benton's watch, I never raised question or rebuttal to any of the demands sent my way. Fear alone made me speak my concerns at that moment.

"Sir," I stuttered, stepping closer to Benton than I'd ever cared to be in my whole lifetime. "Shouldn't I remain here and help with the harvest?"

"Don't be ridiculous, boy. Cain here has paid good wages for you. Now you'll go and you'll work. I'll hear no more of it. If I get one ill-word back, about you slacking off or not doing exactly as you're told, you'll wish you'd never emerged from the womb."

Something told me I might soon be wishing for such things under the watchful eye of Cain Coleridge.

Chapter Two
End of Days

I carried my things behind Coleridge, head down, mouth shut, all the while awaiting the time when he would finally decide to viciously strike me down. After all I had seen too much. I knew his true purpose. The bounties he sought were never turned in to the towns that laid claim to them. He collected the money for his deeds and killed the unsuspecting men, or even women, he was dutifully paid to recapture. No wonder fear crossed the lips of those who dared mention his name.

We rounded the crest of a hill and continued down a long dirt path towards one of the oldest dwellings in Gryphant. It hadn't been occupied in many years. The roof needed repair, the walls had fist-sized holes in them, and the cooking hearth was soiled with some of the thickest muck I'd ever seen. I sighed in disgust knowing that all these dirty little tasks would come to my hands alone.

Once we were settled, Coleridge put me to work doing exactly that. The day dragged on with more and more menial tasks handed out by Coleridge until the calluses on my hands began to bleed. I had been occupying my thoughts with the insipid task of scrubbing down the mixing pot when Coleridge took up a chair at my back.

He'd been busy himself that morning lacing the entry points of the house with a strange looking green plant, a curious task that I dared not question. Now that his work was complete he sat behind me burning a hole at the back of my head with his hard stare. The pressure ceased up on me, constricting my chest and pulling the muscles of my lips into a frown until I could no longer continue with the task at hand. That is when I finally spoke up.

"If you are to kill me sir, I tell you I will not run, but I shall fight to defend my life."

A small sliver of wood jutted out from between Coleridge's teeth as they were bared into what could almost be construed a smile. He rose from his seat at the table, slowly coming towards me. The air suddenly grew very thick. I could feel a strong tightening of my heart and stomach, both twisting in knots, as I instantly regretted ever speaking out of turn. Had I remained quiet Coleridge may have extended my life for at least another hour if not another day. Foolish as I was I had to act the part of the brave man.

"Funny," he said. "You ran before."

As Coleridge edged closer, I threw caution to the wind and took up the broom in my hands like a makeshift staff. It became my ally as I lunged at Coleridge. He returned the favor with quick, sharp actions. Before I knew what happened I was unarmed, pinned against the far wall with Coleridge's hand holding tight to my throat. The mad eyes seemed to pierce my very soul.

"Only a fool chases death lest it serve some greater purpose." His fingers slowly peeled off my throat and something of a smile spread his lips wide. "But□ I salute your courage, ill-advised or not. Perhaps there is something in you after all."

I was befuddled. I dared not move from my placement against the back wall but somehow I found it within myself to lift my tongue to speak.

"Aren't you going to kill me?"

"Think boy, had I wanted to extinguish your life I would've done it back out in the woods where none would be the wiser."

Coleridge went on as he settled back into his chair setting his travel worn leather boots upon the table. "Besides, you are less significant than this chip of wood I hold between my teeth." He paused to showcase the thin strip and then flick it in my direction. His aim was such that the stick almost struck me direct in the eye. "Why would I bother to kill you?" Coleridge continued, "I could just as soon let you languish in your insufferable life as a slave – a fate surely worse than any death I've known."

I felt my cheeks flushing white hot with anger. Who was this man to castrate me with words of such malice? He knew nothing of my life yet he made these observations outright.

The real problem lay in the fact that Coleridge's words rang true. I wasn't a great warrior or poet by any right. As it stood I was just a lowly galley slave with no real memories of the past and no real prospects for the future. As much as I dared to dream it I would never travel the world in search of high adventure. I was doomed to live out my days in the same broken down village until the day I died an old workhorse.

This painful revelation drew the strength from my knees. I slumped against the back wall. My white hot anger was replaced with the stinging of tears. I dropped my head away from Coleridge's gaze to spare myself the humiliation. Not since the day I stood over my mother's murdered body had I shed tears. Crying held no purpose in day-to-day existence. But something in Coleridge's words crushed and hurt me more than any of the multiple beatings Mace Benton had lashed out over the years.

"Those of us with no purpose in life are doomed to merely exist."

Coleridge's words were soft-spoken now as though he were retelling a tale of scripture long since forgotten. Then he rose up and came to me once more. Taking my chin in his fingers he forced me to look up at him. The spark of his eyes had dimmed now as though the madness had crept away for a time.

"Be wary of the purpose you choose, young Calabrese, for some are a cruel and wicked master indeed."

The cryptic-note in his message left a chill running over my body long after Coleridge had left the room. It was doled out like a fireside ghost tale but with much more conviction.

I lay awake that night, trying to decipher the hidden meaning in the message, until the dark of sleep finally pulled me into worlds where the mundane mixed with the magical. All the while, the tune of the traveling performers played on.

The next morning when I awoke I felt very much out of sorts. My own skin was unfamiliar. Demons had plagued me during the night. The dreams had shifted to nightmares and the nightmares had brought with them warnings.

As I awoke I couldn't recall the significance of those warnings, but I knew something unforeseen by my mortal eye was heading this way. My dreams often became some semblance of reality whether I wanted to embrace that as fact or not.

Now, sitting atop my sleeping roll, one hand shifting through my dusty-blonde locks, I desperately tried to remember the nightmare. Bits and pieces came back to me but nothing solid held. Soon I gave up trying and went on with the day's chores.

Coleridge had left early that morning or late the prior evening. Whatever the case may be, he was nowhere in sight. I deemed it best to have a hot meal waiting for him upon his return. Better to sate the man's hunger before his temper flared and he struck the first thing that lived and breathed.

As I took to the stove preparing small dumpling style potatoes in goat's cream my curiosity got the better of me. Allowing the mix to simmer in the cast iron stove I proceeded to slip away towards the back of the sunken hut where Coleridge had his sleeping quarters.

Up to this point I hadn't been allowed to enter the back room. Even in my cleaning rounds I had been forewarned to stay my distance from Coleridge's quarters. Now, my interest grew too great for me to withstand. With Coleridge off for the morning I didn't hesitate to take a hold of this opportunity.

I stood at the threshold momentarily taking long, deep breaths. Feeling as giddy as a child, I edged closer inside, using slow steps to savor my findings. In the simplest of forms this grew into somewhat of another adventure for me. My curious mind was ready to soak up whatever storied past this madman was holding back.

The initial survey of the room left me disheartened at best. It looked no more special than my own quarters out in the stables. There was a sleeping pallet covered in what looked to be a wolf's hide, a handful of inch-thick wood sticks that had been sharpened at the tip, and the remnants of a used smoking pipe. Little else was in sight. There were no ritualistic engravings on the wall, no sacrifices (human or otherwise) chained to the floor, it was just as average as any of the other traveler's rooms I'd cleaned up over the past few years.

I was backing out of the room, the weight of disappointment drawing my head down until my chin grazed my chest, when something caught my eye. Without hesitation I hurried back inside and located an object at the foot of the sleeping pallet.

It was a thick book of scripture bound in a sleeve of leather. A small but sturdy brass lock held the bindings together so that only the owner of the small brass key would be privy to the information held inside.

I bit my lip, gnawed on it until the tiniest speck of blood broke through the surface. Excitement rumbled in the pit of my stomach as I looked over the fine craftsmanship of the leather bindings. It appeared to be centuries old, perhaps handed down through generations until it came into the hands of Coleridge, whether by rites or by theft.

Either way I needed to get it open; the drawing power the tome held was immeasurable. Without the key at my disposal I would need to find other means. I'd break the damned thing if I had to and suffer Coleridge's wrath later. The fire poker sprang to mind. I may be able to force the lock off with that.

As I stood, book in hand, I felt the sense of another presence at my back. I turned too slow and was caught by the nape of the neck. At once my body fell limp, the book slipped from my grasp. The soft leather made a smack as it hit and then slid across the stone floor.

I knew at once who held me in his grasp. These were not the same harsh and forceful hands of Mace Benton that had previously laid down my punishments. There was a finesse involved in the way the hands circled the meat of my neck and a great knowledge of pressure points was displayed as the dark gloved fingers pressed down firm across the carotid artery.

Coleridge had me in his grasp. His heavy breath rained down over the top of my head even as my own breath locked in my chest.

"You're a curious lad, aren't you?" Coleridge asked through gritted teeth and firmed lips. "You've got a wanderer's soul. That's what brought you to Muir Woods, wasn't it? Some juvenile lust for adventure."

Coleridge's grip grew lax around my neck but was forceful as his hand moved up and grasped a lock of hair. I cringed, my eyes forced shut. The veins in my neck bulged out from the pain. Coleridge tipped me backwards, maneuvering me by my hair, bringing me in close proximity to the scroll book that lay upon the floor.

"That, boy, is not for prying eyes. I'd have sworn I made that clear before. Do I have to remind you of the rules at the end of a whip this time?"

"Apologies, Lord," I told him. "I only meant to tidy the room." It was the first thing that came to my mind and I hoped it would calm him.

Coleridge relinquished his hold on me. The relief was such that I remained on the floor, legs tucked beneath me, almost bowing at the feet of Coleridge.

"Mind the warnings, boy. In life they're all that stands between victory and peril." He pointed towards the door, one black gloved finger making the emphasis of his demand for my immediate exit. There was no hesitation. I moved as swiftly as I had the day Tuck and I fled Muir Woods. But in my wake I heard a firm warning spoken from Coleridge's dry lips.

"If I catch you with this book in your possession again, young Calabrese, I'll most likely kill you."

For the next few days I obeyed his instruction, staying clear of Coleridge's quarters and never uttered a word out of turn, but I watched. My eyes marked out every moment of every hour of every day until my study was ingrained upon me like the deepest memory touching my soul.

I watched Coleridge at meals as he took in too much wine and fell to slumber under his wide brimmed hat. I watched the study of maps in the afternoon, while writings were made upon parchment and then hidden away in the elusive leather bound book. In the evenings, as the sun's glow gave way to the crest of a crystal moon, I watched Coleridge load up a satchel with the hand carved stakes, a bullwhip fashioned of the toughest leather, and a small flask that held an indiscernible clear liquid. Then with all the caution of handling fine glass he wrapped that same peculiar plant that decorated the house in soft rags and set it just inside his bag.

Night after night was the same routine. I never heard Coleridge return from his mysterious journey during the night, but each morning he would be there – sleeping or unconscious in front of the hearthstone.

I wondered if perhaps Coleridge was frequenting Gabrielle, Gryphant's local entertainment to men of discerning taste. She was recently widowed, but whatever grief she may be experiencing didn't keep her from sharing her bed with the lot of men living in and traveling through Gryphant.

One warm evening, during the Autumn harvest, she'd even whispered her hot breath upon my ear and offered to make a man of me. I'd been wholly aroused and perhaps would've indulged in such fantasies had Benton not beaten me to it. From then on Gabrielle was nothing more than damaged goods in my eyes. I likened Coleridge to share a similar line of thinking, so entertaining the idea that he was with Gabrielle night after night, didn't seem a sound answer to his nightly excursions. But the pressures of not knowing were gnawing away at my gut like so much spoiled meat. Before I quite literally burst I needed to find the answers.

One night something stirred me and brought me awake well before the dawn. I shuffled about the main floor and took stock of my surroundings noting immediately that Coleridge's satchel and cloak were not present. Coleridge himself was not splayed upon the ground or filling his favorite chair in exhaustion. He'd not returned yet from his evening trek.

Coleridge's strange behaviors were beginning to fascinate me. His complexities showcased a mysterious world. It was more compelling to me than any sage or storyteller I'd ever come across. So I waited eagerly by the door for Coleridge's return, hoping upon hope that if I caught him coming in I could piece together the whereabouts he continued to frequent during the dead of the night.

The hours grew later, one upon the other, and still no sign of Coleridge. My eyes were heavy and growing dim at each passing second. I'd taken to sitting cross-legged on the floor to rest my weary body. Slumped over, head lolling on my shoulders, I began to fade. Once again dark visions invaded my dreams.

Gryphant was burning. I heard the hollers and shouts as prominent as if they were occurring in reality rather than a dream world. Blood stained the grounds. The hard smell of death filled the air. People fled from their homes and littered the streets in a panic looking over their shoulders as an unknown attacker followed in their wake.

I ran the streets with the villagers trying to make their way to safety. Not only the men, but the women and children with fear etched on their faces herded together likes cows moving towards slaughter.

I stumbled and fell, then rose to my feet as swiftly as I could. My heart was pounding. Sweat lay thick on the back of my neck and moistened my brow. A shrill cry broke through the chaos and the panic. I looked towards the sky as a long, dark shadow cast down over me.

Before I could visualize the danger that fell upon me, I was stirred from this surreal nightmare by the presence of Coleridge. He burst into the house, frenzied, eyes wilder than usual. A pained expression drew his lips into a snarl. I saw the dark crimson immediately. It covered Coleridge's cloak still moist to the touch. Streaks of blood ran lengthwise from his brow down across his cheeks. It matted his beard and hair in a clotted mess of color.

At first Coleridge didn't notice me sitting startled upon the floor. He became aware of my presence, mainly by almost tripping over me. He issued a one-word demand from a dry and scratchy throat.

"Water!"

The urgency in his voice pulled me up in a bound and sent me with winged feet to fetch a ladle of water. Coleridge reached out a shaky hand and snatched the ladle, spilling most of the water upon the ground. He drank the remains of it in two gulps. Then he collapsed in a heap upon the nearest chair.

I stood, feet together, staring at the floor. I dared not move, nor speak. My heart was racing as fast and strong as Coleridge's own. The blood that soaked him from head to foot gave away his nightly intentions. He'd gone killing again. Tonight perhaps the victim fought back in an attempt to save his life.

As Coleridge's labored breathing began to quiet into a shallower, balanced pace he cocked his head into the crook of his shoulder and stared with wild eyes at me. For the first time I came to realize that it wasn't madness that was set deep within Coleridge's stare. His eyes held the weight of a collective embodiment of sights no man had ever seen in one lifetime alone, nor would ever wish to. But Cain Coleridge was no ordinary man, I had realized that long ago.

Coleridge spoke suddenly, fervently. "Do you know what horrors lay out there in the night??"

"No, my Lord." I spoke slowly, unsure of the answer that Coleridge sought.

"I never dreamed that a stink hole such as this Gryphant would harbor such devils...I'm so close now."

"Close to what?"

Coleridge's lips curved into a mess of a smile. The streaks of blood lapped over his lips and ran down in fat drops from his chin. "You're a sponge aren't you boy? Ready to soak up knowledge. Good on you....but you're not ready yet. Yes, you're still a work in progress."

The mind reeled from all the possibility that could be unlocked within the last statement. I didn't know where to begin. Before I could utter a sound Coleridge rose.

As the blood splish-splashed off of Coleridge's chin and into his lap he grimaced and ran his forearm across his face, smearing the blood deeper into his grizzled beard.

"I need to get this stink off me."

Coleridge took generous hands full of water from my cleaning bucket splashing it into his face and over his neck. The blood upon him began to thin and finally disappear. I looked on wondering where so much blood had come from if no wound was visible on Coleridge himself.

"Where is the brandy?" he asked as he toweled off.

"You finished it the other night."

"That shall have to be remedied then, won't it?"

I stared at him blankly awaiting my next order. The words he next delivered came as a surprise.

"Come boy, we will venture into town and indulge in some recreations."

Had I known we would be heading to Mace Benton's tavern I would not have been so excited. However, I'd begun to get stir crazy feeling captive in the longhouse with nothing to do but work. A night away, regardless the destination, would prove soothing to the soul and mind.

The tavern was lively this night with drinking and general merriment. A lone fiddler took center stage and played out a rhythm worthy of dancing.

As Coleridge and I entered it seemed as though the world itself had stopped. It grew quiet. No movement was had, no fiddler playing his tune. All eyes stared upon us...or rather, upon Coleridge. He welcomed them with a tip of his hat and then made his way over to the bar.

I followed at his back and watched as those in his way parted like the wave of a fan. We took up a seat at the bar and waited. Coleridge stared long and hard at the barkeep who looked pale and quite faint.

"Are you going to serve me, fellow," Coleridge asked, "or shall I come over the bar and fetch my own drink?"

Benton's hulking form stepped in front of the barkeep and pushed him aside. He looked odiously smug. I cringed at his presence. So far the days with Coleridge had not been the most pleasurable but I hadn't missed that fat bastard Benton one bit.

"A good evening to you, Cain," Benton said with mock sincerity. "I shall serve you myself. What will you be having?"

"Brandy."

"Indeed, good choice."

As Benton poured he turned his attentions towards the other patrons and yelled scathing admonishments, something I had been on the receiving end of many times before.

"We have a true guest gracing us this evening. Let's show him a good time. Play on!"

With that the fiddler struck up a new tune and the chatter and dancing started up again, though this time it seemed that every conversation had to do with the dark suited stranger at the bar.

Benton set his watered down brandy in front of Coleridge and smiled a toothy grin. "You're always welcome here."

I could barely contain my hiss of disgust. What he truly meant, I'm certain Coleridge himself deciphered, was that any paying customer was welcome in the tavern.

Coleridge took a sip of the brandy and his face soured.

"So what brings you to my humble establishment this evening?" Benton asked.

"Brandy."

"The finest in town."

"Indeed."

I smiled at the exchange of words. Coleridge was humoring Benton, playing him for a fool just as Benton believed he held the upper hand.

Benton caught me smiling and snarled in my direction. Then he turned his attentions back to Coleridge.

"How's the boy working out for you?"

"Just fine."

"He's a pathetic creature but useful with a scrub brush," Benton laughed. "If he gives you any trouble just take a riding crop to his hide. That'll take the vinegar out of him quick."

I shuddered at that memory. If I had the opportunity I would've enjoyed marring Benton's grizzled face with his own bottle of watered down rum. But my position in life did not allow me such luxury. I could only sit and fantasize.

"Seems as though you enjoyed those times when the boy got out of line," Coleridge said.

"Hell sometimes I'd turn the crop on him just for fun," Benton told him. I'd been well aware of those times. "It always put a smile on my face to hear him squealing out like a pig."

Benton leaned on the bar allowing his pudgy arms to support his girth as he engaged his conversations of torture with Coleridge. I'd been forgotten altogether as though I were an invisible soul. That seemed to be my lot in life. I didn't even rank a drink.

As Benton continued his bellowing chuckle, Coleridge reached out to take up his brandy. In a flash he bypassed the glass and instead took out both of Benton's arms causing him to fall chin first upon the bar top.

The impact echoed off the walls of the tavern and once again the patrons inside grew silent, all eyes on Coleridge. He stood and leaned over the bar where he could more easily see Benton.

I stood as well, shocked and dumbfounded but rather pleased at the situation. Benton's jaw was split and bleeding. His teeth were marred with crimson and more blood gushed from his chin. He dared not make a move but he seemed to be trying to mouth curses towards Coleridge.

"It seems you are the swine, perhaps you should be the one squealing like a pig," Coleridge told him before taking up his still full glass and dumping it over Benton's prone body. "And the next time I order brandy I want to taste it." He turned to me. "Come Costa, let us leave this place."

Once again the sea of patrons parted at our exit.

As we walked back towards our housing Coleridge spoke freely.

"Mace Benton is ripe for cursing."

The words puzzled me. "What do you mean?"

"There are men and women in this world filled with such greed that they are easily swayed by promises of power. Normal citizens who take on a more deviant nature. Their dark hearts corrupt their very bodies literally peeling back the flesh and leaving them withered and decayed...walking dead."

Even as his words washed over me I still couldn't fathom what he was saying. I vocalized my disbelief.

"Such things truly exist?"

"Aye, but fear not young Calabrese, relieve them of their heads and they can do you no harm."

I'd been walking pace-for-pace with Coleridge up until then. Now I pulled back and allowed him to walk ahead of me as I tried to remember his words and warnings. If such things were true then the world I thought I knew held secrets to it that Coleridge appeared to have become privy to. Then again, perhaps labeling his victims as "cursed" made it easier for him when the time came to end their lives.

The next morning, Coleridge did not emerge from his room. There were times during the day when I could hear muffled shouts of hysterics coming from behind the closed door. Part of me wanted to push through into the room and come to Coleridge's aide from whatever was assaulting him. The other part, the more sane and reasonable part of my mind, stopped me short. The man was mad – better to leave him to his demons.

In the late afternoon when there were no more chores to attend to, and the sun was just setting down behind the black mountains, Tuck came calling.

He was hesitant to step inside so he remained at the door, feet together at the toes, hands laced in between the fingers.

"I haven't seen you in days," he said in a shallow whisper.

"Master Coleridge has kept me very busy," I replied.

"I feared that the madman had spirited you away in death," Tuck said, his voice becoming more audible.

"As you can see I'm still able bodied."

A hopeful little grin spread across Tucks lips. "In that case, perhaps we could take on one of our little journeys today. We're past due for a good one."

I almost shut him down, citing my servitude as the reason, until I had another look at Coleridge's closed door. It was silent now, no screams or muffled grunts came from beyond.

I turned back to Tuck, my own smile showing again for the first time in many days. "Yes we are, aren't we?"

We set out and took the turnoff path into Muir Woods the way we always had when starting out on one of our adventures.

Gryphant had little else surrounding it but Muir, it only depended on one's courage to see how deep into those woods one would go. On this day we walked slow and methodical. The weather had turned during my time with Coleridge and the air now held a frigid chill to it. The first snow had begun to come in with small flurries leaving patches of ice and slush covering the wilderness floor. The chill lent itself perfectly to the tone of discussion we were having – more precisely the one way conversation that Tuck was leading. I had merely responded with quiet grunts and nods right up until Tuck began reciting the history of the man known as Cain Coleridge.

"They say the descendants of the Coleridge line were cursed by a great evil many years ago. They say Cain himself is a madman, a mercenary. He travels from town to town destroying everything in his wake, forcing people to hide in their homes at his passing. They say his family was slain in the dead of the night by Cain's own hands."

I questioned his assessment of Coleridge's character though I did not know why. "Who are they? You're talking cryptic nonsense. Ridiculous tales formed from drunken old men."

"There is wisdom in their words...you used to tell me that. They've lived through raids and death marches. That is why none will step foot towards Coleridge's door lest they be cut down."

"If he'd wanted to eradicate the town he would've done so already," I said and instantly I remembered back to Coleridge's very words: Had I wanted to extinguish your life I would've done it back out in the woods where none would be the wiser.

"Why do you defend him after what we saw in these very woods? He's a killer, you know that."

"I'm not defending him. In fact, I fear for my life every single day while in his service. I just believe there's something more than a simple killer there once you scratch the surface."

"Benton gives you pain through every part of your body, Coleridge gives you fear through every part of your mind, and you practically thank them both for it. Sometimes I can't understand your way of thinking, Costa."

"Then perhaps you shouldn't try."

We were silent for a while letting the solace of the wilderness wash over us. The sun was settling down behind the crest of a mountain. A wash of color curtained the sky and bled it red, a strong reflection of the day's discussion.

For a long while the only sound was the subtle whipping of a small breeze tugging at the branches overhead. We came upon the path where just days before we'd first run across Coleridge, a blood stained knife tight in his hands. My hand tingled as I recalled the drop of blood that had fallen from his dagger and caressed my skin.

I stalked forward through the underbrush determined to discover the body of the man he'd slain that day.

"Where are we going?" Tuck asked as he followed up behind me.

I ignored him and continued walking. We ducked past trees with low bowed branches, into thickets and alongside patches of muddy ice brought up by the changing weather. It felt good to be bounding about again. There was freedom in each step, frivolity, no sustained effort to say and do what was expected of me. I stopped a moment to take it all in, breathed the cool air deep into my lungs and found my pace.

For the past four days I'd been driven by frenetic energy, fearful of each waking hour. I expelled that distaste in one long, hard exhale and then Tuck's words brought it all back inside.

"We should head back. I don't want to get you in trouble with Coleridge. His wrath could prove worse than Old Man Benton."

It seemed the self-same curse that I had known my whole life: always on the verge of discovery and always pulled back by a dominating master.

I nodded agreement towards Tuck and we moved on our way back through the thick of the underbrush. As we walked I took a look back over my shoulder still discontent and then I took a tumble. Something had caught me just above the ankle. I came down heavy and hard nose first into the dirt.

I pulled up to my hands and knees and dusted the earth from my tunic, that's when I saw it, smelled it even, and I fell very still.

I couldn't make out what I was really seeing. It looked like some type of go-between, half-man and half-beast. Coarse hair jutted from the cheeks and jowls. The ears ended in a point and stood out rather than laying flat to the head.

My heart held in my chest at the sight. I imagined the beast leering out with a gnarled paw and grasping my leg, tripping me. On second glance I saw that the eyes were lifeless and the mouth agape. The thing was dead, it had been dead for quite awhile, and death had come at the hands of another.

Suddenly Tuck hooked me under the arm and drew me to my feet.

"Don't touch that, it could carry disease."

"Look at it, Tuck," I said with awe. "It's like nothing I've ever seen before."

"What could've fell such a beast?" Tuck wondered aloud.

We observed the thing, looking over the bristled hair and matted blood. It looked as though it had been butchered. Stab wounds ran the course of its stomach, chest, and even its face. The pattern of the wounds rang a familiarity in my memory that I could not place. Tuck was eager to move on.

"We had better turn back, there is blood on the sun. It could only mean a warning."

"Did you learn that from your soothsayers?" I mocked.

"Believe what you will, but I refuse to tempt The Fates. I'm going back."

Tuck turned to begin the trek through the dense forest from which we had come. He wasn't two steps out before he halted and called back towards me. "Are you coming?"

"I suppose," I muttered. I didn't immediately turn and go. Instead, I stood looking up towards the blood red sky, studying it. There was a warning in its message. Blood would be spilled – things would forever change.

As we returned to the worn gates of Gryphant, Tuck muttered something of an apology for touching on my nerves, then added: "Just be wary, Coleridge is no saint."

When we neared the blacksmith's shop Tuck stretched out his hand to showcase a crudely wrapped package.

"Happy birthday, Costa," he told me. "Sorry it's late."

I gingerly took, the package from him opening it to reveal its contents. I held in my hand carved wood in the form of a new sling.

"My father helped me create that just for you."

I'd not had anything to smile about in quite awhile. This small token of friendship I held in my hand made all the difference at that moment.

"I'll treasure it always."

I hadn't journeyed out away from Gryphant in a month's time and the last time that I had my return had brought with it a savage beating. That had been under Mace Benton's care. Who knew what foul punishment would await me if Coleridge had awoke from his fevered sleep to find his servant boy had gone missing.

A curve of a hill and a dusty trail were all that separated me from knowing my answer to that ill-fated question. As I rounded the small slope and came down the simple path I saw a figure standing tall in the middle of the doorway.

Coleridge's eyes burned like glowing orbs. They were the only thing visible from beneath the brim of his hat. They were visible from many miles off. This time I did not have the same familiar urge to turn and run. I strode forward stopping just short of the threshold and tipped my chin until my eyes could see nothing but Coleridge's heavy leather boots. There I stood and awaited my punishment. Running away was no longer an option. I had nowhere to go.

"Eyes forward, boy," Coleridge told me. "Always look at your enemy."

I glanced up at Coleridge for a moment taking in the dark eyes and then looked to the ground once more. Clearing my throat I said: "Enemy or not you are still my master. I am paying my respects."

"A noted trait of survival for a slave boy, I'm certain. In battle it will get you killed."

Coleridge collected my chin in his fingers and raised my gaze eye-level to his own. "Eyes on your enemy...always, even if you hold court with royalty. Your next attacker could come from anyone, anywhere, at anytime."

Coleridge lumbered back into the longhouse and fetched himself a sheepskin full of liquor. I stood at the doorway for a moment, bemused, relieved that I hadn't tasted the back of a leather clad hand or the strike of a heavy whip. I followed Coleridge inside and, without taking a moment's hesitation to think about my actions, I sat down across from him and rattled off a question.

"Why do you tell me your secrets?"

Coleridge took up a clay pipe and packed it full of dark tobacco. Only after lighting it and taking in several short puffs did he answer my question. "They are not secrets, merely traits of survival every man should know...especially the way the land is ruled these days."

I edged closer in my seat until the thick rings of smoke from Coleridge's pipe encircled my head and caused a tingle of discomfort at the back of my throat. "But why me?"

"I'm getting older. I can't keep doing this forever...even if I do be cursed."

Coleridge paused to marinate in his thoughts all the while taking small puffs from his pipe and blowing the smoke into ringlets across the air. "But don't count yourself special in that regard, Calabrese," he said through his next inhalation. "You are merely the first one I've spoken with at length in several odd years."

I chose my next words carefully even as I repeated what Tuck had told me earlier that day. "Some say you're a saint, others a madman. Which is it?"

Coleridge laughed a low, quick chuckle from deep in his belly. "Foolish sheep." He seemed to speak more to himself than in any regard to me. "They should be honoring me with a feast for sparing them a siege of bloodshed upon their worthless heads. Instead, they chastise my very name...so be it." He turned to me then with his full attention. "Do you agree with their assessment of me, boy?"

"I'm not certain what to think." I paused wondering if I should relate my next words. "Out in Muir Woods that day...I saw you kill a man."

"Things aren't always as they seem. Remember what I told you about the cursed and the damned. There are things in this world filled with such evil that the earth turns black upon their footsteps. They would hollow out your eyes and eat you alive. I am the killer, boy. I hunt these creatures not for bounty but to destroy them, rid the scourge from the earth before the unsuspecting lot are murdered in their beds and slaughtered like sheep in the night. I did not choose this path, it chose me, but I embrace it. The beings I hunt are more dangerous than any man that lives...I am a hunter of demons."

His words chilled me, a rush of cold that swilled over my body and made me involuntarily shiver. Demon hunter? I could only question why someone would willingly seek out beings such as werewolves and cursed beings. But Coleridge wasn't a regular man by any sorts. Much of what he said and did was a great mystery to me and that is what intrigued me so much.

Coleridge had paused in his tale for a long while, twirling the clay pipe between his fingers. Finally he set it on the table and asked: "Would you like to know the truth?"

I could only nod in response. My throat had gone dry and my tongue heavy. The air seemed thick and especially chilly as Coleridge began a tale that apparently started out a long time ago.

"I've been walking this earth for hundreds of years, or so it seems. My early days were spent on a plantation farm similar to this pitiful town we are in now. I can remember little of my life back in those days except to say that as a child I knew nothing of fear or regret. At that time I had the foolish belief that the love of my family would be strong enough to sustain any of the world's evils."

I shifted uneasily in my chair. That sort of love was not something I was familiar with. I held no memories of a childhood painted with love and support. Very little of my core being came from my days as a youth. My father had left our family soon after I came into the world. And though my mother had done her very best, right up until she met her end, there still remained that missing piece of the puzzle that created my very existence. My father was a part of who I was as a whole. I wondered if he were still out there in the world. Sadly, I had come to accept that the fact may never be revealed.

Sometimes it pained me to hear the tales of other's fond family memories, or to see lads my same age accompanied by mother, father, or even siblings. At those moments the world seemed to be even more unfair than I ever realized.

Coleridge pulled away from his tale and put his attention on me as he misinterpreted the pained look etched across my face. "My family was not slain by my hands, boy, regardless of what you have heard." He paused, once again turning inward to reflect. "I merely cleansed the grounds where a cursed home held impressions of an unspeakable night."

I wasn't sure if I really wanted an answer to my next question, Coleridge's eyes had grown dark in such a way that he looked as though he'd gone into a trance, but I found myself asking it anyway. "What happened?"

"It seemed my sister had been spirited away, vanished in the night. My father was frantic and sick with worry. After years of searching we finally found her. She had been captured, bewitched into doing evil's bidding. My father, Abe, rescued her and brought her home...she repaid him with death. I awoke in the night with a sick feeling like a fire-pit in my stomach. Foresight of evil are just one of the abilities I am cursed with."

"Cursed?" I interrupted. "That should be a blessing in disguise to know the whereabouts of evil before they have a chance to sneak up on you."

Coleridge studied me a moment before answering. "You speak as if you know."

My thoughts immediately turned to the dreams. Often they appeared so real to me, like some future that had not yet taken place. It had been that way for as long as I can remember.

"But you don't know, Calabrese," Coleridge continued. "You couldn't know unless you were there and saw the destruction unfold with your own eyes. The urging had drawn me out of bed towards the front parlor where I found my father engaged in a death match with a creature so vile and hideous and yet still holding the same air of beauty my sister had always projected. That night she had finally succumbed to the demon dwelling inside of her. My father was no match. Either the creature held too much strength or he was foolishly blinded by his love. She proceeded to tear out his throat and began to feed on him...until she saw me. While I stood there I saw more than I can tell, and I understood more than I saw. I'll never forget the snarl, lips peeled back to reveal teeth as sharp and serrated as any dagger. And then she came for me."

Coleridge broke off his tale as though it had concluded, but in my mind there were so many more questions raised through the description of that terrible night that I could not let it go.

"How is it you survived?"

Coleridge's eyes flashed. "I killed the bitch."

"But you were a mere boy...like me."

"Every boy must become a man, Calabrese, some just make it there sooner than others. And some don't make it there at all. I was determined to live...though the reasons why escape me now. But back then I was full of life and vigor, so much so that I cut off the head of the beast and burned my childhood home to the ground with both bodies inside."

His eyes locked on mine. Then he issued me something of a command. "Always commit the entire corpse to purifying flame."

I grew uneasy with his tale of bloodshed. At the same time I felt for Coleridge. To have memories of those you've loved and lost is perhaps harder than to have no memories at all. He must have felt my distress for he questioned me in the midst of recalling the disturbing events.

"Do you fear?"

"Yes."

"What is it you fear?"

I did not hesitate in my answer. "You."

"Only demons should fear me boy. You're not a demon are you?"

I shook my head vigorously making certain that I stated an emphatic No. Coleridge had killed his own sister because she had changed into a hideous creature; he labeled Mace Benton as ripe for cursing. Was it that he saw something insidious in people that no other could see, or perhaps he was mad after all.

A question had been gnawing on my mind for days, finally it slipped from my lips. "Where is it that you go in the night when the rest of the world is sleeping?"

"The bewitching hour is when the world is burning with energy. While you simple folk lay in your beds the creatures of the night amass and wander over the land spreading chaos in their wake. But you needn't worry your head on such matters. That is my burden alone to carry, one I've been cursed with for what seems like eternity."

"How is it that such a task came to you alone?"

He sighed. "Just lucky I guess. My mentor once told me I held great powers that were meant for a higher purpose...not just for myself."

I spoke both with a great insistence and a desperate plea. "I could assist you."

"Foolish youth. You know not of what you ask."

"I would be honored, sir, to learn at the foot of a master."

"I am no school teacher, lad. The world out there is an education all of itself. But you have to have the courage to journey out past these walls to find it. Let that be the most important lesson I impart to you."

"The things I've witnessed, the stories you've told me, I can't just dismiss them and continue to carry out my days blind like before," I persisted.

Coleridge pressed his palms to his closed eyes and made a weary sound worthy of the dead. "Perhaps it was a mistake for me to have come this way," he said. Peeling his hands back from his eyes he took in my eager face and lamented my request. "Very well, Costa, I suppose you must learn such lessons at some point – I owe you that much."

My heart raced at his words. The promise of skill passed on from a member of the Coleridge line was something out of a dream.

Coleridge forced his weary body up from the chair and lumbered back towards his quarters with all the effort of a man double his age. He'd grown depleted and pained from the previous night but still he held a rapier wit and vigor in his soul that I couldn't help admiring. He returned soon after with two knives in his hands.

"The first thing you should know is how a proper defense can alter even the best of offenses." He halted long enough to move to my side and pluck the sling Tuck had given to me from my side. "What is this contraption you've been carrying around?"

"It was a gift, sir," I stammered.

"Time to put away your toys, Costa. Life demands of it...especially if you insist upon learning my ways."

He handed the slingshot back, watched, and waited for me to discard it. It pained me to do so knowing how much time and thought Tuck had put into crafting the gift for me but Coleridge's eyes alone insisted I give it up.

Afterwards he took me outside into the cool breath of the afternoon and showed me how to handle a knife. I'd thought it would be obvious, the sharp end pierces the intended target thus eliminating the immediate threat. However, Coleridge prepared me for a myriad of attacks and defenses alike. Parries, thrusts, switchovers, a multitude of combat drills that took us well into the night and all the while Coleridge prompted me with words.

"Challenge yourself. Push your limits. Believe in yourself. See the end result in your mind before taking action."

I captured each of those directions in my mind and tried to implement them into what lay before me but I continued to stumble and ultimately Coleridge came up on the winning end each and every time.

Winded and frustrated I fell to my knees and pounded the round of my fist into the dirt. It was a childish fit but I'd always imagined in my mind that when the day came to prove my skills and worth I would be something of a natural. That proved not to be the case and it bothered me to no end. Coleridge, however, was adamant that I finish.

"Get up on your feet, it's time for trapping," he said.

"Trapping?" I questioned.

"I said up, boy. You insisted upon this now you will come to learn it. The enemy waits for no man."

He clinched me up by the arms and proceeded with forward pressure following with short range strikes. The first open-hand palm strike he left upon my skin reverberated in my ears and left my flesh raw several moments after impact. It nearly buckled me but I pressed on.

"If you're ever forced into hand-to-hand combat with one of these things, and pray that you never are, this training will enable you to strike at your opponent while immobilizing them."

With one last hard strike upon my flesh, Coleridge manipulated his elbow against my own and twisted my arm until I was forced to fall to my knees or risk a broken and lifeless appendage.

He tussled my hair knowing full well that I couldn't defend from him, not that I would've resisted even if my arms were free. Then he let me up.

"That's enough for today. I must rest before the night comes like the restless whore that it is."

I didn't argue. I was exhausted both physically and mentally. I'd taken in a lot that day...in the last few days even. As Coleridge lumbered back to his room to rest I remained outside running over the techniques he'd shown me and the stories he'd told.

After our conversation, I felt a shift in my relationship with Coleridge. I no longer felt like the servant boy bowing to his master's whims and cowering in fear. The fear and intimidation had given way to intrigue, awe, and admiration for who this man really was.

Coleridge was wise above his years, strong and charismatic. He possessed the very qualities that I wished for myself. I followed on his trail back inside the house. His clay pipe remained upon the table. I picked it up and twirled it in my fingers. It was worn and grooved from constant use. With the fire extinguished it had grown cold now. I put it to my lips and dared to dream that I would be even half the man that Cain Coleridge was when I reached that pinnacle in my life. Somehow it didn't seem in the stars for me.

I set down the pipe and picked up my slingshot from across the table. Tucking it back into my belt felt more natural to me than the hand-to-hand skills I'd learned that day. It was all I'd ever known and though I longed to uncover more from Coleridge some things were just too difficult to let go of.

As the remainder of the day waged on into night I pondered over my talk with Coleridge, replaying the terrible tale he'd related from his youth over and over again in my mind until it somehow seemed as though I had been there myself and saw it with my own two eyes.

The transformation of Coleridge's sister, the death of his father, the decapitation, and the burning that followed. I smelled the smoke, the charred flesh singed my nose and I felt like I would retch. A shudder rounded up over my spine and forced me to relinquish the images from my mind.

I waited out the day as best I could, always looking over my shoulder to the heavy chamber door where Coleridge had retired earlier that day. I waited for him to stir, to come back out and continue his ardent tale. Finally the wait appeared too much to bear and I pulled myself away into the outdoors.

There was jasmine in the air outside and the faint smell of something deeper, more pungent. I stood allowing the scent to wash over me as it drew in over the Autumn breeze. I tried to mark out its distinction and the direction from which it flowed. Like any good tracker it was important to find the source of your discontent before it snuck up on you, that much I knew.

Just then Coleridge lumbered out the door dragging his ever present bag of tricks behind him. He noted my strong concentration and quickly filled in the blanks.

"That's death you smell, boy," he told me. "The portal to hell has opened in your backyard."

My blood ran cold. I swallowed hard trying to take in Coleridge's words as mere rambling, but in my soul I knew it was the truth he spoke.

"The scourge of evil are beginning to take up arms," Coleridge continued. "It won't be long now."

"Long for what?"

Coleridge shook his head. "Never mind. It shall be dealt with."

"You must take me with you!" I pleaded. I did not know where he was going, did not know the danger that he spoke of, point of fact he was rambling on like a man gone mad. I only followed my heart's desire and intent.

"Still so eager. A fool who laughs at death." Coleridge said. "Know your strengths and weaknesses, young Calabrese. You've still much to learn. As for tonight, I go alone."

With that a clap of thunder scattered across the twilight sky. Soon a storm would take hold of Gryphant and its neighbors.

Coleridge let the first few drops of rain moisten his brow before donning his wide-brim hat and suiting the familiar bag about his shoulder. He was headed out for another trek into the deepest night, but this time he did something very unexpected. As he passed by, Coleridge clasped my shoulder and spoke directly to me.

"Live your life so that when you die you rejoice. Go forward with courage."

And as a sudden downpour pulled a heavy mist off the ground Cain Coleridge did just that.

Chapter Three
Creeping Death

I'd given Coleridge just enough ground to leave him without cause for suspicion and then I set out after him. I couldn't help myself. He'd peaked my curiosity. Leave something shrouded for so long and eventually one begins to wonder what lies beneath.

He trekked slow and methodical through the now twilight laden foliage of Muir. I followed in a low crouch staying a good distance behind him where I could just make out the trace of his coat as it flowed out behind him.

I'd never been out in the woods past sunset. Something about not having the light to guide me unnerved me in such a way that I kept my head on a swivel, afraid to find an enemy at my back unexpectedly.

Coleridge came to an abrupt stop and I dropped to my belly as swiftly and silently as I could. I didn't want to endure his wrath if he saw that I directly disobeyed him. I just needed to see for myself what he was doing every night.

The incoming storm had been nothing but a tease bringing in just enough rain to moisten the earth so that I now sat wallowing in thick patches of cold mud and ice. My body shivered trying to keep the warmth from escaping. The smart thing to do would be to turn around and go back home, but I'd never proclaimed myself the most intelligent of young men. I always led with my heart not my head and at the moment my heart told me to stay put for something was about to take place.

After a moment's hesitation Coleridge went into his bag and withdrew the strange small plant he'd laced about the entry to the house. It was fashioned differently this time, the leaves had been attached to a rope in a circular manner that slipped over Coleridge's head like a necklace.

I marveled at the strange complexity of the situation, then watched as he began his next task...digging a grave. With the ground still so moist it didn't take long for Coleridge to dig a good sized hole with his bare hands. He left his satchel beside it then hurried off into the darker neck of the forest. I scrambled to my feet and went after him, careful to avoid the hole.

By the time I had made it past the hole, Coleridge had disappeared into the night. I cursed my misfortune then headed back towards the curious makeshift grave. Looking down into the depth of the hole it remained a mystery to me.

I noted his satchel at the side of the hole, usually it remained ever present at Coleridge's side. For a moment I considered taking it with me back to the longhouse for fear he may lose it in the dead of the night. But as my fingers reached towards the leather strap something told me to leave it be, in fact something nagging at the back of my mind told me to get away from that spot as fast as I could move.

It wasn't more than a moment after I ducked down behind several thick firs than Coleridge returned dragging something large behind him. A monster lay at his back. As he drew closer I recognized it as the carcass Tuck and I had found earlier that day. Coleridge dragged the thing, with considerable effort, towards the grave. He intended to bury the beast.

I watched from my hiding place amongst the bushes as he chucked the remains of the beast into the hole. I stayed silent as he moved mounds of dirt by hand over the carcass. But then something shifted in the night just paces from Coleridge.

My chest constricted in fear when the element of danger finally revealed itself. At first I couldn't understand how the carcass had disappeared from its new grave and made its way behind Coleridge then I realized that this was not the same beast but another of a similar likeness.

The protruding teeth, the gnarled claws, a beast of a thing standing upright like that of a man. What pit of Hell had brought forth such an abomination?

With Coleridge in danger I could no longer stay silent. The beast would be upon him in two strides. I pushed through the firs in a scrambled mess of shouts and gestures and it was only then that I saw the silver tipped knife gripped tight in Coleridge's hand. He'd been aware of the beast behind him the entire time. The makeshift grave, the burial of the carcass, it had all been a trap laid out to draw in the other beast. Coleridge had it all planned out except for one variable...me.

When he saw me draw out of the bushes his eyes registered shock for the first time. The beast as well was taken aback, but only for the moment. It stopped long enough to let out a howl up towards the midnight sky and then began its forward assault moving much swifter than a moment ago.

"Get back," Coleridge shouted at me and then turned his attentions on the beast.

They clashed together in an entanglement of limbs lashing out at each other. Despite Coleridge's demand of me I did not move, I could not pull myself away as the two battled. Coleridge held his own end like a man possessed but the beast proved every bit as strong as it appeared and it knocked him to the ground with a solid strike of a gnarled paw.

Coleridge landed hard and stiff losing his wind in the fall. The beast stood before him, a magnificent sight of fur overlaying sinews of heavy muscle. Another howl pierced the night air as the beast toyed with its prey.

Without regarding consequences I moved forward ready to do battle or die trying. But as the beast saw me I halted in my tracks. The curl of its lip and the fury in its eyes made me think twice of my actions. It disregarded Coleridge and came for me. I remained paralyzed with fear.

Something in the weight of its stare told me that it mastered intelligence. Its actions were not random but marked with purpose.

Coleridge scrambled to his feet and shouted with angst. "No!"

He was upon the beast in two strides stabbing it high upon the shoulder with his dagger and once again insisted upon me to remove my presence from the scene.

"Run!"

This time I obeyed.

I turned just in time to see that Coleridge had left his dagger deep within the meat of the beast's shoulder and was now coming fast behind me, faster even. He grabbed my arm, almost pulling me to the ground.

"Do not remove this lest you want to lose your head," he demanded as he slipped the necklace of plant leaves from his neck and placed it around mine. "Wolfsbane shall be your savior. Now keep moving, it's shifted into full lycanthrope by this time."

My mind was a mad scramble that fell in line with the erratic beating of my heart. Wolfsbane? Lycanthrope? I'd only ever heard those words used in legend, mad tales dismissed as falsehoods. Coleridge had been proving a great many facts over the past few hours.

I heard him breathing heavy as he ran the grounds of the woods. His footsteps were amplified by the sounds of another, two pair in fact, moving swift at our backs. I made the mistake of turning to get a visual of our chaser and to see how close he was upon us.

To my surprise I found that a wolf of the four-footed variety came after us. He moved with blistering speed even with his size. It was quite an intimidating sight.

"Don't stop!" Coleridge demanded. His words were an echo on the wind and in my ears right before he was torn down by the wolf at his heels. It took his leg in the snare of his teeth toppling Coleridge.

I wanted to race back to help him until I saw the eyes of the wolf. They were the same pale yellow with the same intensity of spirit that I'd found in the eyes of the man-beast just moments before.

In my hesitation Coleridge took his own action by kicking the wolf square in the jaw with his free leg. This would give us the opportunity we needed to make our escape. I lunged forward and grasped the thick of Coleridge's arm and pulled him up.

"Move, move," he told me, his voice shallow and racked with pain.

I did my best to carry his weight on mine and we lumbered our way to the safe outskirts of Muir Woods. I believe the only reason our escape wasn't thwarted is because the wolf would not cross into open territory.

Its call into the open air signified its frustration and for the first time upon hearing the howl I realized I'd heard it before. It had been the day Tuck and I had made a trek into the thick of the woods and stumbled upon Coleridge for the first time. I wondered how many more of the creatures lay within the trees.

Coleridge was in immeasurable pain but that didn't stop him from cuffing me up beside the back of the head and laying down strong words of admonishment.

"I told you not to follow me. You directly disobeyed me. Such foolish actions could've led us both to an early grave!"

"I accept whatever punishment you deem fit. It was a bad judgment on my behalf. I grew curious and restless enough to disregard your words, but I never expected to see...." I broke off in mid-sentence because I simply did not know how to finish it. There were no words to describe what it was that I saw, at least I had none. Coleridge's time on this earth brought to him a different experience.

"Werewolf. The word you are looking for is Werewolf," he told me matter-of-fact.

My eyes grew wide in shock. "That can't be possible. They are myths nothing more."

At this Coleridge laughed. "Believe me boy there are many things in this world that you will not even believe when you set your own eyes upon them. That doesn't make them any less of a threat."

"That day out in Muir when you'd butchered that man...."

He cut off my words and finished my thought. "Werewolf . That was no man. And the angry little cur we left back their bitching at the moon was his whore."

"That thing is a woman?"

"Only in the daylight hours," he told me. "At night she's been the most elusive of all those devil dogs."

"And you seek out these Werewolves purposefully? Why?"

"Such is my lot in life. My lot, you understand? What happened today cannot happen again."

I nodded and bowed my head in shame. The tone of his voice alone tore me to the core and left me feeling like a hapless child. It was the worst feeling I'd held in a very long time. Not since I lost my mother had I harbored such a pained knot in my stomach from the sense of loss.

My foolish actions alone had caused a rift between Coleridge and I. He'd become my mentor of sorts – he was all I had in this cold world. I couldn't bear to lose him as well. But the damage had been done. Something had been broken.

Coleridge looked down towards his ravaged leg. It had begun to swell around the knee pulling rivers of blood down over his heavy boots. Rather than using stitches or a fired piece of iron to mend his wound, Coleridge opted to wrap a cloth high upon his thigh like a crude tourniquet and then knock back a flask full of whiskey which ultimately put him face first upon the dining table.

I tried to sleep but nightmares of hounds from hell plagued me all night. The smell of the hair still overtook my senses and the high pitched wail still rang in my ears. I drew up time and again in a sweat. It wasn't until the dawn broke over the sky that I found myself drifting off peacefully.

When I awoke much later it seemed the day had gotten away from me. I hurried down from the hay loft where I slept and into the main house steadying myself for a thrashing or tongue lashing for not fixing breakfast. Instead I found a bit of parchment tacked to the dining table with another one of Coleridge's silver tipped daggers.

It read:

It seems the sands in the hour glass have dissipated at an alarming rate. There is only one choice...I must finish this now! Heed my warning this time and do not seek me. I tell you this for your own safety.

You are free Costa, have the courage to follow your heart.

I folded the parchment, tucked it inside my jerkin, and slipped the knife in a loop at my belt. After sitting quietly for what could've been hours I unfolded the parchment and read it again, then refolded it and tucked it away once more.

Night began to fall just outside the window and still no sign of Coleridge. I could no longer sit and wait. Something in my bones told me he would not be returning on his own if at all this time. Words of warning or not I knew what must be done, so I loaded up a satchel with a full line of necessities. Remembering back to all those past nights I'd watched Coleridge fill a fraying sack with wooden stakes and blessed water I tried to emulate that now.

My bag consisted of meager provisions. A sheepskin of water rested at my right hip, the silver tipped dagger at my left. Squaring my jaw I set out. But the moment I stepped foot outside the front entrance my determination seized up on me.

"C'mon," I scolded myself through gritted teeth and forced myself to move. The task laid out before me was daunting, one I wasn't so certain I could handle alone. Reinforcements would be needed.

Tuck seemed almost hysterical as I explained my decision to go into Muir Woods to look for Coleridge and bring him home.

"Have you gone mad?" Tuck asked in half laughter, half shaken fear.

I calmly reassured him. "No."

"You've taken ill then?"

"No."

"But why then would you want to risk life and limb to learn the whereabouts of a cruel and evil master? You're free Costa! Let the bastard stay gone."

I paced amiably back and forth in front of the Blacksmith's Shop. Steam and heat from the iron work were billowing out across Tuck's back as he stood just underneath the archway. Perspiration collected at the top of his brow and his head seemed to have an involuntary spasm as he shook it back and forth in dismay.

Now I cast my line. I needed a strong argument to reel Tuck in on this trek and I had conjured one up on the short walk from Coleridge's long house to The Blacksmith's Shop.

"Don't you see, if Coleridge doesn't return I'll be forced to go back under old man Benton's watch."

A look of concern flashed over the round cheeks and prominent brow of Tuck Goodall. I continued to draw him in. "He'll be merciless with his whims and quick with his hands. And although Coleridge terrified me he never once brought me any physical harm. Coleridge is the lesser of two evils. I have to bring him back."

Tuck stepped down from the doorway and wiped a grimy hand over his sweat-stained face. He grew silent and my heart seized in my chest. I'd never heard him so quiet before.

"But what if he doesn't want to be found?" he finally said. "What if he left Gryphant for good?"

That thought had crossed my mind as well but I had no intention of entertaining the idea. Life was a cruel back tavern joke wrought with futility before Coleridge came. I refused to return to such monotony. If it happened that Coleridge had taken his leave from Gryphant, I would be just as inclined to follow him.

After Tuck had finally agreed to join me on my journey he made it a point to overload us with necessities and non-necessities alike regardless of my protests that traveling with less was more desired on such a journey.

Under the guise of one of our morning adventures, Tuck wooed his mother into packing some slivers of fresh mutton, a wedge of cheese, a full loaf of nut grain bread and fruits. Tuck then loaded his frame with body armor making his bulk double.

The finality came in John Goodall's smithery. This time it was I who belied Tuck's protests as I gathered armaments for the two of us. For Tuck, a halberd and a horned helmet that, once fitted, gave him the look of a Viking...one shaking in his boots.

I decided on , a shirt of chainmail that extended too long past my knees, and I almost settled for a mace until a longsword, fresh from the kiln and polished that morning caught my eyes.

"No Costa, you can't," Tuck protested. "My father was commissioned to make that for someone of very high esteem."

"Who?" I asked, my eyes glinting off the polished steel and perfectly grooved grip. "There is no one in this town who holds esteem, that's been the problem with Gryphant for many years now."

My thoughts turned back to Coleridge. The once mysterious stranger who had swept into town and rocked Gryphant to its very core. He had been a favorable element to the sleepy, predictable nature of the people. Cain Coleridge shook things up and that spark of life in and of itself was reason enough to grow bold and continue my intent and desire to seek out his whereabouts and bring him back.

In that decision I knew I needed weaponry of the finest creation. As my hand went for the sword the distinctive gruff bellow from Tuck's father, John, sounded out as he entered the smithery just behind us.

"What're you boys doing? I told you never to fool around in here."

"Sorry father," Tuck said, dropping his head, ready to admit defeat. I did not share his desires. Grabbing him about the wrist I moved as swiftly as I could past John Goodall with Tuck in tow behind me.

As we made it safely outdoors I called back behind us: "Sorry, won't happen again."

We were almost to the edge of town when John realized we had torn his workspace asunder in our quest for weapons. I could hear his hollering protests just as we entered Muir Woods.

Tuck's body stiffened and his eyes went wide. "I've never heard my father so angry."

"Don't worry," I told him, "you can journey with Coleridge and I."

And I meant it. Three heads were better than one...assuming we ever found him.

Chapter Four
Heroes

We'd taken the same path through Muir Woods more times than could be counted, but this time the journey ahead held a different distinction. The test that lay before us wasn't an imagined task dreamed up to cultivate an otherwise dreary day. This time there was a purpose that was personal in nature.

What I had told Tuck to persuade him to join me was the truth. In Coleridge's absence all rights and claims to my services would revert back to Mace Benton. But there was much more of a reason to be out in the thick of the woods wearing heavy chainmail and a horned helmet that didn't quite sit right.

During my time under Coleridge's watch I had come to know him as a master, a mentor, and now I even considered him a friend. I couldn't just let him disappear into the night without any regard for where or why...especially considering his wounds.

Soon we found ourselves in unfamiliar territory. The trees, the rocks, the bushes, not a thing in sight held any significance to me whatsoever. I'd been out in Muir more times than I could recall, sometimes with Tuck, sometimes on a solo adventure, but each time the surroundings lent themselves to my aide. There was always a simple trail leading to wherever I wanted to go. Somehow we were turned about.

We'd come down a crested ridge deeper into the forest floor among what seemed to be a canyon of sorts. We moved fleet of foot down the trail into the canyon until an uneasy feeling, like black tar bubbling up inside me, halted me in my tracks. Something didn't feel quite right and I'd come to rely on my sense of intuition a great deal on these journeys. If a sign presented itself to me I'd be a fool to ignore it.

"Let's turn back," I told Tuck.

"And head home?" He sounded much too eager.

"No. Let's just get out of this canyon and back onto the main path."

First we moved left following a dry river bed which held loose rock and uneven footing.

"We didn't come this way," I said feeling the flush of frustration heating my collar. "I don't remember any of this."

We turned back, this time breaking right and moved on for a time until I came to realize that not a single landmark stood out to me.

"This is wrong," I said stopping to catch my breath. The travel grew weary and I regretted ever slipping into the chainmail piece earlier that day. It doubled my weight and held unbearable heat upon my skin even through the soft swath of my jerkin.

Tuck flopped down upon a large rock next to me and relinquished his helmet to the ground, no doubt feeling the same ill effects as I.

"Gods, we're lost." He spoke in such a defeatist's tongue that I nearly snapped his head off.

"We are not lost. Now get up and let's keep moving."

"Where?"

"Back into the canyon."

"There's nothing to be gained that way."

"It's our only choice. Let's see it through to the other side."

I didn't like the decision any more than Tuck did, the discomfort of my inner warning playing hell on my memory, but we'd run out of options.

In our descent down we would err on the side of caution, taking every step very slow and measured. The further down we retreated, the darker it seemed to become as the deep crevices of the canyon rose up around us and blocked out the remaining light of the sun.

It seemed the elements of Mother Earth were against us as well. I wondered for a moment if in some telling way we were being warned to proceed no further.

Looking back at Tuck with the brim of his helmet too far over his eyes, and the slide rather than step of each foot, I knew I had to hold strong for both of us. Whatever dark and mysterious forces we were about to contend with in the pit of a black canyon couldn't be any worse than those we'd tangled with before...at least that's what I kept telling myself.

Another half step in and a wisp of fog seemed to come from out of nowhere, wrapping us in clouds of vapor so thick that I could scarcely make out my own hands in front of my eyes much less the safe passage.

Off instinct I pulled my dagger from my waist and extended it in front of me, lashing left to right in the air as I pressed forward. If anything were going to make a jump at us I intended to be readily armed at the very least.

I could hear Tuck behind me, calling my name in an almost fevered hysteria.

"It's alright, Tuck," I said reaching one hand back and blindly catching his wrist. "I'm right here. Grab hold of my belt and follow me through.

Tuck obeyed my request and we moved in a human chain as best we could through the fog. As we pressed further I made out a distinctive mix of smells in the air. It held the elements of coal, brimstone, and the very real and pungent scent of death.

As the fog fell loosely from our shoulders and our path grew clear once again we realized we'd been completely thrown off course.

"Hallowed Grounds." Tuck spoke low, almost under his breath, I had to strain to pick up his words. When I did, I wished I'd been struck stone deaf at birth. I cast my gaze out across the open field that had presented itself in front of us.

As I took in the rampant destruction I realized Tuck spoke the truth. Somehow through our missteps through the blinding fog we'd managed to find ourselves in the middle of an open graveyard known to all as the Hallowed Grounds.

No holy ground lay under our feet here. When my house mother, Cecile, had been alive she'd broken away from the tales of her husband's adventures at sea long enough to impart the story of how The Hallowed Grounds had come to be.

It had been many years before when the grounds that housed Gryphant and its neighbors lay flat, uninhabited by people. Two twin cities were at war, each intent on taking up the land under their own rule. Each side optioned their very best in the attacks. Nobility, kings, and even those of the clergy took up arms. The battle lasted for weeks, raging more vicious with each passing hour. It finally came to be that no man was left standing. Bodies littered the ground. Thousands of corpses of the fallen remained as statues in their final moments of life for many years. Each lifeless corpse grew skinless, and eyeless before they returned to the dust from which they were spawned.

What remained stood before us now – the very real presence of death open and exposed to all who were unfortunate enough to find themselves upon the Hallowed Grounds. Over time markers had been erected, representative of the fallen in their last moments of life. Pillars of granite standing over six feet formed something of a border around the battlegrounds. The sculpted likenesses of five individual gargoyles rested atop them.

They watched over the dead, protecting their lost kings even now. Dead Birchwood trees stood leafless in the field. Dark, thick plumes of smoke billowed up from fires that should've been long since extinguished. Though the battle had been over for some time the air still held a very unsettling aura of that time, as though there were unfinished affairs that needed tending and at any moment the dead would rise up and continue clashing steel upon steel into eternity.

"I want to go," Tuck fell over his words in a messy stutter. For once I agreed with him. The only problem of course lay in the fact that I didn't know how we'd found our way to the gravesite in the first place, so getting out presented a real problem.

"Let's turn and try to retrace our steps." It was the best thing I could come up with though backtracking would prove difficult. The thick smoke had swayed us far from our immediate path. But going any further into the Hallowed Grounds would only be more detrimental to our lives and livelihood.

I turned about, Tuck close at my heels, and started towards what I thought to be the path we'd come in from. Slowly, cautiously we moved until a sharp keening assaulted our ears. I whirled round, dagger displayed in defense, and sought the source of the cry.

"Those sight markers," Tuck said slowly. "They aren't complete."

"What do you mean?" I held my concern at the back of my throat and cautiously turned my attention to the granite pillars. To my chagrin they were not complete as Tuck had said. A very important element was void from each and everyone. The tops were bare. The gargoyles missing.

"What do you think it means?" Tuck asked. I had no answer of my own but we would both soon discover the meaning of it together.

Another ear-piercing wail rang out and it brought our eyes to the sky above. There we found the missing gargoyles. Five of them thundered above. Heavy-set haunches hovering over us as wings of granite held them aloft.

My mouth fell agape, my eyes wide with terror. The gruesome features, once stone now moved in grotesque malevolence as another shrill cry, a warning from above, rang out from first one, then all five.

Tuck almost fell over himself as he backpedaled towards the path we'd stumbled in from. I followed suit and turned on my heel to run, my head whipped back over my shoulder several times to keep an eye on the gargoyle pack.

At first they didn't move. They simply hovered in the air marking us with their eyes. I took it upon myself to react before they did. I returned my knife to its home and, taking up the sling Tuck had built for my birthday, I saddle a good size rock in its cradle, marked my target, and let it fly.

It was a good aim and I wound up taking out one of the gargoyles in the center of the pack. This angered the others and they were swift to move.

Tuck pushed on ahead of me and I took up the rear with one last glance back towards the hell we'd just escaped from, only to find that hell now followed us. The gargoyles were on the move and swifter than I would've imagined a formerly stone statue would be, though I never ventured to guess I would see one in flight either.

The rising smoke from the Hallowed Grounds did not impede our forward movement on the way out which led me to believe that perhaps the accursed grounds drew in travelers to their deaths in just such a way. Tuck moved faster than I had ever seen him go before. I all but lost him in the distance but for the shouting he left trailing behind in his wake.

"What demon curse is this!" he shouted. I wanted to implore him to shut up and move but at the moment my voice lodged in my chest where the pulse of my heartbeat slammed relentlessly.

We scrambled fast up jagged rock, through sticker bushes, and across narrow ravines without a second thought for caution or peril. Our only concern came from above. I dared not look up. The enormous shadows falling over us and the gusts of wind touching our backs with each hard flap of wings were enough to tell me that the gargoyles were close.

My legs moved in jagged patterns, never a straight line, for fear that if I stayed too simplistic in my escape that I'd be snatched up at the shoulders and forever lost.

I noticed Tuck slowing down ahead of me. His head moved left and right in dismay. He was lost.

Somewhere in me I found my voice and hollered in his direction. "Keep moving!"

My voice jolted him. He took off running again. With fire traveling the muscles of my legs, my sandals almost coming apart at the seams, I didn't know how much longer I could continue on. Still I knew that movement, no matter where, was the desired method of escape from these creatures. Then in the distance I saw refuge. The thick of the trees that lined Muir Woods beckoned us back into itself.

We edged closer and the gargoyles gave out a shriek. I dared myself to look back up at them. Teeth were gnashing, claws were out. Once we crossed into the woods it would be difficult for them to follow us through the spread of the trees.

At least one of them wasn't willing to take that chance as he swooped down towards me, intent on plucking me up. I managed to move just in time to avoid a full grab. One claw still pierced my skin high on my shoulder, with such force, it knocked me down sending me into a hard tumble across the ground.

I came up into a crouched position, disoriented for a moment. Dry dirt and leaves stuck to my body. The coarse sand from the trail added to the pain of a jagged gash from when my chainmail tore straight through to my upper shoulder.

An overwhelming heat from pain was enough to bring me back to my senses. I lifted my head noting Tuck had stopped just on the outskirts of Muir. He'd lost his helmet somewhere along the way and his cheeks were flushed.

I could just make out his eyes, panicked, searching inside of his soul for an answer to this predicament. The gargoyles were circling over me like a pack of vultures hovering on a carcass. I raised my voice so I could shout my words towards Tuck in a manner that would coerce instant obedience. Drawing from my own similar experience with Coleridge I used his same authoritative tone.

"Run!"

Tuck's eyes flickered, registering my command. He promptly took off running. As he did, a gargoyle gave chase. It moved with great speed, while hovering just low enough, to enable it to lash out trying to bring Tuck's heavy frame into itself.

The scene before me seemed to draw out in slow, measured steps, even though everything happened in a fraction of a second. Tuck sensed the creature at his back. He didn't turn, only continued running while keeping low to the ground to avoid capture.

He ran straight into the thick of Muir. The gargoyle was so intent on its prey it failed to notice the forest. There was no chance for it to draw up, the impact with the tall pines was inevitable. The creature hit with such force his wings separated from his torso. The body, no longer supported, plummeted to the ground. With one last cry from the hideous beast, it shattered like glass into several thousand small chunks scattering all across the grounds.

Satisfied with the turn of events I brought my focus to the other gargoyles surrounding me. They hovered there, almost as if they were in shock at the destruction of their companion. I seized the opportunity to jump to my feet. My intent was to draw the others into the heavy trees of Muir as well, planning on the fact that they weren't intelligent creatures. Unfortunately, the distance proved to be too great for me because the pain in my shoulder impeded my forward movement.

I would have to make a stand. That singular thought brought a gasp to my mouth. For all my rampant desires to be a warrior of strength and might, deep inside I knew I was just a farm boy. What did I know of battle?

As I lumbered along, my fingers grazed the knife at my side. Something about the touch of cold metal beneath my fingertips brought a sense of power through me like a jolt and I realized then that I did know something about the ways of battle.

My mind drew back to the words of Coleridge, simple yet effective:

"Always keep your eyes upon your enemy."

I would take a chance. With Coleridge's words guiding me, I turned to face my enemy. To my surprise they halted in mid flap to stare down at me. They were watching me, trying to anticipate my next move.

"Not as dumb as I expected." I thought.

Their curiosity ceased quickly and with the crook of its head the one in front, the leader I presumed, dove down towards me at a horrific speed.

I steadied my legs beneath me, keeping them as solid and grounded as tree roots. When the monster came within range I willed myself the courage to proceed with my plan. I allowed it to come a breath away until I could smell the decay and charred brimstone on it.

With aggression, fear, and pure adrenaline guiding me I slashed out with my arm in a wide arc and plunged my knife into the creature. The impact was thunderous and almost took me off my feet. I held strong as the stone enveloped over my extended arm.

Within seconds the beast exploded, showering large chunks of rock over my head from its wasted body. I shielded my eyes from the spray with my free hand but only briefly. Soon the other two would be upon me, no doubt besieged with anger because of the destruction and loss of their leader.

I back stepped, stepping on chunks of ruined gargoyle as I went. My intention was to stake the very next one who dared come near me. But when I retracted my knife I realized I only held the handle in my hand. The blade itself had been broken off during the impact.

Panic overtook me. My chest constricted my breathing and I felt as though I might faint. The remaining gargoyles seemed to sense my fear. They made their descent toward me with great urgency.

I'd lost my sling in the tumble. Without my knife I would have to rely on my wits and instinct alone to save me. A grand lot of good it had done me so far. I kept moving backwards, swinging my arm wildly, hoping the gargoyles could not sense the blade missing from my hand.

It seemed to work. They stopped their direct advancement and circled about until one was on each side of me. They were trying to block me in, pin me down so I couldn't retreat in any direction.

First, the one from the left came at me with talons outstretched. Then the one at the right, a gaping mouth to fill, came in directly after. Instinctively I threw myself out of harm's way ending up chin deep in the scattered dust on the trail.

Above my head I heard a sweet but sickening sound as bodies collided. The two became one large pile of ash and stone. I turned slowly and a rush of excitement overtook me as I realized the gargoyles had inevitably destroyed each other.

The sky was clear, no other enemies winged, or otherwise, presented itself to me. It was over. Victory lay in my hands. There was a great calm in me now. A single tear caressed my face. Death had been so close that I'd felt its very breath and suddenly it was driven away by my own actions.

My triumph fresh in my heart I raced back to Gryphant without a second glance or a second thought as I ran through Muir.

I was eager to find Tuck, calm him, tell him to call off the hunting party he was no doubt desperately trying to assemble to aide me.

When I reached the outskirts of town I felt uneasiness knot my shoulders. I didn't know what lay ahead but my trepidations grew strong. The condition of the gates was my first clue that all was not well in Gryphant. They barely held up. The structures had damage that spoke of blunt force, hard, fast, and furious. I didn't stop to examine them, I had no time.

The moment I passed through those gates I witnessed shock and awe I had only ever heard tales about, mostly recently from the lips of Coleridge. The siege of bloodshed he had spoken of just days before now came true.

Gryphant was besieged by attackers. Strange beings to our lands tore asunder the homes, dragging those who dwelled inside out into the streets to dispatch them. Others set fires, killed livestock, and chased the village children in a mad frenzy.

The young boys and girls held no chance against their wild-eyed attackers. I watched in horror as the ground turned red from their collective deaths. It was a gruesome scene that was all too familiar to me. I'd witnessed such an attack just days before – in my mind. My visions were coming to reality.

Now it all became a clear picture though I still didn't know what we were up against. They stood tall and hunched at the shoulders some bearing horns, others tails. Cloven hooves and razored nails tore asunder my neighbors.

The hideousness alone sent me in a mad dash to the closest sanctuary nearby which turned out to be Mace Benton's tavern. Once my prison, now it offered safety from the madness that had somehow swept through Gryphant.

"Hell unleashed in your backyard."

Coleridge's words were chilling even in my memory. They were a prophecy untold until now.

The tavern was unusually quiet. No patrons lined the bar, no music played, no rowdies feasted on mutton and wine. None were there at all. It seemed as though the tavern had been the only place left untouched by the beings outside who lay waste to all I held dear.

I stayed just behind the tavern door pressing against the smooth wood with my palms and using my bodyweight as a barrier in case I had been followed by one of the beasts. It took a moment to stabilize my breathing. With deep inhalations I steadied myself as they drew to shallow whispers. I heard an indistinctive gurgle and a harsh rasping coming from just behind the bar.

I turned swiftly. My eyes seeking the source of the sound. The sweat slicking my palms seemed to stick me to the door. I was unable, or unwilling, to move forward. Then came a sickening wet-smack followed by a low moan. My heart raced at such a despicable sound. It was a twisted supplication of pain and fear. My own fear gripped me, but it became overpowered by a strong need to know the significance of the sounds.

I moved cautiously forwards. A pungent odor of spoiled meat and human waste grew increasingly strong as I approached the edge of the bar. The creak of the floorboards beneath my sandaled feet drew a low growl from the area just beyond my sight.

Though I couldn't see anything directly in front of me, instinctively I felt the weight of another presence in the room. I was not alone.

Shuffling out of the darkness of the room beyond, Mace Benton began a slow trek towards me. He lumbered, dragging his feet as he walked. I wondered if he harbored an injury. As he drew closer something in the way of his gait brought me concern. I decided to call out.

"Mace, it's Costa," I announced. "The town is in ruin, we must flee."

There was no audible response, just a low moan as he continued towards me. My heart fluttered with concern. He came closer, into the light, and I saw a terrible mask of a face that used to be Mace Benton. Now the skin hung loose and free from his cheeks, the teeth pushed out from rotted gums, and the eyes rolled deep into the back of the skull showcasing the whites of the orbs.

I stepped away, my back jarring hard against the tavern door.

"What evil is this?" I muttered trying in vain to wish away the horrible Benton-like creature who stood in front of me, but he pressed towards me without deterrence. And then once again I recalled Coleridge's words. The night we'd visited Benton's tavern, when it had been full of music and laughter not besieged by despair as it was now. He'd imparted words to me then, words that at the time I couldn't quite understand: Mace Benton is ripe for cursing.

Now they made perfect sense as though Coleridge had been a prophet foretelling the immediate future. Benton was in fact cursed. Nothing would hold him back now.

He lunged for me, the quickness in his step catching me by surprise, and before I could make a move he had wrapped his hands around my throat and began strangling me.

The strength in him seemed to have doubled. There was no way I would be able to pry off the fingers as they bit into the flesh of my neck. Panic ran over me. Soon I would lose consciousness and shortly after that I would die.

Benton's face drew closer to mine and I could hardly endure the stench of rotted flesh. But something in the eyes gave me a glimpse of the old Mace Benton. With the pupils now visible something in the weight of his stare told me that he knew exactly who I was and exactly what he was doing.

This new information lit a fire in me. I refused to go down at the hands of my former handler. If the eyes told the story then it would be his undoing. I used the only tool at my disposal – my fingers– and jammed them deep into his eye sockets. There was some resistance at first followed by a shallow pop and the eyes gave way to the attack.

My fingers embedded down towards the knuckle before Benton finally let me go. With fresh air entering my lungs I took a moment to sustain myself before Benton came for me again. Blinded he came at me wild, but almost latched onto the skirt of my jerkin before I was able to evade him. Using a tuck and roll, I dove behind the bar, slid over broken bits of glass that aggravated the wound on my shoulder.

The commotion brought the Benton-beast towards me, which had been my intent all along. Somewhere behind the bar Benton had always stowed a spiked club in case the bar patrons turned rowdy. It was a simple but powerful weapon. Twenty or so metal spikes ran along the club's head to give it a brutal and efficient crushing force.

In the limited amount of light I was having trouble locating it. My heart raced and my mind spun from the adrenaline. Then I found it. I was within a fingertip's grasp of the club when Benton found me. His hand latched onto my ankle tight and he began to drag me across the ruined bottles of whiskey and rum. My flesh singed under the cuts from the glass. I struggled hard against his attack, until I felt I might exhaust my energies, but I knew I had to reach a solid weapon.

Momentarily I broke from his grip and took the offensive. Using one of the only spared bottles in the bar I smashed it on his head sending bits of glass and watered down rum in every direction. It stunned but it didn't slow, in fact he seemed to grow angrier.

He continued the pursuit, throwing his full body forwards so I couldn't get away. I didn't move, rather I braced myself flat upon the floor and used my legs to buck the falling Benton up over my head avoiding the impact of his frame.

As he landed he took out the corner section of the bar sending splinters of wood across the floor and the spiked club rolled right into my waiting hands. When Benton lumbered back up to his feet I was ready for him.

There would be no hesitation, no remorse for what I must do. I lined up, with a double fisted grip on its base and let the club fly. It whistled through the air. When it made impact with the side of Benton's ruined head, it tore it clean from his shoulders. Not what I had been expecting but effective nonetheless.

I stared at it for a while. I couldn't seem to pull myself away from watching the writhing form in the throes of its death. He'd been a horrible master to me all the years I had known him. I didn't owe him a shred of concern.

For my own personal satisfaction, I lodged a single swift kick into his side, then turned to go. Shelter inside the tavern was no longer an option. Where there was one savage beast there were sure to be many others. I would take my chances in the ravaged streets of Gryphant.

Taking the spiked club in my hands as my only protector I ran out into the street waving it in front of me in an X pattern. It was an unnecessary move. To my surprise the street had grown quiet. The silence was deafening. Not a cry nor howl nor whimper filled the air.

Gryphant was a mess of blood and bodies. Those that did not lay dead in the street would've taken to finding shelter in hopes that the scourge and plague of evil that swept over their homes would subside in time.

At the moment it seemed as though it had. Still I remained cautious, walking along the backsides of the homes, my club as my companion held tight at my side. The smithery where Tuck lived with his father and mother lay just a few markers down from the tavern. As I reached the door I steadied myself before pushing through. I did not want to happen upon another grim scene like the one in Benton's tavern.

With breath held tight in my chest, and club at the ready, I forced my way inside. The door had been blockaded from the inside with several bags full of coal that John Goodall used in firing his kilns. That was a good sign. I had enough sense to realize that the Goodalls had barricaded themselves inside the smithery when the attacks went down. That meant there was a good chance they still lived.

My heart pounded as I tore across the smithery and in through the door that led to the main house. Nothing seemed out of the ordinary. No chairs overturned, no streaks of blood lining the floors or walls. I held great comfort in that. Tuck must still be alive.

Voices carried on the air and I drew deeper inside the house. I moved towards their location even as a knot in my gut drew tight in warning. It was then that I decided never to ignore my instincts again.

I found Tuck well enough, standing in the middle of the room. He was stock still but for the involuntary shivers that racked his body. Seeing him should've been a welcome sight were it not for the disturbing presence of the visitors at his side.

Each of them towered over Tuck by a good foot in height. The one at his right had a long, wiry frame. Jagged teeth protruded from rancid gums. He held the look of humanity gone horribly wrong.

The one to Tuck's left was less putrid at first glance but something about its aura led me to believe he was far more dangerous. His long dark hair contrasted against his pale skin. His dark eyes shone from hooded lids. He ran a skinny finger across Tuck's cheek in a taunting manner.

They had yet to become aware of me. I used the seconds I had at my disposal to slip out of sight just behind the edge of the doorframe. I watched as the two creatures seemed strangely fascinated with Tuck.

The demon leaned in close with its snout taking in a large sniff of the air that surrounded Tuck's body. Tuck quivered and the front of his breeches grew damp. My heart sank in that moment knowing the fear he must be holding inside as he involuntarily wet himself. I wanted to jump in, take his place between the two beings and their macabre probing...until they opened their mouths to speak.

"This one is not the chosen one."

The demon was the first to talk. A low growl in its throat pulled the words out in rough notes. Upon his proclamation the other ran one slender finger down across the meat of Tuck's well-rounded cheek until the tip of his unusually long nail drew the smallest speck of blood. He forced Tuck to look in his direction. Then he spoke.

This one sounded more like a man. His dialect was impeccable. Very polite but very cold. The volume of his words a calm, slow drawl.

"Where is the chosen one?" he asked.

At that very moment Tuck's eyes found me. I don't know whether he'd seen me come in or if he sensed me just then but as our eyes deadlocked on each other I could almost read his mind. The creatures were looking for me.

It seemed unfathomable. Why would a mere farm boy be of such interest to these unholy beings?

As fast as he had looked my way Tuck diverted his eyes.

"I don't know what you want," he stuttered, teeth hammering together upon each word.

"Then you are of no use to us," spoke the dark shrouded being in his soft tongue. "Dispose of him."

Upon his words the demon raked a gnarled claw down Tuck's arm tearing open both the fibers of his jerkin and the tender flesh beneath. He howled in pain and dropped to his knees.

My hand drew tighter around the club until I could feel blisters begin to pucker on my palm. I wanted to run out into the middle of the fray and spirit Tuck away to safety, but my body refused to move.

Warm, salty tears filled my eyes as the demon lay another strike on Tuck, this time high upon the nape of his neck. They were going to tear him apart and I could not bring myself to help him. Then suddenly the other halted the demon's attack and called out loud.

"Are you going to aide your friend or will you just stay stuck to that wall like a sniveling coward?"

Had he seen me enter as well? Were my movements that traceable? No, it was something more. He had sensed me, smelled me even. Either way they knew I was there. They were using Tuck's pain to draw me out. I decided then and there that I wouldn't keep them waiting.

I took a step out from the shadows and hefted the club straight out in front of me, trying hard to stabilize the shaking in my legs before it gave me away, but something told me they already knew.

"That's your big move?" the dark one said. "You waited all this time back behind that wall just to wave a stick at us?"

The air felt heavy. I steadied myself and tried to fill my voice with the same authority I'd heard from Coleridge.

"Let the boy go you bastards."

The fanged smile showed itself again. "While I cannot speak for my companion I can tell you that I was born of both mother and father. Lord Le Carde, at your service."

He gave an irritating little bow before continuing. "My blood lineage runs well. I am a vampire of the highest honor, like my father before me. Your bloodline, however, has threatened the destruction of my own. This I cannot have."

They were coming for me now. The dark one, Le Carde, stayed back just enough so that the demon could be the first to engage. I held steady, my club, in front of me one moment then snatched and shattered into bits the next. I suddenly found myself at the complete mercy of the attackers.

They were enjoying themselves much too much. Toying with me, baiting me with false advances, they forgot all about Tuck.

For the most part he was forgettable. A scared little rabbit in soiled trousers, not much of a threat. Sometimes the weak become the strong. Somewhere, something inside of Tuck switched over and he became a fierce protector. Lashing out with the first thing at his disposal, a wooden chair, he broke it across the back of the beast before me just as his barbed teeth, smelling of rot and dripping with saliva, were inches from my face.

The blow staggered the beast, angering him enough to turn his attention back to Tuck. Tuck's eyes caught me in his sights. He bellowed, at the top of his lungs, in a manner I had never heard him before.

"Run!"

I'd issued that command before when the gargoyles had hung over our heads and Tuck issued it to me now. But I couldn't oblige him. I wouldn't leave my friend.

Being the closer of the two, Le Carde was quick to silence Tuck. He lashed out with a long, skinny hand, grabbed Tuck around the throat lifting him until his toes dangled over the floor. His round, white cheeks began to flush pink. As he was held aloft, his face changed to a dark shade of blue. His life was slipping quickly away.

"No!" I shouted in protest which turned the attention of the demon back towards me. He slammed me against the back wall pinning me there, forcing me to watch the destruction of my friend.

Le Carde's vice grip was strong. Tuck tried in vain to pry the slender fingers off his throat. Le Carde turned back to me, a wicked smile creeping over his face as he relished my pained expression. Without even regarding his prey, he ended the little game with utmost ease.

A slight flip of Le Carde's wrist snapped Tuck's neck like so much dry underbrush. A hollow pop sounded, followed immediately by a mangled crunching. Tuck fell limp. It was a nightmare. The kind of nightmare where you experience something terrible but you are frozen, unable to move or retaliate, no matter how hard you will it. I didn't even have time to mourn. Le Carde dropped the body to the ground like spoiled meat and then he came for me.

My own hide remained at the mercy of the rabid demon before me. The demon pitched me high over the better length of the room. I landed with a painful crash through the splintered wood of a nearby table.

I was breathless from my fall. My head swam, I was so dizzy I was on the verge of unconsciousness.

"You fool! Don't let him out of your grasp. Their bloodline is a tricky lot." I heard Le Carde admonish the demon.

The demon grunted a reply. The two of them began a mad search for me, tearing up furniture and breathing in my scent until they finally found me.

They stripped away the bits of table that had fallen upon me. I couldn't move. My eyes were the only part of me still working. As I looked up, I could see the distorted image of the two of them standing over me.

There was hunger in their eyes. They were eager to get a hold of me. The demon extended his gnarled hand. I heard a shout. Had it come from my own lungs? Then much to my surprise, I witnessed the spilling of blood as the demon's head was removed from its body in one clean swipe.

Dark crimson blood, almost black in hue, spilled from the exposed neck landing all over my face, blinding me.

An altercation ensued. I couldn't make out any of the details. I heard hollering and the thud of the demon's body hitting the ground next to me. Frantically I cleared the blood from my eyes looking up in time to see Le Carde with his hands upon John Goodall, Tuck's father.

He was trying to extinguish John the same way he had killed his son, by breaking his neck. This time, I would not allow it.

I grabbed the first thing I found next to me, a chunk of wood that had previously been a table leg, and launched myself into the melee. My first swing caught Le Carde upside the back of the head. It was enough for him to release his grasp on John. Then he turned towards me.

The evil little gleam in his eye was replaced by evil fury. He wanted to draw blood. His once handsome features now looked almost feral. The spikes of his teeth drew down towards the bottom lip and he flicked his tongue over them.

My second blow, with the makeshift club, lacerated Le Carde's cheek, knocking the sinister look off his face as it staggered him. His countenance now held a look of shock. John Goodall came around to my side to join me, a twelve inch sword secure in his hands, I almost sensed the fear that crawled over Le Carde.

He hissed at us, reared back and retreated into the night faster than either John or I could register.

"Come back here you cowardly bastard!"

John made a move to go after Le Carde but his strength failed him. He dropped to his knees, more out of anguish than pain.

I gathered myself as best I could and went over to his side. My body had taken a savage beating that day. I held it together only because of a hide forged thick from constant abuse.

"You mustn't let them get away with this," John said. "They must be punished for these wicked deeds."

"Who are they?"

"Demons, creatures of Hell sprung up to lay waste to the land and kill...." He broke off, a twinge of pain lodging the words in his throat.

I reached out to embrace him, knowing full well that the anguish he felt was due in most part to the loss of his boy. John would not have any of it. He shook off my grasp and then lifted his blade. I recognized it as the one I'd been admiring in his smithery.

"I worked seven weeks on this sword. It was going to be a surprise gift for Tuck." He paused as he passed it over to me. "I want you to have it."

The sword, made for someone special, from father to an unsuspecting son, now lay in my hands. I was reluctant to take it.

"I can't accept this. I'm just a farm boy, how can you expect me to find the strength to conquer these demons?"

"You are more than you know, Costa. Powerful blood runs through your veins. That is one of the reasons I never tried to claim you as my own."

"What're you talking about?"

I'd never spent all that much time with John. We'd always exchanged pleasantries and talked in passing of weapons and weather and other useless nonsense. Now he was ardent with his words. His eyes the embodiment of passion.

"Go back to your dwelling, gather only what you need, and then get out of this town and don't look back."

I stood then, sword in hand, turned from the ruined smithery with the broken remains of the Goodall clan still inside, and went back towards my home not once looking back.

Coleridge's lodgings had remained untouched during the raid but still held the air of death all around it. The walls were cold, colder than the brick and mortar that held them in place. There was something more, something deeper that filled the rooms with a chill.

I hurried with my packing. I wouldn't bring much, just provisions and solid weaponry the best of which I knew I would find in Coleridge's room. I was no longer concerned that he'd be upset with murderous rage if he found out I was in his quarters. Cain Coleridge was not returning.

His room held the faint scent of tobacco and brine. The prominent satchel did not hold court, vanished with its master somewhere deep into Muir Woods. Most of what I would need to take with me already lay with Coleridge...wherever he was.

I scoured the room looking for more, when I came across the book. The leather bound bit still locked in place. This time the small brass key accompanied it, staring at me and hinting. Finally the contents were mine to discover. Cain Coleridge's thoughts and history were laid out in front of me.

There was a loose note, on parchment, tucked inside the front flap, folded tri-quartered, and addressed to C.C. I unfolded it to reveal a map. Words were scrawled out over the top of it, they simply read: Seek the Master of Weapons.

Coleridge had known he would not be returning. He'd left the book and these words intentionally, knowing that I would find them. I felt a strong sense of loss, everything I'd ever known had been taken from me, ripped away so fast that

I could not even grab a breath before it had been knocked out of me again and again. I had no other options now.

Packing the book and my belongings I set out intent on following Coleridge's last words. I would find this Master of Weapons.

Chapter Five
Seeking the Master

At first it didn't feel much different than any other time I'd ventured into Muir Woods. The air still held the same hint of jasmine; the forest floor made the same soft crunch from the leaves underfoot; everything held the same distinction as the times Tuck and I would go on our adventures.

A staggering difference came to me the moment I crossed an unfamiliar threshold. Tuck was no more. The two of us would never again journey out together. I'd lost my companion. My mission to find the Master of Weapons would have to be sought alone.

A terrible pain hollowed my gut and brought stinging tears to my eyes. This was no enemy I could fight with my fists or the steel at my hip. It was grief – I'd felt it years before when my mother had been taken from me unexpectedly, and I held it inside me again now.

I'd promised myself then that I'd never allow the sorrow to take hold, I would never cry for my losses. I never have. The burden I carried with me now proved too great to bear. I crumbled to one knee hanging my head low enough to smell the dirt at my feet.

The trees stalking high above me could offer no solace. Tiny patches of dirt below me grew moist as my tears fell free. I watched as they pooled together allowing myself a moment to dispel the pain I felt. Afterwards, I straightened up, stood tall to the world and continued on my path towards The Master.

The path split into four different routes. To the East lay the Hallowed Grounds and the Gargoyles we'd tangled with before. I would definitely avoid going in that direction. North and West brought with them mystery, and South brought me back home, which at the moment seemed like a welcome choice except the fact remained that Gryphant was no longer my home. In fact it hadn't felt that way in a very long time, but now there were no ties to hold me.

So I would push forward, but the question still remained...which way? My instinct was to fish out the world map and compass from my satchel, but part of me disregarded the need. I'd been a studier of maps since I was very young, always marking out paths to explore when I got up the nerve.

I closed my eyes and thought back as a cool wind picked up through the trees and caressed my face. The map was there in my mind's eye as detailed as though it were directly in front of me. I marked my path following the curved line from Gryphant all the way up towards the crested hills of Ravenwood where the Master of Weapons was said to be.

After seeing it, remembering it, I decided that the shortest distance to travel would be straight ahead. I would go North.

Feeling confidant in my decision I proceeded without any further hesitation. The path looked clean, smooth and inviting. There was nothing to fear here, only my imagination.

I'd always imagined just what it would be like to break away from the monotony of my homestead. Instead of being confined to the four walls of my room, I was going to branch out and see the world in all its glory.

Now, as I stood on the precipice waiting to make that transition, I found my feet reluctant to move. Questions once secure at the back of my mind were now edging to the forefront to undermine my courage and conviction in my journey. What if the world was not glorious? What if it was a cruel and vicious pile of muck the same as Gryphant had been for so many years? Who was I to be taking up arms and heading out to find the Master of Weapons? I'd never lifted anything more than a wet mop – up until the prior morning anyway.

They were questions needing answers. I felt no impending desire to sink into those dark areas of my mind, to have an inner dialogue with myself. Surely this kind of thinking would drive me mad. Time was of the essence. In only a few short hours the sun would shine the last of its golden rays giving way to the dark of night without so much as a warning of twilight.

My eyes were useless in the dark. I needed to cover as much ground as I could before that time to set up camp for the night in a fitting area. I knew Muir Woods from the grand scope of trees that bowed over at their eight feet of height to the smallest speck of sand marking out each path. I did not intend to stay on its edge and risk being whisked away in the night never to return such as Coleridge had.

Space and soundless night were the only things laying before me. The journey ahead was a double-edged sword, more prominent than the fine piece of craftsmanship that was secured at my hip.

Running my finger over the hilt I remembered Tuck in his last moments. If nothing else, I owed his family.

Everything I ever dreamed of lay ahead just beyond a thicket in the night. But behind me I was leaving the only world I ever knew. Friends, memories, the creature comforts of home that – though checkered with pain and loss – were the grounds I'd been reared upon.

And Coleridge.

The memory of my time spent with him lay back in Gryphant. The moment I pushed past those ominous bushes standing like soldiers at the edge of my path, I would leave all of that behind me forever.

I made a forced effort to move, disregarding the pit of nervous energy bubbling up in my stomach. Coleridge was gone, Tuck was gone, it was time I moved forward with my life.

Cinching my pack higher upon the width of my shoulders I made my way to the thick underbrush and was stopped for a second time.

A sharp puncture dug into the exposed flesh of my calf. I drew back, immediately, when I felt a searing pain run up my leg. Bending to check the damage, I saw a thin scratch running across the meat of my calf, around to my shin bone.

The wound was a small one but the stinging sensation ran deep. I wondered if I'd been clipped by some sort of animal lurking in the bush that I'd unwittingly disturbed.

Crouching low I edged back towards the source of my discontent. The bushes were armed, small but prominent thorns were laced about the shrubs...each and every one of them. The thick underbrush was going to claw at me, pulling me down until I became lost inside the heavily grown thicket.

I tended my wounded leg once more. The scrape throbbed and seemed to be alive with the intensity of fire. Scanning the bushes as best I could in the fading light I weighed my options.

The thorns stood out more prominently now that I knew their full power. My leg stung in such a way that I wondered if the tips held a subtle poison. For a moment I considered turning back, leaving my task by the wayside and returning to what I knew best.

It only took remembering my misery, toiling long hours in a tavern bar, while watching others live out the life of my dreams to shake all thoughts about quitting from my mind. Besides, Gryphant was in ruin. It would take long days into weeks of rebuilding before it became something again. All the rampant destruction would plague me every waking hour if I went back. It seemed I had no real choice after all. I had to press forward. There was no going back. But I lacked the strength to do it. A great fear of the unknown gnawed at the far reaches of my mind holding me back.

Hefting my shoulder bag down I reached inside seeking the only thing that could bring me comfort. My fingers ran over my sling and the fruit in my pack, before finding the supple, soft leather. Withdrawing Coleridge's journal I felt the empowerment I needed to keep moving. The words inside were Coleridge's legacy left to me to follow through with. I could not let him down.

My fingers closed tighter around the leather binding. I felt a sensation of power buzzing through me. I knew I was capable of undertaking what lay ahead. Coleridge had faith in me, that made it easier to have faith in myself.

Restoring the book to its home in my satchel I waited not a moment more before plowing full force into the thorn bushes. I felt the little pricks immediately. Each one held its own distinction as it grazed my flesh. I tried to quicken my pace hoping an end to my torment would come soon.

The pain was excruciating. I began to grow dizzy. All my strength was required to absorb the blows from the bushes. I feared I would not make it through. My legs would give out beneath me and I would be forever lost upon the border of Gryphant.

Staggering, almost blind, I discovered an opening about fifteen paces or so in front of me. I wondered if my eyes deceived me, if it were a hallucination brought on by the pain racking my body. Still, I knew I couldn't stand much more. If the clearing really did exist it was worth taking a chance.

Utilizing the full distance still in front of me I took off on a bound and leapt towards what I hoped would turn out to be sanctuary. With my head tucked under me, my shoulder hit the ground and just like that I was free of the thorn bushes.

I lay still for a moment, allowing the coolness of the earth and the softness of the grass beneath me to soothe my worn body. I'd never imagined such a border patrolled the outskirts of Muir Woods. It seemed almost as if the thorn bushes had been strategically set to dissuade those who wished to exit...or enter.

My adrenaline slowed. If I were to close my eyes, at that moment, I knew I would doze off. I had to keep moving. There was still so much ground to cover. I shifted to a sitting position with considerable effort. My body suffered the dull ache of worn limbs and a weary soul. A furious stinging came from my wounded shoulder and ran its torturous heat deep into the meat and spread up along my neck. Tender little pin-sized holes puckered my flesh from where the thorn bushes left their mark. I'd barely started out on my journey and already I felt the worse for wear.

The contents of my bag had spilled out every which way. It took precious time to gather everything back up. I was moving much slower than before. My mind wanted to move, to pick up the pace, to be further along before nightfall, but my body had other ideas.

I needed rest.

Everything was catching up to me. I'd been running for a very long time. Running from my dissatisfying place in life, running out of fear for the future, and running from the troubled past of my childhood. I'd never really allowed myself to stop so I could take it all in. Now, with new burdens on my back I was over-flowing with pain and distress.

Exhaustion pulled at me, begging me to stop, but I pressed on. It forced me to look inside myself, to conquer any fears clinging to me still. There wasn't any room for doubt. Doubt would only get me killed. It became a necessary evil to look back upon the boy I used to be and reconcile him with the man I was becoming.

A dark blanket covered the sky. Not even the stars were out to light the way. I considered settling down for the night. My body was already weary and racked with pain. Every muscle ached. The little nicks in my skin had not subsided either. It felt like needles running the course of my body and the culmination lay in my wounded shoulder. It throbbed and ached. I could barely keep the weight of the sword up so I returned it to the scabbard. So far it had done its job well. I was happy to have it as my companion on this journey.

My thoughts turned to Tuck. I thought about how his face would've beamed as his father unveiled the sword as his own. There would've been tears but they would've been warranted as John Goodall showed his son how much he valued him and Tuck realized his own sense of worth. Now my own tears fell, knowing those words would never be spoken between them. Tuck would never know his full potential as the good man he would've become.

I unsheathed the sword once more. It glistened in fine reflection under a heavy crescent moon, perfectly crafted with love. I bent one knee and planted the tip of the sword down into the ground. Bowing my head, I spoke not to the Gods and I did not lose myself in prayer. My words were for Tuck. I vowed vengeance in his name. In the death of my friend I became reborn.

Sometime during the night I awoke, troubled in my sleep by demons past, present, and in the unavoidable future. I lay there a long while looking up at the blackened sky. Finally, when I knew sleep would not return, I sifted through my bag to withdraw the bound leather book.

I'd not had much chance to become familiar with the pages in my rush to leave the town in its decay. I unwrapped the leather bit and opened the tome. The pages were worn and weary and they made a sound like the dead shuffling upon the earth.

Inside there were labeled and detailed drawings of sights I hoped I would never lay eyes on. Deep in my heart I knew that humble request would not be answered. I'd already seen much but I knew I had yet to even begin. Those perils splashed across Coleridge's pages awaited me, as they had awaited him. At least I had his experiences to guide me.

I flipped through it seeking ardently the monster who had stolen Tuck from me. I'd been sheltered for too long. Even the bar dweller's tales had never accounted such horrible beasts as the ones I'd seen in Gryphant and now amongst these pages. I needed to know what I was dealing with.

Coleridge had written at length on the subject of vampires.

In the center of the book lay a worn paper folded in thirds. I unfolded it to reveal dictation and renderings of various weapons, most of which I had no knowledge of. The scripture written there spoke to me as the words almost leapt from the page.

"You must master many weapons in your quest to vanquish the servants of hell."

In just a simple sentence it detailed mine would be an arduous apprenticeship, that is if I could ever find this Master of Weapons whom I sought.

I lay the book aside. My head had grown just weary enough now that I could return to slumber. As my eyes shifted closed I began a dream, a vision really, of a nightmarish creature spanning bat-like wings and a ghoulish face of fangs. The image startled me in such a way that I jerked awake and to my sudden shock and horror I found the ghoulish vision was very much a reality standing before me.

It watched me with eyeless, dark sockets. Its long torso leered up and a flicking forked tongue taunted me. The nightmarish plague seemed to be rising up just as Coleridge had warned and prophesized. There was no rest for the wicked in their attempts to take over the four corners of the world. There would be no rest for me either in my attempt to thwart them.

Staggering back in a foggy, sleep induced daze I lumbered for my sword. The ghoul did not make chase. It simply moved forward in slow, purposeful strides. Its methodical movements carved fear in me more than if it had waged a full on attack.

I hefted my sword double-gripped in front of me. The creature was not swayed. Sweat moistened my brow, my muscles grew taught in anticipation. We circled each other with nothing separating us but the campfire that lay between. Then, in a lapse of judgment or a sudden burst of confidence, I leapt over the fire, sword raised high, and came down with the edge of the blade towards the ghoulish head.

The creature reacted by lifting the crest of a wing up across its body. I smiled inwardly, mistaking the movement as a shielding out of fear but when my sword met what looked otherwise to be a flimsy sheen of skin it reverberated off the wing and almost toppled me over onto my back.

Now, it was the ghoul who smiled as he came for me. Undaunted I proceeded to strike him again and again, each time producing nothing but the same result of unyielding failure.

The ghoul remained steadfast with his approach lowering his winged arms long enough to spit a hiss towards me. In that movement I noted the spindly body. The torso seemed withered and dry, a fine marking point for the tip of a sword. I hoped in secret prayer to myself that only the wings remained impenetrable and then I awaited my opening. It came not a moment later when the ghoul lashed out at me with both scaly hands.

I drew back my arm, tucked my elbow, and forced the head of my blade forward. The penetration of sword to body resulted in a dark scream from the ghoul. Its chest ripped open as I buried my sword almost to its hilt inside of the open cavity. A putrid smell of decay and waste emanated from the exposed rotting heart. I was surprised to see a heart at all thinking instead that the beast was born of darkness alone.

I shifted my sword up into the still beating heart and split it open. A thick green puss ran out and then exploded from it almost lobbing itself into my eyes. Instinct alone kept me from being blinded. I shielded my eyes with the thick of my forearm taking the majority of what I came to realize was poisonous. The ghoulish beast, perhaps once mortal, had grown dark in its own decay and now held a poisoned heart.

I drew back instantly as the flesh of my arm stung and sizzled beneath the poisonous spew. The ghoul itself had been rendered helpless at the severing of its heart. I watched as the body drew to dust and fell amongst the rest of the dirt at my feet.

My adrenaline still pumped heavy through my veins. I made haste and wrapped up my campsite, the stinging flesh on my arm hindering my progression. It was no longer safe. Dark of night or not I had to keep moving. I had never felt so physically helpless before. My stomach had turned over on itself leaving me breathless and unable to stand straight for long.

I walked the remainder of my path in a daze thinking ridiculous nonsensical thoughts having no merit to anything. Still such visions kept my mind from harking back on the grotesque features of the ghoul at my campsite or the haunting laugh of the vampire Le Carde before he tore out Tuck's throat. My delirium was welcome.

I staggered my way a few more miles out, riding on fumes of spent energy and nothing more. My feet dragged but they moved along one after the other. Determination, if nothing else, remained unfailing...until I saw the chasm spread out before me.

Had I been moving in a rapid pace I would've plunged right in. The width of the chasm was massive but in the dark of night it blended well with its surroundings. I stopped just short of the edge and peered over into nothingness.

It looked as though it went on for an eternity, that anything that had the sad misfortune to fall in would travel in a perpetual fall only wishing to hit bottom. The expanse of it carried on in every direction. There was no way around it.

I grew confused and frustrated enough to have to consult Coleridge's map even in the darkness. There were small markers, basic line drawings, nothing to indicate the chasm at all. Could this be right? Had Coleridge not encountered this area? Impossible. He could not have made it down to Gryphant without coming across the chasm from some point.

My mind reeled with such questions. Giving into my exhaustion I fell to my knees at the mouth of the chasm feeling desperate and lost. Somehow I'd made a mistake, had taken a wrong path, perhaps gotten mixed up in the thorn bushes and come out in an unpopulated area that wound up in a dead end.

I could feel my pent up energy and vicious determination slip and fade away. My quest to find the Master of Weapons, to carry on Coleridge's legacy and leave one of my own had come to an end before it started.

If I turned back now, which seemed like my only logical choice, I would go straight back to the remnants of Gryphant and there I would live out my days.

My shoulders slumped forward in defeat. Suddenly I felt very tired and before I knew it my forehead pressed against a patch of grass, my cheek following, and I gave in to the exhaustion that had been building in me.

I slept.

I would have no visions this time. For the first time in many nights my slumber was inviting, warm, and dreamless. It was waking that brought the real nightmare. My body lay still across the grass, as my eyes came awake I shifted to move and found I could not.

Each limb had been staked out, stretched to its limit down to my fingers and toes. I saw nothing that bound me but still no amount of force or will would move me.

In desperation I cried out. "What sorcery is this?"

"No sorcery at all."

I heard the voice sound out clear as day but as I shifted my gaze as best I could I saw none to which it belonged.

"Who's there?"

My heart started jittering in panic. Unable to move, a stranger lurking in the night, these were surely the makings of a bad situation. With all I'd been through so far a multitude of undesirable outcomes ravaged my mind. That trait perhaps had been my undoing for the majority of my life.

I'd always related situations with the most negative of outcomes. It came from years of living in turmoil. Now it seemed as though those thoughts and fears had manifested into something horribly real.

"Who's out there? Show yourself!" I hollered again trying to keep as much conviction in my voice as I could muster.

"I'm right in front of your nose. You needn't shout."

My head swam in confusion and my eyes searched the night frantically trying to locate my most unwanted visitor.

Just then a speck of a shape sauntered forward stepping up onto the tip of my nose. I had to adjust my sightline, and my disbelief, to make out the tiny man who now occupied the space at the end of my nose. He was fitted in tiny leather boots, a green wool jerkin, and a matching stocking cap. His face was weathered but distinguished from what I could make out.

"Who...who are you?" I stuttered.

"My name is Angus and you are trespassing."

"This is open land." I argued.

"This is Cri land and your big tromping feet nearly destroyed our entire village square."

"What village? I didn't see anything."

"You didn't bother to look. The signs are everywhere, as clear as day."

With the wave of his tiny hand, Angus produced a wooden sign post no bigger than the likes of my thumb.

My anger grew within me, steaming my brow until it was red hot and I was ready to burst.

"You're magical? You did this to me...tied me down. Let me up immediately!"

"I'm afraid I can't do that. Rules are rules, you must learn your lesson. You can't just go stomping people's homes whenever you please."

"How can I be expected to see such a ridiculous sign at that size? I protested.

"You look with your eyes and the logic of your head instead of your heart." Angus shook his head. "Talos is going to have a hard time with the likes of you."

The name rolled over me, through me, down to my marrow. I felt as if I knew it somehow, or if I didn't that I should.

My body started to shake as I struggled once again to get up.

"I have you laced down good and tight with strings of mithril. You might as well not fight it. Your muscles will ache in the morning if you persist."

I stopped at his warning, stock still and petrified. My fate lay in the hands of this tiny Gnome and his other named acquaintance who had yet to let his presence be known.

"Who is this Talos?" I asked.

"You'll meet him soon enough." Angus told me. Then he reached into a small pouch that rested on his hip and drew out a fistful of what appeared to be dirt or a fine, grained gold dust.

"Sleep now." he whispered the words and I could scarcely hear him, but the message drew loud and clear when he blew the dust upon my lids and I fell unconscious.

Chapter Six
Awakening

"Awake."

Now the gentle urgings of a voice I didn't recognize pulled me from my strange little dream world.

As I came around fully, I realized I'd been moved. No longer was the grass at my back, nor were the tiny ropes pinning my body. Angus, the little tormentor, no longer stood upon my nose lecturing me. Instead, I saw a man with long white hair, braided to his waist, adorned in a soft, flowing cloak. He stood over me, a weathered cane in his hand that he gently tapped against the floor until I woke.

I was in a bed softer than the fur of a newborn pup. From what I could see of my surroundings, I was being held in a loft.

"Where am I?" I muttered. My energies were spent leaving me with limbs too heavy to lift. I couldn't even draw up my head to look at the man as he spoke to me.

"You'll have many questions. Answers will come in time. For now, your body needs nourishment. You've been asleep for many days."

He left me then. I fell back into my foggy world of dreams. When I awoke, sometime later, a table had been prepared in the corner of the room. All manner of cured meats, cheeses, soft grains and fruit were laid out in front of me. I'd never seen such a feast in all my days – at least not one meant for my enjoyment.

The aroma of spiced meat rub and apple cider drew me out of bed. That day I feasted like a king. After eating I didn't know what to do with myself so I stayed in the room, seated at the edge of the bed, perfectly still.

Was I a captive? If so why the grand meal? Perhaps a sacrifice to some strange God that needed to be fattened up before the slaughter.

My wounds were treated but my belongings were gone. This unnerved me. The Book of Scrolls from Coleridge held my path, my mission. Without it I was lost again, doomed to wander aimlessly.

There were no windows in the room, just a solid wooden door that pulled open the moment I began running thoughts of escape through my mind. The older man entered holding his ever present cane in one hand and my satchel in the other.

"How did I get here?" I asked. "The chasm...Angus. What happened with Angus?"

"Angus is well," the man replied. "He is patrolling the border of the chasm keeping watch for those who wish access to Ravenwood...which is where you are now."

"He works for you then?"

"In a manner of speaking."

"You can't keep me here against my will!" I shouted, leaping up to my feet to confront him.

"You're free to go whenever you please. I hold no one against their will...however, it is I that you seek." He paused. "My name is Talos, I am Master of the Weapons."

"Master of the Weapons?!" I was relieved, shocked and confused all at the same time. I couldn't fully believe my eyes, particularly when I saw his. They were pure white orbs, lacking any sight as well. How could this blind, old man be who I sought?

"Those are my belongings," I said.

"Yes, I was bringing them to you. I sensed your panic at their disappearance."

"You sensed my panic?"

"You hold much hostility. Not everyone is out to get you."

"It's the greatest method of defense to regard everyone as a potential enemy."

He gave a gruff laugh. "You sound just like your father, young Calabrese."

"How do you know me? And what do you know of my father?"

"I trained your father in the arts of war when he was a young man of your age."

"You're mistaken," I told him. "My father was not a warrior."

"So you spoke? He told you everything?"

"I've no memory of my father."

Talos sat down for a moment, as though pondering, then he stood, towering over me as I craned my neck to look up at him expectantly.

"That is all for now."

He began to leave with me still standing there on the floor, dumbfounded.

"Wait!" I called after him. "What am I supposed to do now?"

"That is your decision. As I said I hold none against their will."

He stood still in the doorway. I knew he was waiting for me to make my decision. I couldn't go backwards there was nothing left for me there. If I did I'd wind up right back where I started – cursing the Gods for my lowly existence.

I needed a fresh start and inside Ravenwood under the tutelage of the weapons master seemed as good a place as any to spring forward from.

"I'd like to stay," I told him.

He nodded, a small grin twitching the corners of his lips. "Good man. Your time here begins tomorrow but this evening I'd like you to join us in the courtyard for our mandatory meeting. This way you can get to know your fellow students."

Fellow Students?

I wasn't expecting that there would be others. In my mind I justified my solo training as the benefits of being a friend to the greatest hunter in the land. Little did I know I had just set myself up to live in a school.

Chapter Seven
The Bitch and the Brawler

What had I walked into? In my race for power and glory I'd signed myself up for challenges that were beyond my comprehension and level of skill, though I didn't realize it yet.

I came to know Ravenwood as Talos' training grounds. It housed some thousand acres of land high up to the north almost reaching The Peak of the Gods. Ravenwood fell in an octagonal pattern with several gates housing different access points. Not one of the gates were marked. Consequently, I became turned around immediately. The assistance of a map would've been more than welcome at that moment.

The first gate I found came open with ease displaying sleeping quarters. Several sleeping pallets lined the walls, many bags and satchels lined shelves sitting upon the floor in neat rows, the belongings no doubt of those who occupied this room.

The energy inside was at once thick and heavy with judgment as it poured from the eyes of several young men paused in their activities to watch me as I entered. I knew that discretion well from my days in Gryphant. It made my loss of Tuck much harder to bear. The boys were of varied ages, heights, and races, but they were a pack banded together to stake out the new guy who, as one voice called out, was apparently known to them as:

"Fresh meat."

He held a medium build under the stretch of a green tunic. His eyes were an unsteady mix of cloudy grays and they sized me up and down looking for the flaws I might hold. I returned the favor marking the spike of dark hair that rose up over the middle part of his scalp just short enough to showcase the prominent point of a set of Elven ears.

I didn't want any trouble, especially with someone from the Elven race, so I disregarded the comment he'd thrown my way and tried to offer my hand to him.

"My name is Costa."

"Nobody cares, whelp." He backed away then stretching out his arms in a grand show. "I am Paralay Dante, they call me the Elven sensation. But that doesn't matter either. What matters is that you'll find my name at the top tier of each and every challenge the Weapons Master throws at us. I'm untouchable because of me...not because of my lineage." He pointed in my direction, holding his stance, staring at me for a long while before concluding his point. "You are a lazy pile of dog meat who's been fed from his mother's tit for far too long."

"I don't know you, friend," I said, still trying to manage a cooler head. "More importantly you don't me."

"I'm not your friend and what I do know is that ever since you got here Talos has been treating you like fragile glass. That sickens me."

Paralay snarled, his top lip curling, his nose twitching just like a mongrel dog. In his expression I read the basis of his anger. He was jealous, plain and simple. In Paralay's mind Talos had been doting over me and giving me special treatment that he and the others at Ravenwood had not received. It was an absurd notion and I tried to explain.

"I never asked for any of this," I told him. "I'm simply here to learn and Talos is helping me to do that...nothing more."

Paralay scoffed. "Poor little broken down ruin of a whelp."

He looked me up and down again trying to size me up then breathed a strong inhalation that flared his nostrils wide.

"I can smell your lack of fortitude. You won't survive here."

The gray eyes flickered with obvious disdain and Paralay made his exit, brushing hard against my shoulder. The other boys followed him out in a steady line like sheep to their shepherd leaving me standing all alone, just as it had always been...just the way I liked it.

I continued my exploration of the grounds making my way outside into the courtyard. Immediately, I felt at home. The space was well kept. A small garden was there forming a circular pattern of flowers around a freestanding fountain of granite. The image depicted the goddess Aphrodite holding a small urn in her arms where crystal clear water flowed freely and collected at the base of the fountain itself.

The goddess of love had always been touted as being the most beautiful of all women. I'd never had a reason to debate that statement until now.

At the edge of the fountain sat the most stunning vision I had ever seen. The girls in my town had been pretty, some very pretty, but none of them had ever stopped my breath the way this beauty in front of me did.

My eyes took in every bit of her from her cinnamon colored skin to her silken, dark locks traveling the length of her body ending in a wisp of curls at the small of her back. I marked every detail as if somehow I had become a painter who wanted to reproduce the image on the flat of a canvas.

She noticed me staring at her. Her blue-green eyes were a storm at sea. A long silence filled with magnetic energy flowed between us for what seemed like eternity. She cocked her head to the side, squinted a questioning look with those magnificent eyes, and smiled at me. My heart nearly silenced then and there.

"Who are you?"

It took me a moment to form words but eventually I managed to get out something that sounded like "Costa."

"I'm Talisa. You must be the new boy."

Something in the words new boy made me feel woefully out of place but at least she hadn't referred to me as "fresh meat" the way Paralay had. I'd always been something of a loner. Even though Tuck and I had held a bond as tight as brothers I'd always felt like a misfit around others in Gryphant so I kept to myself. Here, in Ravenwood, it was a new start. I wanted to have at least one ally to turn to. One as beautiful as Talisa would be extra special.

Feeling my nerves fade I grew more confident and stepped forward to join her at the edge of the fountain.

"It's a pool of reflection," she told me. "It mirrors events from your past, whatever it is you've yet to reconcile with and let go. Everybody sees something different. Look inside, tell me what you see."

I hesitated. My past was just that and I wanted to keep it that way. I didn't see any significance in drawing from events that would be better left buried. But Talisa had a convincing way about her and I found myself looking over the edge of the fountain into the small pool there.

It took a moment but images slowly began to form within the water causing it to ripple and swirl. I was drawn back to my childhood when all of my faith revolved around my mother, so gentle and caring and suddenly taken away from me leaving me in a broken home.

The images shifted and I saw Coleridge on the outskirts of Gryphant. He was watching from afar as a younger version of myself hefted bales of hay and scraped up the shit left behind by the farmer's pigs.

He turned to me then, looking directly at me through the pool of reflection and he mouthed something over and over again. I leaned forward trying to make out what he was saying. He spoke to me here and now through some form of sorcery.

When you are in doubt, be still and wait.

When doubt no longer exists then act with courage.

Slay without mercy for you shall be given none.

Startled, I jerked back abruptly trampling a row of yellow sun-kissed flowers under my feet. Talisa hopped up and reached for me. The touch of her fingertips upon my arm sent a shiver over my entire body.

"Are you alright?" she asked.

I didn't answer and instead moved forward to look again into the pool. The waters were still. No images surfaced and worst of all Coleridge was gone again from my life.

"The images...they vanished."

"Yes, that happens. Sometimes the memories are so strong that it pulls much energy from the host. It takes time to get back to a state of remembrance. Perhaps if you come back later you'll see again."

I forced my gaze from the pool and took in Talisa's lovely features. She seemed to hold a warmth to her that was as inviting as a fire pit on a cold winter's night.

"That was not my past that I saw. It was of the here and now."

"Sometimes the pool can bring forth treasured things from anywhere, anytime. Once my father reached in and pulled out an apple from the Garden of Eden."

"This place is very odd."

"What makes you say that?"

"Many reasons. For instance, the Weapons Master, Talos. He seems very frail, old. Like he's long since past his prime. How could he possibly teach me anything I don't already know."

I smiled at her ready to back up my words with a small demonstration designed to impress. But as I looked upon her once delicate face I noted the creased brow, the dip of a frown, and the squint of the sea green eyes that now held anger within them. Then the tongue lashing began.

"You know nothing more than to run your mouth Cocky Costa," she mocked. "If your head wasn't as thick as granite that frail old man, as you call him, could teach you a great many things...including manners."

She began to storm off. I called to her hoping to convince her to stay.

"Talisa wait, what did I say?"

She turned back, began to speak, and then grew even more upset storming over to me and pushing me back until I almost fell over my own heels.

"You're nothing but a walking brute!" she screamed. For a moment I thought her mad until she bent down to the patch of yellow flowers and began to tend to them with care.

"Oh, I'm sorry," I said kneeling to help her. She raised her eyes to me and I reeled from the pure amount of hatred I saw embedded in them.

"Get out of here, Costa!"

I muttered out another apology and then did as she requested and left the courtyard as fast as I could. So far I had made quite an impression on the others who were staying at Ravenwood and this was only the beginning.

After that I stopped exploring and decided I would head back to my room and stay there indefinitely. Things weren't working out here. I felt more alone and desolate than before I'd left Gryphant.

I walked, taking a slow stride, holding my satchel limp in my hand and debating whether to just leave and never return.

"What did I get myself into?" I thought. Then a voice called my name stopping me in my tracks. I angled my head right, left, looking for the source of the caller and wondering if I'd been hearing things until Talos stepped forward.

"Where are you going?"

"I was just going to put my things in my quarters," I lied.

"Time for that later. Come with me now."

I followed Talos in silence, watching him amble along with effort on damaged legs and a weary back. He looked weathered as though the years had taken a strong toll on his body. I thought about what Talisa had told me and I lamented that perhaps Talos's years invested in the arts of war and knowledge would in fact prove useful to me. After all, if Coleridge had learned the trade from Talos then so would I. Besides all that, I was happy to see him.

"I'm glad you found me," I told him.

"You found me, Costa. That journey you took is something that you should be proud of."

I paused a moment to ruminate over the attack on Gryphant, Mace Benton's horrible turn, and the lingering face of the vampire Le Carde that would forever haunt my memory.

"Perhaps," I said, shaking off the momentary shiver that tingled up my spine. "But I meant that I'm glad I ran into you right now. It's nice to see a friendly face."

Talos turned his head and smiled at me. His leathery skin drew up at the cheeks with much effort and a powerful, hypnotic intensity filled his sightless eyes.

"Friendly, aye?" he mused. "This mug has been referred to as a lot of things in my days but that's a new one."

"I just meant I was glad to see someone who was at least sociable. I feel out of place amongst the others."

Talos questioned me with the arch of an eyebrow. "Oh?"

"It's very much like back home. I don't fit in with any of the groups. And there's an underlying expression of disdain coming at me that I don't understand."

"Your battles are not with the others. Once you've accepted yourself for who you are everything else falls away. The opinions of those around you will not affect you."

"At the moment they aren't making it any easier."

As we walked I caught sight of Talisa coming my way. She walked with such straightforward determination that the hem of her dress blew back and exposed her thighs. She still managed to catch my breath, upon first sight, but I couldn't forget the way she'd gone on the offensive and attacked me just a short while before.

"Like this girl approaching us now," I told Talos. "She must be a touch off in the head. Why I'd reckon she could put the vengeful snap of a harpy to shame."

Talisa stopped just in front of us, cringed at me, then bowed before Talos.

"Father," she said.

"How are you my daughter?" Talos returned.

I almost toppled over from the exchange of greetings.

"I'm quite well, father."

"That's good, Talisa, because I heard wind that perhaps you had gone a touch mad in the head."

Talisa looked my way and in her icy glare I realized she knew I'd been the one who'd said such words. Now it became clear why she'd gone on the offensive when I'd spoken ill of Talos.

"Never mind the rubbish that comes from displaced mouths," she said, her harsh undertone completely evident to even the most displaced ear.

"I didn't realize the two of you were related," I said.

"You didn't realize a great many things," she snapped. "I'll see you later, father."

She leaned up on her toes and kissed Talos's leathery cheek. I tried to offer her an apology, but she wanted nothing more to do with me.

"I'm a fool." I said aloud as I watched Talisa round a corner and disappear from sight.

"Depends on who's looking. I of course see nothing."

Talos's wry humor brought a twitch of a smile to my face despite the ongoing rabble of the day. I finally felt able to relax.

I followed Talos outdoors where the west wing of Ravenwood ended. There were people scattered around partaking in conversation. When Talos entered, they all fell in quiet lines. Even Paralay's overactive mouth grew silent at the appearance of the Weapons Master.

Talos stood before the gathered crowds and directed me to stand up at his side. It was uncomfortable to say the least. Many eyes looked my way, some with curiosity, others with malice. Paralay himself burned a hole right through me.

"Good day to you all," Talos' voice boomed out over the morning air. "We have a new man, Costa Calabrese, who has come here to attend my study. I'm asking you to show him the same respect you would to me. Our first session begins in the morning. Please be prompt. You may go on about your business now."

At his word the crowds slowly began to disperse.

"Go," Talos told me. "You should find your fellow peers more receptive to you now."

The next day I found out exactly how receptive my peers were.

"You're never going to make it through," Paralay chastised me as I lay nose first in the dirt trying hard to regain my wind.

I had been ill-prepared for the tasks that lay ahead of me. In my time, back home, running through the trees of Muir, or even working hard to toil the land for my daily chores, I'd always imagined myself to be in fairly decent condition. This level of physicality was an experience quickly changing my line of thinking.

Remembering the pact I'd made with myself the last time I lay upon a cold ground, I forced myself up to my knees first and then back to a standing position.

"I'm not finished yet." I puffed out the words with ragged breath and was greeted with condescending laughter. They were trying to break me, they'd been working hard at it all afternoon. Each trial that Talos set before us, whether it be a test of speed, strength or agility ended with Paralay mocking my attempts.

"Concede defeat."

My feet were stable beneath me now. Although my eyes felt leaden with exhaustion, I still managed to hold Paralay's gaze while defending my position there in Ravenwood with one simple word: "Never."

Paralay crooked his head and smiled a tight-lipped grin. "You will."

He stepped away to be with his entourage of followers. So far none of the others had made any attempts to get to know me at all. It seemed Paralay had them all dangling from a string like puppets.

His bragging was odious but paled in comparison to the run of his mouth denouncing any who posed a threat to him. It was his defense in lieu of nerves and his own lack of confidence.

If he mattered not, which he didn't, I should've walked away without counting his opinion of me. But I'd finally had enough. The anger welling in my mind and body was set off.

We'd broken from forms to refuel our bodies with large legs of mutton and freshly picked ears of corn. I needed to slake my thirst. The air was much drier here than I was used to. It burned my lungs with each breath I took.

I found my way to the water barrel and ladled out full bowls of water to quench my thirst. Suddenly, I felt a bump, then solid pressure against my head. I found myself face first in the barrel with water surging up my nose and into my ears.

I jerked my head up quickly from the water causing a cramp in my neck which added to the fuel of my anger firing up inside me.

"Who did that?" I coughed out trying hard not to choke on the water filling my throat.

"You should be more careful," Paralay said through shouts of laughter.

Something in his words or the Elvish gleam in his eyes, dredged up the familiar animalistic rage within me. I went on the offensive using the first thing at my disposal.

When the ladle struck Paralay it made a pleasing thunk off his skull. He staggered, touched his forehead where a small gash was prominent. It took him a moment to register why his fingertips were now stained with his own blood. The first blow had caught him off guard, the second one made him angry.

I wasn't expecting his defenses to remain so sharp after being racked in the head. He kept his wits about him. When I let the ladle fly again, he ducked under its assault catching me by the waist, to tackle me to the ground.

We struggled, rolling about on the ground, each striking solid blows before being thwarted by the other. The onlookers circled us, cheering us on, imploring us to maim or cripple the other like savages. Only one stepped in to break it up.

"Enough of this!" Talos' words seemed to echo from the sky like a thunderclap. He broke through the pack surrounding us, then used his cane to strike us both in the places it would hurt the most.

We pulled back from each other, panting, bruised, blood encrusting my lip and there was a good sized welt on Paralay's brow.

"I will not tolerate brawling amongst my own, unless it is sanctioned by me. Is that understood?"

So sanctioned it would be.

Up to this point, we'd been mastering our intellect, training to use our bodies as weapons, and to defend ourselves. Now, we would use all of those learned skills, one-on-one, just Paralay and myself.

Talos set us up in front of a course of obstacles designed to test our speed, agility, balance and strength. It ran the length at the back of Ravenwood's housing and presented itself across uneven ground littered with mud puddles and pits filled with water hazards.

I had expected to be facing Paralay in some form of physical combat but Talos had refused it stating how he would not allow the room for injury brought on by angry young fools. Instead, we would race.

"The first of you to the end shall be the victor and this petty rivalry will end there."

It seemed simple enough. The Elf was quick and spry but only my disdain for him rivaled my confidence in defeating and humiliating him in front of his followers.

We began with the strike of a gong in a long distance sprint. I edged Paralay out, taking up the lead in a matter of seconds. But before I knew it the first obstacle seemed to come from nowhere.

Barbed ropes zig-zagged out in front of me. There would be no going around, I'd have to tackle each one. Some were low enough to jump, others were meant to be crawled beneath, but all had a very real element of pain to them if you struck them. Fortunately, I managed to negotiate them without incident. I punched over the last hurdle landing in an awkward tuck and roll. When I came up I looked back to find Paralay at my heels.

I needed to increase my distance quickly. Moving ahead I found my next obstacle. Hanging vines dangled from overhead, below a pit of water, and on the other side the inviting crest of dry land.

Avoid the water at all costs I told myself.

I took a hold on one of the vines, tightened my grip and hoisted my body up and over. Wind tussledmy hair and pulled at my clothing as I swung over the pit. It seemed simple enough until I released myself too short from the edge.

At first my feet were firm and planted upon the solid ground and in the next instant I slipped off the side. I managed to catch myself and I clung there dangling over the pool of water, trying hard not to slip.

Paralay caught up to me at that moment. He landed gingerly and then turned in my direction. I extended one hand out towards him. It was a foolish move but desperation led me to it.

"Help," I strained out the word as my chest constricted against the side of the pit.

"You must be joking," Paralay laughed.

My extended hand fisted up and anger fueled my body. I exploded, using my hatred to propel upward and get back on level ground. I was halfway up when Paralay struck. He swept first one, then the other hand out from under me. I spiraled backwards and struck the water with a heavy splash.

I'd never imagined how cold it would be. The first impact felt like ice running over my body. Jarring little needles of pain raced over me that put the thorn bushes outside Gryphant to shame.

When I surfaced Paralay was nowhere in sight. That mattered little. My first dilemma to solve would be how to get out of the frigid water. The rope would not suffice as it did not reach far enough down.

I had to swim quite a ways until I came to a net of webbing. It reached great heights, intimidating at just the sight, but it proved my only exit. I began to scale it hand-over-foot. My sopping body made it that much harder to pull myself up. I vowed to take it out of Paralay's hide the moment I caught up with him.

Finally I reached the top of the net. Once up high I could see the rest of the course and Paralay negotiating it without effort. He navigated a small maze and came across a set of swinging rings like he'd been born on them.

He would win if I let him.

Climbing down would take too much time. Throwing caution to the wind I double gripped the net and launched myself up and over. The ground seemed to rise up and meet me. I came down hard on the other side, momentarily knocking the wind out of my body. After taking a moment to assess no serious damage had been done I forced myself up and continued the race.

I struggled to finish. I had no energy left. My legs felt heavy, my labored breathing was burning in my chest. By the time I got through the rest of the elements Paralay had already surpassed me.

Talos and the others awaited me there, waiting for me to finish. I almost dragged my body over his marking point of the finish.

"Paralay is the victor," Talos said raising Paralay's arm. Then he stood over me as I gulped in heaving breaths of air mixed with anger, resentment, and humiliation. "Do you know why you failed?"

When I heard the cheering from the others I allowed my emotions to take over me.

"The bastard used cheap tactics to get ahead."

"Can't accept losing graciously?" Paralay taunted. He knew what he had done. I wanted to peel his skin right off his hide.

"Enough," Talos said. "What's done is done."

I turned on him then. My fury with Paralay and my frustration in my disappointing display with the challenge leading my words and actions.

"You think it's so easy, old man? Then why don't you run it!" I hollered and then I struck Talos solid upon the shoulder. The crowd around us gasped. I flinched as I felt the thick musculature tap my hand. Talos didn't move at all.

"Is that a challenge, Costa?" he asked.

I'd not known what I'd been thinking at the time but I could not lose face now, not when I already initiated the actions. "Yes, I challenge you."

"It's important to realize what you're getting yourself into. Your father once challenged me. The results were not in his favor."

"I am not my father."

"Very well, I accept your challenge. However, I have not run this course since I tore the ligaments of my knee." He motioned with his cane towards his right leg. I couldn't help but scoff as I looked over him, not seeing then what a powerful enemy he could be if pushed. All I saw was crude matter standing before me, matter that was old, battered, and blind.

"I don't believe you ever have gone through this beast," I said motioning over my shoulder towards the trail Paralay and I had left behind. "You dream up tortures for your students that you would never rightly endure yourself."

"Strong words. Are you sure you don't want to retract them?"

I thought over my response, it didn't take me long. The beast grew alive inside me and ire fueled me. "Why? No one's ever stood up to you before?"

"No, I just wouldn't want you to choke on them later."

He was smug, arrogant, and above all else crafty. Lessons in all things, I should've been paying more attention. We set ourselves up at the tail end of the course...the sprinting distance that marked the finality of the race.

"The sun is setting," Talos said. "I do not wish to risk life and limb to prove a foolish point. The two of us shall race from this point."

"All too easy," I said.

Then Talos asserted himself. "Costa since I accepted your challenge that leaves me to make any amendments I see fit for myself, agreed?"

"Whatever you wish. I'm aching to show the Elven miscreant over there how you run a fair race."

Paralay's eyes twitched and the snarl of his lip signified his irritation. This pleased me. He'd been under my skin since I'd first arrived, I saw it only fitting that I return the favor.

"Very good then," Talos said. "The parameters are such: we race a straight race, just the two of us, and to even things up you shall be blind folded."

"That's trickery!" I protested.

"You agreed, everyone heard it," Paralay's words stung at me but I would be remiss to back down from the challenge at hand. So I agreed. It wasn't until the black silk cloth looped over my eyes that I began to doubt myself.

The world around me had gone dark and for the first time I realized just how it was living as Talos did, the difference being at the end of the race I could return my sight.

We commenced at the sound of the gong that cracked the air. I thought it would be fairly simple to accomplish the task, all I had to do was keep a straight path up to the end. The details turned out far more difficult to carry out.

Without my sight at my disposal my senses were in an uproar, confusion circled me. I veered off and found myself tripping up over my own two feet. Then it was over, just like that, Talos the victor.

I threw the blindfold to the ground and cursed aloud, this drew Talos to me.

"Tell me the lesson in this, Costa."

Even though he couldn't rightly see me I kept my head down, eyes away from his own, ashamed to be in his presence. But angry above all else. I returned my words with a bite in them.

"Lesson?" I scoffed. "The only reason you defeated me is because you had me blindfolded."

"You're right," he said.

I looked up then, a deep frustration in my soul. The whole experience at Ravenwood up to this very moment had been baffling to me. "Then why?"

"Because, Costa, the terms of battle will not always be in your favor. If you are to study under me, they most certainly will not be to your liking. I've heard nothing but excuses from you today. Perhaps this is not the place for you after all."

Panic cinched my chest as the meaning of his words tore through me. "Are you telling me to leave?"

"You're not ready. Go home."

Talos turned his back to me. I could feel the weight of his disgust rolling off towards me. The gentry had been shocked silent. Their stunned faces stared after me. Paralay held his smug grin, it had been a good day all around for him. For me it had been humiliation and disappointment. I should never have journeyed here. I'd gather up my things and be on the move by morning, but one thing troubled me.

When it was all said and done I realized I did not want to leave. I sat at the door to Talos' chamber for the remainder of the day, even opting to miss mealtime and instead stayed seated upon the cold floor.

Finally Talos came to retire for the evening. He stopped short of his door and cast his gray gaze down towards me. I knew he sensed me there. I bowed my head and stared at the floor as I spoke.

"You can't kick me out. I have nowhere to go."

Talos said nothing. I felt a great knot of discomfort well inside me. I didn't want to be at odds with the Master, he was all I had really. But it was on me to make amends.

"I'm sorry I struck you." I muttered the words, embarrassed for my previous actions. My temper had gotten the better of me. "I need you to help me...please."

I kept my head down, fearful of Talos' response. He owed me nothing, less than nothing after my childish behavior. He stepped around me and opened the door to his chambers with a lumbering creak.

"Come inside, Costa," he told me. I said not a word more and followed Talos inside.

The room was far more organized than I had expected a blind man's chambers to be. Not a scrap out of place.

Everything from tapestries to the linens on the bed roll matched in color and design.

There were books too, lined on shelves spanning across the walls in every direction.

Books? I thought. An odd choice for a man who cannot see to read them. I lifted one from the shelf and studied it. Words were replaced with strange bumps along the pages. I traced my finger along them, fascinated at the sensation that ran on my fingertip...I could almost make out the word in my mind.

Talos took the book from me and set it back in place.

"You have sticky fingers. Do you know why you failed today?"

"I'm not ready. I need more training."

"True, but you failed before you even began."

"What do you mean?"

"In your mind you'd already lost. The minute I took away your sight you told yourself all the impossibilities of racing blind. A true warrior can conquer any element just by focusing his thoughts alone."

"How do I do that?"

I received a quick, hard wrap across my knuckles with the blunt end of Talos' cane.

"Stop telling yourself no. You must train yourself to see only the outcome that is favorable to you."

"That's so hard to do."

"Aye, I didn't say it would be easy but once you trust yourself and believe in yourself you will know how."

"Will you show me?"

He grew quiet for too long. I knew I needed his guidance, I had no one else. Everyone I'd ever looked up to had left me in one way or another. It had become tiresome to walk my path alone. I'd been trying to build from others by taking in as much information as I could from afar. They were mostly drunken fools who wandered into the tavern, their best days behind them.

I'd made that judgment of Talos when I'd first met him, but slowly I came to realize his knowledge far surpassed any other I'd spoken to...perhaps even Cain Coleridge. I'd be a fool not to listen with an open heart and mind.

"The last time I took on an apprentice it didn't work out well for me." He paused. I waited with my breath held tight in my chest for his response. "Your father was even more stubborn than you are."

"Why do you keep speaking of my father? Who was he?"

Talos' cloudy eyes regarded me for so long that I wondered if he had been struck deaf as well as blind.

"Please," I told him. "I must know."

"Sit young Calabrese."

I sat upon the floor, legs crossed under me, and awaited Talos. He fetched something from a stack of neatly lined books and scrolls that were laced with small flags of varying size, markers for Talos to register which tome was which.

He shuffled forward across the hardwood floor and extended the piece of parchment.

"Here, take it."

I reached out and grasped the parchment by one of the yellowing corners. At first glance it looked as though it had been in hiding for many years.

"That was left here for you...by your father."

I looked up, his words startling me. For so long I'd known very little of my father and now pieces were falling into place. I took a moment before reading, uncertain what lay before me. My heart pounded with anticipation. When I finally began to read it, the words recounted on the page stilled my heart:

Costa,

I have never been a man of letters. Over the years I have recounted my knowledge and experiences within a book of scrolls so that the world would know of the evils that lurk in its belly.

For many years it has been my task to seek and destroy the creatures the Devil calls his own for the protection of humankind...even as they persecute me in my mission. Over time I grew quite successful in my conquests thus causing the minions of Hell to rally, determined to extinguish myself and my entire lineage.

I had hoped to spare you from such horrors, but it seems you are fated to the lot of a demon hunter just as I was. Fate chooses us, we do not choose our Fate. My last regret is that I could not prepare you further for the dark road ahead.

I realize now that my attempts to grant you a normal existence have left you woefully unprepared for what lies ahead. Know that my distance from you over the years was sought in your best interest.

You will need proper training if you are to do battle with the evil scourge. Talos shall be your mentor and your guide during your many travels. His words and his steel were all I needed to help me brave the cold nights when I was a boy of your age. It is my final wish that you will find the same comfort in his teachings.

It will not be an easy road, go forth with courage. You must embrace your fate and continue my work. It will not be easy. Find whatever solace you can in my words but be prepared for the ills that shall come from not only beast but of man. People will not understand.

With that said I shall not saddle you with goodbyes but I shall pass on my love – take it or leave it as you see fit. I believe one-hundred percent in all you do. Now you must believe in yourself if you are to survive.

Your Father,

Cain Coleridge

I felt the breath and strength leave my body reading the signature at the bottom. But it was there, gleaming up from the page where it could not be missed.

"This cannot be," I said looking up at Talos for some answers. The Weapons Master had history with Coleridge. He knew my own father more intimately than I ever would. For the last remaining hours we had spent together we had grown into what I considered friends but Coleridge hadn't found it within him to tell me I was his son then and there. I wondered why he had even bothered to tell me at all.

"Your father was not a saint," Talos began, almost reading my mind. "He was a very troubled young man with a very storied past when he came under my care. It took almost everything I had in me to reign in his fiery spirit in a way that he could harness it for his use rather than let it consume him. We came to many breaking points but Cain finally found his path here. Once he did he allowed it to consume him– which to this day I still regret."

"What path?"

"The path of the demon hunter, the one that you are now on."

I shook my head. "I never chose such a path. The only reason I sought you out was to try and make some sense of everything that has happened to me in the past few months. But I'm tired now and I'd like to be left alone."

"Your soul is weary."

His words encompassed the truth. The weary soul that Talos spoke of came from a battle for my own identity between Costa Calabrese the farmhand from Gryphant and Costa Coleridge, kin to the greatest hunter and destroyer the world had ever known. It was a hard fought battle to say the least. The worst part was not knowing which outcome I would prefer.

Talos remained quiet, waiting, he knew I had more to say. He allowed me the time to form the thoughts in my head to speak with clarity on the issue at hand.

"Is it true that he killed his family? Burned his home to the ground?"

"He related that to you?"

I nodded.

"He must've held you in high esteem then. Coleridge's past was not easily persuaded from his lips."

I fished out the book of scrolls and held it outstretched, allowing Talos to run his fingers over it.

"Coleridge left this for me. It chronicles a lot of his past."

"Yes, his past as a demon hunter – his rebirth. His life before that not many are privileged to hear...not without the promise of certain death."

"Then you must tell me. If he truly is...was my father then I must know."

"Cain Coleridge lived a normal existence until evil came into his home." Talos spoke as though he were dictating from a piece of parchment. Speaking in a flat tone, his words were chilling to the ear. "His sister, infected by a demonic nature, transformed before his very eyes and slaughtered her father before turning on Coleridge himself."

"So it is true?"

Talos stared at me with his sightless eyes for a long while. I began to grow uncomfortable under the weight of that stare. It implored me to remain silent until his tale was complete.

"Without a second thought, Coleridge decapitated the creature and set fire to his family home, with the bodies of what were once his sister and father still inside. From there he wandered aimlessly from town to town getting caught up with the local rowdies and causing trouble. He grew tired of the bar drunks he ran with, going off on his own leaving a trail of misery in his wake. He was lost, very much the same way you feel lost now. This is when he met me."

"It was fated."

"Perhaps. Though at the time I regarded him only as another angry young man intent on destroying himself and anyone else who happened to cross his path. As it turns out I crossed his path one night in a pub on the outskirts of Lao."

"What happened?"

"Your father was brazen back then, a drunken fool who felt he could best any challenge. His minor successes against minuscule fighters prompted him to challenge me. I held something of a reputation myself back then, not this old fool you see before you now."

He waved his hand up and down his body in display. I took in his outward appearance for a moment: the long white hair, the hunched shoulders, the sightless eyes. At first it would seem that Talos' best years were behind him, but something in the way of his stance or was it the sinew of muscle bulging from his exposed forearms, telling me that he could still best any who challenged him. Even a young fool such as myself.

"Cain was intent on carving a name for himself," Talos continued. "He didn't know the legacy he would soon unfold...I did."

"How is that possible? Do you have the gift of foresight?"

"It's just as I've always said. There are certain things that you do not see, you feel them. Your father's attack upon me was raw but full of promise. I knew right away his powers were meant for a higher purpose, just as yours are now."

"When did he leave this with you?" I said squeezing the page in my hand until it crumpled under the weight.

"He had a messenger bring it to me not long ago. He foresaw his imminent death. He wanted to leave you these words so you would know the truth."

"What truth? For all his bravery going against evil as he did he was a coward for leaving me...for leaving my mother."

I felt overwhelmed. My father had always been a nameless, faceless savior. Now I had a face that I could envision, characteristics and mannerisms to look back on. Cain Coleridge would be forever burned on my mind.

"I don't know if I can do this, if I can be this demon hunter. Coleridge held such power behind him, such great knowledge of the world."

"He was just a man of flesh and blood," Talos said as a smile, looking foreign and out of place, crossed his lips. "You're tough. I sense great things in you. The beginning of your journey is carved from the past of your blood. You cannot change the decisions of others just as Coleridge could not change his decision of leaving you so long ago. It is best to embrace your fate and make it your strength. For now you must rest, Costa. You've had a long day. There will be many more ahead of you here."

"You're allowing me to stay? Today I failed you."

"Yes, and you struck me."

"Apologies, Master." I bowed my head in shame.

"It won't be the last time you'll want to strike me. I'm firm but fair. If you are to study under me as my apprentice then you will learn tolerance."

I nodded in respect and made my way back to my own quarters.

What followed was a long and arduous apprenticeship under Talos. As time went by I came to know Talos as wise beyond his many years. He instilled in me a great many things. Most of all he built my confidence. Because he believed in me, I believed in myself.

He kept me segregated from most of the others so I could properly focus my energies. During the day I built a strong foundation by training with various weapons and defense methods. At night my mind soaked up knowledge from books and parchments...some spanning centuries in time. I built my body and mind into formidable attributes. Most days I reflected on Coleridge's letter, his first and last words to me as my father. As I let it soak into me, I realized it sounded more like a death sentence passed down without a scrap of encouragement from father to son. My path and my doom became imminently clear.

Chapter Eight
Weapons of Great Importance

A Year's Time Has Passed

The candle light waned. The storm outside no longer rattled the doors. Talos sat silent as I waited for his assessment of my tale.

"You've been here for many moons now. In that time, you've grown into a solid young man, however...." he paused to draw emphasis to his next statement. "You know as well as I do that you still have much to learn."

I frowned, because I strove very hard to earn his respect, to win him over with my talents by showing him the changes within myself while under his tutelage.

Talos was aware of the concern on my brow, with a simple scenting of the air. I knew he was sensing the shift in energies... it had been one of the main focal points of our teachings together. He insisted I expel my pent up anger.

"Was it not your own assessment that it has been a time of learning for you?"

"Growth, mentor," I insisted. "I have changed. I'm not the self-same whelp I used to be."

"Aye, you've become a vessel to fill but you still have room to take in more. Remember, the moment you feel you can no longer learn anything from this world is when it is time to leave it."

I hung my head as I took in his words. Sometimes I hated it when Talos was right.

"Very well," I sighed. "What else must I know before I can begin my journey. It's been so long since I ventured outside these walls."

"Patience comes from experience...that comes in time after many mistakes along the way. The key is to learn from your mistakes. You mistrust, that makes you weak."

"But I trust you."

Talos grew silent. His faded eyes held my own until I could no longer look upon the ghostly orbs. Finally he said: "Perhaps you are right. You have been here at great length."

I could not contain my excitement. "You're letting me leave?"

"Pack your things," he told me. "Wait for me on the morrow."

The next morning my abundant joy turned sour as I saw a roadblock to my happiness standing at the path leading out of Ravenwood.

Paralay leaned against the charcoal brick that made up the archway at Ravenwood's gate. I'd been so wrapped up in my detailed training with Talos my time with Paralay was sparse.

He still held the same arrogance and frustrating smirk he always had, just across more chiseled features. He'd foregone the spiked hair for a cropped cut as close to the skull as one could get without being completely hairless.

His eyes shined with mischief as I came forward. My teeth clenched under the weight of my disgust. Even after our time apart I still held disdain for the Elven warrior.

"What are you doing here?" I asked, holding the tension in my jaw so that my words had to press through gritted teeth.

"I was told to wait here." Paralay was as cool as ever. Unflinching as though nothing could ever unnerve him.

"By who? Who told you to wait?"

"Talos. He and I had a long chat last evening."

I felt a great discomfort knot up in the pit of my stomach. I wasn't sure just why until I saw the satchel high on Paralay's shoulder.

A smile spread his lips wide. I almost let my fist fly directly into his straight, white teeth, but Talos made his appearance before we could come to blows.

He was draped in a loose fitting brown and white robe. His ever present cane held fast at his side, on his other side his daughter Talisa.

I'd not seen her in a very long time. Though I'd tried hard to seek her out, it had always been in vain. I heard she'd made a journey to Oceania, the village by the sea, to learn the ship trade.

Time had done her well. A feather-stitched long coat fell over her like wisps of sea foam. Her crystalline eyes stared at me, and for a moment I thought I saw the trace of a smile.

I stared at her as she approached with her father and for the first time I noted Paralay's hard stare as well.

He was enamored of Talisa also. You could read it on his face like a prophet read his runes. As he caught my gaze he scowled, then sheepishly turned his head away, an embarrassing flush across his cheeks.

"Good," Talos said, "you're both here."

We turned and paid our respects with a bow of our heads. It still made me marvel he could sense our presence.

"Why both of us?" I asked, my tongue laced with aggravation. Even though I held a great deal of respect for my mentor, he still owed me an answer to my question. This was to be my departure day, my trek into the world to carry on my father's lot in life and finally avenge his death. Unless Paralay were there to wish me well on my journey I didn't see any reason for his appearance this morning.

"Today marks a big day for all of us," Talos explained. "It's the ending of one journey and the beginning of another just as profound."

Sometimes Talos made statements sounding like cryptic nonsense. This time I needed him to be more succinct with his answers.

"What are you telling us? I thought today I was to leave this place..." I stopped and stared long and hard at Paralay. "...alone!"

"This mission calls for more than one hand upon it."

Now Paralay spoke up. "I don't need this whelp, I can do it on my own."

"You don't even know what it is yet," Talisa added, her voice a sweet song on the ears.

"It matters not. I fear nothing," Paralay told her. He was trying hard to talk a tough game.

"A wise warrior would accept his mission with a silent tongue regardless of the requirements," she returned.

"I'm glad you feel that way, daughter," Talos said. "Because you're going with them."

Upon hearing this unfortunate news, Talisa lost her stoic, dignified stance to became a haughty, spoiled little brat.

"Me? But father you can't mean for me to travel to that frozen tundra with these two fools!"

Paralay and I had been listening to the same conversation but somehow we picked up different words as our main concern.

"Fools?" he asked. "Surely you meant fool."

My question seemed a bit more relevant than his ego driven defense. "Frozen tundra? Where are our travels to take us?"

"Costa asks the only question that demands any answer," Talos said.

I smiled. It felt good to be validated.

"The three of you are going to borrow essence from The Gods and bring it back here to me," Talos continued.

"The Gods? Then we're going to The Peaks?" Paralay's voice took on a quiver that I had never heard from him before.

"What peaks?" I wondered aloud. My study of maps and travel had taken me as far West as Oceania and as far East as Lao but I'd never once come upon any peaks that were namesake of The Gods.

"Frozen peaks," Talisa said. "Where nothing green thrives, only a cold, cruel wasteland of nothingness."

"There will be no more debate. It is time to leave on your mission."

We all fell silent nodding with respect. Whatever Talos deemed fit to be, was to be, irregardless of any argument from us.

"Each of you will have an equal part in this. Talisa will be your guide. Paralay will be in charge of any strategic attack plans, but overall Costa will lead you."

I heard a grunt of disdain come from both Talisa and Paralay. The discomfort of this trip had just been amplified by Talos' announcement of my leadership. I didn't want to disappoint him by any means, so I said not a word though inside I dreaded the hours that would be spent – the three of us alone on a frozen mountain top.

I watched as Talisa hugged her father goodbye, a part of her seemed to cling to him and did not want to let go.

"Be safe my daughter," Talos said. "The map shall be your source, the Earth your guide."

Paralay followed a handshake with a cocky boast of a strong, solitary effort leading to the completion of the mission.

Then I stepped up.

"So all that talk of me getting out to walk in my father's footsteps...it was a lie?"

"This is your final training exercise, Costa. What happens out there on the Peaks of the Gods will determine how you will set forth all the rest of your days."

We traveled in silence for the better part of the journey. Heavy packs and thick fur laden clothing were on our backs. I wondered what awaited us up there in the high mountain air where the temperatures were at their coldest.

I was born of desert winds and harsh sands, little rainfall, let alone a frost. Even the mild chill, spreading down from the peaks to caress the exposed skin of my cheeks, drew a shiver over my spine.

"There is something you need to know about the destination we are headed towards," Talisa said. I heard a faint echo of her words in the distance. I knew we were getting higher.

"The sun never shines," she continued. "It grows so cold that even your breath crystallizes before words leave your lips. Everything is sheathed in ice."

"It's also been said a vile wizard inhabits the mountain peaks," Paralay added. "Once a mighty God he was shunned by his people. When they wouldn't pay him tribute he cast down frost upon them, forever encasing the town in ice.

"That's just a fable," Talisa said, her tone full of disgust. "There's nothing up there, nothing at all."

Paralay raised his voice. I could hear a small rumbling in the distance as he laid into Talisa. "I speak the truth, and you should keep your mouth shut about matters you know nothing of."

Before more tongue lashings, or even blows, could be thrown I stepped into my role as leader.

"That's enough."

Paralay had other ideas. He hooked my collar in his fist and drew face-to-face with me.

"Just because Talos is quite literally too blind to see how inept you are does not mean I share any interest in his decision to put you in charge."

"Let him go, Paralay," Talisa demanded. "How dare you speak ill of my father after all he's done for you."

Paralay relinquished his grip just a moment before I swiped it off of me.

"Little miss follow-the-rules is no doubt going to report me, aren't you?"

"If she doesn't I will," I said. "Now keep your mouth shut and let's keep moving. We're losing daylight."

I expected another bloody altercation to erupt. My guard was up. I was prepared. Paralay held back, bit his tongue even, accepting my words as both warning and order. As we continued, our breathing became more difficult with the ascent. It was a long journey. We finally made it to what looked like civilization. Upon closer inspection, we were shocked to realize the entire village was frozen stiff.

Livestock, oblivious to everything around them, were frozen in their tracks. Each house was sheathed in ice. No sign of life. Not a soul in sight.

"It's the wizard's wrath," Paralay spoke in a whisper. "I told you, but you didn't believe me. Now you believe because you see it too!"

I looked to Talisa who froze out of shock rather than the elements or any wizard's curse. Her mouth agape as she looked over the once prosperous village now forever entombed in ice.

"Soon his wrath will spread into the valley below," Paralay continued. "Everything will be destroyed...Ravenwood, everything."

"Then we need to stop him." My heroism at that moment came more from my eagerness to impress Talisa than any sort of want or desire to protect the valley.

But she disagreed, adamantly. "No, our mission is to retrieve the Essence of the Gods, that and nothing more."

Feeling a need to defend my declaration I stood behind my statement.

"We have a duty to protect humankind."

The words sounded more like my father's than my own. Paralay corrected me.

"No, we don't. We haven't proper training to deal with the likes of a wizard."

"He's right," Talisa agreed.

"You believe your father would send us up here ill prepared?"

"I know my father prepared us for what he told us to do, nothing more. If we try to be heroes it'll surely be our deaths."

I lamented as we moved on. Part of me regretted not being able to step forth as Cain Coleridge surely would have to erase the scourge amongst the people. The other part was relieved, in the knowledge, a battle with sorcery and magic would not be an obstruction on our journey.

We wouldn't be free of all obstructions, however. In order to proceed the three of us would have to cross a giant body of water, in front of us, frozen just as everything else had been.

"How do we cross that?" I asked.

"Very carefully," Talisa said.

She may have been joking, but as it turned out we had little other choice. We headed out onto the icy plank, after any heavy equipment was removed from our packs. It was a time consuming effort to cross with the utmost care. Even though we were dressed for the frigid weather the cold air on the ice was biting.

We tried to hasten our efforts, while still moving cautiously. As Talos had instructed Paralay was the one to lead us forward across the ice as we linked hands to make a human chain.

"I can see the other side," he called back to us, "We're almost across."

Coming up on the last few inches of the crystal lake, a sudden loud crack disturbed me. Talisa was sandwiched in between us, so I was forced to raise my voice to get Paralay's attention.

"The ice is coming undone, we need to stop."

"No, keep moving."

He kept us moving, dragging Talisa by the arm as I followed. Just as I feared the ice beneath our feet began to unravel. Long streaks of open ice appeared on all sides, threatening to pull us deep within.

"Stop!" Talisa panicked as the ice broke up in patches beneath her feet. "We're going to fall in!"

"I'm fast, we can make it!" Paralay told her.

"And you'll drag the rest of us to our death in the process."

She pulled free from his grasp. Breaking the chain the three of us ran for safety. With each step dark lines laced through the ice beneath our feet. For once Paralay's boasts were founded on truth. He was fast and he made it to the other side within seconds. To his credit he turned and helped Talisa to safety as well.

I didn't have the same fortune. My foot cracked through the ice bed and I lurched forward onto my stomach. Talisa instinctively reached out to grasp my hand. She fell to her knees in the snow bank as the rush of water encircled my leg threatening to pull both of us into the lake.

"Paralay, help me!" she shouted.

The two of them managed to pull me to safety. My body was racked with shivers. I twitched and jerked as every muscle spasmed.

"We have to get him warm," Talisa shouted.

She threw her weight atop me then and I felt a strong sensation of warmth pool over my entire being from her petite frame.

"Wha...what...are...you doing?" I stammered the words out through chattering teeth.

"I'm trying to keep you from freezing," she responded. "Paralay, get his lower half."

At her order Paralay wrapped himself around my legs and held tight to me. Talisa's crystal eyes locked with mine. Something enigmatic shined from them. As her body warmth soaked into me I felt my strength and vigor return. The shivering began to subside and Talisa shifted her weight from my body. I reached out and held her fast to me.

Our breath mingled in the cold air and I could feel the pulse of her heart rising up through our fur laden clothes. Its rhythmic beat seemed almost to call to me.

"Are you ok?" she asked.

My grip upon her locked her in place atop me. Slowly I released her. To my surprise she lingered a moment longer before righting herself. I stared after her then turned my attention to Paralay who still clung to my legs.

"You can get off now."

"That's gratitude," Paralay said as he dusted the snow capped earth from his knees. "Next time I'll leave you to rot."

"Enough of that," Talisa hissed, her words forming a crystal cloud on the air. "We are a unit like it or not. We are strongest when we work as one."

"She's right," I said offering my arm towards Paralay in a show of truce.

He accepted my arm and pulled me to my feet. "Very well."

The morning had taken its toll so we decided upon rest as soon as we found a safer area. Many troubles weighed heavily on my mind. It felt good to have a rest from it all even if it would be short lived.

One thing that still harbored ill within the three of us was the company of the other. Sharing space would be something that would have to be dealt with if we were to survive this journey together. I opted to take my position as leader and open up the channels of communication, starting with the one I despised the most.

"How can you be so certain there is a wizard that dwells here?"

Paralay turned to me, "Because I've been here before."

Looking over the rim of his cup, the fire we had built danced within the structure of his green-gray eyes bringing on a demonic display across his countenance making me shudder.

"Back in the day, when I was a welcome member of my Elven troop we journeyed towards these parts. A massive blizzard hit the peaks that year. We took shelter in the town you just saw, only it was brimming with life at the time. As long as they made sacrifice to the Weather God he let them live on in peace."

"Living in frozen temperatures the likes of these does not seem very peaceful," Talisa said bringing herself closer to the fire pit to further illustrate her disdain for the frost-bitten weather.

"They made do until they became desolate," Paralay continued. "There was very little to spare, they could no longer appease him. The Weather God grew angrier, casting down hail storms upon the town. We offered to try to help. Such foolishness cut our numbers in half."

"You mean they died?" I asked.

"Yes, the nature of this land was never meant to be set foot upon by our race."

"Then why did you agree to come now?"

"Revenge," he said quietly. "I knew a girl in those days, Trinity. She was young and pretty...looked a bit like you Talisa."

He smiled her way pausing to reminisce. Trinity's face no doubt lingered on his mind and in his heart the way I knew Coleridge's would forever haunt me.

"It was at her insistence that we tried to aid the townsfolk. When we had almost made it to the highest peak, to find where the vicious bastard hid, he cast down a sheet of snow so fast and furious it swept us back down to the start of the trail." He looked around taking in the sights with his Elven eyes then pointed to the earth at his feet. "Here in fact. It took us days to recover, most of us had been swept away never to be seen again. Trinity was one of the damned. I wanted to go back then, find the bastard and kill him for what he had done. But I didn't own the strength and I could not go it alone."

"But you told Costa not to fight him," Talisa said.

"I've grown a lot since then," Paralay answered. "I know how to pick and choose my battles. Just setting foot upon this mountain peak again is victory enough in itself. I feel Trinity's spirit all around me. For once I feel at peace."

He grew quiet, solemn, sipping his cup. I noted a deeper level to him now that I'd not seen before through the arrogance. He held his head high with the pride of his lineage. I had mistaken the confidence of his bloodline with conceit. He demanded of himself and as such demanded the most out of others.

Talisa kept the communication going with a question simple enough drawing from her lips but difficult for Paralay to answer. "You loved her?"

"She was the only one I felt I could be myself around. When she was gone I didn't fit in anymore. I found myself falling into more and more trouble."

"What'd you do?"

"Petty things really. But when I picked up with a guild of thieves it marked my end within my home. I'd found my calling as a thief, and I felt welcome among my brothers. But I shamed my family and for that they sent me away."

"They sent you here," Talisa recalled.

He nodded. "Yes, and for the first time in a long time I've learned what it's like to feel like family is around you and supports you."

Talisa reached out and grasped his hand tightly in her own. I felt a sudden pang of jealousy course through me. The weight of her body upon mine, and the softness of her breath as she hovered over me before, brought me warmth and chills all at the same time.

I'd been mostly silent as Paralay told his tale but now I wanted to speak out, if for nothing more than to break-up their bonding experience.

"You and I share similar backgrounds," I said.

"I didn't know Calabrese was an Elven name," he joked. Talisa laughed with him. I could feel my ears burning but I continued my own story and this time I drew from what I held closest to me at that moment.

"My true surname is Coleridge."

I watched over the fire as their eyes grew wide with shock. Their reaction troubled me. I recounted Coleridge's letter and his warning of those who would fear me, hate me even.

"You lie," Paralay said, his words did not hold much conviction.

"Why would I invent such a tale?" I argued.

"Because it makes you somebody where you were nothing before."

"Stop it Paralay, that isn't fair," Talisa demanded.

The dynamic between the three of us seemed a mad swirl. One always attacked the other as the third took whatever side they opted for at the moment. I'd hoped we could push past such trivialities but Paralay stayed consistent, attacking me at every open spot.

I did not need Talisa's defending this time though I still welcomed it. Having her account for me held wondrous possibilities. But I wondered where her allegiance would go when she found out that I did indeed speak the truth.

I didn't bother with words then, I simply located the letter I had tucked away in my satchel and handed it across to Talisa.

"What's this?"

"Read it," I encouraged.

She stared at me a long while then unfolded the page and began to read. I poured over the words myself as they were forever etched on my mind. When she finished she folded it back up, bypassed Paralay's outstretched hand, and handed it back to me.

"So it is true then," she said.

"What did he show you?" Paralay asked in disgust. "Some sort of love letter?"

Talisa turned to him. "No, it was words from Cain Coleridge himself. Written in his scripture, in his blood."

"Why can't I see it?'

"Because they are personal words passed on from father to son," she said, then turned to me. "You shouldn't have even let me see it."

"I wanted you to get a better understanding of who I am and the reasons I'm here."

"Why are you here then, Costa?" Paralay asked. "Kin to the greatest hunter of all time should be high upon a throne, not a frozen mountain peak."

"Because I did not know him as such. He came in and out of my life too swiftly. I'm just trying to put the pieces of my life together now that they have been scattered to the four winds."

There was a long silence as each of us ruminated on thoughts deep within ourselves. Mine of course turned to Coleridge. I'd been hearing such different tales about him, some of greatness some of weakness, and all the while I just wanted more time with him so I could decide for myself if he were a good man or bad. For if he were bad, and I of his blood, what did that make me?

"Costa," Paralay called to me. I looked up awaiting another ill-advised quip to pull from his lips. Instead, he extended his arm in a fashion of friendship. "Perhaps you're right. You and I do seem to be cut from similar cloth."

"Yes," I agreed, "we're both damaged goods."

We enjoyed a hearty laugh at that. It would be the last to be had for quite a time.

Upon waking we could scarcely see daylight. Even the fire had burnt itself out. And the temperatures seemed to have been steadily dropping all the while.

"So do we call this morning?" Paralay joked as we packed our things.

"It unnerves me," Talisa said. "I say the quicker we accomplish what we set out to do the better. What do you think Costa? I mean my father did anoint you as leader."

Their eyes fell upon me looking for my guidance. I'd come through quite a bit in my time but I still wasn't arrogant enough to think I could handle this on my own.

"What say we all?" I said looking towards Paralay.

"I've no interest to stay here a moment longer than we need to."

"Agreed then," I told Talisa. She looked relieved.

After studying the maps, we charted out west into what turned out to be more peaks than valleys. Every forward movement from then on would be a vertical climb.

My lungs burned and my legs ached. I silently said a prayer and a thank you for all the training Talos had inflicted upon me. At the time it seemed like torture but now, hanging off the bit of a cliff with loose stones underfoot, I understood.

Somehow we'd lost our group order in the climb and Talisa wound up bringing up the back end. Paralay and I had negotiated a particularly hairy crag of rock with little effort, but Talisa struggled a bit.

"Stay here, I'll go help her," I said.

Paralay nodded, happy to have the rest as he drew large gulps from his water skin. I went back to the edge of the rock where we'd just come up and looked down for Talisa. At first I could not see her, the perpetual night had been playing with my eyes ever since we'd set out at the beginning of the day. As I adjusted my sights I found her pressed to the wall, holding on for dear life, too scared to move.

Instantly I dropped to my stomach and extended my hand down to her. I felt the sting of regret strike me like Talos' blunt cane knowing now that we never should've left her at the back.

"Talisa," I called, "Grab my hand."

I reached, flexed and extended my fingers trying hard to grasp any part of her and hoist her up. She looked up at me then, her eyes shone like two crystal gems. They were more luminous than I'd ever seen. I almost lost my concentration until her soft voice called out.

"Costa, please help me!" she was panicked and frightful.

I reached again, waving my hand out in front of her. "Take my hand I'll pull you up."

"Where are you?"

I halted. The shock of the words hitting me. As I looked again I realized she did not see me. Blind, like her father before her. But how so suddenly?

The answer would have to wait. For now I needed to get her to safety.

"Reach above you, I'm right here."

She let go with one hand, waved it over her head, and then clung back against the rock.

"I can't, I'll fall."

"No you won't I won't let you."

Paralay came in from behind me then. "You fools are going to anger the Weather God with your shouts. He'll send down sheets of ice and snow and bury us all up here."

"We have a situation here, Paralay," I told him. "Talisa cannot see. She can't climb up. Help me grab her."

"Can't see?" he was as confused as I but he moved as instructed. With me still at the edge of the cliff, Paralay climbed back over the side. When he reached Talisa he gently eased her off the wall and helped her up to me.

As soon as she grew close enough I grasped her tight and drew her to me. Her feet touched solid earth but she would not let me go. She held fast to my neck and buried her face against my shoulder to weep.

I didn't break away. The scent of her, like a jasmine field, filled me up with such warmth and such longing. But as her tears flowed from her and moistened the shoulder of my heavy cloak I felt her pain and it made me want to protect her, shelter her from any harm that may befall her.

"No helping hand for me?" Paralay asked as he scrambled up the cliff's edge. When he saw Talisa in my embrace his eyes squinted into daggers aimed right for me.

I had to let her go then lest I risk a new rift between us all. She pulled away, wiping the tears from her eyes while pacing to compose herself. What I noted after a moment was Talisa was still walking blind. I caught her arm forcing her to stand still.

"What's happening?" I asked, concern filling my voice.

"My eyes are useless in the dark," she said. "I can make out shapes, but nothing tangible. As we go higher into this frozen abyss and the light is completely shut out I cannot see around me."

"Night blindness," Paralay said. "It's a rare trait passed on by...."

"My father!" Talisa shouted. "I share his gifts and his flaws."

"You are not flawed, Talisa," I told her.

"Not yet, but as the years carry forward I will grow completely blind." She grew quieter. "Encased in darkness for eternity. I cannot live in such a way."

We had no words to comfort her. From then on we kept a chain so that one would never be set away from the other two for very long. It became quite a task to scale the summit. The height, width and depth of some chasms made me begin to wonder if we were ever going to make it out alive. Our map reader had been stricken blind. We were going on instinct alone. I only hoped it would be enough to carry us to our destination.

Out of the cold gray desolation we finally broke ground and made our way into the most majestical thing we could've seen...our long lost sun. It peeked out, just a crest of it, and caressed our faces with its warm kiss.

We had made it to the top. Before us lay a great dome of ice fashioned brick by brick, stone by stone, into housing that spanned the height of a great castle.

"We have arrived," Talisa said, a bright smile upon her face as the sun lifted her curse of blindness.

"It cannot be. The Weather God dwells here," Paralay muttered. "I can feel it in my bones. How else do you explain a castle of ice that does not melt in the sun?"

We all looked back and forth at one another, fear now hollowing out our guts. Talisa's magical eyes lingered upon mine.

"This is our destination."

I pondered but only long enough to gather my courage. "Let it be then."

Even at Paralay's protests, and my own lingering doubt, we entered the icy dwelling. It was a miraculous hall laid out in crystallized structures from the furniture to ornamental sculptures of flowers taken directly out of blocks of ice.

Not a soul in sight. In fact it looked as if no one had been there in a very long time. I remained fully aware of every inch of my surroundings but my muscles relaxed and I allowed myself to breathe fully.

"Where is this water we must fetch?" I asked Talisa.

"There is nothing on the map that shows this dwelling. It could be anywhere."

"Perhaps this is the Essence of the Gods," Paralay said. "Let's just chip off a piece of the wall and take that back to Talos."

I shook my head. "No. We will know it when we see it. The Gods make grand spectacles for themselves."

"What could be grander than an entire castle sculpted of ice?" Paralay protested.

I had no answer for him until we edged farther through the hall and came upon the exit at the other side. What awaited us there drew our breaths in a gasp. Such glorious beauty was illuminated in a grand design of flowers in full bloom, lush green grass, and thick full plants. They all culminated around a spring bubbling up from the ground, extending its watery limbs every which way in an invitation to those who found it.

"It's beautiful," Talisa said, her eyes now able to focus clearly once again. She began to step toward the spring and at that moment something in the deep recesses of my soul had me lash out and stop her.

"What is it?" she asked.

"We are not alone."

Upon my proclamation we were joined by three visitors, a man and two women. They stepped from the dense foliage and the women, dressed in wisps of colorful cloth began a dance around the spring.

The man stepped before us and I noted his legs, they were more goat-like than human, with thick hair covering the full length of them right down to the hooves that replaced his feet.

"Grand morning to you all," he said.

Paralay and Talisa seemed taken with our new visitors. I remained edgy. Something inside me called out a warning though I did not know the source of my discontent.

"Who are you?" I asked, hand on the hilt of my sword.

"They call me the Satyr," the goat-man said. He motioned over his shoulder. "Those are my Nymphs...protectors of the spring. We don't often get visitors up this way. Would you join us for a song and a dance?"

He produced a fashionable flute and began a lively tune. The Nymphs pulled away from the spring and each of them took hold of Paralay and Talisa by the hand.

They began a dance around the spring. It was very peaceful. My head began to lull itself on my shoulders. My eyes grew heavy. My hand slipped from my sword.

I heard words then, floating on the air or coming back to my memory I could not be clear on, but they spoke to me and I listened:

When you are in doubt, be still and wait.

When doubt no longer exists then act with courage.

So I waited, the music of the Satyr's flute filtering through me, my companions dancing in a trance with the Nymphs, and then I found the reason for my discontent and it came direct for me.

Before my eyes the Satyr's cherubic face became a mask of protruding cheek bones with twisted teeth. I stepped back in shock to see the Nymphs had also taken the form of hideous beasts.

Demons...here? It couldn't be, but it was. I knew in my soul they were here for me.

They had baited us with delicate grace and charm. Wooed us with music and laughter tainted with magical deception before moving in for the kill. It was unexpected but somehow I knew what to do:

Slay without mercy for you shall be given none.

No words would ever ring more true.

The demon before me was advancing. He held death in his eyes, death for me alone, but I had to put the welfare of my companions ahead of my own.

"Run!" I shouted out to them, hoping they hadn't succumbed to their trance. For my good fortune, and theirs, Talos' training was instinctive in all of us. Paralay and Talisa realizing the peril they were in reacted defensively. I reacted the same way as my assailant lashed out.

During the short time I had been preparing to hunt them, I had learned demons enjoyed attacking with their bare hands, as if ripping apart a human body were the equivalent of slaughtering a farmer's pig for supper.

Using the speed and agility I'd enhanced through my training with Talos, I took to a knee and rolled out of harm's way. For all their power the beasts lacked adequate quickness. It was best to keep distance between us.

I withdrew my sword, taking a chance to look back towards my comrades. Paralay was already on the verge of dispatching his demon. Talisa, on the other hand, had trouble ahead of her. She used her mind and wits for battle, not her strength. Using evasive tactics would only last for so long before she had to engage in combat. It was anyone's guess how well she would fare.

I'd sooner die myself than return to Talos with the corpse of his beautiful daughter in my arms. My demon would need to be dealt with swiftly so I could assist Talisa. I moved to draw his attention but he halted. At first I believed it was fear holding him back, then he produced the flute he'd piped as the Satyr.

Did demons have a sense of music? I didn't want to wait to find out. Whatever tune he'd played before had rendered us all in a stupor. I lunged forward, using my sword to hack off the hand which held the flute. It tumbled to the ground, the shrieks of its owner echoing through the skies.

I took my sword overhead and cut the head of the thing off at the neck. I swung with all of my might. There was hardly any resistance as my sharp blade separated the thing's head from its neck in a spectacular spray of blood. It crumbled in a heap spilling dark crimson out over my boots. Paralay dispatched his own creature at the same time.

"Get that demon off Talisa!" I called.

"Not demons," Paralay said in a pant, "Shape-shifters."

The description struck me cold knowing the evils my father spoke of had so many variables to fight. But I hadn't time to argue or question Paralay. Talisa needed our help.

She was taunting the beast, trying to circle it, out run it. Rather than produce any weapon she held her water skin in her hands, filled with the Essence of the Gods.

I moved on her attacker, hoping to cause enough distraction so she could escape. The thing whirled round taking in both Paralay and I with its blood red eyes. We formed a triangle, the three of us surrounding the beast.

"We've got it outnumbered," Paralay chuckled then moved forward.

"No, don't!" I shouted but it was too late. The moment Paralay advanced the creature struck out, backhanding him with such force that he slid three feet away.

I moved in next tackling the thing about the waist. It grabbed my cloak to tear me loose from its body. The creature hefted me high in the air, with its hands around my throat. Talisa stepped in then, showcasing her own bravery.

With my throat constricted I could not dissuade her. She mounted an offensive upon the creature that surprised me. Her father had schooled her well in the arts of hand-to-hand combat, but she was no match for the manner of beast we were dealing with at that moment.

It reached back a hand swatting at her. She fell back out of my sight. I felt dizzy. A great swell throbbed in my head as the oxygen left me. But Talisa had effectively distracted the creature long enough for me to gain some leverage.

I used my legs to climb up the beast's torso until my thighs took it around the head and neck. Now we each cut off the wind from the other. Even on the verge of passing out I held my ground until we both tumbled to the earth.

Soft gurgling noises sounded. I was dismayed to find they were coming from me. My reprieve came not a moment too soon. Paralay, now recovered, dove atop the beast from the rear gouging at its eyes.

Free from its grasp I took in as much air as I could. My vision remained cloudy. I stayed upon the ground to clear my head but I couldn't stay there for long. Commotion ran all around me. I shifted up ready to help my comrades in the fight.

Paralay was dispatching the remnants of the final beast, it was Talisa who needed my aid. She hurried to me, water spilling from holes that had been torn into her water skin.

"Costa, the Essence!" she shouted. "We're losing it to the earth."

"We'll go back and get more," I told her, my voice hoarse from the abuse to my throat.

"Look around you, we can't."

I turned back towards the spring dumbfounded. The lush flowers, the thick foliage, and the spring itself were drying up before my very eyes.

"Illusions," Paralay said. "Just like the images they portrayed for themselves."

"So there never was a spring?" I asked. "How could Talos not know this?"

"It was here, once," Talisa said. "Just like Paralay's wizard. Now everything has dissipated."

"Except the water you hold now, we have to get it into another container," I told her.

We scrambled to empty our packs to find something useful. I snatched my own water skin from my side, emptied its contents upon the ground in a splash, and tried in vain to transfer the Essence from one skin to the other. I changed tactics before losing what we'd fought so hard to obtain and tipped Talisa's skin to my own mouth to take in the Essence of the Gods.

"What're you doing!" Paralay shouted. He reached out for me trying to stop me. I forced him back with my free hand.

His panic was forthcoming but I'd had no intention of drinking it. Instead, I used my mouth as a tool to transfer the water into my skin. The remnants tingled upon my lips. I felt flush with energy I'd never known before.

"You had no right to do that," Paralay said. "Now the water is tainted. Talos won't be pleased."

"I did what I had to do in the moment," I told him forthright with no apology in my tone.

He muttered a curse as he began packing up our gear. Distance, I thought, would be the most appropriate thing at this time. Let cooler heads prevail. Everyone was wound up after our impromptu meeting with the devil's spawn.

"What's it like?" Talisa asked me as she lightly traced my lips with her finger.

My soul felt on fire but it was nothing from the water skin bringing on such enlightenment. Her touch alone caused emotions in me to stir that I had never truly known before.

"It's hard to explain."

"Perhaps it's just best to see for myself," she said coolly. Her fingers laced up over the back of my neck and through my hair. She pulled my head down until I was level with her and she pressed her lips against mine.

Such softness and power all at the same time.

She pulled back, licked her lips with a sensuality that brought shivers to my spine, and then stepped away without a word.

I stood there like a stone statue ruminating in the afterglow of her presence until a leather satchel bounced off my head.

"Are you going to help us or not?" Paralay demanded.

I nodded, forgiving him his temperament. That, I had come to learn, was Paralay's nature. We were an enigma the three of us. I caught eyes with Talisa on the way back down the cliffs. I know unraveling her mystery promises to be most intriguing.

We arrived back at Ravenwood physically exhausted, but with a zest of soul coming from the completion of our goal. Dropping our supplies in a heap by the archway we hurried to find Talos, proud in our accomplishments.

He sat amongst Talisa's garden sanctuary by the statue of Aphrodite – no doubt praying for his daughter's safe return. When we entered, he stood, a smile turning up the corners of his leathery cheeks.

In our rush of excitement Paralay and I almost passed over the paying of our respects until Talisa dropped to one knee and bowed. We followed suit, then I rose to extend the sheepskin holding the Essence of the Gods.

Talos took it gently from my hand. We waited breathlessly to find out the significance of the water. He opened the skin to empty the flask into the fountain pool behind him until the flask was bone dry.

I waited, leaning on my toes to see if the mix of water were somehow going to display a showcase of magic. Nothing happened.

"What does it mean?" Talisa asked. I was grateful she had voiced the question on all our minds. "The water, what was it for?"

"Quenches the thirst," came Talos reply.

I believe we were all confused at this point. I couldn't help questioning my mentor's actions myself.

"You mean you sent us to fetch a pail of plain water?"

"You're reading the surface again, Costa," he explained. "Water is a powerful element able to take on any form to adapt to its surroundings. But not one of you would've agreed on that fact unless it had been labeled as it was: The Essence of the Gods. Some things in life are given power simply by your own reaction to it. That is what you were meant to learn."

"We tested the Fates," Paralay protested. "Just crossing the threshold alone could've angered the Weather God and had him bring his wrath down upon the valley."

Talos turned to Paralay, his milky eyes almost consoling now. "There is no Weather God, Paralay. The people of that town lived in fear of the weather itself. In their minds they saw a great master of the elements because they believed that if there was a God then they could try to appease him. They were not ready to accept that the weather would come and go as it pleased regardless of their many sacrifices."

Paralay bowed his head in shame. "I feel like a fool. All this time I believed as well."

"No, you fought valiantly," I told him. "Without your aid those demon creatures would've overpowered us."

"Demons?" The shock in Talos' voice drew my spine rigid with fear and contemplation.

"Yes, mentor, there were demonic forces awaiting us at the top of the mountain when we went for the Essence...er, water."

"This is troubling," he muttered, running his fingers through the shag of beard that grew from his chin. Then he clapped his hands together drawing up as tall and straight as his weathered body would allow. "What matters is that you bested them. The three of you, when faced with the elements of very real danger, learned to adapt to each other, rely on each other rather than go against the flow of one another's energies. I salute you all."

We saluted him back with the bow of our heads. I felt a great sense of pride welling up inside of me. The completion of the mission and the attainment of our goal solidified in me the confidence to carry on as the man I'd set out to be. But one element still eluded me. I would never feel complete until I knew that part of my life that had been hidden from me for so many years. In order to truly know myself I would have to walk the path that my father had carved out before me.

As the stars quietly took their places in the night sky Talos held a grand dinner in our honor. Paralay and I had dressed in our best tunics in anticipation of sharing the head table with the Master and his daughter.

We regaled him with tales of our climb up The Peak of the Gods. He seemed most interested with our account of the battle fought against the demon scourge. His brow creased in deep contemplation. He spoke not a word until we had finished. He leaned forwards and whispered to me.

"They were not meant to be there."

He stopped to study me. One heavy hand dropped upon my shoulder, his face searching the air around me.

"Have you spoken to anyone about your lineage?" he asked.

I felt a great weight of discomfort course over me. My shoulders tensed under Talos' hand and I knew that lying to him would be futile.

"Yes, mentor. Talisa, Paralay, and I discussed stories one night up on the mountain. I told them I was Coleridge's son."

His silence stopped my heart.

"Was that wrong, mentor?"

"What's done is done," he told me. "But in the future perhaps it would be best to keep that part of your past private."

My discomfort was growing. I wanted to shake Talos' hand from my shoulder so I opted to reach out for my goblet of wine hoping that he would withdraw his grip. The goblet went from table to mouth and back again with no movement from Talos whatsoever.

"I know my father held a hated reputation amongst most people. I don't necessarily revel in being the son of a slayer, but I didn't think it required such secrecy."

"The Dark Lord has eyes and ears everywhere, Costa. For now your silence can mean ensured safety for yourself and the company you keep."

As his clouded sightline traveled towards his daughter Talisa, he finally withdrew his hand from my shoulder. I realized what he meant. I was a tainted soul now. I walked my father's path with my father's blood coursing through me. All the minions of Hell roamed the Earth seeking me out to eliminate my blood line. They had located us there on the mountain peak from the whisper of words on the wind. It had been I alone who brought grave danger upon the heads of my companions.

I followed Talos' stare across to Talisa's perfect face. She smiled at me. I remembered the softness of her lips as they had brushed against mine. Regretfully I turned away. I could not bear the thought of harm coming to her because of me. Now I understood why my father lived his life alone.

At the conclusion of our meal I had stuffed so much food into my belly that I felt ready to burst. The wine fogged my head. I felt dizzy enough to turn in for sleep that would last ages. But Talos held one more surprise treat in store for us.

He excused the rest of the students. Talisa, Paralay, and I were invited into his chambers. I tried to hide my staggering as best as I could. Such an embarrassment it would be if I fell flat on my face during his presentation.

"The three of you have made me very proud. Your determination has brought you through some very difficult tests I've laid before you and your continued courage will no doubt bring you great successes in life. As we now part, I would like to present each of you with the tools of your trade, for which I'm known."

Weapons.

Up to this point we'd each been utilizing short swords and daggers as our primary resources of defense, except for Talisa who refused to carry a bladed weapon. Talos' gift to each of us this day was a hand crafted piece of weaponry that best suited our own individuality.

For Paralay: a mate for his short sword. Dual blades made of fine mithril, the lightest yet most durable steel known to man. He demonstrated his skills, spinning the blades in unison as though they were extensions of his own arms. I was impressed.

Talos then stood before Talisa smiling down at his daughter. She returned his smile with a reminder.

"You know I will not carry a weapon designed to kill."

Talos nodded. "Yes, but I must insist you have some method of defense other than close quarter contact."

With that he clapped his hands together, as he drew them apart he produced a long staff from midair. I didn't think there was anything else Talos could do to awe me...I had been mistaken.

The staff was carved of fine, sturdy wood. Etchings from the far East laced its body in grooves. Talisa collected it. She looked comfortable with the weapon in her hands.

"It's beautiful." she said.

"Yes, beautiful," I agreed though I was not looking upon the staff. Talisa caught my stare. She blushed, then turned away quickly to thank her father with an embrace.

Now it was my turn. Before he passed me my new weapon of choice, Talos had words of wisdom to pass on.

"Costa, you have your whole life before you – why not forget the past?"

"If I am ever to truly know my father, or that part of myself that is undiscovered, I must walk in his footsteps."

I didn't have the heart to tell him the truth. My lot in life would be to hunt and destroy as my father had before me I would be committing the foul beasts to their grave in an act of vengeance.

Talos nodded his head, lamenting my decision, and turned over my weapon.

"Costa, for you I have secured something very special. It has been in my care for ages, passed down through generations. Rampant misuse of power by a few apprentices made it necessary to shield the knowledge from those who were not prepared to use it wisely. Its known only one other master in its time...your father."

He handed over a magnificent combination of wood and steel: the repeating crossbow, providing the means to kill without risking a deadly encounter. The bolts that came along with it varied in size, shape, and dimension. A pouch across my back handled sharply carved stakes, silver tipped arrows, and bolts equipped with enough holy water to at least stun any foe from the devil's pack.

"All of you have made me very proud. When you leave me now each of you will be skilled in the arts of weaponry. Do not forget the lessons learned here or abuse the skill you now possess.

Each of you has a destiny to fulfill. When your path grows dark and you can no longer see your way forward that's what I'm here for."

He turned to me then, grasping my shoulders, penetrating my soul with his invasive, ghostly eyes. His words brought me comfort, a smile, and a few tears.

"Your father would be proud of your accomplishments." He paused, to let out a long winded breath. "There have been days where I've longed to have the youth and strength of someone such as Coleridge – to live one day in his skin."

"We prefer you as you are, mentor," I told him.

"What makes you say that?"

"Because we love Talos. Each of us aspires to be like you. Your teachings have made me a man of great merit. I would not be half the man I am without you. I am forever grateful."

"You are very welcome, my apprentice, but your heart and your will got you this far...not me."

"I believe you had something to do with it as well."

I clutched him in an embrace, letting the strength of our bond enhance my resolve to travel the land to conquer not only the demons walking the earth, but the ones that still gnawed at my soul.

Chapter Nine
Concerning Vampires

Our mission, and subsequent battle on top of the peaks, had been the culmination of a long, arduous apprenticeship. In that time I'd built my body and fashioned my mind to deal with what inevitably lay before me.

Now that we'd graduated from Talos' care I felt my energies shift again. The great adrenaline rush and focus now dwindled down into a new pit of dark determination within me. Change was in the air, I knew what lay before me – that didn't make it any easier to accept.

My body's defiance told that story in simple movements. The backs of my legs drew taught with every movement. Knots coiled my back like little ripples up and down my spine. Even the simplest twitching of my thumb resulted in excruciating pain.

Everything had caught up with me. I lay in bed allowing the warmth of the shag covering to coil around me, trying to rest my mind so I could attain some level of comfort.

I began to drift off, letting the safety of Ravenwood be my sanctuary. It was time to move on – carry out my fate like my father before me. It troubled me to embrace such things. Even though I knew I had to accept the changes, a part of me preferred to imagine it would all work itself out.

I pulled the coverings up over my head in an effort to remove myself from the outside world. That lasted not but a moment. A dark whisper brought my eyes open in a snap.

"Costa, there is a great evil afoot."

At first I imagined my father stood over me, Cain Coleridge with his dark scruff of hair peaking from beneath a wide brimmed hat and the piercing, hooded eyes staring down at me.

The eyes glowed like a full moon at twilight, pale and lacking pupils, that's when I realized it was Talos who had awakened me.

"What's the danger?" I muttered, still halfway on the precipice of the dream world. "Come, get your belongings and meet me in my chambers."

Talos left. I dressed before rinsing my face and the dryness of my mouth with water. Inside Talos' chambers it felt colder somehow than the rest of the grounds. I couldn't help but regard it as the danger he spoke of that lingered on the air.

He turned to me then, handing me a cup filled with hot spiced cider. It warmed my body but my soul still felt the chill creeping over it. I waited in silence for Talos to reveal why he needed to wake me in the middle of the night. "The demons are rallying," he told me, a hint of anger pulling at his words. "It's just as I feared. They've come to discover your connection to Coleridge." He sat then, slowly, the weight of his troubles too much for his aching joints. "It seems I failed you."

"You haven't failed me, mentor. I am grateful for your help and guidance throughout this time. I wouldn't be who I am today, if it hadn't been for you."

"My attempts to protect you haven't worked. The danger is out there...it will find you."

I sat next to him, settling a reassuring hand upon his shoulder. Funny how things had turned full circle –I was comforting him now. The student aiding the master.

"We knew this day would come. It's time I accepted my calling, to face my destiny head on."

Talos nodded. "So be it."

I'd spent a long time reconciling the person I was now with the troubled soul I used to be, preparing to face this inevitable day. Was I ready? Only time would tell.

I located Coleridge's journal and folded back the pages until I found what I was seeking. It seemed I always indirectly fell upon the passage that suited the situation at hand, as if my father had foreseen each obstacle that I would face.

"Remember; always go with your first instincts. The troubled man would be wise to keep his innermost thoughts to himself. Find a place in your mind to go willingly to escape from the evils of the world. But when the darkness consumes your mind, you will find you cannot run away from what's in your head."

Preparation for this journey differed greatly from the travel to the peaks. There would be no need for layers of clothing to keep the chill of the elements at bay. I filled my bags with the most useful of items, paying special attention to elixirs or herbs which promoted healing.

By a quirk of fate, my path, quite possibly my doom, had become clear. I couldn't allow fear to hold me back even as it bubbled in my stomach and knotted my shoulders. With a heavy breath I finished with the book of my father's words, tucking it away into the bag at my side and cinched the crossbow Talos had given to me up over my shoulder with a leather bit. Then it was time to go.

I scanned my quarters for the last time. So many memories were locked within every corner. Though it was time to go leaving behind this part of my past grew considerably more difficult than when I'd left Gryphant.

Ravenwood felt like home. Those who resided there were my family. Leaving behind my brothers and sisters in arms would prove most difficult.

Entering the courtyard, I found at least some of my loved ones refused to let me leave so easily.

"Did you really think we'd let you slip out without us?" Paralay asked with a grin. He leaned nonchalantly against one of the stone pillars, arms crossed, a full satchel at his feet.

A second set of baggage belonged to Talisa. She was dressed in skins that ran the length of her body from head to toe, hair swept back and tight to her skull – fashioned as though she were ready for battle.

Looking at her delicate features, remembering her plight on the frozen peaks, reminded me of my father's words about the importance of his isolation from others. I couldn't accept their decision.

"I must walk this path alone."

They remained defiant. Talisa hitched her bag across her shoulders. She smiled at me and dismissed my words as a mother would do to a small child.

"Don't be silly."

I set my hand upon the strap of her satchel, my intent to relieve her of her bags and her foolishness.

"You don't understand what I'm facing. The dangers I'm about to encounter are not something either of you should have to deal with."

"And why should you?" she asked stepping back from my grasp. I could almost detect a sense of urgency when she spoke of my plight. I was warmed by her concern for me. Irregardless of the feelings developing between us, or perhaps because of them, I had to stand my ground.

"Because it is my fate, my destiny."

"A man makes his own destiny," Paralay scoffed, then in a much more serious tone he delivered words straight from his soul. "My destiny lies with you, Costa, no matter the element of danger."

"As does mine," Talisa added."

The camaraderie we'd formed during our short time together was an unbreakable chain. I knew better than to try and argue any further. My companions would travel with me as I willingly sought out all the powers hell could throw at me.

My training was in place. I held armaments at my back fashioned by a renowned weapons master. Paralay and Talisa were at my side. I was ready to face the accursed horde as my father had before me – but where to begin?

Talisa, Paralay, and I journeyed by foot. We stopped to rest at a sleepy little town not far from Ravenwood. It was rotten in such a way that many of the inhabitants slept on the streets – no homes to speak of to call their own.

Talisa tried fiercely to dissuade us from our decision to stop.

"The place makes my skin crawl. Let's move on to something more inviting."

"The next town is another half a day's travel," Paralay told her. "We need to stop and rest to gather our strength."

I made a point of wrapping my arm loosely about Talisa's shoulders to comfort her.

"It'll be fine, girl. There's nothing inhabiting this place we can't handle."

She huddled close within the comfort of my cloak and whispered up to me.

"When night falls I fear I won't be able to discern friend from foe. You will have to be my eyes."

"I won't let you out of my sight."

Paralay had gone ahead of us marking our path in search of....

"Food!" he called back over his shoulder.

We hurried to catch up with him in front of a tarnished structure. The door barely on its hinges and the roof had collapsed in more than one spot.

"What destruction could've befallen this place?" I asked aloud. Looking over the damage, I equated it to my last days in Gryphant when the savage demon attack laid waste to all I'd known growing up.

Those memories still haunted me, but I held deeper ones in my heart now. It was a balance of light and dark to keep me sane. Spiraling into madness, like my father before me, was a concern I held at the forefront of my thoughts.

The same held true for Talisa and her inherited blindness. She clung to my hand like a young child as she looked over the building in dismay.

"Are you sure it's safe to eat here?"

"It's worth a try," Paralay said. "My belly is rumbling."

We moved inside. Any doubts concerning the level of satisfaction we would receive were quickly erased by the aroma of smoked meats filling the room. One room, small and quaint, housing very little by way of decor or even amenities to dine.

Some chairs were scattered around a handful of tables. A few patrons sat eating, not one looked up at our entrance. At the back of the room a man stood beside a pit of rocks and fire roasting a small animal. We made our way towards him. He glared at us from under hooded eyes.

"Three pints of your finest ale, innkeeper and rustle us up some of that pig you're roasting as well."

Paralay's demands were met with a curt response. "We've no ale here."

I stepped in to take over the questioning. "We've traveled some distance. We'd appreciate any hospitality you can offer us."

Paralay scoffed. "You sure don't sound like Coleridge, you're much too soft."

"Never mind about my father," I told him under my breath, my words a warning trailing on the air. It was too late. Upon hearing the Coleridge name the innkeeper perked up and sent us over three plates full of meat direct from the bone.

"Ah, see," Paralay said settling in to dine. "Drawing from lineage has its advantages."

I refused to debate him in front of the townsfolk, instead I turned my attention back towards the innkeeper.

"How do we wash this down?"

Not a word was spoken, instead he gestured towards our water skins.

Perfect I thought.

Though the meat smelled of fresh herbs and spices while roasting over the open flame it left a lot to be desired by way of taste. It was dry and stringy, not like any mutton or pig hide I'd ever sampled before.

My companions' faces held the same expressions as they bit into the meat. Even watered down ale would've been a welcome respite at that moment.

"Seems the pig is over cooked," Paralay said as he tore at his meal with his teeth as best he could.

"It's not pig," the innkeeper said, his voice gravelly and low as he puffed on what looked like a stick of charcoal dust. "'Tis vermin."

We all stopped eating then.

"Surely you jest," I told him matter-of-fact.

"Look around, son, did you see any livestock coming in?"

I shook my head slowly as an unpleasant rumbling entered my gut and though I wished deeply that he wouldn't the innkeeper continued with his tale.

"We do what we can to survive."

Talisa made a small squeak, then covered her mouth and ran to the corner to retch. I felt inclined to follow but remained weighted to my seat from pure shock alone.

Paralay was undisturbed. He continued with his portion. My instinct was to check on Talisa, but something at the back of my mind told me to probe this man deeper. I sent Paralay after her in my stead. The sight of him gnawing on the charred flesh grew unnerving, it reminded me very much of Benton's swift turn to an accursed, rancid, corpse-like human.

I studied Paralay's gait as he walked away hoping not to see the ragged shuffle-step of a man gone over into a demonic state. There was no evidence that he'd been cursed. My mind was just playing tricks on me. With my fears firmly dissuaded, and Talisa safely in Paralay's capable hands, I turned my attentions back to the innkeeper.

"Who are you?"

"They call me Dragus."

"Well then Dragus, what evil has befallen this place?"

He remained quiet, staring at me from under hooded eyes.

"I can sense something upon the air, now tell me what I want to know before I pull you across this bar and throttle you."

My father's blood did indeed run through my veins. Even this man Dragus knew it.

"They come in the dark of night, a plague upon our streets. No locked doors or windows barred can keep them from obtaining what they seek."

"Who?"

"Vampires. They drag the bodies still kicking and screaming back up to the hills where they make their dwelling to dispatch them one by one. Sometimes in mid-day I can still hear the screaming."

I shook my head in dismay. "That is a wild tale."

"These abominations must have come back because of the resurgence of hell's minions. If you are who you say you are, hunter, then you can stop this corruption from returning to Calyx. We're on the verge of extinction."

"I owe nothing to you or your perverse little town," I almost spat my words. "I'd be doing you a favor to let death sweep over this place and erase it from any map."

Talisa and Paralay finally pulled me outside. I shook free of their grasp and paced a frustrated line in the sand.

"Is this what I'm meant to become? A do-gooder for every despicable miscreant within walking distance. No wonder my father went insane."

"Aye, it's a heavy burden to carry," Paralay agreed. "I say let them rot."

"Your father chose his path because he felt he had a duty to uphold," Talisa said. "He held instinct and skill none had ever known before. Talos once told me Coleridge thought it a disgrace not to use his gifts for something other than himself. Perhaps that's why he faced these demons, because he knew no one else could."

I took in her words and washed them away a second later. "Coleridge was ego driven. He went after these beasts to sate his own appetite for blood and to quench the everlasting guilt he felt for destroying his own family."

"But I heard tell that he had no choice regarding the death of his father and sister."

"I'm not talking about his upbringing," I said. "I'm talking about me! He left me, left me to suffer at the hands of a tyrant with no real memory of the past. That isn't easy to get over, and don't think that I haven't tried to."

"That may be true but couldn't you think for a moment that maybe all of this isn't about you? We have a chance to do some real good here."

"Or make some profit," Paralay added. "Go back and tell those fools that we'll save their stinkin' city...for a price."

I looked after both of them. Everyone had their own agenda... including me. I held a foul taste inside my mouth. It was a combination of carrying out a destiny that I'd not asked for and a longing to become that special someone that garnered respect and fear at every turn.

"We'll save their precious skins," I said. "But we'll do it my way."

Now, more than ever, my anticipation was growing. There was something to be said for the thrill of the hunt. If the innkeeper's tale had intended to scare, it failed miserably. I'd heard a similar fable before.

In my days tending Benton's bar I'd heard many strange tales – mostly fabricated nonsense spun by drunken bards. But these vampires were a devil species I already knew well. The face of Lord Le Carde still burned in my memory. His long dark hair against pale-sick skin, the blood-red eyes, and the inch long fangs would be forever ingrained on my very soul.

Would he be amongst the lot of vampires if we found them? Doubtful. We were many miles from Gryphant where I'd first run into Le Carde. After burning daylight in a mad, frenetic pace towards the hilltop where it was said to have sightings of hell unleashed, the three of us sat around a campfire prepared to rest. Talisa already set herself down for sleep, closing off the outside world until the light of day returned and brought with it the promise of her sight.

Paralay and I had no words. We needn't speak any for me to know what lurked behind those shifty eyes.

I kept to myself. The inner darkness I'd once held at bay now creeping back over me in a wash as I contemplated how future events would play out.

Now more than ever I understood my father's nature, how his mission to seek and destroy became all consuming. Nothing and no one else mattered.

"Find one focus and do it well," Paralay said. They were not the words I'd been expecting at all. Thus, I had to break my silence which had most likely been his intent.

"What?"

"Your mind is torn between who you are and who you feel you need to be to honor your father."

He set me off, a spark of fire igniting the tumultuous aggression I struggled to keep at bay daily.

"Shut your mouth, Elf. You've no idea what it's like to carry such a name...it's a burden."

"No, but I do empathize with not fitting in, not knowing who you are or where you truly belong."

I stood then. He'd hit a nerve, though I would never admit it aloud.

"So what?" I said as I paced back and forth in front of the fire. "Does that mean we've bonded now?"

He settled down against his bed roll looking up at the stars as he gave a glib reply. "Of course not."

I remained up, pacing off my energy, balling my hands at my sides ready to strike out.

"Get some sleep, Costa," Paralay told me. "You'll need strength tomorrow."

I knew he was right but as I settled on my bed roll I couldn't get myself to drift off. Time passed deep into the night until the campfire burnt itself down to ash and embers.

My body finally settled in a sweet spot and I let my heavy lids shut tight. Thoughts of tracking and tactics entered my mind forging the dreams of a hunter. I didn't know exactly what we would run into on the morrow but I was intent on being prepared for whatever it may be.

As I drifted further into dreamscape a chill swept over me. I found my thoughts shifting to that all too familiar world where dreams and reality merged into one. Something dark and sinister surrounded me as I wandered amongst the ruins. I felt the coldness of the caverns I traveled pull over my entire body. Then, out of the darkness and the shadows came a face I would not soon forget.

The blood red eyes, teeth pointed into sharp stakes, and the twitch of a grin just before he ended Tuck's life with the flip of his wrist.

Lord Le Carde, his face was unmistakable. In fact I could almost smell him, the rot and decay permeating from his every pore. He stood before me, arms outstretched as if he were going to embrace me.

"Welcome," he said.

He came forward then. I found myself watching his actions as a bystander. Le Carde's attention no longer fell on me, instead his deadly reach went for Talisa. I didn't know how she had gotten there, nor I for that matter. Things were spinning out of control and before I knew it Le Carde had Talisa in the grasp of his long, skinny fingers. He drew her close and took a sizeable chunk out of her neck with the point of his teeth.

I wanted to shout but found my voice locked in my throat. He tore out her jugular and as her blood splashed over my face I jerked awake.

I looked over my shoulder to find Talisa still sleeping soundly. The discomfort of the dream still weighed heavily on me. Le Carde was here, close, I could sense it. I would not allow those images to become reality. I knew what I had to do.

In the middle of the night I stole out of the campsite under cover of darkness. Talisa and Paralay meant well. I was grateful for the companionship...up until now. Tracking Le Carde was something I had to do on my own. It had fast become a selfish little desire of mine that grew all consuming.

I'd forgo Talisa's map of the land and instead base my choices on raw instinct alone to guide me. Under Talos' tutelage I'd grown into my intuitive nature. Where confusion once lay, now, I had an insight.

My pursuit brought me across deserted plains – all flat lands. Sand crusted underfoot and I felt as though I'd been walking for days. The sun began to rise; I was losing the cover of night. More pressing than that became the weight of dizziness clouding my head.

I'd grown tired in a short span of time. My feet dragged behind me. The sands underfoot began to draw up and whip around me which puzzled me for there was no wind. My pace slowed as I shielded my eyes trying hard to trek forward through the whirlwind of sand. I began to recognize a most foul odor in the air.

"That's death you smell."

I heard Coleridge's words at the back of my mind. As the odor grew stronger so did the fog in my head. It intensified enough to drag me to my knees. My hands fell forward as I sought to brace myself. In the coarse sand I came to find the remnants of a human skull, withered and broken but distinctively human.

It was at that moment, I knew the smell of death was a warning...a message of my own destruction. Something in the air was toxic and dragging me to my doom. The cloak about my shoulders grew extremely heavy. I lurched forward from the weight of it and fell face first upon the sands.

So tired...my eyes grew heavy. Soon I began to forget why it was that I had come that way. Everything else mattered little; all I wanted to do now was lay down and rest. I tried to retain my senses but even as my thoughts protested and called for me to rise my body had other ideas and it won out with a compelling argument.

I fell asleep even as my own voice called out a warning that such actions would surely lead to my own skull decaying under the hot sands.

I awoke moments later. My eyes took their time to focus. At first I thought I must be in a dream as I saw a vision of splendid beauty hovering over me. As my eyes cleared I could make out Talisa's delicate features. Her countenance a mask of worry and concern that wrinkled her tanned forehead.

"He's coming around." Her eyes kept my gaze as she called out but she wasn't speaking to me.

Just then Paralay came in behind her. "Good, it'll give me a chance to put him back down. What were you thinking trying to shake us like that?"

I couldn't answer him, my tongue had gone dry and I still felt the veil of exhaustion floating over me. All I could muster was a shake of my head.

"Still have trust issues, aye?" he said. "Get over it."

When Paralay walked away my eyes focused back on Talisa and I noted the welling of tears.

"You could've died," she told me. "You wandered into the Forgotten Realm. Stepping foot inside drains you of your energy. Once the sands stir up you lose all sense of direction and thus settle down for sleep never to wake."

"Yeah and they say the weak of mind forget why they came that way in the first place," Paralay added.

I tried to argue with him but I only managed to mutter my words and mesh them together to come up with something that sounded like tiplsdrn.

Talisa set a finger upon my lips to silence me. "You move too fast. Rest now. When you regain your strength we will set out...together."

I took in her words, her face, and drifted deep down inside myself where I forged my energies and readied for attack the moment I came round again.

Along the winding road I'd traveled in my life I'd lost bits and pieces of myself, regained some, and added anew. What I found in my journey was the pleasure of knowing, at least for a little while, I had friends who cared enough to watch my back. If it had not been for them I'd have joined my childhood companion, Tuck in the hereafter.

As it was I stood to face another day. My body felt weary with a soul to match. At that moment I may have been happy to join Tuck, but I wasn't finished yet.

This time Talisa's skill with the map guided us direct to the point. We arrived at the foot of a crested structure. It seemed as though it had been chiseled into the face of a mountainside. Small, curved slopes acted as windows. A T-shaped doorway at the top of the East end of a central tower appeared to be the only way in. Not the most inviting of doorways I'd ever run across.

A strong sense of fear overtook me then and I began to have second thoughts. Something in me held me at bay, taunting me, telling me I was not the hunter of hunters, but still the self same young boy who merely dreamed of adventure but never truly lived it.

Talisa must've noted my hesitation for she came alongside me where Paralay could not hear and whispered to me.

"We don't have to do this. We can turn around right now and head back to Ravenwood."

The thought was a nice one. Ravenwood and Talos would be a welcoming sight. I could live out my days there growing old and gray. But I would never know peace. I would be forever haunted by my father's disappearance and his words would be a catalyst in my mind. It was not to be.

"No," I told her with an adamant shake of my head. "There is nothing to be gained back there. If this is the demon lair then we are to make our stand here and now."

"This is where the innkeeper's words directed us."

"Let's hope he wasn't persuading us into a trap," Paralay said as he unsheathed one of his short swords.

I fitted the hood of my cloak over my head and pressed forward, the comfort of my crossbow resting comfortably against the small of my back. Unknown dangers awaited us inside this cavernous structure. If the innkeeper's tale rang true we were willingly pulling ourselves towards a great evil that none had been able to thwart before.

Strong and steady we moved inside, our feet scraping off a dusty path in front of us. The dwelling was strewn with a mess of trinkets thrown every which way. Broken bottles, destroyed paintings, marble statues and bits of gold lay in piles.

The interior remained almost completely intact with many of the original ceiling support beams still in place. We'd found nothing at the bottom caverns. A large stairwell hinted at rooms up above. One by one we made our way up to the next level of the cavern. The air grew dank and cold, piercing the soul with such a frigid chill. I felt my heart race faster with each step.

As we reached the top, noises halted us in our tracks. They came from a long corridor and it sounded as if there were a party in progress. The three of us looked at each other and silently agreed to press forward.

I took the lead walking ever so slowly. Torches upon the walls lit the way and I grew concerned that our falling shadows would alert any who might be up ahead of us. But what we found were two large armored doors.

"The noises come from inside," Paralay whispered. "If the vampires are stirring it'll be too dangerous to go after them. We must come back later."

"We don't know what lies beyond these doors," I told him. "It could be anything."

Slowly, perhaps foolishly, I peeled back one of the heavy doors and peered inside. At first sight it looked as though it were a simple dinner party. Both men and women filled a long table drinking red wine and carrying on with laughter. As I looked again I found it to be a most disturbing vision.

'Twas not wine that they drank but blood, tapped from the neck of a poor soul by some crude device that resembled a spout. He hung upside down and they drained him into their cups until he went pale.

I shuddered to think of such torture. These beings truly were soulless and they needed to be halted in their scavenging of human life. Looking out over the table, all of them were merrily distracted in their gluttony. My eyes scanned each face seeking the one who would make the best target to start with as I silently loaded my crossbow.

I turned to motion behind me for Paralay and Talisa to arm themselves, thankful I had led them in and they had not endured the shock of the sites I had seen. Most likely that display alone would've sent them running for the exit.

As I turned back to the vampire dinner party I felt my own urge to flee. Sitting in one of the cushioned back chairs, goblet of blood in hand, and staring at me was Lord Le Carde.

He winked at me, drained the remainder in his goblet, and in a flash that hideous countenance was a breath away from my own face. He moved with lightning-like speed, tearing open the door he caught me by the cloak and pitched me inside the room.

I came up overhead and landed back first upon the dining table. The vampire lot made a unanimous hissing sound, abandoned their goblets to the ground, and came over me to feed on the new blood that had been handed to them like a gift.

Luckily for me I was not alone in this quest. My companions came to my aid immediately, jumping into the fray and pulling the vampires off of me before any real damage could be inflicted.

With the pack off of me, I tried to shake the senses back into my noggin. My head pounded. When my eyes focused once again I found that I was directly underneath the vampire's hapless victim as he swung to and fro from the ceiling fixtures. They'd not time to cork the spout at his neck before the altercation had erupted, so fresh blood dripped down to splash across my shirt and chest. It was warm and thick. This unnerved me to no end. I quickly shifted off the table top to find myself once again facing Lord LeCarde.

The turbulence behind me had not subdued but I couldn't pull myself away from my battle with LeCarde to see if my companions needed help. He was my only focus. We stayed squared off, face-to-face. I looked into his hideous eyes, the memory of that day in Gryphant came flooding back over me. He'd escaped me once before, it wouldn't happen twice.

I moved forward, he as well, but before we clashed I dove past him into a tumble. He whirled around with great speed but not fast enough to thwart my intent. I stopped just near my crossbow, the bolt still chambered, and drew it up eye-level with Le Carde's face.

I couldn't tell you the exact moment I relinquished the trigger on the crossbow. Nor can I describe to you how it traveled the distance between myself and Le Carde. What I can recall is the moment of the bolt's impact upon his wicked face. He tried to deflect it but all he managed to do was knock the bolt off course with his head and direct it into his eye.

The impact was blue-black blood splattering across his pale face, into his hair, and upon the cavern wall behind him. Le Carde let out a wail which drew the attention of the other vampires.

I no longer had my back to them so I was better able to take in the scene. Some had fallen at Paralay's hands. Others held hateful grasps upon my companions, but as they noted their leader Le Carde in trouble the vampires abandoned their kills to aid him...or so I thought.

The moment the bolt went through his eye the vampires threw one last wicked hiss, and departed from sight in the most unusual way. Their forms shifted drawing their limbs within themselves and scaling down into the shapes of bats.

Wings flapping they flew over my head and out the back of the cavern to escape. I shielded myself until I was certain they were gone. When I looked up I saw that Le Carde still stood. He had removed the bolt and with it his eye. One blood red orb and one hollow cavern stood staring at me with all the hate in the world encompassed in that one good eye.

"You will pay for this with pain," he told me. "Even your family will suffer from the pain I inflict upon you."

As he spoke I wasted no time. I loaded up another bolt, the one filled with holy water was my choice. I took a wild shot towards his wicked heart. He just wouldn't allow me the pleasure of a quick death. Following his fellow vamps, he sprouted wings. Taking to the air, to make his departure he flew to where I was, leaving me with a harsh scratch upon the cheek.

I tumbled to the floor from the impact of the blow. When I looked up he was gone. No matter how much I wanted to go after him I couldn't. My attention turned to my friends. Paralay and Talisa were busy tending to their wounds.

As I approached the two of them, I realized how much I owed them for their loyalty to me. I had no words. They'd returned time and again to aid me even though I pushed them aside.

We made haste to leave the same way we'd come. I felt a deep sorrow stemming from my failure. I'd failed Tuck. Le Carde had escaped his punishment. I tried to persuade myself that it wasn't my fault. After all, I'd not expected to see an average size man transform himself into a bat.

As we walked I ran the events over in my head. Nothing laced together, the seams remained frayed.

"We were woefully unprepared," I said aloud. "Next time...."

"Next time?" I didn't know who held more shock and disdain as both Paralay and Talisa seemed to speak the same concern in unison.

"You're the ones who talked me into aiding the village Calyx. If you want to go...just go. I've told you again and again."

"Our concerns lie with you," Talisa told me. "You're apt to get yourself hurt or even killed in this pursuit."

"My concerns lie with myself alone," Paralay said. "I'm happy to fight at your side Costa but the only way we survived the last encounter was through sheer luck. What makes you think we can hold our own against that lot?"

"I'll refer back to my father's notes. There has to be something to aid us. In the meantime, let's head back to Calyx and shake up that innkeeper."

I wasn't looking forward to returning to the town of Calyx with its burnt out houses, and charred vermin for food. Talisa hated the idea even more. She protested until she ran out of breath. Then she fell silent and sullen. But the devil's face was known in Calyx. I knew that is where they would return eventually.

We found the innkeeper Dragus unreceptive upon our return. The moment I stepped foot back inside the door he armed himself with the pitchfork he used to turn the meat on the grill.

"Put that down before you wind up eating your own arm for supper tonight."

My warning was strong but truthful and the innkeeper knew it. He lowered the weapon and glowered at me. Then sunk his head and motioned us inside.

"You didn't succeed," he said. "I knew you wouldn't."

"How? How did you know it?"

"Because they are indestructible!" His voice shook with his words.

"They must have a weakness...somewhere." I almost sounded like I was trying to convince myself. "Will they be coming tonight?"

He nodded. "Yes. You stirred them up. They will be angry...and hungry."

"Let them come. We will meet them straight on."

I looked back towards Talisa and Paralay who had been treating their wounds with whatever clean wraps they could find. They each held my gaze for several moments before nodding agreement. That night would be marred with blood, from whom it would flow remained to be seen.

I sat alone that night, waiting inside one of the only other homes that still stood erect. My only company was a flicker of light from a waning candle and Coleridge's scriptures. I leafed through them, poured over the same words again and again, seeking something that would give me a small speck of hope that I could defeat Le Carde this night. That I could be the demon hunter my father was before me. And then I found it.

Concerning Vampires:

These things I have proof by inference. Though they exhibit great strength their powers cease at the coming of daylight. Face a vampire with courage and calmness and he shall cower in fear. For all their purported strengths their weaknesses are greater still. Any wound the vampire takes shall affect it for all its immortal life, impairing its ability to hunt. They hold great appetites that can only be sated by human blood. Vampires will hunt their prey like any great north man stalking deer. They mark their territories to bleed out villages in their respective names. Know these markings well, for if you come upon them you will want to prepare immediately before the sun sets and they come out of hiding. Time spent preparing is never wasted.

It went on to describe methods for tracking, trapping, and eventually killing the lot but I decided to defer the pages for later as something in Coleridge's thoughts gnawed at me. I took up my candle and went out into the night seeking the source of my discontent. Moving up and down throughout the town of Calyx I finally realized what was troubling me.

Paralay had taken a spot upon the rooftop of the inn to keep watch on the grounds below. I made my way up to him to discuss my findings.

"What's the matter?" he asked.

"There's no writing on the walls."

"Say again?"

"According to my father's writings if a town were truly the hunting grounds of the vampires it would be marked with signs labeling their territory so no other would dare hunt there."

"Then what of the innkeeper's tale of the demonic forces coming in the night and spiriting away the hapless townsfolk?"

"A lie."

"Why would he want to spin a yarn like that?" Paralay asked. "What could possibly be gained?"

"I don't know," I told him. "But I mean to find out. Where's Talisa?"

"Down below. She wanted to get some sleep. You know how she is with the night."

My heart froze in my chest before he even finished speaking. Talisa had been left alone within reach of the innkeeper, Dragus. There was no telling his plot against us. I feared for her life.

"She's in danger."

Those three words were all I could get out before leaping from the rooftop. Riding off pure adrenaline I dropped from the roof like the very enemy I meant to take down. I landed with delicate grace, my cloak following after me and wrapping about my shoulders in a fond embrace. My boots slipping ever so slightly in the sand I made my way inside searching frantically for Talisa.

What I saw brought flashes of painful memories back to me. The night that Tuck died grew gruesomely vivid in the forefront of my thoughts. I smelled the blood, tasted the terror. Just paces from me now Talisa lay cowering in fear. She swung wild and blind at her assailant who stood over her, a stoop to his shoulders and tiny fangs pointing out from his weathered face.

Dragus reached for her, trying hard to snatch her leg even as she kicked like a mule. After taking a blow across the knuckle of his hand he finally moved to grasp her hair instead. As he pulled her to her feet I heard him speak his intent, unaware that I was present.

"Come you little bitch, stop struggling and accept your fate as one of the damned."

Talisa was screaming now. I'd heard enough. Vaulting over chairs I hurried to grab Dragus by the scruff of the neck. It was all I could do not to splatter the innkeeper's head against the far wall. But I needed answers and I knew I would be able to wring them out of this deranged little fellow.

I allowed myself one well-placed solid wrap of his head off the stone hearth where charred remains of vermin still lay. He groaned, holding his head, then had the wherewithal to go for me so I knocked his head once more until he complied, by staying where I put him.

Shouting, almost spitting my words, I bombarded him with questions.

"Why did you lie to us? What is going on here!?"

"The master," he muttered. I stared at his tiny fangs and the dark circles brewing under his eyes. He was not of this world but still not the hideous visage that Le Carde and the other vampires bore.

"Who?" I asked as I stretched his neck.

Paralay entered just then. He saw that I had Dragus well in hand and went to aid Talisa. My interest remained with the pudgy innkeeper.

"Who?" I repeated.

"Lord Le Carde, he awaits fresh meat."

The name he spoke made me want to continue turning his head until I heard a pleasing snap at the base of his neck. But I refrained.

"The vampires don't attack here do they? You feed them, don't you...you vile little swine?"

"No, no," he protested. "They come, they hunt. But Le Carde is of royal hierarchy amongst the vampire clans. He likes his meals brought to him. Please, I am but his servant. I had no choice. He made me this way."

His sniveling almost made me feel sorry for him...almost.

"What of us? You led us into a trap that could've meant our doom."

"No hunter. It was my last effort to be saved from this immortal life. So that I may find rest again as a normal man. You've no idea how much I must suffer, only allowed to feed on small vermin when the scent of precious blood is all around me."

He looked over at Talisa and made an obscene gesture with his tongue. I'd had enough.

"You still want to be saved, Dragus?" I asked. "Do you still long to be released."

His eyes were wild. The anticipation of my words drawing excitement throughout his body as it twitched in my hands. "Yes hunter, I do!"

"Very well then."

I kept hold of Dragus by the neck with one hand so that I could manage my dagger with the other. Slipping my dagger from the holster at my side I quickly ran its tip up and into the heart of Dragus. Blood poured from his chest soaking into my cloak and the front of my tunic. Undaunted I pressed harder, deeper, watching the eyes as they flickered and the light of life was extinguished.

In that moment I knew how my father felt on that fateful morn so many years back at Muir Woods. Plunging the blade deep into his enemy, the world's enemy, and watching with satisfaction as one less evil creature would be breathing life that night. At that moment I was truly a Coleridge.

Chapter Ten
Demons and Destiny

We would mount our offensive there inside Calyx. According to Coleridge's journals, the vampire's held various weaknesses, when capitalized on it could make all the difference between victory and death.

We were not going to take any chances this time.

It had been a fitful night. None of us slept as we awaited an attack on Calyx. My eyes felt grainy from the lack of sleep but I'd managed through worse. My adrenaline pumped hard with anticipation. We had ravaged the town for supplies. The majority of the villagers who still lived were more than willing to help us. They'd lived in fear for far too long. Had I not already had incentive to proceed with the mission their forlorn faces would've been enough of a catalyst.

Once armed we set out to fulfill our plan. We moved the remainder of the townsfolk into one dwelling and set ourselves up in another. Traps would be set in various corners of the house. Then we would wait. As I unrolled a coil of wire across the staircase, I found myself thinking about Talisa. I feared for her. I couldn't remove the image from my head of Le Carde's teeth tearing into her throat. Nightmare or not, I knew the situation at hand was very dangerous. It could very well be the last night for any of us.

I steadied myself, knowing in my heart of hearts, I would have to take this to its end, as quickly as possible. So I set myself up behind a doorway waiting for the vampires to show themselves.

It remained quiet for too long. My haunches started to ache as I squatted behind the door. Paralay had returned to the rooftop to get a better look at the incoming pack. Talisa secreted herself on the second level even though she protested we made sure she was armed with something more than just the staff Talos had given her.

I had taken her long staff, sharpened the ends of it into good stakes, then littered the floor around her with metal traps previously used to hunt small animals in the forest. Tonight this hunter was well aware that if a vampire stepped foot in the trap it would surely break its limb, leaving it a helpless, easy target.

Sweat stained my brow from the anticipation. I took shallow breaths to help in keeping very still. The sight and hearing of the vampire clan were said to be far superior to any mortal alive. That is why Coleridge and Talos both had been so adamant about training not just the body but the mind, for battles would not be won through physicality alone.

Soon I heard the rumbling and I knew they were coming, even before Paralay returned inside and told me. He headed to an adjacent room used for cooking. As soon as he disappeared from sight the vampires surrounded the house.

Vampires had an uncanny sense of direction, avoiding the other shelters, they came directly for us. All our intentions, the planted traps, our resolve to end this nightmare, would now play out amongst this battleground. It was evidenced as the first beast broke through the doorway. As it entered I went into action using all my strength to strike at its legs with the edge of my sword.

The wail the beast emitted was painful to my ears. It crumpled in front of me. I took my time lopping the head clean from its shoulders.

It was a satisfying sight but I wasn't able to relish in it long before Lord Le Carde jumped into the fray.

He was upon me before I knew it. He knocked both the sword and the crossbow out of my hands. I heard the weapons skid across the floor, in the darkness, then felt the pressure of his blow across my cheek. The contact knocked me around until I fell against the wall.

A small candle had been affording some semblance of light in the room with just enough light so I could see my enemies as they entered. Le Carde reached out two long skinny fingers and extinguished the flame, dousing the room into darkness.

The odds were stacked against me. It was my danger now. Even with only one good eye he'd be upon me in moments. Weaponless, sightless, I had to rely on my training. I harkened back to my challenge against Talos and his insistence that I run the race as he was...blind.

In that moment it required a different kind of strength, a different kind of functionality to progress through the test at hand. Even though I'd failed that initial test I walked away from it with a lesson that would prove to aid me in my current situation.

My ears would be my guide. There was a prickly sensation on my skin alerting me to the presence of my enemies. I was going to have to rely on my intuition as well. I'd never before tried to harness the gift of foresight, but it was fast becoming a welcome ally.

Threats were posed all around me. I heard Le Carde growling in the darkness. There were other growls, hollers and shouts from around the rest of the house where Paralay and Talisa were stationed also. Pressing my back flat against the wall I tried hard to distinguish the different sounds around me to enable me to take in my surroundings even as shadows fell over them.

Le Carde came closer, I could smell him. The pungent odor of rot and decay edged closer and closer towards me. It felt thick on the air. I could only hope my intuitive nature would lead me to safety.

Without further hesitation I made a move. Exposing my back to danger I raced forward towards the staircase praying in the darkness Le Carde would not see the wire, hoping it would be his downfall. I had almost made it to the landing, racing with speed not known to most men, when I felt the snag on the back of my cloak. I'd been caught and yanked off my feet.

His strength seemed insurmountable. I tried to clear the cobwebs. My eyes focused on the shadowy figures moving past me, behind me, and even above me. I began to fear I wouldn't escape. I would stand and fight...if I could stand. Something pinned my cloak to the ground. I craned my neck to see my assailant and found myself eye-to-blood-red-eye with Le Carde. He grinned his familiar grin as he went for my jugular. I managed to roll to one side avoiding his attack by mere inches. I wouldn't be able to avoid him for long, luckily I wouldn't have to. As if in answer to my prayers a light from above came to disperse the darkness.

The fire lit torch, thrown by the hands of my Elven friend, landed amongst a pack of vampires who hovered around me. I didn't even realize they had been there. As the fire illuminated their faces they cringed and drew back.

Paralay wasted no time. He was able to capitalize on the surprise attack because the vampires were blinded by the light. Swinging his short blades with ferocity he leveled heads, cleaved skulls, and slashed throats.

The vampires converged and went on the attack. I went after Le Carde, trusting Paralay to take care of the others. Take out the leader and the rest shall fall. I knew in my soul he was their leader.

I tackled him around the waist and pinned him to the ground. He was not getting away from me, this I silently vowed. I retrieved a bolt from my quiver and brought it down in a spiking motion intent on piercing his remaining eye right through to his brain. It was not to be. Le Carde moved just a fraction of a second ahead of me to avoid the blow.

Then he caught my throat, pinching it tight. I felt like he was trying to rip my head clean from my shoulders. We struggled. I won my freedom from his strangle hold by flipping him overhead with the sole of my boot planted firmly against his stomach. He took to the air landing gracefully upon his feet.

"Your move," he said while stretching out his arms.

Punishment. I wanted him to suffer as I had suffered when he gloated about ending my father's life and then he took Tuck from me as well. Instead, Le Carde moved up the stairs faster than a bolt of lightning. My heart constricted in my chest as I thought of Talisa and the vision I'd had before.

Paralay moved with grace and speed in his own right but he was outnumbered. I retrieved my sword from the floor, rushing to his side to even up the score. We matched each other swing for swing until I heard a heart-wrenching scream come from the loft upstairs.

"Talisa!" I cried out.

"Go," Paralay told me. "I have them...help her!"

I wasted no time arguing. The Elf went to work with precision in every swing of his sword. Grabbing up my own blade, I jumped the rail and took the stairs two at a time until I reached the upper quarters where Talisa was stationed.

She was unconscious, in the arms of Lord Le Carde, though his appearance wasn't what I was accustomed to. His royal coat and button down shirt had torn away to reveal sinews with bulging muscles. Large leathery wings sprouted from his shoulders and spread out the entire width of the room. Long talons wrapped around Talisa holding her close to Le Carde's chest. I feared her dead.LeCarde snarled at me. His once handsome face and regal aura replaced by stake-like fangs and a forked tongue. He was hardly recognizable save for the missing eye that I had taken from him before.

I threw caution to the wind coming at him with my sword held high over head. He caught the blade in one hand and shattered it to fragments as he threw me to the floor . It was my misfortune to come down on one of our own traps. The teeth of the trap locked around my wrist, almost severing my hand. I hollered in pain which drew a familiar grin across the lips of the vile Le Carde devil.

With Talisa in his arms he no longer concerned himself with me. He started towards the window with her. I knew if he made it out to the skies upon those bat wings I would never see her again. I couldn't allow it but I lacked the strength to even stand let alone make chase.

With my arm still trapped I dragged myself across the floor to take up the staff I'd adjusted for Talisa. Le Carde had his back to me as he stood at the open window. With a silent prayer, I set myself and launched the staff with my one good arm across the room. It found its mark directly between his shoulder blades.

The scream tearing loose from his body rocked the entire house. Talisa fell from his arms. Le Carde turned back around to face me. I saw the staff had gone straight through his chest, piercing his dark heart.

He still struggled to hold onto his life, lurching across the room towards me, as I remained trapped. Blood poured down from his open wound. His growing weakness brought on a change in his form. The wings returned to his back and his talons returned to skinny fingers as they struggled with the stake through his heart.

"This time you die you bastard!" I shouted and as if my words were some sort of magic spell Lord Le Carde let out one last penetrating wail, arched his back, bursting into fragments which scattered all across the room.

I shielded my face with my arm to avoid his blood but reveled in his death. It was a glorious sight I took with me as I fell unconscious.

When I awoke it was to a most welcome sight. Paralay stood over me looking worse for wear but still standing.

"We keep finding you like this," he said.

"We?" I asked. "Talisa?"

"She's tending to your arm."

I looked over, my wounded arm was now free of the trap. I saw her wrapping it gently with a cloth. Her lip was split and a small trace of blood ran down from her neck but she was alive.

"I thought I'd lost you," I told her.

"No," she said. "I'm afraid you're stuck with me for eternity."

"Both of us," Paralay added.

Before the night was done I made a point to round up the fallen corpses and commit the bodies to flame. It took some doing to gather up the remnants of Lord Le Carde but Coleridge's journals insisted on great care being taken in the disposal of the corpses after death.

As I watched the bodies burn into the night, I recalled his tale of the child who had watched as his family's bodies became nothing but ash and I wondered if it had been a vampire who'd taken his father's life under the guise of his sweet and unsuspecting sister.

I placed my arm about Talisa, still nursing her punctured neck, and decided not to dwell on such matters tonight. Instead I rejoiced in the site of Lord LeCarde and his minions burning. I had my vengeance.

My eyes danced off the flicker of the flames until something drew me to the hills just outside Calyx where a shadowy figure on horseback kept watch on me. In the distance I watched as he tipped his hat to me then turned and rode away. A small grin crossed my lips. I knew it was my father. The words of his journal came back to me:

There's more, much more that awaits you.

Seek & Destroy

Beware

"The Path to Heaven must First Lead Through Hell...
let that be your only warning."

Chapter One
Rulers of the Sea

"You must respect the sea but trust it not." Talos' eyes shifted, the hazy sunken orbs looking within to a time when he himself had been a sea faring man. "The sea is a dark and dangerous mistress with many predators lurking beneath its depths. Never underestimate that which you cannot see."

It was an accurate and fair warning especially coming from a blind man. I'd heard similar disturbing tales from my house mother Cecile many years ago. Her husband had ignored the warnings to respect the sea and was forever lost within it. My companions and I wouldn't make the same mistake.

When Paralay, Talisa, and I found out we were to cross the Black Sea we lamented because this time we would have to acquire assistance. At the moment, Paralay was holding his own, even against a much bigger opponent. Wiggins was burly and had height to him as well. The fight had been decidedly in his favor to start with as he used his power to pummel the young Elf. But as soon as Paralay found his pace, things took a turn and Wiggins was now on the losing end facing Paralay's speed and dexterity.

"Slippery little fella, isn't he?" Captain Davies said with a nudge of an elbow against my arm. I nodded approval and smiled in the knowledge that I had backed a winner in this bet.

Captain Davies was simply enjoying the fight for its entertainment purposes. It mattered little that his first mate was on the receiving end of a chair splintering across his back. Wiggins took the hit like a champ, dusting off the debris from his shoulders and marking Paralay with a solid swing from his clubbed fist.

"Shall we let them carry on with this?" I asked. "Someone is liable to get really hurt."

"What's the matter, Calabrese? Afraid you're on the losing end now?" Davies taunted. "No, we're seeing this through. I don't pull out of bets when that much cash is on the line. Not to mention my boat."

"Fair enough," I replied, keeping my smile from his view

Captain Davies and his crew of Regulators were said to be the rulers of the high seas – pirates, known best for smuggling, looting, and pillaging. His ship, Misery, had been specially constructed to compensate the demand of any and all paying customers no matter how litigious.

For our missions we always traveled light. We never brought anything that wouldn't be an absolute necessity. Consequently, we had not been fortunate enough to procure enough to pay our way across the Black Sea so I presented a wager to The Captain instead. Should Paralay win the fight we would have clear voyage to our destination. If, on the other hand, Wiggins were victorious we'd lose the armaments we'd brought along setting us back days in our mission.

I knew full well Captain Davies and his crew thought it to be a sucker bet. Just looking at the size difference between Wiggins and Paralay one would assume to know the victor straight away. But I had confidence in my Elven friend. He'd been trained by the best in the land and he'd even bested me before. It was a sucker bet all right, the Regulators being the suckers.

My companions held their doubts about dealing with such ruffians but I was sold immediately on one fact alone: they were human.

Human faults and frailties I could deal with. It was demons that plagued my soul. Cursed by the hands of Fate to hunt and slay the spawn of Hell, I've seen more than I can tell or even begin to understand.

My gift of foresight has been both a blessing and a curse. As a hunter of demons I was expected to seek out evil wherever it may tread and extinguish it before the forces grew in number and corrupted the earth. I never expected I would come across evil so magnificent as in the form of a dragon – rulers of the underworld in their own right.

The vision had come to me in a dream, as they usually did. So vivid, so real, as if it wasn't a dream at all but a piece of the future snatched from space and time and showcased to me like a play.

This particular dream raised my body temperature so high that it brought me awake and drenched me in sweat from head to toe. It started out like any other, I didn't know where I was or why but then suddenly from the charcoal sky a dragon bellowed out a glorious roar. His leathery wings beat heavy like funeral drums causing torrents of wind to whip around the unsuspecting lot of innocents standing like sheep below it. Then the dragon descended upon all of us in a rampage, blowing toxic fire from its mouth and nose and leaving nothing but burned flesh and charred remains in the wake of its attack.

When I woke I wasted no time in relating my vision to Master Talos as always. He would usually calm me enough that I could manage to go back to sleep, or at least rest my eyes long enough to feel somewhat reenergized by morning. His words this night shocked me.

"Sark must be destroyed!"

Talos had known this day was coming. Ever since the resurgence of evil had been corrupting the land many of Satan's minions who'd once lain dormant were now taking up arms and satisfying their need for rampant destruction.

"The dragon Sark is something of a pet to the dark Lord," Talos had continued. "He has been unleashed upon the unsuspecting world to hunt and play."

"How am I to stop a dragon? I am merely a man of flesh and blood." I told him.

"Your father's blood runs through your veins, and the generation of hunters that came before him as well." Talos shook his head. "If you do not believe in yourself by now, Costa, then perhaps the world is in fact fated for destruction."

I hated hearing the disappointment in his voice. Talos had become more than a mentor to me in the past few years. His instruction on the ways of weaponry and defense were only surpassed by his knowledge of life itself. I could not let him down.

It was up to me to stop Sark. When I told my constant companions about our next mission they thought I'd gone mad. But as always Paralay and Talisa would be at my side no matter how dangerous the task.

A part of me knew what I must do before I set out to do it. As Talos had said, it was in my blood. My father's words came back to haunt me.

"The portal to hell has opened up in your backyard."

Because of all the trouble Paralay, Talisa, and I had run into before I knew my father's words rang true. I knew he was out there somewhere. I knew it in the depths of my soul, part of me has always known. My instincts became certainty when I'd seen a shadowy figure in the distance watching over me. Cain Coleridge watched from afar as the three of us battled evil so singularly personified in the form of the vampire Lord LeCarde. He watched me as he always had when I was but a boy…from a distance.

I'd not told the others, for all they knew my father lay dead somewhere at the hands of the very demons he faced night after night. My mission had become two-fold now. I would follow in my father's footsteps to battle back the forces of hell, but it had also become my lot in life to seek out Cain Coleridge. I had many questions gnawing at me that only my father could answer.

"Regulators!" Davies bellowed, his voice chiming off the thin walls of the pub. "Mount up."

Paralay had swayed the advantage back to his favor…just as I'd anticipated. The Elf had much stored aggression. Those that mistook his size for his skills more often than not wound up just as Wiggins had, face down on the floor.

"Fair is fair," Davies told me, though I suspected from the look on his face that he was more than a little perturbed. He walked over to Wiggins and gave him a solid kick to the ribs. "Get up you filthy sack of laundry. It appears as though we will be taking our new travelers to their destination."

Due to Wiggins loss to Paralay, Captain Davies and his crew had no choice but to take us across the Black Sea and honor their bet. What they didn't know, what we could not tell them, was that they were traveling towards a pit of hell. Some secrets should never be revealed

Though they were a rowdy bunch, the Regulators welcomed us on board their ship without attitude. Even Wiggins extended a hand to Paralay, accepting his defeat like a sportsman.

I believed Captain Davies ran a tight ship, and though their reputation as violent pirates preceded them, the Regulators fell in line when commanded. As leaders of our respective packs, both Davies and I shared something of mutual respect for one another – we could relate.

That night in the galley a welcoming party ensued. Meat and fruit lined the tables and plenty of ale to toast Paralay's victory over Wiggins. Having worked in a tavern for the better part of my youth, and seeing the evils alcohol did to men, I rarely partake in drinking. Tonight I made an exception and raised a pint to my good friend as the Regulators hefted him upon their shoulders. The ale held a nutty aftertaste to it and appeared darker and richer than anything I'd run across before.

"Nothing but the best," Davies remarked as he sat next to me. He clinked his glass against mine in salute then tipped back and drained the ale in a full gulp. I followed suit merely to blend in.

"I never had the satisfaction of experiencing such pleasures," I said. "The innkeeper back in my hometown of Gryphant used to water down everything that crossed the bar."

"That is an offensive crime. The lout should be punished."

I thought back to Mace Benton, my former house lord and a tyrant of a man, and remembered decapitating his cursed head from his shoulders. A small smile touched my lips at the memory.

"He got what he had coming to him," I told the Captain.

"All men do," he replied.

Paralay staggered towards us, officially inebriated. His words slurred as he spoke them. "They tell me there is a great treasure awaiting us when we reach Dragon Isle."

My jaw clenched at the mention of our true destination. I had only ever told Captain Davies to take us across the waters of the Black Sea towards Oceania. From there we would travel by foot towards Dragon Isle and Sark. I was hoping to procure The Misery for our return travel as well. If they knew our destination involved tangling with a demonic dragon they would not be so generous with safe passage.

"You've had too much to drink," I said to Paralay trying to soothe the Captain's prying ears.

"No, Costa. Wiggins will explain."

Paralay called over the grisly looking first mate who seemed equally as drunk as the Elf did. He had to speak his words twice before I could understand him.

"The Dragon Dagger. It's a relic of mighty kings and dragon lords and I am to be its next master!" He paused in his proclamation as he caught Captain Davies' hard stare. Then he rephrased himself. "With your permission of course, Captain."

Before Davies could reply, Paralay began to instigate Wiggins.

"How are you to be its next master? A relic of kings and lords handed down to a drunken pirate? Ha!"

Inebriated or not Wiggins wasn't going to cater to insults. He let fists fly and before long a brawl ensued within the galley. Captain Davies and I remained seated, taking up more ale, as bodies were pitched overhead, crash landing all around us.

"Does Wiggins speak the truth?" I asked between sips of ale. "Is some sort of dagger in play here?"

"Aye, Wiggins speaks a little too much," Davies replied. "The Dragon Dagger was forged in the Fire Kingdom of The East. It is said to be enchanted with magical gems."

He took a long swig of ale and then regarded me with a chuckle. "You didn't think we were just going to haul your asses across the most dangerous sea known to man without some sort of profit for ourselves did you?"

"Profit?"

"Of course! An enchanted dagger is a hot item on the market."

"You're peddling magic?"

"We're pirates, Calabrese, we peddle whatever turns a profit. Weapons, artifacts, people, anything."

"People?"

"Anything," he repeated.

My thoughts went immediately to Talisa. I had not seen her for the majority of our sea voyage. I'd been too distracted by the brooding Captain and his band of jolly pirates. We were traveling in and out of storms. I knew her eyesight would be troubling her as we lost the sunlight behind thick, dark clouds.

"Excuse me, Captain," I said rising. "I must tend to my people."

As I left the galley the chaos continued behind me. I heard the Captain take charge and bellow for the crew to cease in their madness. Poor fool. He knew nothing of real madness lest he faced the beasts I had over the course of the past year.

Chapter Two
Misery

All my thoughts turned to Talisa. She haunted me daily. I could barely function with day-to-day activities. Her very presence caused my heart to race and my breath to catch in my chest. I'd battled demons, vampires, and death itself but this one woman it seemed would soon be my downfall.

When I found her she held her head low over the side of the ship relieving her dinner out to sea. I felt a twinge of uneasiness knot up my side as I approached but her sea sickness isn't what concerned me. At her side stood one of the Regulators I had not seen before. A tall, wiry lad with short dark hair caressed Talisa's shoulders and held back her hair while she vomited.

A strange sensation surged up in me and I just couldn't shake it. I learned long ago to trust my instincts, to go with my gut as they had never proved me wrong in the past. My father had held an instinct for danger as well. It seemed as though we demon hunters could just smell evil in our wake. But this time my warning signs had given way to something other than the dwelling presence of evil, something much more prominent tugged at me…jealousy.

Ever since the first time I'd seen Talisa I'd known there was something special about her. The way she carried herself and didn't back down against even the fiercest enemy. Her soft and simple nature. Even the vulnerability her inherent night-blindness left her with did not sway me from my growing affections, in fact it made me want to look after her all the more. So seeing her in distress just now I grew angry that someone else had their arms about her, comforting her, instead of me.

"Talisa, are you all right?" I asked.

My words drew their attention and as I looked closer I came to realize the man with his arms around Talisa was not a man at all but instead a woman. I had not been aware there were any others on board the ship. My jealous instincts began to subside but something still made me feel uneasy.

"I'm ok," Talisa answered. "Maybe just a bit embarrassed."

"Don't be," the woman told her. "It happens to the best of us."

"What happens?" I asked, the uneasiness still harboring in the pit of my stomach. "Who are you?"

"My name is Lazara," she replied. "I'm first mate amongst the Regulators. Talisa was having a bout of sea sickness."

"I thought Wiggins was first mate."

The two of them shared a laugh together. I did not see the humor.

"More like first brute," Talisa said. Obviously her ailment had passed.

Lazara stared at me and finally acknowledged my query. "Pirating is too important to be left up to men."

Something about her shifty eyes and her androgynous nature had the fine hairs on the back of my neck standing up. I stepped past Lazara to speak with Talisa but my attention never left the other woman even with her at my back.

"Anyway, Talisa I need to talk to you about something…that is if you're feeling up to it."

I turned round and looked Lazara square in the eye. "In private."

Taking Talisa by the arm I led her back towards the lower deck without so much as a salutation for Lazara. But before heading down the stairs myself I threw one last look over my shoulder towards the assumed first mate.

She remained at the balustrade without the slightest hint of movement. Had I not known better I would've thought her to be a permanent fixture of the ship. As I watched her I noted a brief glow emanate from her eyes. My hand instinctively went for the crossbow at my side. I held off drawing it, but I knew I would have to keep a close watch on that one for the remainder of our journey together.

I took Talisa to my chambers to discuss my findings on The Dragon Dagger. Once inside I found myself getting tongue tied. She stood at the port-side window allowing the moonlight to illuminate her vision. As it cascaded over her delicate features she looked like a goddess out of some sort of fable told by poets and bards.

Regaining my bearings I struck up some candles to shed more light to the room and then broached the subject of the dagger and Captain Davies ulterior motive for taking us across the sea.

"That scheming bastard," Talisa said at the conclusion of my tale. "I knew we couldn't trust these ruffians. We should've traveled to Dragon Isle ourselves."

I shook my head. "No, we never would've made it. We need their expertise to traverse the rough seas ahead. Just be sure to watch your back while in their company. None of them are to be trusted, understand?"

She nodded. I reached forward and grasped the slopes of her bare shoulders to emphasize my point.

"None of them," I repeated.

Something in her eyes changed, not the light or her affliction but a sensory emotion. It felt like a great tugging pulled me in towards her simply from looking upon those eyes. My movements were no longer my own. I leaned my head down and brought my lips towards hers. To my surprise and delight she did not pull away. But before we could consummate the kiss, Paralay stumbled in bloody drunk and boisterous.

His faced swelled with bruising and his clothes were tattered but a smile remained nonetheless.

"One-to-one," he said. "That means round three."

He stared at us a moment as though it took that long to register that we stood in the same room with him.

"Hey, what're you two love birds doing in here by yourselves?"

We both drew away immediately. Paralay's reference of love birds caused Talisa to blush and sent my heart aflame but I couldn't let on to the Elf that anything out of the ordinary was taking place.

"I was just telling Talisa to be extra careful while we sojourn with the Regulators. It's important that we don't draw too much attention to ourselves while on this ship."

Looking over Paralay's drunken features I could tell that would not be an easy task for him to follow.

"And for Heaven's sake do not mention our true reason for this journey. If they find out we're seeking Sark they're liable to throw us all over board, understand?"

He did not seem to register my words. I glanced at Talisa with bewilderment and then tapped Paralay on the chest to which he promptly passed out upon the floor.

"Oh dear," she said.

"That's precisely what I want to avoid," I said. Then I hefted him up off the floor and deposited him into my own bed. "I'll let him sleep it off."

"Where will you sleep?"

The softness of her voice stirred my heart once more and I ached to continue from where we had been interrupted, but the moment had been lost…or so I'd thought.

"I'll manage," I told her.

"You could stay in my quarters," Talisa said. Her hand grazed against my arm sending a tingle rushing over my body and awakening my loins.

"A woman's quarters are her own. It wouldn't be right." I stammered out my words feeling like I had reverted back to the awkward farm boy I had been a few years back.

"I'm inviting you," she told me. "I don't think you'll get much sleep in here with Paralay having fitful drunken dreams."

"If you insist."

"I do."

She took me by the hand and I followed her down the hall to her sleeping quarters. The ship held great storage, plenty of room for smuggling and transporting anything that turned a profit as Davies had suggested.

The size and structure of the ship was one of the reasons it had been a favored vessel for so many years. Even when Misery changed hands from Captain to Captain it never lost its legacy. She simply outdid every other ship on the high seas and that is why I had sought her out in the first place. I knew first hand how reputation spread from mere deeds alone. Even if you're not seeking such attention word seems to get around.

Our sleeping quarters were not lavish by any means but because they dealt in various forms of transport there were enough private rooms to make long journeys more comfortable. I had insisted to the Captain when we boarded the ship that Talisa receive the largest of the rooms. When I told him she was the daughter of The Weapons Master he offered up his own. To our surprise she declined, citing no special treatment regardless of who her father was.

I wish I could say the same. But when you're the son of the world's most feared and famed hunter of demons life's rules inevitably change. There are those who praise me, others who try to challenge me. I cannot walk the streets without someone recognizing me. It has started to become something of a burden. Time and time again I have to turn them away when they try to obtain my services for their towns. I am nobody's savior regardless of how much they want to pay me. I do what I do because it is in my blood line. I have no choice.

At the moment I allowed Talisa to take charge. For the first time in a long time I gave up the need to be in control. I couldn't let my guard down with anyone else. Only with Talisa have I ever felt as though I could fully relax. With her I let down my guard, break down my walls and allow her to see the real me, not the face of the stone cold hunter I show everyone else. Without such an option in my life I fear losing the real me altogether. Talisa anchors me to reality.

Her room was brightly lit on all sides by candles. The glow was warm and inviting. I wanted to sweep her up into my arms and set her upon the bed, gently undress her, and make love well into the night. Instead I stood and waited like a slack jawed yokel.

"See," she said. "There is plenty of room here for you to stretch out upon the floor."

The floor. Now I felt the fool. But I did not let on.

"Looks perfect."

Talisa blew out all the candles save but one which she took to bed with her. From my spot on the floor, head propped in the crook of my arm for comfort, I watched her move with such grace that it would put even the Goddess Aphrodite to shame.

As she sat upon the bed tying up her long dark locks in a coil atop her head she caught me staring at her. I tried to avert my gaze but it did little to erase the fact that I'd been watching her every move.

"Goodnight," she said.

"Yes, goodnight," I replied and then turned my back to her in a failed attempt to appear disinterested. Deep down I longed for her every breath, every curve.

Soon I began to drift off. I dreamt of our time on The Peak of the Gods, the frozen tundra beneath our every step. The cold tore through you to the marrow. I remembered falling in between the cracked ice and how the icy water bit at me like a thousand stabbing knives. It grew colder and colder until my body began to convulse from the shivering. The dream bled into reality and I continued to shiver on my spot upon the floor until I awoke to a warm hand upon my cheek. Talisa stood over me with concern upon her face.

"You're freezing down here," she said. "I didn't account for the drafty floorboards out at sea."

"I'll be all right," I told her, half certain I remained dreaming.

"Come to bed with me."

Her words drew me awake but still sounded like a distant dream. I'd only ever hoped to hear her speak such things. I tried to remain a gentleman.

"Are you certain?"

"Yes. We're both adults. There's no reason we can't share the same bed if it is the most logical reason."

"Agreed."

I removed my boots and slid in beside her. Her small body radiated warmth and comfort. I felt spellbound. This temptress had me at her beck and call. I would give her the world if she asked for it.

We both lay on our sides, face-to-face, our noses almost touching. Our breath mingled together on the small space of air between us. I could not bring myself to move or even to speak.

"Goodnight," she told me once more, her voice a dark whisper on the air.

I muttered something of the same and turned away from her. My body had lost all traces of the cold as I burned with desire. I tried to remain the embodiment of self control until her hand grazed my cheek and turned me back to face her.

Without another word, without another thought, I kissed her lips. She tasted so sweet. Our bodies pressed against each other, her bosom treading lightly across my chest. I started to undo the bodice of her dressing gown feeling the soft, supple skin beneath.

My fingers traced the lines of her cleavage, back up to her neck where I lingered on two dominant puncture marks that had healed into scars. I cursed myself for allowing her beautiful honey skin to be marred by the vampire Lord LeCarde. I'd almost lost her that night. But she was here now in my arms where I had always wanted her to be.

Treading lightly across her skin with my lips I sought her exposed nipple and took it in my mouth. She gasped and ran her fingers through my hair pulling me closer to her.

"Costa," she said quietly. "I've never been with a man before."

Her words halted me and I drew away. A look of concern washed over her. I had no words.

A chaste young woman untouched by the hands of man bedding down with a hunter-killer could not be permitted. She was the daughter of the greatest weapons maker in the land, my mentor Talos; she deserved better than to experience her first sexual encounter on a leaky vessel with drunken pirates strewn about. I had to put a stop to it.

Ignoring her protests and questions I took it upon myself to leave the bed, then her room, without so much as a "goodbye." What could I say? No words would suffice. I knew what had to be done. I just hoped she would understand some day.

Back in my own sleeping quarters I found Paralay up and about. He held his head in the palms of his hands looking a ghastly shade of pale.

"Are you sea sick?" I asked.

"Ale sick," he told me. "What happened with you and Talisa?"

I was surprised at the question. "I thought you were unconscious."

"For the most part but I still heard her invite you to her room. So what are you doing back here?"

"Never mind." I was adamant in my response but he still continued to press the issue.

"Did you fail her?"

"It's not your concern."

"I believe what happens between my traveling companions is a major concern of mine, especially now that there will be an unbearable awkwardness between the two of you."

"There won't be. What happened or didn't happen between us is for Talisa and I to deal with. It won't jeopardize the mission at hand."

"I should hope not, Costa," Paralay said as he once again staked claim upon my bed. "I'd hate for Talos to find out we did not conquer Sark because you were too busy seducing his only daughter."

I could only imagine Talos' wrath should such a thing take place. With a shake of my head I settled upon the floor for the remainder of the night. It was dark and cramped with the dampness of the sea once again causing me to shiver. I thought about the warmth of Talisa's bed, the sweetness of her kiss, both so inviting and I knew I would dream of her. Just as I had been dreaming of Talisa every night since I'd met her, except when the visions of the demons took over control of my thoughts.

Chapter Three
Some Things Strange and Sinister

For the first night in many years I did not dream. I barely slept. My head held too much worry to welcome deep and meaningful sleep. I had intermittent bouts of rest where I just closed my eyes for a few hours, but I always awoke during the night. My thoughts plagued me; my past deeds plagued me. The one thing my father's journals didn't prepare me for was how it felt to kill.

Even though the demonic forces I faced did not belong to humanity some of them still looked human enough. Talos had shown me the skill to defend myself from death. My father Cain had told me the weakest point on each enemy I would face. Neither of them could prepare me for what it felt like in my gut and my heart and soul when I actually had to deliver that death blow. Most of it was instinctual, the will to survive took over and I did what I had to do. But afterwards each death stayed with me.

I imagined the same thing occurred with my father. He'd never had any companions with him to unwind, or share the details with. His isolation had been by choice. If I'd had a choice I would've opted for my father to be with me now. I needed him. I needed him to help me understand a great many things. Even in our brief time face-to-face he had been selfish. He discussed his woes and his heartache. That made me very bitter now. Who could I discuss my troubles with? They were few and far between. My father had fated me to be just like him even as he went out of his way to not let that happen.

The next morning instead of joining the others in the galley for breakfast I decided to seek out Captain Davies. I thought it best to avoid Talisa for the time being as well. She would have questions I could not easily explain.

The Captain remained in his quarters opting to take a hot plate in with him rather than sit amongst his crew. I knocked once then took it upon myself to enter.

"You were missed at breakfast," I told him.

"I prefer to enjoy my meals with a little peace and quiet. What's your excuse?"

"I hardly eat anymore."

"Troubled mind of a killer?"

The reference irked me. "I only kill those deserving."

"I could say the same."

"If you only knew the likes of what I've come across you might actually be thanking me."

"You hunters are so arrogant in the portrayal of your tasks. As if it makes you nobler than other men just because you've run across the spawn of hell. What do you think I've seen out here on the sea, Calabrese? Creatures of the deep are just as unrelenting as the demons you face, except out here there is nowhere to run."

He continued to eat at a leisurely pace as if he'd just imparted an anecdote or a fable. I'd inherited my position in life when my absentee father had believed I had come of age. It wouldn't have been my first choice, especially considering in his journals he'd related how others deemed him a pariah of sorts. I'd assumed the misinformed reactions of others were why my father had always labeled himself a bounty hunter rather than stating his real mission. Walking in his footsteps I had chosen to do the same as I saw fit to draw less attention to myself. It appeared as though Captain Davies knew otherwise.

"You need not worry about concealing your true destination either," he said through bites. "I take it upon myself to know everything that goes on upon my ship."

"And you find no concern with our travel to Dragon Isle?"

Davies looked up and smiled, a silver tinted tooth shining back at me. "If I did you never would've stepped foot on The Misery."

He pushed his empty plate aside and stood to fetch something from his bureau.

"Besides, as I said we have our own interests at heart as well. I've been looking to gain the Dragon Dagger for some time, but there hasn't been adequate reason to venture all the way to Dragon

Isle…until now. With a famed demon hunter in our pack I am certain to claim the dagger as my own."

"I'm not going to help you pilfer goods, Captain."

Davies turned round to face me, a strange weapon held tight in his grip and pointed right at me. I'd never seen such a piece before but my instincts warned me of great danger. Both wood and metal merged together in a narrow shaft with a trigger point that Davies had his finger set upon.

"What manner of weapon is this?" I asked, even as my hand moved towards the crossbow slung at my back.

"This, Calabrese, is a firearm. One of the most advanced forms of weaponry to come along since that crossbow you are reaching for."

My hand froze just fingertips length away from my crossbow. I had to hand it to Captain Davies, he didn't miss a step. To my relief he lowered the firearm and turned it around to showcase its method of use.

"It is centered on black powder, an explosive substance that is only found in the most remote of regions. You drop a metal pellet inside the shaft, pack it down tight with powder, and when the time comes to blow a hole in your enemy you pull on the trigger and send the pellet right through their forehead."

I watched as he stuffed the barrel of the gun with fine dark powder and then pressed it down firmly with what he referred to as a packing rod. The actual use of the firearm would remain to be seen. Captain Davies was particular about blowing holes in his ship. But that didn't keep him from bragging.

"Take that knowledge back to your Weapons Master. He might learn something about how the world is changing around him while he sits up on that hill. Maybe it will urge him to venture out…see the world." He paused, laughed, and rephrased himself. "Oh that's right, he can't see anything."

His words and lackluster attitude began to annoy me. Talos was not only my mentor but also a good and trusted friend. I didn't have many of those so when one of them was on the receiving end of verbal or physical abuse, warranted or not, I raised my defenses like a good dog and went on the attack.

"Perhaps I will inform Talos," I told Captain Davies. "He would get a kick out of seeing a weapon that takes so much effort to utilize that one would be dead before he ever got off a shot."

Check and mate. I had stung Davies with that and he knew it. But before he could retaliate Wiggins burst into the room.

"What outrageousness is this?" Davies bellowed. "Go back out and knock before you enter, you buffoon!"

"Begging your pardon Captain." Wiggins bowed his head and stepped back outside the door.

Davies turned his attention back to me. "You cannot find good help these days."

As instructed, Wiggins rapped a knuckle upon the door and only then was he permitted entry.

"What is it?" Davies asked him.

"Tsunami headed this way!"

I would've thought the situation comical if it didn't imply our immediate demise. The skin of Captain Davies eyes almost peeled back as they grew wide in terror. He ran past me with Wiggins on his heels hollering commands every which way.

I'd not had enough formal knowledge at sea to truly know what we were up against. The word Tsunami had been used by my house mother Cecile when describing foul bits of weather her husband had narrowly avoided in his travels.

She'd said the sea had grown angry, rough. Any ships that had not prepared themselves for every given scenario were almost always splintered against the jagged rocks of the shoreline, the crew scattered out to sea.

I tore away to the porthole inside the Captain's stateroom and took a look outside. My heart nearly stopped in my chest as I saw a massive wave building upon itself and heading in our direction. I could feel The Misery trembling beneath my feet and I echoed its sentiments.

My thoughts, as always, turned to Talisa. I had to make sure she made it safe below before the wave hit us. As fast as my legs could carry me I went in search of her and found her at the railing on the port side, once again Lazara stood with her.

"Talisa!" I hollered.

She saw me coming and turned her back to me.

"She doesn't wish to speak to you," Lazara told me.

"Silence bitch," I said in my frustration, "We haven't time for this, we're in danger."

The wave was coming fast, it would hit us at any second. Talisa still did not regard me. She was in very real danger of being swept out to sea. But something in Lazara's stare halted me in my step. Her eyes, an unusual cluster of grays, now flashed a searing yellow from within.

I had seen that look before and had stored it at the back of my mind to concentrate on more pressing issues. Now it could no longer be ignored. Lazara's eyes didn't just happen to have an abnormal pigmentation, nor did the light glance off of the pupils just so to cause them only to appear yellow. She had flashed them on purpose as some type of warning to me.

"What evil are you?" I asked, disregarding her warning and continuing my approach.

At my words Talisa finally turned around. She had anger on her face and hurt as well. It killed me to know that I had been the cause of her discontent but at the moment we had more important things to worry about.

"What are you saying, Costa? Back off!" Talisa almost growled at me and then she stepped in front of Lazara to act as her shield.

She thought she was doing the right thing, protecting her companion. I could respect their kinship knowing how difficult it must be for Talisa to always be surrounded by nothing but foul, brutish men. She found a friend, a common bond with Lazara being the only other woman on the ship. But my instincts told me that Lazara was hiding something and I intended to find out just what that was.

Unfortunately I would not get that chance. We were hit. At first the movement around me seemed slow, very slow, as though my own mind had manipulated what I saw in order to better process it. The next minute there was chaos.

Because the waters had built up with a rage that could not be defied the initial size of the wave grew to be about ten feet tall. As such when it hit us it came from above. The force of the blow crippled all of us including The Misery herself.

I felt like I had been struck in the side of the head. My ears rang and I lost all sense of visibility. The last thing I saw was Talisa being pulled over the railing into the murky depths below. I didn't even have time to scream out before we were struck again. This time the wave flipped us.

The Misery for all her strengths could not withstand this brutal attack. Anyone who had not been below decks found themselves at the mercy of the sea, which included myself, Talisa, and Lazara.

I had never fancied myself a very good swimmer. In fact, truth be told, I preferred dry land under my boots. So finding myself thrashing about in the sea, waves coming down over my head, water simultaneously blinding me and shooting up my nose, I thought this was my end.

The next wave knocked me under. Below the depths of the water it seemed so much more peaceful. I floated below the surface, my eyes adjusting to the darkness that cloaked me. I could no longer hear the screaming from the crew or the cries The Misery called out as the waves mercilessly pounded her body. I only sensed me.

I began to descend further towards the ocean floor. I didn't struggle, I allowed it. It seemed much easier not to fight. Let the sea claim me. Perhaps then I could find a sense of peace. Then I heard my father's voice. He called to me somewhere under that water and I knew it wasn't imagined. We held a connection the two of us. I'd sensed his words and warnings once before and now, wherever he was, he called to me again.

"You're better than this, my son," he said. "Quitting is not an option."

This time his cryptic wording did not immediately cast out a line and reel me back in. My body and mind were tired, very tired of the despair and the weight of my new role in life. I fought him. I spoke back.

"I don't want this anymore. I don't want to be you."

"There is a purpose to life, my son. When you are ready you will be shown. For now you must get up!"

If nothing else, I always held perseverance. I'd been knocked down before but I never stayed for long. As I grew older, my duties more intense, it began to get harder and harder to stand back up. But once again I would do just that. If not for me, then for Talisa and Paralay and Master Talos. Others were counting on me. I couldn't stop here. It wasn't my time. Not just yet anyhow.

Chapter Four
Shipwrecked

The sea was a cruel mistress indeed, a vicious bitch in fact. I came awake on the shoreline with my face buried in the sand. My memory failed me. All I could remember was being tossed head over heels several times and the harsh sting of saltwater running coarse over my throat with such a burning that I'd swear to swallowing acid.

I pulled myself up onto shaky legs still trying to regain my bearings and take in my surroundings. No evidence of life shown for miles.

"Talisa." The name tumbled off my tongue and pulled the strength back into my body. She'd been at the rail of the ship right next to me when the wave hit. That much I remembered. She was never far from my mind.

Her petite frame had been ravaged by such an intense wave. She'd been swept off that deck as though erasing a memory. There was no telling if she were lost out to sea or not. I knew I had to try to locate her before nightfall for both our sakes.

My cloak had been torn from my shoulders but that was the least of my worries. The crossbow Talos had given me upon graduation from Ravenwood Academy had been claimed by the sea as well. Every arrow bolt taken. Only an empty quiver hung loose from my waist.

Undaunted I moved forward across a large stretch of open land. Nothing but sand and sea were underfoot. Finally in the distance I made out a shape lying across the sand. I raced forward hoping in my heart that I would find it to be Talisa. When I reached the body I found a huddled mass of limbs curled into the fetal position trying to keep warm. I tugged on the shoulder and revealed the face of Paralay staring back at me.

His teeth chattered and his eyes grew dilated. He muttered something over and over again. I couldn't make it out until I leaned forward, ear to his lips.

"Sea God," he said.

I shook my head. "There's no God of the Sea. You're imagining things like your Weather God up on the Peaks."

"No!" he was insistent in his distress. "The Sea God grew angry with our intrusion and destroyed The Misery for it."

"If that were the case The Misery would've been destroyed a long time ago the way Captain Davies and the Regulators carry on with themselves. It was the sea itself that interceded with our travel. There is no God."

"Ha, a man who believes in demons but not gods. You are positively prime evil Costa."

I ruminated on his words for a moment then hefted him up across my shoulders. He was in no condition to walk himself.

"Come, we must find Talisa and the others before night sets and we see what true evil exists here."

We'd been going up and down the shoreline for what seemed like a millennia. I feared the worst but did not impart my concerns to Paralay. One of us needed to remain strong, both mentally and physically. He'd become quite cumbersome across my shoulders but I trudged on regardless. The make of any hunter worth his salt lay in his conviction to get the job done regardless of circumstances. My job as it lay before me now was to get my friend to safety.

I would've hefted Paralay around all night if I had to, but as fate would have it we came across some friendly faces about a quarter of a mile down the shoreline. Captain Davies and Lazara had set up a makeshift shelter of palm fronds that they huddled beneath trying desperately to strike up a fire. My heart almost burst when I saw that Talisa sat with them. She saw me too and hurried over to help carry Paralay into the small camp.

"Is everyone all right?" I asked, gently laying Paralay down.

"All is well," Lazara answered.

"Except for my crew," Captain Davies added.

Paralay pulled his head up from the sand just long enough to ask about Wiggins.

"Dead," Davies told him. "All dead."

The Captain was forlorn. I understood his distress. He'd been traveling with the same crew for many, many years now. You grew a bond, something of a kinship with those you traveled with. Each put their lives on the line day after day for each other. Shared adventures, stories, the good and the bad. Comrades were a very important part of one's being when traveling through a world so cold.

I knew in my heart that Talisa was more special to me than anyone I'd ever traveled with before or any I'd meet after. My heart leapt at the sight of her and I needed her to know as much. I took her aside where the others could not hear and hoped that my words would not fail me.

"I thought I'd lost you to the sea," I said. "How did you manage to get to shore?"

"I don't remember much, just fighting the waves as they tossed me around like a rag doll higher and higher until I felt as though I were flying. I did not fear, I felt very calm and in control. Then I found myself on shore and soon after I located Captain Davies and Lazara coming out of the surf."

"That's an amazing story."

I reached out my hand and gently caressed Talisa's cheek. Her skin felt so much colder than I remembered that I almost bristled at the touch. She must've had just as rough a time out in the belly of the ocean as I did.

"I'm glad you're all right," I told her.

She set her hand upon mine and her cheeks blushed up illuminating her pale skin back to the honey-bronze I had grown accustomed to. "I'm glad you're all right too."

Finally I drew up enough confidence to approach the subject of my growing affections for her. Facing death, or an unknown future, made you appreciate the things you have in life.

"About last night…."

Talisa silenced me, laying a finger across my lips before I could complete my sentence. "You don't need to explain."

She held such a sweetness of soul that I had never known in anyone before. I knew then and there that my life would never be the same. I took her hand in mine and held it against my chest.

"I would like to try," I said. "It's just that you're very special to me. I want our time together to be just as special."

She smiled and brushed a quick kiss across my lips. "It will be."

Night came much too swift and with it a bitter cold that hit us down to the marrow. We made do with what we had, huddling around the fire to keep warm, but in the morning we needed to find shelter that better suited us than simple shrubbery. I held my doubts that the island we'd landed upon had any sort of life upon it at all.

According to The Captain we'd been blown way off course. Being a master of trails herself, Talisa marked our whereabouts as mysterious lands that few dared to travel. I quickly began to see why. We seemed to run into ocean and sand no matter what direction we took. I began to long for something of a makeshift path, anything that looked like a marker point.

For the first time since I was a boy back in my hometown of Gryphant I felt very lost, very unsure. In the shipwreck I'd lost my father's journal along with everything else in my pack. Without it I had no sense of security. His words had always been a comfort to me knowing that if I didn't have the answer for a difficult situation myself I could turn to the pages and find what I was looking for. Now where would I turn for the answers? Within? Even with all the training Talos had given me, and the real world experience I held as a hunter of demons, I still did not trust my own skill enough to lead us where we needed to be. Maybe therein lay my problem.

Paralay had recovered enough to walk on his own merit, which aided me a great deal. We were all lacking in energy what with the little nourishment we could sustain from eating off the land. The Captain aided us in distinguishing which plants were edible and which poisonous. I took great note of his teachings as I'm certain I would need it in future travels. Up to that point the only plant life I had familiarity with was wolfsbane.

"We're going in endless circles," Lazara moaned. "Why not take our chances directly in the thick of the jungle?"

She pointed out the dense foliage that crested the sand dunes just north of us. To that point we'd been walking the border of the jungle, not daring to step foot inside for the Captain's fear of being swallowed whole.

"I told you why," Davies answered her. "And it only appears as if we're going in circles. That's your mind playing tricks on you."

I'd been keeping my distance from Lazara but never lost her from my sight. What happened on the ship before the wave struck still lay firm in my memory. I could not accuse her of anything yet because I still did not know what I had seen. And now my head had grown fuzzy from the aftermath at sea. I couldn't discern anything tangible. Perhaps the storm at sea actually had danced off her eyes at the exact second I caught her gaze. On the other hand we may have a demon in our midst. I could not afford to make a wrong assumption, in either case, especially when Lazara and Talisa continued to remain so close.

"I have a suggestion, Costa," Paralay said coming along the side of me so his voice wouldn't carry down wind. "But I do not wish to insult the Captain's lead. I thought you might ask him."

"Me? Why me?"

"Because you lead our party just as Davies leads his men…or led as it were. That makes you equals. Being under you I am not allowed to speak out of turn."

"You're not under me Paralay."

"Of course I'm not! But just the same Talos has put you in our lead. Everyone recognizes your father's deeds as nothing short of amazing. They respect you. I'm just a thief."

"You're more than that but I understand what you're saying. Tell me your thought and I'll relate it to the Captain."

"The trees, they should be our allies," he told me. "I fancy myself a great climber. If I can get to the peak of one of the taller trees I can scout our trail for miles so we need not walk aimlessly."

I looked up at the tall palms that bowed over the jungle terrain we'd been avoiding. They were plenty high. A good climber could in fact use the perch at the top as a scouting position just as Paralay said.

"Are you sure you're up to it?" I asked him.

"Being tossed around at sea took some of the vinegar out of me but I am well now."

So it was agreed. I pulled Captain Davies aside so the others would not hear and related Paralay's suggestion. He seemed almost elated in his acceptance, as though he'd been putting on a front the whole time and his sense of direction was in fact failing him.

We watched as Paralay started at the bottom of one of the taller palms and as he found his footing he scampered like a small squirrel up and out of sight.

"Brave lad," Davies whispered to me.

"No other I'd want at my side," I replied.

"That's how I felt about Wiggins…Lord rest his soul."

The Captain's despondency was clearly evident. I could see now that he lost not just a crew but his companions as well, and maybe even a part of himself had been claimed by the sea.

"I see something!" Paralay called down to us.

"What is it?"

He hurried down to relate his findings. "Shelter, looks like a small dwelling not twenty markers from here."

"Thank the Gods," Talisa said.

"Don't thank them yet," Davies told her. "We don't know who lives there. They may not be hospitable."

"Then we'll just have to go knock on the door," I told him.

When we came upon the shelter we were no longer concerned about who inhabited it. It became clearly evident from the boarded up windows and sunken in roof that no one had lived there for quite some time.

The inside of the dwelling had not held up much better than the outside. Warped wood flooring, cobwebs laden thick with dust, and the stench of dead filling every corner. But to our surprise the place came fully furnished. A modest dining area occupied one corner, a handful of rooms each held a bed and a bureau with enough fresh clothes for each of us to change from our ravaged wardrobe. They even had a chest that unfortunately upon opening revealed nothing but spoiled provisions.

"Cook it long enough and should be just fine," Captain Davies said examining a piece of meat.

"I'd just as soon starve," Talisa told him.

"When you're on the high sea you make due with what you have girly."

"I'm not averse to roughing it, I just don't want spoiled meat walking around in my belly."

"We'll find you something else," I told her. "In the meantime we should all get some sleep."

"Agreed," Captain Davies said. "And be mindful of the Night Stalkers"

I halted in my step. "The what?"

"Nocturnal assailants that prey on you while you sleep."

"Prey? How so?"

"They whisper in your ear causing frightful dreams."

"Doesn't sound like much to worry about," I told him. "My dreams are usually frightful anyway."

"Heed the warning. You'll awake confused, agitated, sometimes still believing you're in the dream state and that is when you can run into trouble. I had one fellow who walked himself right off a cliff once."

"Are these just sea faring assailants? Why have we not heard of them before?"

"As I told you before with the gun, Calabrese, there are many things that you do not know yet."

"So how do you battle a dream?"

"With this."

He rolled his sleeve and showed us one of the many inked markings that lay across his skin. "This tattoo is a protector that wards off evil spirits in the night."

"I'm not putting that thing on my arm," Talisa told him.

"Suit yourself," Davies told her. "But I learned about such things from a Shaman. They know much of dreamscapes and the wicked that you can run into even when you're not awake."

Captain Davies caught me staring. His knowledge was extensive in many areas. Even though Talos was and always would be my mentor I knew that the mind thirsted for knowledge from different sources. The moment one stopped learning in life was the time for him to go to his grave.

"What say you demon hunter?" he asked me.

"Show me what I must do."

As the others retired for the evening Captain Davies and I stayed on the main floor. We'd managed to get some old candles to stay lit long enough so he could tattoo the marking on my arm. The process was some of the worst pain I'd experienced. He used a needle dipped in ink and forced it against my skin with just enough pressure that it soaked straight through the dermis.

I likened it to something of the method used for crucifixion. Finally my blood dispersed and my nerves began to numb enough that it became nothing more than a dull sensation.

"You've learned quite a bit from your travels. How long have you been at sea?"

Captain Davies pondered, shook his head as if disbelieving his own answer. "For as long as I can remember. I practically grew up on a ship. The Misery originally belonged to my uncle. He left it to me upon his death. One drunken night I was foolish enough to lose her in a game of cards. Spent the next year trying to get her back. Finally I just stole it from under their noses."

"That's quite a tale," I said, harking back to my own misfortune with card games. My very freedom had been gambled away by a foolish and drunken mistake. Hard lessons for a young man to learn followed for many, many years.

"She belonged to me in the first place," Captain Davies continued. "I swore then that I'd take good care of the old girl…and I did. Now she's scattered out to sea somewhere with my crew. There'll never be another like them."

"You still have Lazara."

He scoffed at my assessment. "She's new blood. I picked her up not too long ago."

"New blood? She told me she was your first mate."

The Captain had a good laugh about it. I wasn't laughing at all. Lazara had blatantly lied to me, and to Talisa. One more reason not to trust her.

"Ha! Is that what she said?" Davies replied. "She has a healthy ego I'll give you that. But she always keeps to herself. Very odd if you ask me."

"Why is that?"

"Because any woman who is more interested in bedding down with another woman is just odd…it's not natural."

His explanation took me by surprise but it explained why everytime I saw Talisa that Lazara wasn't far behind. I knew that Talisa would have many suitors chasing her around but I never expected I'd have to vie for her affections against another woman. That was a battle I wasn't sure how to win.

When the Captain had finished his artwork upon my arm he retired for the evening. I stayed up to design a form of weaponry to replace my crossbow. The thought of wandering around foreign lands unarmed made me nervous to say the least.

Inspired by Captain Davies pistol I fashioned something similar that would sit at my wrist for easy access and travel. Without my arrow bolts I had to make due with rustic style arrows carved from wood and stone. Those of us who had secured daggers to our boots or legs still held them there even with the sea ravaging us, but those alone would be nothing if we ran into real trouble.

I used my own dagger to carve out the patterns and then secured the mechanisms with bits of twine. Satisfied with my creation I strapped it to my wrist for easy access and loaded an arrow in its chamber.

As the night waned my eyelids grew heavy. I managed to get a larger fire going in a pit where the stone hearth for cooking once stood. The warmth of it grew inviting enough for me to curl up on the floor and rest my weary head.

Sleep came to me swiftly. As I lay I dreamed of mermaids and dragons, mythical creatures that one would have to see with their own eyes to believe they truly existed. I'd seen much in my short time upon the earth and even with all I'd seen there were still some things I could not believe in.

My hazy eyes came awake to look upon the markings that now forever lay tattooed upon my arm. Night Stalkers. Assailants who attacked you while you slept. It was a ridiculous notion but I'd come to learn to be better safe than sorry.

As I began to drift off again I noticed a shadowy figure moving towards me. I shifted awake and pulled myself up to a sitting position to get a better view.

"Who's there," I called, ready, willing, and able to test my new weapon's accuracy. I was very proud of its completion. Part crossbow, part pistol, all in the compact size of the slingshot I had been so fond of in my youth.

I aimed but dared not fire as the figure moved into the light and I saw it to be Talisa who approached me. Her eyes glowed within the light of the fire and she knelt down at my side.

"Costa," she whispered. "I know what you want."

Without hesitance she leaned in and kissed me full on the lips. I felt lightheaded and aroused all at once. Then she pulled away and stared at me. Her eyes were luminous even shrouded in shadow as her back faced the fire.

"I want it too," she told me. I remained at a loss for words and left myself at her mercy. She gently took my new weapon from my wrist and set it aside then she proceeded to remove my shirt. Her fingers trailed the grooves in my chest and abdomen. She followed with her tongue.

I became breathless. This was another side of Talisa I'd never known before. She was so sensual and passionate. I looked down at her in the darkness and she looked back at me, an impish little grin across her lips as she began to undo the belt of my pants. I smiled back until suddenly it dawned on me. Her eyes, she saw me full and well in the dark of night. Either Talisa's night blindness had suddenly been cured or it wasn't her.

"Get off of me," I demanded.

She seemed confused. "Why?"

I grabbed her shoulders, made sure I took control of her. "How is it that you can see? The firelight alone should not be enough to combat your blindness."

"Oh," she simply said, then the eyes flashed that same blazing yellow I'd seen on the boat and Talisa transformed into Lazara right in my grip. But that wasn't all. Lazara continued her transformation. Sharp fangs pulled down from her teeth and her nails became like razors. That hideous snarl she'd always greeted me with became much more vile as her face formed into that of a demonic nature. Shape shifting demons, the worst of the lot.

She tried to tear at my jugular using her teeth while her arms were trapped in my grip. Her strength was impressive and I knew I wouldn't be able to hold her off for long. I reared back wishing I had a weapon at my disposal until I realized I did.

Locking my limbs around Lazara's own I rolled across the floor and pitched her as hard as I could into the fire that blazed just behind us. She landed with a thud amongst the flames and lit up immediately, but that still didn't stop her. It did, however, give me just enough breathing room to grab my new weapon from the floor.

No doubt hearing the commotion Paralay, Talisa, and Captain Davies hurried down from their upstairs quarters just in time to see me try out my makeshift mini-crossbow. I launched the arrow of rock and stone from its chamber and watched it pitch direct into

Lazara's forehead. She tumbled backwards and fell against the stone hearth. The flames lapped up over her again and this time she did not get back up.

"By the gods what have you done?"

At first I couldn't understand Talisa's concerns until I realized my predicament. They had not seen any of the altercation. They'd simply seen me kill Lazara. Captain Davies was none too pleased. Paralay had to hold him back from assaulting me.

"You son of a butcher!" he shouted. "I'll kill you!"

I tried in vein to defend my point of view. "She came at me, tried to kill me under the cloak of night."

"How did she get the jump on you with your natural senses?" Paralay asked.

I had no immediate answer. What could I tell them, that she had made herself to look like Talisa and seduced me?

"She surprised me while I slept. Apparently your protective tattoo didn't work, Captain."

"He has gone mad just like his father," Davies insisted. "The Night Stalkers have him, I warned you! We must implement candling before we succumb as well."

"Candling? That's barbaric," Talisa said.

"What is it?" Paralay asked. I also grew curious but I knew better at that moment than to try to question anything.

"A method used to extract the demons that have burrowed themselves deep into the victim's brain," Davies explained. "Calabrese has obviously been possessed."

"This is ridiculous, outdated nonsense," Talisa protested. "There's no way…."

"I'll do it. I'll allow Captain Davies to perform the candling."

She looked at me, shock upon her face. But it wasn't anything compared to the horror I'd seen etched across her beautiful features just moments before when she saw me as a killer. I couldn't let her think of me that way. Even though she defended me now I knew there was a part of her that still feared me.

Captain Davies set me up on my side lying upon one of the tables. He then stuck a candle that had been whittled down to size into my ear canal and lit it at the top. The practice was said to dispel demons by sucking them out from the cavity of the skull where they dwelled. It was also said to be nothing more than a myth. But I had grown desperate.

My desperation didn't come from my interest in having the demons drawn from inside me, for I knew the ones I harbored were there to stay. I was desperate to quell Talisa's fears no matter what it took.

I'd never seen such fear in her eyes as when she'd looked at me moments ago. It was as if I had become a stranger to her. I never wanted to see that fear on her face again, and certainly not from anything I had done to create it.

The Captain hovered over me like a high priest dealing out ritualistic rites of passage and he praised imaginary gods.

"Great mystery in the sky, teach me how to trust my mind, my intuition, my inner knowing and the senses of my body. Demons be gone!" he shouted, as if chanting and hot wax dripping across my face were all it would take to dispel would be demons. But something strange did occur. We heard an ominous sound ring out. It did not come from me or the so-called Night Stalkers inhabiting me, it sounded from outside.

They all tore away to the windows to find out the source. I carefully plucked the candle from my ear and joined the others. Perhaps no demons had been extracted but I could certainly hear much more clearly than I'd remembered.

Outside just past the breakers of the shore we saw quite a vision. I could scarcely make it out until Captain Davies recognized it as his own.

"The Misery!"

Chapter Five
And the Dead Shall Walk

The Misery stood tall and proud before us. She didn't have a mark on her. Captain Davies almost fell to tears. My usual skepticism ran its course.

"How is that possible? We were turned upside down."

"She righted herself," Davies said. He held too much excitement in his voice. Something told me to proceed with caution.

The two of us took up torches and went out to search The Misery for survivors and supplies while Paralay stood back with Talisa. I did not want her wandering around a ship in the middle of the night with her eyesight hindering her. There was no telling what was on that ship. With all the tales I'd heard growing up, and the demons of the sea Captain Davies had suggested, I preferred at that moment to err on the side of caution.

We had to wade out about waist level before we could get on board The Misery. I was beginning to hate the sea. What I wouldn't give to be back home on dry land surrounded by cliffs and mountain tops. The sea faring life did not suit me.

Once on board a chill overtook me. Something didn't feel quite right and I knew better than to ignore my senses.

"Let's get whatever we can carry and get off of here," I told Davies, in fact I insisted.

"I'm certain I can make my baby manageable again. Then we can get out of here."

"Check it in the morning, right now just supplies."

"Who the hell died and left you in charge, Calabrese? This is my ship and I'm going to check for structural damage, understand?"

The Captain abided by his own rules and nothing I said or did was going to change that fact. He made his way down towards his chambers and I to mine. The eerie chill of silence quickly shifted when I saw what lay below.

The Regulators, all belly up and bloated like dead rats. Stephenson, the first I came across had been pinned down by supply crates. His sternum had been crushed causing him to bleed internally and drown on his own blood until it poured out from his ears, nose, and mouth.

Edging past the disgusting corpse I began gathering armfuls of whatever I could find: food, clothing, mostly armaments. Luckily Paralay had enough foresight to pin down his swords. He'd become very adept at using those fine blades and thus very protective so he secured them where the others would not find them. I secured them to my back and carried on hoping to find my crossbow or Talisa's staff. Instead I found more bodies.

In the hallway, at the foot of a long flight of stairs lay Wiggins. His once powerful frame now nothing more than a twisted mass of limbs. I noticed immediately that his head didn't sit quite right on his shoulders. As I inspected further I concluded that he'd fallen down the stairs and broken his neck upon impact. It seemed that most of the deaths were not a direct result of the waves upon us but more possibly the panic that had set in leading the Regulators to make fatal mistakes. Staying calm in the face of danger was a particularly useful trait to learn, one of my first in fact.

When my arms could no longer carry another item I called out to the Captain that it was time to go. An inch or so of water still remained on the decks of the floor and it grew more and more difficult to walk through with the bundle I carried.

"I'm going to leave you!" I called out.

Finally he stepped out from his chambers. Packs lined his back neatly secured and not as burdensome as my load.

"Do you need some help there Calabrese?"

"Don't mock me. Grab a load and let us leave this place. I don't wish to stay here a moment longer."

"Having terrible vampire flashbacks?"

"What're you talking about?"

"Nothing. Here this is the way out."

He pointed towards the stairs and then stopped short when he saw Wiggins lying lifeless at the bottom.

"Damn the fates."

"Fate is what you make of it," I told him. Then as my arms began to grow numb from the load I forced a satchel into Davies hands. "Carry some of this. We need the provisions."

He did not expect the weight and it caused him to stumble back, striking one of his packs against the wall. Something fell out and made a splash in the water below us. I readjusted some items in my load and reached for whatever had fallen.

"No leave it, I'll get it."

The Captain seemed very skittish now and it made me lunge for the item even faster. As I fished my father's book of scrolls from the water I knew exactly what he didn't want me to see and why it had taken him so long to finish up in his chambers.

"Were you going to tell me you had found this or just keep it for yourself?" My voice remained calm but inside I felt my anger seething. "Something else to turn a profit, right Captain?"

"Not this time, demon hunter. That wealth of information is staying with me."

"Over my dead body."

"If that's the way you want it."

The Captain lunged at me then, I had a feeling he would. My first instinct was to strike him with the nearest item at my disposal, which at the moment was my father's journal. It rang his bell quite good. He staggered back, almost tripped over Wiggins, but then lashed out at me once more. By this time I had been able to free myself up from the burden I'd been carrying so when Davies went for my throat I parried him and employed an arm lock. He in turn grabbed my hair.

"You thieving bastard!" I shouted.

"You're lucky I didn't kill you while you lay upon the table with that candle in your ear."

We struggled, taking turns slamming each other into the walls of the ship. The smack of flesh off wood was enough to wake the dead…and it did. Amidst my duel with the Captain we were joined by a third party. Wiggins, his head still flopping around unnaturally from his shoulders, stood up.

"By the gods, Wiggins, you're alive," Captain Davies said. He believed to be looking at his former first mate the way he'd known him for so many years, I saw otherwise.

Wiggins eyes held no life. His chest did not rise and fall with breath. He had not come miraculously alive. The dead had risen and my guess was that it did not end with Wiggins.

Scraping sounds, moaning, and shuffling were echoing throughout the ship. In my experience the animated dead were not a friendly lot. They were employed by the forces of hell.

"Captain," I said slowly gathering up weapons and my father's journal from the ground whilst keeping an eye on Wiggins. "We best be going now."

The Captain wasn't a foolish man. Upon second glance at Wiggins he concurred with me. "I think you're right."

Wiggins had other plans for us. He reached out with lightning-like speed for the closest prey, which happened to be Captain Davies. The former first mate began to throttle the life out of his Captain. Davies didn't hesitate. He pulled his pistol from his coat and shot Wiggins point blank in the head.

The blast knocked him backwards and allowed Captain Davies a solid breath back into his lungs but it didn't stop Wiggins from coming forward once again.

"Come, we must get back to the house!" I told Davies. We ran back inside his chambers and went for the small porthole window.

"We'll never fit through that," he told me.

"Not as it is."

I retrieved Paralay's swords from my back and sent several blows against the watered down wood paneling around the window. It proved enough for me to kick out a good size hole after that.

"Now we'll fit."

Wiggins entered behind us just then and took hold of the Captain once more. This time Davies wouldn't escape. I watched in horror as Wiggins tore out Captain Davies jugular with his teeth and swallowed down the hunk of flesh like a sliver of rawhide. Then he came for me.

I stood my ground, hefted both swords and arced them together until Wiggins rotten head fell from his shoulders and made a splish-splash on the watery floor.

"Blades don't need reloading."

Wiggins may have been down but the rest of the Regulators were still on the move. They either heard the commotion or they smelled my human flesh and grew insatiable for it. I wasted no time and hurled myself from the window into the murky depths below.

Paralay and Talisa were waiting at the doorway when I made my way back.

"That took a long time, we were growing concerned," Talisa said.

"Where's the Captain?" Paralay asked.

"Reunited with his crew," I said breathlessly.

They stared at me in confusion.

"The Regulators have been reanimated from death. They're on their way here…now."

"You're talking madness again," Paralay said. "How do we know you didn't kill the Captain yourself?"

"You should know enough by now from what we have encountered before that I speak the truth. We haven't time for you to question me. They'll be coming for all of us…soon."

"My God," Talisa gasped.

"God can't help us now," I said. "Only one man can."

Chapter Six
Zombie Attack

My father's journal had been a lifesaver before. Notes upon notes of all manner of creature were described within its pages. I didn't know how much time we had before the Regulators would be upon us but I took the initiative anyway to look for help from within.

It took me longer than I hoped. Usually I had the great instinct to turn right to the page I needed. But my mind was cloudy, focused on many things all at once. I found myself lingering on a passage that seemed to have no real purpose for being there except to warn me directly.

"Love is best left for those who can enjoy it. Never seek the affections of a woman. Disengage yourself from such thoughts now. The joy does not compare to the sorrow, and in our line of work that sorrow is inevitable."

I wondered if my father had been thinking of my mother when he'd written that line or if another had captured his heart…the way Talisa had captured mine.

Finally I found his words on the walking dead.

"Organization is the most important factor I can impart to you when it comes to surviving a zombie attack. You must organize before they rise for you won't have a chance to once they are in your midst. Keep moving, keep low, keep quiet and always keep alert. You mustn't let fear dissuade you. Keep your wits and your head…chop off theirs. Know that no place is safe, only safer. The zombie is a relentless enemy. If you can avoid them do so."

The entry hardly passed for a survival guide. What I gathered was that my father had perhaps run into a zombie maybe once or twice but he had not been foolish enough to get pinned down in a rustic house while a group of them shuffled towards the door with death on their minds.

How do we keep winding up in these predicaments?

There seemed to be no real answer to that question except to say that trouble had a way of finding me.

"We need to use our surroundings to our advantage," I told Paralay and Talisa. "Same as last time with the vampires, only the Regulators won't be half as smart."

"They weren't that bright to begin with," Paralay said.

"We'll make our way up the stair case and destroy it behind us," I suggested.

"But we'll be pinned down. How will we get out of here? We'll be at their mercy."

"Not necessarily. We can slip out the upstairs windows and make our way into the jungle behind us."

"Captain Davies was adamant about staying out of there."

"Captain Davies is dead, and unless we want to follow we will have to take our chances."

"Agreed."

"I have a present for you."

I unloaded Paralay's swords from my back and handed them to him.

"My swords…fantastic!"

"Let's get a move on, there's no telling how fast they can move."

As if on cue the front of the house was assaulted by the zombie clan of Regulators. They tore at the boarded windows, smashed in the front door, and made their way inside before we had a chance to organize. The very first rule my father insisted on in a zombie attack and we had already failed.

That didn't mean we'd lose our heads in a crisis. Paralay tossed over one of his swords to me and we began to run towards the stairs. Any further debate over my plan had been tabled, now we just rode off of pure instinct.

The zombies were surprisingly fast. Before we made it up to the mid-point of the staircase they had caught up to us. As the last one to go up I was the first one targeted. Stephenson, his lungs still dripping from his chest cavity, reached out a gnarled hand and took a good fist-sized clump of my hair.

I almost fell backwards into the waiting arms of the Regulators but managed to catch my balance. Stephenson's breath smelled of decay upon my nose He pulled and twisted my hair, controlling my head in the process. I thought instantly of Wiggins ripping out Captain Davies throat with just his teeth alone. My heart quickened in its pace. Death stood waiting for me and one of these days He would collect.

Today was not that day, however. Having my companions at my back is something I had tried to dissuade before but had not regretted having. That certainly remained the case as both Paralay and Talisa scrambled to my aide despite their own safety.

We all tried in vain to pry Stephenson's grip from me but it appeared as though his strength had grown. The other members of the crew were coming quickly behind him having torn the door from its hinges and even ripping out the window box to get inside.

"Stand aside," I heard Talisa say to Paralay. I could not make out what she was doing only that she had brandished a dagger and advanced. Instead of attacking the zombie Stephenson she went after me, my hair to be exact. She hacked away with her dagger until the only thing Stephenson held in his hands was the length of ponytail I formerly had running down my neck.

Free to move I took the initiative to dispatch Stephenson the same way I had fallen zombie Wiggins. Stephenson's head tumbled to the ground right at the feet of the rest of the crew. They collected his head from the ground and paused long enough in their confusion for the three of us to make our escape.

When we got to the top of the landing all three of us worked diligently to destroy the staircase. We only managed to put a good size hole in the top of the step before we had to turn and run. The Regulators were still coming and nothing short of fighting the entire lot was going to stop them. That wasn't something we were prepared to do even if we wanted to.

We barricaded ourselves inside one of the upper chambers and took a moment to catch our breath. It felt as though we'd been running ever since we crashed upon this accursed island.

"We can't stay here. It isn't safe, only safer," I told them reciting my father's words from the journal.

"Then let us not waste anymore time. We need to get as much distance from those things as possible," Paralay said going over to the window. "I don't want them at my back when we are moving through the jungle."

"Talisa, stay close to us," I told her.

"I'll be fine, I'm growing accustomed to the blindness."

"Nevertheless, if anything happened to you I'd feel responsible."

"There's no time for that now," Paralay told us. "What say you? Are we all ready?"

We agreed and made a swift exit out the upper window. No sooner did our feet touch the ground than we heard the door buckle in. The zombie lot had made their way upstairs.

"Move, now!" I said.

We ran straight into the thick of the jungle before us leaving behind one danger for a possible new one that yet remained to be seen.

Chapter Seven
The Maori and The Maiden

"This is no jungle, it's swamp land," Paralay said.

Paralay spoke the truth. The stretch of land before us held more depths of water than any solid ground. It also smelled more rank than the breath of the zombie's.

"We'll have to make do, we can't turn around now," I said.

We moved as best we could with no real sense of direction and wading through thick patches of murky water. Paralay took the lead and I could hear him ahead of us cursing the late Captain Davies and his crew.

I stayed back with Talisa. She seemed to bc faring quite well in the dark of night. But I was still glad she couldn't see me. I knew I needed to apologize for a great many things and I preferred not having her look upon me as I did so.

"Back there with Lazara, that wasn't me."

"You scared me. I thought you had changed."

"I know, I'm sorry. Sometimes my demons get the better of me. I guess that's why my father always chose to walk alone."

"You're not your father, Costa, just as I am not mine. We share similar traits but we are our own person in the end." She paused. "I'm sorry about your hair."

I ran my hand through my new shorter locks. "That's all right, it's an improvement."

Talisa joined me in a laugh and then blindly sought my hand. To simply have her hand in mine gave me such a sense of peace that I hadn't had in a long while.

Half drowned, exhausted, and soul weary we had no idea how we would conquer Sark. But our mission still lay before us, that's if we could ever find our way out of the accursed swamp.

"I'm exhausted," Paralay called from the front. "There's no end to this place."

"I'll take the lead," I told him.

As much as I hated to release Talisa's hand I had to be fair to Paralay and give him a break. When I made my way out in front I was glad I did for my senses immediately picked up on something.

"We're being followed."

"The zombies?" Talisa asked.

"No," I told her. "Something else."

We didn't need to wait long to find out what, or who had been trailing us. I cursed myself for not being able to pick up on the energy before. I was too caught up with my feelings for Talisa to allow any outside interference. Now it would cost us. I was beginning to understand my father's warning about love not being in the cards for a demon hunter.

Our predators came down from the trees, out of the thickets, and even up from the swamps. They were small they wore flax coats, short capes, or simple waist-blankets and many wore nothing at all.

It looked to be a warrior scouting party which meant there were more, perhaps hundreds, back at a campsite somewhere. The scouts were armed with tear-shaped clubs carved from polished black stone, solid wood, or even bones, and all varying in size. But each one ready to split a skull like a melon. Whoever they were they meant business.

Paralay began to draw his sword and I motioned for him to stop. We were outnumbered and surrounded. There was little we could do especially in such an environment. We were at their mercy.

They rounded us up, took our weapons and supplies. I lost my father's journals for the second time. Then they tied our hands behind our backs and marched us through the swamps.

I kept watch on the ones that guarded Talisa. Bound or not if they got out of line I intended to kill every one of them or die trying.

Just as I expected they hauled us to a campsite that we never would've been able to find on our own. Whoever these people were they had dug in tight within the swamplands making the surrounding marshes and jungle vines their home. I preferred four sturdy walls and a roof over my head but at the moment nothing the three of us said had any relevance.

I'd kept something of a level head up to a point but now came time to panic. They began to split us up, sequester us into two groups. Which meant Talisa being broken off from Paralay and I.

"No!" I hollered, struggled, and took a shot over the head for my troubles.

Talisa called out for them to stop. Her voice sounded so soft and gentle even clinging to the negative air. The savages hardly seemed to care. They continued to lead us away in opposite directions.

The next to get split were Paralay and I. He turned to me and spoke with strength and valor.

"Don't let them break you…no matter what. Stay strong."

I nodded and watched as they pulled my Elven friend away kicking and screaming as he went. Then it became my turn. Two guards of fairly good size remained with me. Each held their ever present sticks in hand as well.

I'd learned a fair share of hand-to-hand combat techniques, not only from Master Talos but my father Cain Colerdige as well. If need be I held no doubt that I could best my burly captors even with my hands tied behind my back. But I didn't want to risk it just yet. I couldn't take a chance of putting Paralay and Talisa in jeopardy without first seeing where this led.

They took me towards a small hut of sturdy sticks and vine. My head still throbbed from the blow I'd received earlier. I began to grow dizzy. The guardsmen at my sides had to hold me up to keep my face from planting into the moist earth beneath me.

Inside the hut sat another staunch fellow. He had tribal paintings tattooed the length of his torso and up around his arm. Face paint marked his status as something of a high chief.

The guards pitched me in front of him without regard that my hands couldn't be used to break my fall. My knees absorbed most of the blow and it brought me back to the times in my youth where my days consisted of beatings on a regular basis.

Their leader (I could only assume he was something of a leader to them, from the way they regarded him with such respect) looked me over like a piece of prime stock until his guards handed my belongings over to him.

Paralay's sword he handed back to them, it was my father's journals that took his interest. He poured over every page and I watched and waited. My dizzy head almost pulled me into slumber until I heard their chieftain utter the word tabu.

I knew well enough what tabu meant. It seemed my father's storied history didn't sit well with these swamp dwellers any more than it did for regular folk. I sat quietly and patiently awaiting the wrath they were certain to bring down upon my head. Instead, the leader spoke and he did so in perfect English.

"You are the demon hunter?"

"You've heard of me?" I asked startled.

"Of your kind, yes. It is said you hold great powers. That you can combat the forces of evil like no other."

"Routinely. I suppose it's my lot in life."

"Is that so?"

I nodded.

"Good. Then I have one more for you."

The conversation had taken quite an unusual turn. The simple fact that we were having a conversation at all rather than them splintering my skull with their big sticks surprised me. But it seemed for once my name, or my father's name, would get me out of trouble instead of into it.

"You want me to flush out a demon for you?"

"You won't have to flush her out. She comes at the same time every night…to feed."

"She?" A sick part of me grew intrigued. With the exception of a few irregulars such as Lazara, up until that point I'd been mainly facing your average variety male demons. A female would prove to be a new and unique challenge.

"We call her The White Maiden. She is a very dainty, beautiful woman but there is an underlying secret."

"What is it?"

"We don't know for certain. Only one survivor ever escaped her clutches. He told us she had transformed into something of a hideous beast."

"I've come to notice that as not such a rare trait," I said with a smile. My knowledge of all things demon had expanded tenfold since my tutelage under Master Talos and even more so while traveling the great expanse of land the devil's spawn inhabited.

"We need you to assist us in dispatching this creature, demon hunter. Our numbers are dwindling as The Maiden grows bolder with each night moving closer to our village."

I chose my reply carefully and emphatically stated: "No."

They were all shocked to say the least. I received another wrap across the head for my efforts as well. The blow sent me down nose first and they had to haul me back up by the arms to get me to pay attention to their leader once more.

"You believe you're in a position to negotiate?"

Again my answer was simple and straightforward. "Yes."

They moved to club me once more until their leader halted them. He finally rose to his feet and came forward. Even on my knees I was the same height as he. I knew better than to judge someone off mere appearance alone. I'd learned that the hard way back when I'd challenged Master Talos to a blind foot race.

"You're either very cocky or very confidant, demon hunter."

"Or very foolish," I added. "And do call me Costa. My inherent title dismays me to hear."

"How so?"

"It isn't something I'd ever have asked for purposely."

"But you have a rare gift and we need that gift."

"Exactly why I'm so confidant…and cocky," I mused. Paralay's influence no doubt. I could see that they were all getting fed up with my roguish behavior so I decided to cut to the chase. "Release my companions and I'll aide you with The Maiden."

The tiny leader pondered it for a moment then motioned to his guards for action. I awaited my short life to flash before my eyes and my inevitable death to come directly after, but instead they cut loose my bonds. I was free as requested…if only that had worked in my younger days.

"What about my companions?" I asked as I massaged the skin around my wrists, tender now from rope burns.

"Free to go but we'd like to ask all three of you to be our guests at a banquet this evening."

"A banquet? Here in the middle of the swamplands?"

"The Maori make full use of whatever land we are permitted to use."

Indeed they did. I had never seen rustic lodgings scrounged off the land in such a manner. Jungle vines laced through each other in large coils to form roofs and even doors. They laid out the dining area with large rocks and plank wood that had drifted ashore. The makeshift village was actually quite quaint; however there was nothing they could do to keep the rotten stench of swampland from blowing in with the winds.

The Maori's gala celebration included leek soup and some wild berries indigenous to the surrounding area. Certainly not the grand feast we'd had upon graduation from Ravenwood Academy but not lacking in entertainment by any means.

Once The Maori considered us their saviors, or tabu, they began to treat us like royalty. First they offered up new clothing for us. Since The Maori themselves didn't have much use for clothes out in the swamplands they could do little by way of new garments but they did manage to repair the tears and holes in the wardrobe we had been wearing up to that point.

From there we were invited as guests of their leader, K'hmad, to sit at his table and enjoy the night's festivities. Dances native to their people were performed and stories were regaled well into the night.

At this point Talisa and I slipped off. The soup, though unique looking with its rich greens, went down smooth. The entertainment delighted the eyes and ears as The Maori told their tales with a form of theater. But the two of us found much more pleasure from just looking across at one another. The outside world could've crashed down around us and we wouldn't have been any wiser lost in each others gaze.

I walked with her hand in mine with the deep of the night sky above us and the sounds of the gala behind us. We had no words for each other, just a feeling of electricity that had sparked up again since we'd come ashore from the storm at sea and had continued all the way up through dinner. I took it upon myself now to lead Talisa back towards the sleeping quarters.

The Maori lived in thatch huts, several of them dwelling inside at a time. They were hospitable enough to jam several more into their groups so that Talisa, Paralay, and I could have our own places to sleep. Tonight, however, Talisa would not need hers.

I brought her back to my hut, closing the door behind us. One thing I'd come to learn during the shipwreck, the zombie attack, and my ever uncertain future as a demon hunter was that life is short. I needed to seize moments of bliss wherever I could find them. At that moment Talisa embodied that bliss and our time together was at hand.

She lay across the bed made up of palm fronds and I joined her. I kissed her then, long and passionate. Parting her lips I explored her mouth with my tongue and she met me with her own. But I didn't want to rush anything. Her very presence mesmerized me and I wanted to soak it all in. Every line of her face, every curve of her body, all of it captivated my heart.

There had been girls during my training time with Master Talos that had shared my bed with me, but none as fair as the weapons master's daughter herself. Bedding down with some of the female counterparts in Ravenwood had almost become something of a right of passage with the students, even if Master Talos had little or no idea about the goings on. I always suspected that he did.

Master Talos had a grand talent for knowing what went on around him at all times. Being stricken blind had never been a deterrent for him. I could see now that Talisa meant to follow in his footsteps with her own affliction.

I untied her shirt and allowed her to slip my own off over my head. We took our time undressing each other, feeling each other's bodies. This moment, our unification as one would be a moment we would not soon forget and I intended for it to be special… especially for Talisa. She trusted me enough to give herself to me when she had said no to others in the past. In her words I knew the answer as to why.

Love, pure and simple love, I had not known such an intense and euphoric feeling in all my days. I had never even known what it had been like to have the love and affection from my own parents. With my mother's untimely death, and my father's disappearance from my life for all those years, I'd never really managed to allow myself to have any kind of feelings for anyone. The closest I had come was my good friend Tuck whose savage murder at the hands of the vampire LeCarde still haunts me.

But now I had Talisa. Beautiful, sweet Talisa who had given my life new meaning and joy. My father couldn't possibly have been in his best mind when he had written a warning to stay clear of love. What kind of a life could you have if you did not merit yourself the ultimate pleasure of connecting with someone intimately on all levels? A life lived without love really wasn't lived at all.

Talisa smiled and wrapped her lips around my finger. I let her tease my fingers for a few moments then withdrew my hand and laid it across the slopes of her breasts. She stared up at me with her crystal blue eyes and I kept her gaze as I entered her. I took my time, slow and gentle, so as not to harm her.

The connection felt so overpowering that I groaned even as Talisa gasped in delight. We stayed there united and rhythmic for a very long time. Each stroke, each caress of our bodies, each climax from Talisa, all held extra special meaning. This was love, true love. When I came it overwhelmed me. I gritted my teeth and rode out the wave of bliss as it almost transcended me to another plain…or so it felt. At that same moment Talisa climaxed as well, shouting to the heavens so loud I almost feared The Maori troop were going to barge in seeking the source of the disturbance.

She shifted positions and she collapsed across my chest. I held her there, not wanting to let her go. For the first time in a long time I'd found a spark in my life. I wasn't a loner anymore. I had something worth fighting for, worth getting up in the morning for, and something I could lose. That scared me.

We went from heaven right back into the jaws of hell. With only a few hours rest under our belts we had to set out to face the White Maiden. The Maori man who had been one of the only survivors of her attack knew few details that could aid us, only that she had come in the deep dark of night, the witching hour when everyone else slept. I knew that time of night well. Most demons crawl the earth at the times when men slept in their beds completely unaware of the insidious beasts.

Demon hunters rarely slept. We always kept one eye open ready to combat the threat should it come at us during the night. This particular night pulling myself from Talisa's warm embrace proved almost too difficult a task.

I tried to shift silently from her delicate hands but she woke anyway. Staring up at me her blue eyes were so lustrous, inviting, and full of love that it melted me. It gave me hope that perhaps my heart had not been forged of stone after all.

"Come closer to me," I insisted and bear hugged her against my chest. "I never want to let you go."

"Good," she replied. "Because I never want to leave."

I had no choice but to leave, begrudgingly. We had all agreed as a unit that only Paralay and I would confront the White Maiden. Even though Talisa had begun to grow more accustomed to her impaired vision it still remained a factor that would make her more of a liability against such a powerful opponent.

With one last kiss to Talisa's sweet lips I headed off to meet Paralay. He awaited me on the very edge of the swampland the Maori called home. They had given us a map and supplies earlier in the night and wished us luck in our endeavor to which Paralay had replied: "I make my own luck."

My luck ran hot and cold. I suppose having both elements of good and bad running the course of my life kept me in balance. We didn't have to travel very far. The Maori used a carved out path to seek supplies and food out in the Mysterious Lands.

"Why don't the fools just choose a different path?" Paralay questioned as we once again found ourselves wading through pockets of thick, murky water.

"I believe they've already intruded on the Maiden enough times now that she is beginning to edge closer and closer to their dwellings."

"Well I hope you received good payment for this job at least.

"Not really. I bargained for your life."

I nudged my Elven friend and we had a good laugh. It took our minds off the fact that we were out chasing demons in the middle of the night again.

The grove the Maori said held the whereabouts of the White Maiden seemed so out of place amongst the swamp and its stench. A beautiful clearing opened to the edge of a pool of water formed from years of rainfall.

"Makes sense now," Paralay said stooping to gather water in his hand and quench his thirst. "With nothing but sea and swamp surrounding them the Maori come here for drinking water."

I remembered back to Master Talos' final mission for us on top of the Peak of the Gods. He had said water to be one of the most powerful elements on Earth believed to hold both purifying and healing powers. An elixir of life so unpredictable in nature that it drives men to their collective deaths just to obtain it.

I knelt to drink myself and that's when I saw her. She had a much smaller frame than I had anticipated. Having dealt mostly with the larger, male variety with their massive snarled snouts and gnarled fingers I hardly expected the beauty that stood before us.

Dark hair contrasted with a pale face and white robes that fell loose from her body. She looked dainty with a tiny waist and petite feet, almost like a glass figurine and not a person at all. But she wasn't a person – or so The Maori had said. According to them this beautiful young woman was their spirit attacker, the White Maiden.

"The Maori must've gotten it wrong," Paralay said. "That is no demon, that's an angel that stands before us."

Perhaps. I even speculated it myself. But after the incident with Lazara I'd come quick to learn how appearances could be deceiving.

"Don't get too close, Paralay."

Even as I spoke he edged closer to the water where the woman had come up from. Before I could stop him he had stepped inside the pool. His motion disturbed the calmness of the water sending ripples across its face and over to the White Maiden.

"So beautiful," Paralay muttered. His words floated on the air and his eyes glazed as though he had fallen into some sort of trance.

The White Maiden beckoned him closer to her. She drew him in with her beauty. As captivating as she appeared I still held my head about me. Something wasn't right, I could feel it in my bones. Many Maori men had disappeared in this very location, perhaps by the hands of this woman. I did not intend to allow Paralay that same fate.

I moved into the pool after him. The water splashed up around my thighs and across Paralay's back. My movements did not affect him, in fact they did not even register. However, as the result of my intrusion, the White Maiden showed her true colors.

It did not take long, seconds in actuality, but when I saw it before me I felt as though the earth had stopped spinning and everything slowed. The once beautiful, dainty features of the Maiden pushed and pulled like leather stretched across a workman's table.

Something looked to be pushing its way through from behind her skin until the skin itself shed in large flakes. The white robes fell away to reveal a long, thick torso. The hair and face fell away to reveal a diamond shaped head with slits in the eyes. What stood before us no longer resembled a girl by any facet of the imagination. Instead we looked upon the largest python I'd ever laid my eyes upon.

The body, a miraculously blinding white, extended for what seemed like miles. The sliver of eyes followed every small movement we made, or rather I made. Paralay stood motionless. His eyes had no spark to them. He remained in a trance.

"Paralay, wake up!" I shouted.

The only response I received came from the white python. She hissed at me, the sound though guttural boomed across the night sky and sent more ripples across the water. Paralay was knocked off his feet and disappeared under the surface.

I wanted to go after him. Even though the body of water appeared shallow I had no way of knowing just how deep it actually could be. The more I learned of these treacherous beings from the underworld the more I despised them. They had far too many tricks up their sleeves and even though I had somewhat of an advantage, my father's teachings in his scrolls, I still could not contend for every single method of attack from every single creature.

Though my father was well traveled there was no mention of giant water snakes or maidens in white throughout his entire journal. Perhaps it was a chapter that I needed to write myself, supposing I survived this attack.

I had Paralay's sword at my back and The Maori had given us each a small spear they called taiaha. Everything seemed so futile and worthless against a creature of such magnitude. Nevertheless I squared my shoulders and sent the spear flying. My aim proved as sharp as always.

The taiaha struck gold just underneath the python's eye, lacerating it and sent thick, dark blood into its eyes.. I moved off instinct trying to capitalize on the situation. As I came closer to the creature I stopped in my tracks. It towered over me, taller than any of the largest trees I could remember from my days in Gryphant.

I held the short sword in my hand and still felt at a complete disadvantage. Then Paralay emerged from the water. His eyes were wild and he held the companion short sword tightly in his grip ready to attack.

"Where is the bitch?" he asked.

"Right in front of you," I told him.

The python bowed its head as though she had heard us and delivered a curtsy. Then she flicked her forked tongue straight into our bellies and launched us backwards into the water.

My vision clouded as I went under but I managed to regain my bearings quickly before the giant head came crashing down with fangs as sharp as stakes.

I dove out of the way, out of the water, and back onto dry land where I felt more comfortable fighting. Paralay latched onto the head and began to hack away at the python's good eye. Sometimes I still marveled at the elf's courage.

Running to the side of the beast I hacked into the body with wild arcing swings. We had the foul thing. She was moments away from being decapitated until she struck me from behind. I'd forgotten about the tail.

It lashed up and hit at my legs. The force of the blow knocked me down immediately. My legs went numb. I couldn't move them at all. I had to drag my body away before the tail came down again and broke open my skull from its weight.

Paralay had his own troubles. He was in dire straits without my help. The python had shaken herself free from his attack and now he found himself pinned underneath the waterfall. It poured over his shoulders, impairing his vision and movement while the python crept in to kill him.

"Get the hell out of there!" I called. I tried desperately to make it over to him, or at least create some type of diversion but all my efforts seemed futile.

Then help came from the most unlikely of sources. Talisa, armed with fire, came from seemingly nowhere to aide us. She held a bow in her hands with arrows that flamed at the tip and she let them fly one after the other towards the giant serpent.

It shrieked as the arrows lodged in its body and the fire they emitted began to char the scales right off its back. With Talisa engaging her attack, it gave Paralay enough time to make his move. He leapt from beneath the water and brought the length of his sword down into the snout of the snake. It split down to its very jowls and in an instant the python no longer held shape, instead the Maiden in White returned to her original form and only moments later she fell dead in the water turning it a dark crimson.

With the feeling returning to my legs I came to a wobbly standing position and hurried over to embrace Talisa. Paralay looked over at us and I could see his eyes grow heavy with hurt. It was no secret to me that he held feelings for Talisa. I'd never intended to cause him any pain. We don't have a choice with whom we fall in love. You can only avoid such feelings for so long before you succumb to them. That is why I knew my father's warning held something else behind it. He masked a hurt from a lost love.

Paralay's hurt now turned to bitterness and he lashed out. "Talisa, what in the hell are you doing here? I thought we told you to stay back at camp."

Talisa absorbed his anger with a smile. "Because I knew the only one who could bring down a powerful woman would be another powerful woman."

"I'm just glad you came when you did," I told her. "We owe you a debt of thanks for saving our skins."

"You don't owe me anything," she said, and then turned to Paralay. "We're supposed to be in this together."

He ignored her. "Speaking of skins, let's take the rest of this carcass back to the Maori so we can get out of this accursed swamp."

"Agreed."

We wrapped up the White Maiden as best we could in mud and tree vines then brought her body back to the Maori village. The experience was very unnerving having a demon so close at your back and expecting her to rise up and go on the attack again. She remained dead all the way to the village where we plopped her down in front of their leader even as he slept.

He almost jumped from his skin as we woke him, then scuttled backwards as far away from the body as possible, snatching up his own taiaha and poking at her.

"She's dead," I told him. "But I must insist you commit the body to flame. Evil must not be allowed to reanimate."

"Reanimate?"

"Yes, like the walking corpses out on the shoreline," I explained. "The remains of our crew who somehow became infected with a curse that brought them back into this world as soulless, mindless zombies."

His face had grown pale at my description. "We shall burn her at once."

Chapter Eight
Draconia

None of us wanted to stay in the Maori village any longer than we had to but the night's demon hunt had left us all weary. I decided it would be in our own best interest if we bedded down for one more night or at least a few more hours. We needed all the strength we could muster before going up against Sark.

It also afforded me the opportunity to make love with Talisa once more. She had grown bolder, this innocent girl I'd first met many years back, and not just in our adventures together, but in the bedroom as well.

Her rambunctious nature simultaneously aroused me and peaked my curiosity. I'd never known her to be anything but demure and here she was nibbling upon my neck with hard pecks and then taking my bottom lip between her teeth and biting me.

"Ouch!" I shifted and stared at her in surprise. "That hurt."

She held a devilish grin and licked her lips to lap up the blood, my blood, that had broken through.

"Sorry," she told me. "I'll make it up to you."

I lay back while she straddled me, taking me inside her with one fluid motion. We were so perfectly matched. One heart, one soul, forever entwined. The dynamic exceeded any physical component. I felt her energy pouring through me with each stroke of her body over mine. Each tender kiss left me more breathless than the last and in my heart of hearts I knew my life would never be the same now that I had found my other half.

As we lay in bed I held her close to me, cuddling her small frame, though it felt like I just couldn't get her close enough. I began to wonder if my instincts foreshadowed the future. Perhaps our time together was limited. Talisa must've felt it too for she started to doubt the validity of our mission at hand.

"Why must we battle this dragon? It's madness," she said. "Only fools willingly go in search of such danger."

"It's what we do…what I do." I shifted positions so I could look upon her as I spoke. She seemed so innocent looking up at me with those crystalline eyes and that delicate soft skin. "I never knew who I was before, Talisa. I had no purpose in life but to indulge another man's whims of torture and abuse. Many nights I'd look out into the horizon and dream of the day when I would break free of that prison to forge a life anew.

Never in my wildest of dreams did I imagine I'd become a killer of killers. But that is my lot in life and I've learned to accept it as such just as my father before me.

I don't know why I must do the things I do, I only know that they must be done and I am the one to carry out such deeds."

She leaned up and kissed me. "You're a very brave and courageous man Costa Calabrese. I love you."

Her words seemed to cripple me. For a moment I wondered if I had imagined she had said such beautiful things but then my heart told me it was true and I wept.

"I don't remember the last time I heard those words spoken to me…if ever," I stammered, overcome with emotion. "I love you too."

The dawn came too quick and we began to prepare for our departure. Only one thing hampered our leaving

"Paralay is gone," Talisa told me.

"Gone? Gone where?"

"I don't know, I've searched all over."

"He has to be here somewhere."

I finished packing up some of the edible plant life and weaponry The Maori were insistent on giving us for our journey. We were hardly in a position to refuse what with most of our belongings awash at sea or still back on the cursed Misery. So we'd have to make due with spears, clubs, and leek soup.

Fighting Sark with our armaments from Talos proved difficult enough. I did not like our odds given sticks and stones while being undernourished. Our only hope lay in the finding of a random town that held a special smithery and a bake shop on our route. And now Paralay had disappeared. Things began looking very bleak.

I counseled with the Maori leader to find out about Paralay's whereabouts. Hopefully he had not gotten into any trouble with the Maori that would find him locked in a brig or stock.

"Your friend must've left under the cover of night," he told me.

"How do you know this?"

"Because my guards would've seen him otherwise. He must've slipped out while we slept."

"Where would he go?"

"You're the hunter, why not track him?" He mocked me, even after we had dispatched their White Maiden, he still held disdain in his voice for my profession. I allowed it to slip by if only for the fact that I did not have time to debate.

Paralay's antics were proving increasingly frustrating. Ever since we'd stepped foot on The Misery he'd been acting more and more rowdy and insubordinate. To run off now when we needed him to face Sark was the last straw.

I returned to Talisa who played with some of the Maori children. She looked very much at home with the young ones. My thoughts wandered and I began to wonder what our children might look like some day.

"Did you find him?" she asked, noting my return.

I didn't know what to tell her. Without Paralay it seemed even more bleak and futile to continue on with the mission at hand.

"No. He left sometime last night of his own accord. I suppose we can track him down."

She shook her head. "No. If he wants to go then let him go. We cannot wait for him. I'm tired of rewarding him when he has one of his whims take over."

I felt somewhat shocked to hear her speak so harshly but I could tell by the crease in her brow and the grit of her teeth that she'd had enough of Paralay's antics too.

"Very well," I said. "We'll press on without him. But I think we should turn back. Go home to Ravenwood and regroup."

"Don't be ridiculous, Costa. We've come too far to turn back now."

I took her gently by the shoulders and moved her away from the prying ears of the children. "I worry for your safety."

"I can take care of myself…and anyone else who comes along. So stop treating me like I'm glass. We're in this together now. The two of us. Forever."

I repeated her words with a smile on my face and in my heart. "Forever."

I didn't know where Paralay had gone and I didn't much care but I did know that he would've found a way out of the swamplands that didn't include backtracking towards the zombie crew. His resourcefulness never failed to impress me.

Sure enough I found a few good sized footprints making their way out over the only patch of dry land that seemed to exist on the accursed island. I even welcomed getting sand in my boots. Regardless of what magical properties water was touted to have the sooner I got away from it the happier I'd be.

Talisa and I marched by foot for miles taking only minimal rest. I began to fear that we had made a grave mistake, that Paralay had been whisked away somewhere by another demonic creature and Talisa and I were doomed to follow that same fate or else be forever lost on the Mysterious Lands.

I pulled out my father's journal at our next rest stop hoping to find some comfort from his words. Something, anything to help me keep going. My fingers curled back the pages past the vampires, the werewolves, and even more hideous creatures we'd yet to come face-to-face with. I began to wonder what did it all mean? Why did it matter whether these things were thwarted or not and who was to say that it was my job to do it?

Talisa leaned over my shoulder and skimmed the pages with me. I felt her body against my own as she pressed into me. My words began to pour out of me without hesitation or contemplation.

"When I was younger I'd always look for the thrill of adventure," I said. Part of me regaled Talisa with this particular story but part of me said it aloud for my own sake. "My friend Tuck and I would make it a point to go out as far as we dared in the thick of the woods just to feel as though we conquered something, that we were brave."

"I'm sure you were, even as a child."

I shook my head. "I was a fool. Even though I lived my days under the rule of a tyrant it still remained simple and straightforward. But I cursed the Fates everyday for my mundane lifestyle. I asked them to enrich my life, make me a great adventurer, and they handed me this. A hunter of demons. Will it ever end?"

We'd been sitting on a large rock that had begun to make my ass grow as numb as my soul. As I stood I lost control of the pages in the book and they were taken by a gentle breeze that came in off the shoreline. One of them pulled loose and took to the air. I reached once, twice, and missed it each time. Talisa tried to catch it as well but to no avail.

The parchment curled and wafted across the air with reckless abandon. I watched it in frustration. It seemed to beckon me to follow it and I did just that. I was at the mercy of a piece of parchment. I suppose I could've just let it go but the book of my father's writings were all I had left of him until I found him again. And in that realization I remembered my true course.

It wasn't about defeating the demons. And it wasn't about the adventure, or carving a name for myself. All of this had to do with my father Cain Coleridge and my attempts to know who this man was…or is. His journals had led the way thus far and they would continue to aid me in the most mysterious of ways.

Talisa and I hurried after the loose journal page and it brought us to the answer we sought. Safety, salvation, a tiny village met us just over the horizon. We looked at each other not believing our own eyes and having to count on each other to discern reality from a mirage. It was real all right.

We hurried there, almost running, hoping to encounter friendly faces in the village. We had no maps, no sense of direction from being turned about on the high seas, finding signs of life out in the midst of this swamp and jungle didn't exactly inspire tranquility but we had no other option at our disposal.

"I wonder if Paralay is here," Talisa said as we drew closer to the tiny town.

"If there's a tavern I'd bet money on it," I replied.

As we came closer, we noticed that the town didn't grow any larger. The seemingly forced perspective of a town in the distance in fact was the actual size. The housing structures were an odd mushroom shape made of solid wood and coral. People, little people, packed the streets at every turn. I'd not seen such hustle and bustle since my childhood home of Rhone, and it had been a mining community thought to have riches hiding within the lands.

I grabbed the nearest person a small man who held a stature of about four feet.

"You there," I said, "Where are we?"

"This is the one and only Draconia."

"Draconia?" I repeated. "I've never heard of it."

He almost laughed. "Draconia is the largest tourist village for fans of Dragon Isle. Where have you been?"

"On the wrong side of the island it appears," Talisa told him.

"Oh no don't go on the west side, there's nothing there for miles."

"So we noticed."

He smiled then, his toothy grin almost blinding us. "That's because everyone is over here, in Draconia."

"And this is all inspired by dragons?" I asked.

"Yes, they're magical creatures."

"They're destroyers of nations," I said crimping tighter to the man's arm. He grew alarmed and I opted to let him go. No sense in wearing out our welcome before we ever really set foot inside.

"Come Costa," Talisa said pulling away from the man. "Let's get indoors. This accursed sun is blistering my fine skin."

I'd had my run in with little people before only much smaller, the size of a thimble in fact. These folks residing in Draconia looked to be an entire race of Dwarves. I had never had the distinct pleasure of meeting a Dwarf in all my days. There were a great many things I was learning on this trek.

We walked until we found what looked to be a pub and forced our way inside, ducking our heads and craning our necks just to get through the door. We were greeted by a cheery faced female Dwarf with dark hair in a peasant dress.

"Ah, visitors," she exclaimed. "Will you be sitting or would you prefer to kneel at the bar."

"Um…we'll sit."

She brought us to a table that looked only big enough to suit one full grown human and we lumbered over to sit as best we could.

"What'll you be having then?"

"Anything, we're starving," Talisa said. She didn't seem to mind the cramped quarters as much as I did. But I soon didn't mind either. I found myself staring across at her, unable to pull my gaze from her beautiful face until she blushed in embarrassment.

Our hostess came back to the table with plates that appeared half full at first glance until I realized the portion sizes were doled out for the Dwarf race.

"Excuse me," I said before she left. "I just find it curious that a town which prides themselves on being a tourist attraction wouldn't make provisions for other larger races."

"Costa don't be rude," Talisa scolded.

I shrugged. "Just an observation."

"No worries," the woman said. "Thing of it is, you folks are our first humans."

"Really? So an Elf with short, dark hair didn't pass through this way?"

"Can't say that he did."

As the woman left us to enjoy our meal Talisa looked at me and sighed. "No Paralay."

I could tell she was disgruntled. She worried after him like a kid brother, we both did. It concerned me that he had just disappeared without giving us word. I wondered if my growing relationship with Talisa had wounded him more than he let on.

We ate…quickly. Even with the small portions Talisa left most of her meal on her plate. I was happy to indulge in her food as well. Then came the arduous task of locating the town smithery. It did not surprise me when they told us the town held no such shop. However it did carry a souvenir shop, laden with dragon fixtures no doubt.

I urged to continue with the mission at hand citing that if night fell we wouldn't be able to fit in the half-size beds that the local inn no doubt held. But Talisa's curiosity was peaked and she insisted that we have a look at the souvenirs.

Little did we know in the midst of that small town we'd find one of the finest craftsmen to come along since Talos. The small shop included hand carved statues, religious icons, and fantasy figurines.

I marveled at the attention to detail in every image noting epic battles known throughout myths and legend. Included amongst the displays stood one titled "Hunter" that depicted a man that looked something like my father standing against a massive, hulking shape too gruesome to look upon without getting chills.

The shop keeper sat upon a finely crafted stool, another of his creations no doubt, and watched us in silence as we walked amongst his work. Finally I came over to him and looked him in the eye as he sat.

"Tell me good sir," I said in a low whisper. "Have you ever forged weapons."

"We are a peaceful community. There are no need for weapons here."

"The world outside these walls is dangerous indeed. Has no one ever asked you before?"

A smile curled his lips and I knew then that he held a secret. He stood, motioned me to the back with him, where the others could not hear. He pulled away false wall panels to reveal a discreetly hidden collection of weapons. Swords, three in all, lined the walls. They were diverse in size, one long, one short, and a third of similar design that extended far from the hilt in a cross-like manner.

I reached out to touch the beautiful blades and the tiny artisan halted me. He took the time to pull the blades down and hand them across to me so I could better marvel at their structure.

Each hilt had been fashioned of human remains. Each blade forged and molded to the sharpest steel. They were lightweight and very functional. Any one of them would be adequate protection from an enemy attacker. For the dragon Sark I wanted them all.

"These are fine blades, my friend. How much do you want for them?"

He shook his head. "We don't sell weapons here."

"A trade then?"

He raised a brow. His leathery skin wrinkled up in question as he pondered my suggestion. "What did you have in mind?"

"Classic striking staffs from the Maori clan."

"Maori? They actually exist?"

I nodded.

"Let me see!"

Sitting back in his chair, he looked as though he were salivating as I brought the staffs to him. With his craftsman's eye he looked once, twice, and even three times over the structures of the weapons. Then he uttered but one word. "Beautiful."

"A deal then?" I asked.

"I always knew the Maori were not just legend. Seeing taiha such as these only proves justification for my instincts. Yes, you have a deal demon hunter."

"How did you know who I was?" I asked as we traded the weapons. The small man stepped down from his seat, making him look much tinier than he already was as he walked across the shop to collect one of his treasures.

He came back and handed me the figurine depicting the likeness of my father battling evil incarnate.

"For you," he said. "Keep it."

I nodded. No more words needing to be spoken. My father's legend reached far and wide. Captain Davies knew me, why should I be surprised that this Draconian Dwarf would know me? My lineage was grand indeed.

I returned to Talisa, our new weapons in hand. She looked me up and down, her eyes like fire as they took in the steel I held in front of me.

"Any longer and I would've just had you dispatch the little fool and be done with it."

"What?" To hear her say such words, in such a harsh tone unnerved me.

"Do you know why this town of littles is flourishing? Because Sark and his dragon brethren regard them only as snacks. Bite size little morsels to snatch up in between feedings on human bodies." She stared at me a moment and then pointed to the bone blades in my hands. "Don't believe me? Where do you think the shopkeeper got the remains to make such fine handles?"

"Perhaps you're right," I said handing over the cross-shaped sword to Talisa. "That just means we have to double our efforts to get rid of such a menace."

She looked over the sword for a moment and then handed it back to me, opting for the double blades instead.

"You keep that one. I feel more comfortable with the other ones."

I'd never known Talisa to welcome a weapon in her hand. It appeared she was changing on this journey. It seemed a lot of things were.

Chapter Nine
Dragon's Lair

The Draconian weapon maker indulged our request to locate the nesting grounds of any dragons in the area. He pointed us north, towards what they called the Roof of the World. The Draconians insisted that the dragons were beautiful creatures. Precious beasts rarely seen but that should be respected for their majesty like a unicorn or Pegasus. I didn't bother reminding them that the horned and winged horse from centuries past had never been known for burning entire villages to the ground with a single breath.

I had expected something of a cave to house our winged foe but Talisa and I found ourselves climbing the crest of a cliff. Our breath drew heavy and ragged and our senses were diminished by an odor most foul.

"What on earth could smell so bad?" Talisa asked, going so far as to put up her shorter sword so she could cover her nose with her free hand.

I tolerated the stench as best I could, wanting instead to take in the odor and pinpoint its nuances to decide whether or not it proved useful to us. The mix seemed something of charcoal, excrement, and rotten flesh. I could barely stomach it. Finally about halfway up the cliff we found the reason for our discontent.

It looked like a nest that you would see from any manner of bird only on a much larger scale. The entire top of the cliff housed the nesting grounds of our dragon, Sark. Sticks and grass weren't the only things making up the nest itself. Human remains, some still fully intact, others mostly devoured, filled out the holes. Sark himself was nowhere in sight.

As I came upon the scene first I tried to dissuade Talisa from approaching and taking in such a horrible vision. In her rebellion she pushed past me to take a look for herself. She didn't seem fazed at all.

"All dead," she said. "Such a shame."

"Where did they come from?" I wondered aloud. "No misguided traveler would accidentally wander up a mountain top."

"He must go out to feed. With the wingspan of a dragon Sark could go anywhere. We're lucky he didn't find us out at sea."

It was a sobering thought and entirely true. According to my father there were none more deadly than a dragon. I had read his passages at length before we had ever set out on this mission. I'd found nothing to put me at ease. Cain Coleridge had merely penned one warning in regard to dragons:

"In your foolish pride do not attempt to battle a dragon head on anywhere at anytime. For none are a more deadly creature than the devil's pets and the world is their playground. Pray now you never need face one. To do so will surely be your death...demon hunter."

I suppose now would be the hour where I would find out if he were right in his assumption. We could hear some very distinctive noises coming from just below where we were standing. Someone, or something, had been following us. I'd allowed whomever it was to believe they had the upper hand but now the game was up.

Reaching over the side I caught the intruder as they were coming up. To my surprise he was wily and quick and slipped free of my grasp. We both drew our swords and came up blades to each other's necks in a standstill. That's when I realized I held my weapon to the throat of Paralay.

He laughed and withdrew his. I kept mine where it was. Any other time I would've been happy to see him, at the moment my fury overrode my sense of friendship.

"What gives Costa?"

"Where the hell have you been?"

"I thought I'd get a head start, let the two of you sleep in."

"How kind of you," I said in sarcasm. "But there's only one reason you would want to do that and it had nothing to do with a notion of generosity towards Talisa and I."

"What then?" he asked, eyes squinting.

Paralay had decked himself out since we'd last seen him. Whether he'd gathered equipment and clothing from the Maoris or the Draconians couldn't be said for sure but I did note heavy leathers covering his torso and some loose coin purses hanging from a leather bit wrapped double around his waist. Nothing out of the ordinary for a traveling man but to the discerning eye, the eye of a hunter who is trained to notice anomalies, one thing stood out.

"More likely you decided to go in search of the Dragon Dagger."

Using my sword I quickly cut free the only coin purse that stood full against the others. It sat at Paralay's mid-back, tucked away where others could not see. He tried to stop me but I moved much swifter than he.

Sure enough inside the pouch lay the dagger. The hilt was crested with jewels, the blade itself curved almost the length of a scimitar. A magnificent treasure to be certain, but one that did not belong to any of us.

"Once a thief, always a thief," I said.

"Damn you Calabrase!" Paralay shouted. "We don't all have famous names we can ride off of. Some of us have to make ends meet the best way we know how."

"Do you think I enjoy this plight I'm forced to endure?" I asked him.

"Quiet, the both of you," Talisa said. "Your voices carry on the wind up here."

"So?" Paralay asked.

"So if you haven't noticed we are standing on the dinner table of our enemy who is sure to return soon."

She was right…how I hated that. As if waiting for his cue Sark made his presence known with a most horrible shriek. It pierced the air and rattled the earth under our feet as he made his appearance. Nothing in my father's journal could have prepared me for such a sight. This was no ordinary dragon, it was straight from the pit of hell.

Sark held the form of a regular winged beast, massive in shape and structure, but without skin and scale. No wings flapped, only shafts of bone sprouted from his back. His tail was a large stretch of bone. Talons and feet were replaced with bone. Every rib and tooth were visible. The eye sockets held no orbs. The devilish horns didn't sprout through the skin of the forehead, they merely grew up from the skull.

He crept up over the side as though he'd been hiding in wait for us all. Out of fear or foolishness Paralay decided now would be our best chance at success by knocking Sark off the side to his death. He raced forward, blade in hand. In his rage I feared he would get himself killed. Sure enough Sark needed do nothing more than swat him away with the bat of a hand to send the Elf sprawling straight into the lap of one of the human remains.

By now the thing had bested the side of the cliff and its full form stood before us. Its mass blotted out the sun. Talisa and I became his next intended targets. I came to stand beside her. If this were to be the end I intended to go down fighting next to the woman I loved.

Sark drew back his bony skull and lashed forward with his attack. It did not come from teeth or talon but from the fire in his belly. My first reaction was to shield Talisa. As I threw my arms around her our swords crossed together in front of us. Bone and steel linked up and as they did they reacted as something of a shield. Sark's flame tore over us, around our bodies and over our heads but it did not burn our flesh.

In his anger he drew back to blast us again and it was then that I saw the black heart displayed inside his ribcage. It looked as though it floated there, unhinged. A heart was a heart regardless of nature. It was a source of power that spread life and once extinguished would hopefully fell its host. Without my crossbow at hand there was only one thing at my disposal that could be used as an airborne weapon. The Dragon Dagger.

They said it held magic, I only hoped that were true. With hope and a prayer to guide my shaky hand I let the dagger fly. It sailed with precision up between the third and fourth rib plunging straight into the dark heart of Sark just as he went to emit another blast of fire from his mouth. The fire never reached us, instead Sark swallowed it back down causing the bones of his skull to implode from the pressure. His head literally erupted flame.

Pieces of bone fell down around us. With the host head and heart now gone it would only be a matter of time before the body came crashing down as well. Talisa and I moved as fast as we could to take Paralay back down the cliff. I only looked back once to take in the sight where a dragon, the devil's pet, had been felled at the hands of a demon hunter. That would be one for the books. An entry even my father had never been able to enter. Somewhere inside me I felt pride stirring up and then the madness of reality struck me cold in the face again.

What I saw I could not believe and I began to wonder if everything that had happened since we boarded The Misery had been a dream. Captain Davies and the Regulators; the Maori; the White Maiden; even Sark all had to be a wondrous dream. That was the only way to explain the fact that as we made our way down the cliff I found myself staring face-to-face with me.

"Surprised to see me."

"Surprised to see me," I replied.

My legs grew shaky and I had to release Paralay from my grasp. The other me smiled, his grin marked by protruding fangs.

"This was really the only way for it to end…brother," he said.

My mouth fell agape. A brother? How could it be so? But before that question could be answered he extended a long, skinny finger and beckoned for Talisa. "Come to me my darling."

"What? No!"

I turned to protect the love of my life only to find that she wasn't quite herself anymore. Her beautiful eyes had grown dark as night, her teeth pulled down into sharp points. She held the wound upon her neck which I only now came to realize as bite marks.

"Talisa, no," I begged. "Stay with me!"

As I reached for her hand she reared back and struck me full force across the cheek. Her strength had grown tenfold and the blow sent me spilling to the ground in a heap. I watched semi-conscious as she made her way to the side of the vampire version of myself, my apparent brother from the dark side. They looked like the bride and groom from hell and as they disappeared into the night I could only imagine if that was where they were headed.

I had promised to protect her from harm and I had failed. Now they had her. This must be why my father had warned against falling in love. The pleasure did not outweigh the pain I felt as my heart broke.

And so I screamed. Sometimes all you have is the scream. I wailed into the sky that had turned dark with ruined ash from the corpse of Sark. My scream echoed across the lands out in the distance where not only my father had disappeared but now Talisa as well and with her went my soul.

I would have to find both of them now if I ever had a chance of coming back from the darkness, back from the pit of hell. Without Talisa in my life I was emotionally ruined. Without my father I wasn't whole. What would be left of the Demon Hunter now?

Chapter Ten
Once A Hunter

"Demons are everywhere. They come at you when you least expect it disguised as your friends, your family, someone you love. They can even crawl into your mind and disguise themselves as you.

They are quite hideous though they've been known to hold recognizable human qualities. Half beast, half man. They stand upright with hunched shoulders, a devils tail and hoofed feet balancing them.

Demons are driven by desire alone, much like humans who chase dreams of wealth and lust. But the demons have only one desire…to kill. They are quite literally heartless. That puts me on even ground with them and gives me added advantage to the hunters of the past. I no longer have my heart either."

As I sat extolling the distinct description of the demon lot and my tales of pursuit to the tavern dwellers of Gryphant's pub I couldn't help but feel a certain amount of poetic justice.

When I had been a boy, in this very town, in this very bar, I'd sit and listen to travelers speak of their journeys in such a manner that it captivated me. Now I was the one telling the stories to a new lot of young men with adventure in their hearts.

"What happened to your heart?" one of the young women asked. She had a beautiful face to be sure with pouty lips and a pretty smile. But she was nothing compared to the woman who had tore my heart out. My only reprieve came from the fact that she had not literally pulled my heart from my chest like any good demon.

"It's a useless appendage to have in my line of work," I told her. "I got rid of it."

"That's a bunch of horseshit," someone called from the back of the room. When he stepped up into the light I saw it to be my old friend Paralay who chastised me.

I'd not seen him in months. After our time on Dragon Isle we returned to Ravenwood…just the two of us. Telling my mentor Talos the circumstances of how we lost his only daughter had been one of the most unbearable moments of my life.

I didn't even know what to say. Someone who resembled me swept Talisa away in a vampire-like frenzy. It made no sense to me and I had seen it with my own eyes. But Talos had known, he'd known about my brother Cris, said my father had many dalliances in his time and one night he'd bedded down with a vampire who had taken the form of a normal woman.

A child of both demon hunter and vampire was born to the world. That abomination was my brother Cris. I surmised that as the heartache my father wrote of in his journal. Talos had known all of this the entire time and he'd not told me. That felt like another betrayal. Was there no one I could trust in this world? I couldn't live with that reminder day in and day out so I left Ravenwood and came home.

Gryphant had been rebuilt since the initial demon attack so many years before. Homes had been refurbished, businesses continued to grow, but nothing would ever feel the same as it had before. At every street corner, on every wall, I saw death. Gryphant had changed its face but its soul still shed blood. Or perhaps it was me who was the one who changed, as my former good friend pointed out.

"Costa Calabrese came from shit, that's how he learned to dole it out so well."

"Get the hell out of here, Paralay."

"That's a fine story you told just now, but false. The man who you speak of, the demon hunter, had more backbone than the drunken lout I look upon now."

One thing I've come to realize as I get older is that I hate people. I told them not to push me and they did it anyway. Paralay pushed me now and I no longer had the tether to hold back my raw rage. That calm, rational Costa who compartmentalized things had gone with Talisa.

I exploded up from my seat at the bar and smashed my still full glass across Paralay's head. He always wore his hair closely cropped so his skull sustained most of the blow and it sent him spilling backwards over one of the tables. I knew that wouldn't be the last of it though.

Paralay had fight in him. I'd seen him battle back from the brink of death against foes twice his size. He didn't disappoint now. Springing to his feet he launched himself into my stomach and simultaneously slammed the small of my back into the edge of the bar.

As I winced in pain I couldn't help remembering our very first fight out at Ravenwood so many years before. Each of us had been trying to prove to the other who was the better man. Some things never changed.

I wrapped my arm up and over Paralay's head as he peppered my stomach with hard punches. His assault was relentless even as I squeezed the breath from him. I couldn't withstand many more blows to the stomach without retching booze so I reached down to Paralay's belt and plucked him up off the floor. Using all the strength I had in me I tossed the elf up over my head and back behind the bar where he landed with what must've been a lot of pain smashing over bottles of liquor.

Satisfied with my win I reached out for the only salvageable bottle of brandy that remained on the bar and saluted the crowd before tipping it back. As I drank Paralay popped up from behind me with drinking glasses in hand and shattered them across both sides of my head.

My eyes rolled into the back of my head, I dropped the bottle to the ground, and I followed falling unconscious across the floor. When I came to I found myself propped up against the wall of the pub outside in the street. Paralay sat across from me holding a wet cloth to his wounds.

"The owner kicked us out," he told me. "He said demon hunter or not he wouldn't have his business destroyed by a drunken brawl."

"Why are you here?"

"I'm looking for a demon hunter, know any?"

"No."

"What happened to you?"

I stood, shaky, but ready to walk away from him. "I think you know the answer to that question."

"It isn't your fault what happened to Talisa."

"Isn't it? I was supposed to protect her and I failed. What part of that isn't my fault?"

"We were both there, Costa. And besides that all three of us knew the danger we were facing when we went out there. Talisa knew what she was up against. She didn't need our protection. She could always take care of herself. It's now that she needs our help and you're just going to walk away."

Even for all his words to try and stop me I didn't. I walked. I turned my back on Paralay for the second time and I walked away without a second glance. This time he called after me.

"She loves you."

Now I broke down. It felt as though my heart had been sliced with a red hot knife and all the twisted emotions of love, hate, despair, and anguish came spilling out of the open wound. Funny, I just swore I no longer had a heart. Seems I had been wrong.

Paralay gave me my moment. When I was ready I turned back to him with fresh tears running down my face. There had been a time before when I never wanted anyone to see me cry. To me it showed weakness and didn't contribute anything to day-to-day life. Now I didn't give a damn what people thought of me.

"I know how we can get her back." He told me.

"How?"

"Witchcraft."

"You hate sorcery."

"For Talisa I'd do anything. What about you, Costa?"

"I'd give up my soul."

"You may have to do just that."

Chapter Eleven
Magic

Paralay decided to rest before the long journey ahead. I sought reinforcement from my father. His words no longer gave me the comfort that they used to. What I read off the page now I took as little more than science and superstition. Any inspiration I might have derived from my father's teachings before were now reduced to pure and simple tactical facts.

I had researched on vampires before when we'd faced Lord LeCarde and his clan. But I needed to know how Talisa had been turned and what, if anything, I could do to change her back. Everything else stayed a secondary thought on my mind until I read a passage in my father's book:

Vampires seek to expand their clan by seducing mortals. Once the unsuspecting is in their grip the vampire will puncture their skin, usually upon the neck with their teeth. This is something of a rite of passage and will begin the transformation from human to vampire.

The human has only one chance to escape such a horrible fate. They will not become a full vampire until their first mortal kill. Before that time the vampire lot that impregnated them with blood must be destroyed.

For all the myths and legends of the vampire clans they were nothing more than Satan's lackeys. If they bled I could kill them. I'd done it before and I would surely do it again. Brother or not nothing could keep me away from Talisa. If I had to dispatch my own father to bring her back I would do it.

In the morning Paralay and I hunted the witches.

"Where did you find out about this coven?" I asked.

"Master Talos. He said they came together from four families of untold magical power, one from each family. Bliss, Charity, Hope, and Faith."

"Why would they help us?"

"We'll have to persuade them."

"Persuade them how?"

"You better let me do it. I have more experience wooing ladies," he smiled.

I was in no mood for Paralay's charms. "I'd just as soon persuade them with my steel."

"Keep your weapons sheathed," he warned. "I don't want them on the defensive before we even get a chance to explain our situation."

As we walked on I noticed the area around me growing very familiar. The burnt out trees, a faint scent of charcoal, sawdust littered over the path to cover tracks.

"Where are these witches located?"

"In Rhone."

Rhone. My birthplace. The very last time I had seen Rhone my mother had been killed. I don't remember how or why or who I just remember death and that my young life had been turned upside down ever since.

Funny thing, when I stepped foot back inside my birthplace it felt like nothing more than any other town in any other place. This was no longer any home I knew.

Unlike Gryphant, Rhone had not been rebuilt. The shattered remains of what was once a prosperous city now lay scattered in large chunks of debris. No housing, no pubs, no signs of life at all were present.

"Are you sure we're in the right place?" I asked.

"Yes. Talos said Rhone…why?"

I shook my head even as a chill ran up over my spine. "No reason."

"Who goes there?"

The voice rang out like a chime on the air. We withdrew our weapons even after Paralay said not to. Both Paralay and I had gone back to basics once returning to Ravenwood. He with his dual short swords, I with my crossbow. They did little at the moment when we couldn't see our attackers.

I decided to speak openly, try to flush out the witches with words. It's something Talisa would've done.

"We seek your service."

"Of what do you seek?"

Before I could answer another voice called out across the skies.

"They seek a woman!"

"Yes," I replied, feeling foolish shouting to the sky. "Talos, the famed Master of Weapons, his only daughter has been taken away by evil. We need to get her back."

Finally the witches made themselves known. They did not hold the appearance I expected. I'd heard witches were wicked looking creatures, devoid of any manner of feminine beauty.

These women were lovely. All four of them had hair down to their waist, blonde, red, black, and brunette. The color of their hair seemed the only thing that separated them. Each one had long, flowing dresses as dark as night and lips that would bring envy to the purest of roses.

I held my breath as they approached. One of them broke from the pack and came right towards me. Her eyes, a rainbow of colors not discernable as one solid, stared deep into my own. She took my chin in her hand and smiled at me.

"There's more to it than that, isn't there boy?

"Will you help us or not?" I said pulling free of her grip only to fall into the hands of the redhead.

"Not until you openly admit your hidden truth."

"What truth?"

"We told you everything," Paralay said. "Come Costa, we don't need them."

"Tis true love you seek," the redhead said setting her hand upon my cheek.

"Yes," I admitted. "She was taken from me."

The dark one stepped up then and the others fell in line behind her. "We are not the devil's spawn as those who don't understand our ways have labeled us so harshly."

Their story sounded much like my own and my father's before me. Labeled as Pariah's even though we only ever sought to do good.

"Our coven follows the right hand path. White magic – good magic," the dark one said, she introduced herself as Faith, the blonde one Hope, the redhead Charity, and the brunette Bliss.

"We will help you find your love," Bliss added. "But we will need something first."

Paralay removed a pack from his shoulders. He'd been carrying it around since we agreed to hunt for Talisa. Now he relinquished it to the witches.

Faith removed the item from the bag which turned out to be the head of a ram. She smiled. "You've done your research."

"I don't know why you need it, I was just told to bring it," Paralay told her.

I glanced at my friend but could not keep his gaze. All the while I'd been meandering around like a drunken fool he had been setting things in motion to get Talisa back. At that moment I felt like such a failure. So when the witches instructed me to follow their lead I did not hesitate, I did not ask questions. I did what I was told so that I could get her back.

They cast a circle with stones and had me stand in the center. Then they called to the four elements of earth, fire, air, and water, what they called the Lords of the Watchtowers.

"This is a safe space," Charity told me. "You can speak freely here."

"My entire life I have lived for myself. I only truly ever felt alive when I was staring death in the face. Until the day when I first saw her and realized I wanted to start living for someone else."

"Look inside yourself," Hope told me. "Who do you see?"

"Talisa."

As I spoke the images of my mind spread out across the sky for all to see. Paralay stepped back away from the circle with his eyes and mouth opened in shock. I knew his aversion to all things magical.

The images portrayed memories of Talisa from my mind's eye in happier times. They seemed almost real enough to grasp and then she spoke.

"Please don't cry for me. I was not whole until the day I met you. I was born again when you loved me. And your love for me will keep me alive for eternity."

She blew me a kiss and then the images shifted. Talisa was no longer the sweet and beautiful girl that I had fallen in love with, instead her teeth grew to fangs and her eyes went bloodshot. She was a vampire.

I heard Faith speaking, and then Hope, Charity, and Bliss joined her in something of a chant. "You will not find love. Everyday will be the same. You may as well not have even been born."

"What is this dark magic?" I heard Paralay call.

"Great One, we offer up this sacrifice to you O'Lord!" Faith cried out holding up the head of the ram Paralay had slain. The weather seemed to shift at her calling. Dark clouds rolled in over a once perfect sky. Fire sprung up around the circle of stones trapping me inside.

"Your woman sits at the side of the Dark Lord," Charity told me. "That's where you'll find her…if you survive!"

On her words a gateway opened beneath my feet. I began to descend into Hell. Without hesitation Paralay ran past the witches and jumped the fire to try and catch me. Instead, he wound up being pulled with me straight into the bowels of hell.

Chapter Twelve
Hell

We were surrounded by brick, walls of brick and little else. It looked to be something of a tunnel. I remembered falling but not much more. Paralay sat at my side reluctant to move.

"Where are we?"

"In Hell."

"Come on then, Costa. Pull out your writings and see what your father says about traversing the pit of evil."

I located my father's journal and found very little to go on.

"It says to always carry a map when in the realm of subversive spirits," I told Paralay. "And to travel in good company. Always knowing who your companions are before setting out."

"No worries there," he replied.

"Easy for you to say."

"I know you feel wronged, cheated even. But Talisa turned her back on me as well. It's not just you who lost her, Costa, it's both of us."

"You're right, I'm sorry."

He set his hand upon my shoulder to reassure me. "Don't apologize. Let's just go in there and bring her back. Are you ready to walk through Hell with me?"

I reached my own hand up and clasped his in a gesture of friendship. For a moment my heart felt something of itself again knowing I had someone willing to fight at my side.

We headed down a tunnel towards nothingness. I waited for Hell to jump out at me. I expected my own personal demons to leap out from the shadows and try to bring me to my knees. It seemed very quiet for the bowels of Hell, perhaps too quiet. In my travels I'd always come to know silence as a great indicator of trouble ahead. Quite the antithesis of what one would expect, but factual nonetheless.

Paralay knew it too. The still of the air had an eerie chill to it. Something was destined to leap from the shadows and detain us or die trying. We edged along slowly, Paralay watching the rear as I took point. When my sense of danger grew so extraordinary that I felt my gut turn over I stopped. My gut instinct never failed me.

Up ahead at a crossing point a pack of wild dogs blocked our forward movement. These were no ordinary dogs, the Hounds of Hell stood before us with blood soaked spittle lacing through their teeth. Apparently they'd already killed tonight but that wasn't enough to stop them from feeding again.

The Hounds were known to protect their Dark Lords. They held no preference for who came their way, all were suspect. No bias, only bloodshed. Any normal man would be torn asunder from just one. Paralay and I stood against several hounds. But then again we were not normal men.

"Be ready," I told Parlay as I watched with a keen eye and studied the limbs braced against the stone flooring. The eyes flared into deep shades of red. Their snarls grew in capacity until loud barks came from the pack in unison. They prepared to move on us.

They started a run towards us, each moved individually but they kept a solid unit, a pack of wolves made up of many but fighting as one. It was something of a military strategy, one I'd learned from Talos. Before that time I'd always fancied myself to be alone, now I regarded having my own pack (Talisa and Paralay) as something that should not be dismissed.

But the good of the many still rode on the shoulders of the leader. They were only as good as their weakest link. Using that knowledge for my own advantage, and the attainment of victory for me and Paralay, I would exploit that weak link by picking them off one at a time. Using my crossbow I set the first one in my sights and fired. The arrow bolt tore through him with great ease.

At the same time Paralay used his best defense, the two short swords, and took down another advancing predator. The next round belonged to me. I had to reload swiftly and fire with pinpoint accuracy as the dogs came in at blistering speeds.

This time when the arrow flew I managed to take down two of them at the same time. Blood burst from their heavily muscled torsos and they landed in a combined mess upon the floor.

One would think the deaths of their comrades would cause the others to flee in fear, but they continued in pursuit even more aggressively. Now we would have to change our tactics. I shouldered my crossbow and pulled my own sword from its sheath. Then Paralay and I advanced meeting the dogs as they came for us.

It was a fine, bloody display. When it was over a man and his elf stood tall amongst the dead hounds at their feet.

"I hardly broke a sweat," Paralay said with a grin.

Not all dogs would be so easy. Those in the guise of men were especially detrimental.

At the far exit a beast appeared to be watching us. He stood back watching and waiting. He stood with stooped shoulders, and a head full of teeth. Large, sinewy muscles bulged from beneath layers of thick fur as he watched us with dark eyes.

"What by the gods is that abomination?" Paralay asked in a voice so low I almost lost his words on the air.

"Werewolf," I replied. "Half-beast, half-man."

"Why doesn't he attack us?"

It was a fair question. The fact that I did not have the answer didn't unnerve me as much as the fact that the werewolf didn't attack us. I knew not the ways of werewolves except to say that this one held familiarity to it.

"I've seen this bitch before."

Paralay's shock made his words much more vocal. "That's a woman?"

The werewolf began to move forward. She lumbered, favoring a wound in her upper shoulder, an old wound inflicted by my father some time before. I'd never forgotten that night. The night I'd found out what Cain Coleridge was, not the bounty hunter he'd claimed to be but a killer of killers, would forever be branded in my memory.

The were-bitch had bitten him that night, almost killed him because of me. Now I had an opportunity to right that wrong. I stood my ground, Paralay at my side, and we readied for battle as the wolf came at us.

One swing of a wild paw told me this would be harder to accomplish than I originally thought. The wind of the blow tore past me and I just managed to jump back in time before being gutted.

I took a swing with my sword and Paralay with his. We wound up crossing our own steel together. The beast was quick, that much I remembered. Her strength and fury hadn't subsided through the years either. If anything she'd grown even more temperamental.

She came at us again, both paws flailing through the air. We had no choice but to back up or risk getting our heads smashed together. Eventually we ran out of the room. A wall at our backs pinned us down. We were ripe for the killing. One single shot from the werewolf would be our demise. I stepped out in front of Paralay.

"When she strikes run past us," I told him.

"No way, we're in this together remember?" he replied. "Between the two of us we can stop her. She's outnumbered."

My heart nearly stopped as I saw that wasn't entirely true. The odds became even as another werewolf came from behind the first. One would be hard enough to handle, two nearly impossible.

For the first time in a long time I felt fear. But it was not fear for myself, or even for Paralay. I feared never seeing Talisa again. That she'd be lost to the darkness forever. That was enough fuel to fire me up for an attack. But I found reinforcements from a surprising source.

The she-wolf took a hit, a very damaging blow, but it didn't come from Paralay or I, it came from behind. Wolf on wolf, they engaged each other with such hatred and fury that we'd be fools to try to intervene in any manner.

"Why are they fighting each other?"

"Territorial rights?" It was just a guess on my part. For all my studying and preparing for my life as a hunter I still found surprises every single day.

Paralay and I were still in danger. The wolves battled back and forth, tearing at each other limb from limb right in front of us. We couldn't go around, over, or through them. Once one defeated the other we'd be back where we started.

"We need to be ready to strike whichever wins," I told Paralay.

He nodded just as the fight ended. The female fell to the ground, her throat exposed from a large gash from the male's claws. The male stood over her, he'd been battered but not enough for us to relax. We'd had no time to plan, our instincts took over at that point and we landed a double attack on the werewolf. He stopped us both cold.

It would never cease to amaze me how the wolf could act so much like a man while looking like a beast. The werewolf caught our swords in his hands and even as the blades sliced open both palms he still held fast to them, pulling them from our grasps.

Weaponless I went for my crossbow. Pulling it from my shoulder I knocked loose my bag and sent the contents spilling to the ground. My father's journal fell at the werewolf's feet. Disregarding the swords and us he reached down to pick up the journal. That would've been the perfect opportunity to strike but something halted me. Some internal feeling of familiarity, something much deeper than anything I'd ever felt before.

I looked upon the werewolf, he seemed fascinated by the journal. Sounding so anguished it would break even the hardest of hearts the beast let out a loud howl. It bounced off the walls and echoed deep into my mind.

"He's calling for others, shoot him!" Paralay said.

Off instinct I fired my crossbow. The bolt whistled through the air and pierced the werewolf in the chest. He stumbled back, blood bubbled up through his teeth and poured from his mouth.

For a moment I wondered if the arrow wasn't enough to do the job but then the wolf succumbed and fell backwards against the far wall. He slid down in a strained effort to keep himself upright and managed to leave a trail of blood behind him on the wall. That's when I knew my shot had landed fatally. The bolt had gone straight through, piercing his heart. But the wolf didn't die right away. He sat upon the floor, still clutching the journal.

"We need to finish him. Take the head right?" Paralay said moving forward and collecting his sword.

He stood over the wolf, sword over his head ready to strike down. The wolf didn't put up a fight. His head drooped forward as though he knew what was coming. He looked very sad. Then he began to change.

I halted Paralay before he landed his death blow. "Wait, something's happening."

We watched as the beast turned back to the man he once was. As the transformation progressed I noted the structure of the face, the likeness of the hair, it all came screaming back to me. But when I saw the eyes, the dark eyes of knowledge and despair, that's when I knew.

"Father?" I muttered.

The transformation completed and sure enough before us sat my father, Cain Coleridge, bleeding through the chest where I had shot him. The she-wolf had bit him that day some years back when I'd interrupted his duties. Once bitten the transformation began to eat away at him rapidly. Knowing that he didn't have a lot of time left Cain had left Gryphant in haste. It all made sense now. He had told me as such in the letter he wrote me.

It seems the sands in the hour glass have dissipated at an alarming rate. There is only one choice...I must finish this now! Heed my warning this time and do not seek me. I tell you this for your own safety.

You are free Costa, have the courage to follow your heart.

"What have I done," I said aloud sinking to my knees in front of Cain.

He tried to speak then, coughing up blood at first and then finally managing to get out his words.

"Talos taught you well."

I shook my head, tears filling my eyes and anguish filling my already broken heart.

"No, it was you…it was always you."

"My wounds are grave son."

"I'm sorry, I'm so sorry."

"Have no regrets, Costa. You did what you had to do. It's up to you to end this now."

"How?"

"Use consciousness, reason, compassion, and love as your weapons. The demons will be rendered helpless."

"I cannot do it alone."

Cain glanced over to Paralay. "You're not alone. You never were. You're lucky in that regard. Going through life facing down demons by yourself is a lonely man's work. You've grown into quite a man Costa, people are drawn to you. Find a little more faith in yourself and those around you."

"I have so many questions for you…why did you leave me? Why did you come back? Why didn't you ever tell me I had a brother?"

"I can only tell you I have always loved you. I did what I thought was best at the time. I'm dying son. This is your time now. Costa, you need to do what you think is best."

Paralay put his hand on my shoulder and whispered. "Talisa."

One name, a whispered reminder of all that was good and right in the world. I could not let her light be extinguished by a darkness that I'd sworn to fight, that my father had sworn to fight. I could not let that darkness envelope me either. Now, at this my darkest hour, I had to be stronger than I ever imagined possible.

"I have to go, father," I said taking his hand.

"I'll wait here." He tried to manage something of a smile and then his hand slipped from my own and my father was gone again, this time for good.

I stood over him watching as the last traces of werewolf faded and left only a man in its place. He seemed so peaceful.

"We can't just leave him here," I said softly, still disbelieving what I had done.

"There's no time," Paralay told me.

He almost had to drag me away. As we went, I kept looking over my shoulder at my father, slumped against the wall, his journal still in his hand.

"Are you up for this?" Paralay asked me as we walked blindly deeper and deeper into the bowels of Hell.

"There's only one thing on my mind Paralay."

"What's that?"

"Revenge."

Paralay stopped me. "No. Let's just get Talisa and get out of here. There will be time to fight the forces of evil another day……when we're at full capacity."

"You can go if you'd like," I told him. "But I'm going to finish this…now."

In my life I'd taken advice, orders, been subjective in my approach towards matters and even followed my father's teachings in his journal word-for-word. Now was my time. I knew what needed doing for myself to feel whole again.

I pressed on and after only a moment of hesitation Paralay followed. I knew he wouldn't let me down. Travel in good company…indeed I had done that. But we were always meant to be a trio. Missing our third part did not sit well with either Paralay or me. It was time we got our third part back.

When we found Talisa she lay crucifix-style upon an altar of sorts wearing a long black dress of lace. My wayward brother stood over her pooling blood into her mouth from a slit in his wrist. It was some sort of ritualistic ceremony that I intended to halt immediately even if it meant chopping off his hand.

I don't think I'll ever get over seeing my likeness staring back at me, fangs protruding from his gums, eyes as cold and dark as night, skin like a pale moon. How I could go so many years without knowing I had a brother disheartened me…to a degree.

I'd not known my father until recently. Why should I be surprised to know of more lost bloodlines announcing themselves. My father quite easily could've fathered many bastard children in his travels. But I was the chosen one. Only I would carry on his legacy to combat evil while my brother chose to join their legion.

Cris saw us coming and looked up with a smile, not bothering to stop in his dirty work.

"My father protects me, you have no power here."

"Your father lies dead in the hall," I told him. "I killed him and before I leave this world I plan on doing the same to you."

"Oh Costa, so poetic," Cris laughed. "My father is the Dark Lord, not some foolish old man who wandered the earth like a nomad."

Paralay, the only one with any sense left in his head, stepped forward and took charge.

"Get away from Talisa."

"Who is this, your sidekick?"

"I'd rather have him at my side than the likes of you," I replied.

"No worries there, brother. I prefer the company of a beautiful woman."

Cris motioned down towards Talisa who seemed to be enjoying the bloodletting just a little too much.

"Enough talk. Let the girl go."

"I can't do that. She's one of us now."

Cris pulled his hand back and I watched as the slit on his wrist fused back together within seconds. Then he took Talisa by the hand and helped her off the altar. She looked so different from the girl I'd known and loved.

Her eyes were no longer the magnificent crystal blue I remembered. Instead they had become dark and cold. Her skin held the same pale luminescent sheen as Cris'. I longed to see her smile again but when she opened her mouth I saw nothing but the hideous fangs of a beast, not the beautiful girl I once knew.

The two of them descended from the altar steps, hand-in-hand, looking like the epitome of a bride and groom from Hell…which was befitting considering our surroundings.

We paired off, Talisa at Paralay and I with my brother. They came at us. We would dole out our unmerciful and righteous justice upon them swiftly. Cris was cocky and arrogant, wrapped up in his appearance and he overestimated his natural abilities. He was the complete antithesis of myself.

But he did mirror me in one way: he was too young and too eager, that would be his undoing. As he came at me with reckless abandon I sidestepped him and drew up my crossbow, locked and fully loaded, eye-level with his head. As he turned around I let the bolt fly.

It was quite an interesting sight to watch my features accept death. When the arrow plunged into Cris' forehead it did not knock him back. He merely stood there, almost in shock, with blood pouring down into his eyes.

His hands lumbered up trying to pull the arrow out by the shaft. He'd lost all sense of what went on around him. I could not fault him for that considering that his brain had been pierced. This left him open and vulnerable enough for me to dispatch him the way my father had always taught me: remove the head from the shoulders.

With one clean sword strike I did just that then turned to see how Paralay was fairing. He'd been dancing around, using his extraordinary quickness to keep Talisa at bay. Finally as he saw me cut my brother's head clean off he took a stand and struck Talisa right in the mouth. She fell to the floor unconscious.

He looked over and no doubt saw the concern on my face. "Would you have rather I staked her in the heart?"

I shook my head and scooped Talisa off the floor. "Come, according to my father's notes she is not fully under their control until her first kill. We have to find the source of this evil to save her."

"I'm with you," Paralay said. "To the end."

I nodded with respect towards his choice of words knowing in my heart that may well be our fate.

Chapter Thirteen
The End is the Beginning is the End

Many things in life are unexpected pleasures. Falling in love, finding your life's true purpose, learning a new skill, all of these are little nuggets of treasure that can be folded into the memory and held close to the heart as good moments. Meeting The Devil face-to-face was not one of those moments.

He was massive in every sense of the word. Broad shoulders, big hands, and a head of horns and a spiked tail very ominous in structure. He sat on a throne of gold waiting for us.

I set Talisa down gently and then armed my crossbow. Paralay withdrew both short swords. We were both sweating, either from the heat or our nerves was unknown, but it matted my hair and ran down my spine in rivers.

The devil stood. Not a word was spoken by anyone. I preferred to take action. Lifting my crossbow as quickly as I could I send the bolt flying towards him. I'd aimed for his black heart, wondering if he even had one. The arrow never found its mark. The devil caught the shaft in mid-air before it ever reached him and then he snapped it in half.

I'd angered the devil and now he came for us. To my chagrin Paralay's courage overshadowed his good sense and he hurried in front of me to meet the behemoth. He had no chance. Within seconds the devil swatted him aside like a horsefly. The blow sent Paralay hard into the wall. I heard a sickening crack upon impact and watched in horror as his body contorted in such a way that I knew his back had been broken. Whether the elven sensation still lived or not remained to be seen but I had no time to find out. The devil came for me this time.

My own sword outstretched I stood my ground, placing myself between the devil and Talisa.

"I may fall this day but you will not have her!"

"Fool," the devil said to me, his voice a low groan on the ash of the air. "I'll have you *both!*"

I would go down swinging, that was for sure. But in my soul I knew there was nothing I could really do at this point. Death would soon be calling.

The fates play whimsical little games sometimes and I found myself at this moment seemingly caught between space and time. My eyes somehow deceived me yet again but it indeed was truth that I saw.

Looking as though he'd already danced with death himself, my father, Cain Coleridge, burst inside the chambers that the devil called his own and threw himself upon the dark lord.

I'd thought I'd killed him but here he was once again at my side protecting me like I always longed for him to do when I was a child. He'd already begun to morph back into his werewolf form as though calling upon it to aid him in the showdown against the devil.

During their struggle Cain looked back over his shoulder and called to me.

"Now son, the holy water!"

I knew what he meant, the reason he still stood now. My crossbow bolts alone were very vicious indeed but my father knew it wouldn't be enough to stop some enemies. That's where Talos came in to play with an arrangement of weapons that would assist a demon hunter against his greatest of enemies.

It didn't take me long to find the arrow I was looking for. I had a special compartment sectioned off for such a fragile piece. All glass and filled from tip through shaft with the purest of water blessed by a holy man.

Through fresh tears I cried out that which I had never been afforded the opportunity to say before. "Goodbye father!"

He looked at me, his face still only a hint of wolf but still mostly the countenance of Cain Coleridge and he spoke as prophetic as the writings in his journal.

"Love is the way."

The devil cringed as though his ears burned and he grew sickened at the very words. Evil so singularly personified as the devil himself could not appreciate the value of love and all it had to offer. With a dark heart love only got in the way. But for perhaps the first time in my life I knew my heart was pure and it urged me now to do what I knew I had to do.

My crossbow unloaded the arrow filled with holy water and it pierced my father's back through his heart for the second time that day, but he would not go alone this time. The arrow continued into the chest of the devil and shattered sending the holy water coursing through his veins. Talos had been right…water was a powerful source from which to draw.

A burst of flame so powerful it could blot out the sun erupted from the bodies of both my father and the devil. I threw myself on top of Talisa. My first instinct was to protect her at all costs.

The flames pooled over us. I felt the heat, felt the fire scorch my skin and the blistering begin. My hair burned (thank the Gods it wasn't long anymore) and my clothing started to char.

I thought of Paralay in the corner and Talisa underneath me. We were all mortals. Fire was unforgiving by nature. Surely this would be the death of us.

"Wake."

A familiar and friendly voice called out. My eyes came awake, blurry at first but then I saw Talos standing over me. His usual blind stare saw right through me.

"A dream?" I asked.

"No, a nightmare," he told me. "But you pulled through and now you're back here at Ravenwood safe...all of you."

I tilted my head and recognized my chambers inside Ravenwood. Then I saw Talisa and Paralay both seated by my bedside. Paralay had lived though I could tell in his eyes he'd never be the same physically nor emotionally. But Talisa had come full circle. She no longer had protruding fangs or blood red eyes. And when she leaned towards me she did not try to tear out my throat, instead she kissed me her sweetest kiss and whispered the most beautiful sound I'd ever heard.

"I love you."

"The scourge of evil is at bay," Talos told me. "You can rest now."

"I am a demon hunter, like my father," I replied. "There is no rest for the wicked so there shall be no rest for the hunter either."

"Then you have our swords," Paralay told me. I was happy to see him stand and walk towards my bedside, labored but walking nonetheless.

"Always," Talisa added.

The three of us had always been and always would be bonded tighter than blood. But my blood still flowed with the energy of my father and I knew that wherever he was he'd be watching over me, watching with a protective eye like he always had before.

Talisa and I sat alone in the garden where we first met. She held my hand and smiled at me.

"This is a dangerous life," she said.

"Being a hunter brings with it a dangerous element to be sure," I replied.

"I meant being a hunter's wife!"

She nudged me in the shoulder with a playful jab and then took my hand again. Our rings momentarily struck together and I watched a small spark come off them. It made me smile.

"One day we'll have children," she continued. "What will we tell them?"

"When they have questions I'll have answers for them."

She took my face in her hands, her crystal eyes staring hard at me. "And you'll *be here* for them?"

"Always."

"Good," she smiled and brushed a kiss on my lips. "That's all I needed to know."

I watched her walk back inside and waited until she was out of sight, then I brought out a leather bound book with empty pages of parchment inside.

Even the best intentions, those laid out in advance, sometimes did not go as planned. I intended to be there for my children, to let them have the father I never had, but if somehow the spirits took me away before all of that they would still have their answers.

I began my story at the beginning. The day I found out I was a demon hunter.

Heroes Call

"The past is not at rest.
The sins of the father will be passed down
to his sons and daughters
Through the 5th and 6th generations.
A hero must answer the call…"

Prologue

In the realms of dragons and sorcery, demons and gods, kings and commoners, he carved out his legend by his own hand.

He ravaged the land for his own doing. The mere mention of his name brought fear to all he encountered.

Until he met her.

His was an endless bounty. He vanquished all who crossed his path.

Until he met her.

An unruly fighter with an iron will. He cared for no one but himself.

Until he met her.

Chapter One
Dreams

It's funny, you think you have your demons beaten and then they return to you in the form of your loved ones. Mine started as always in the form of dreams.

"I am sent here by the chosen one. So shall it be written. So shall it be done. Child of light, be it daughter or son, is to be destroyed."

The thing spoke with a soft tongue. It didn't hold malice in its words. No guttural growl hid at the back of its throat. I saw no hoofed feet or scaly horns. There was no evidence that The Destroyer held any demonic qualities at all other than a most unfortunate name.

But still at that moment while I lay broken in despair, defeated by the tricks of my very own mind, I knew somehow I had to find the resolve deep down within myself to overcome my enemy once again.

I woke with a start to a silent room. Nothing but shadows crept along the walls. The beast remained locked within the prison of the dream world. My own prison had been created from circumstances largely out of my control.

As the son of a famed and feared hunter of demons it had become a natural transgression to fill his hunting boots...whether I wanted to or not. With my comrades in arms by my side we slayed demons, dragons, and the accursed saving mankind from certain destruction. But those days seemed so long ago now.

My wife Talisa lay next to me sleeping soundly. Her dark skin held a healthy glow from the impending birth of our first child. Pregnancy agreed with her. I knew she would make a great mother as well. It was I who had become troubled.

As silently as I could I slipped from the bed and stepped over to the window to look out at the night sky. The moon had grown full and round. It glowed like a beacon hovering in the air. Pure white. Not a trace of blood on the moon. Things were at peace in the world.

Except for me.

In the days following our last battle when the demons turned to ash and the storm clouds cleared from the sky, Talisa, Paralay, and I settled into new lives away from the violence.

I'd brought my bride home with me, home to Rhone where it had all started. My birthplace had gone through its own battle with hell. It had been burned to the ground by raiders and became the spawning ground for evil for many years.

Rebuilding Rhone had been one of the first things I'd insisted on once I retired from the hunting trade. So far Talisa and I had made it a nice and peaceful place to live.

'Twas the peace that troubled me.

Peace only meant calm before the storm.

And now the dreams had begun again. Dreams of death and destruction that haunted me every night. Talisa said I was just restless. I knew better. Many a time my visions had manifested into reality. I couldn't take that chance now. I had too much to lose.

I looked back over to Talisa. Her face was framed in moonlight. She looked angelic. That suited her just fine. She was my angel. I needed a balance of light against the darkness that surrounded me in my work.

Though my head had grown troubled I knew her touch would calm me. I crept back into bed and rested my head upon her growing belly hoping the love of my unborn would protect me from any more bad dreams.

Funny, the child protecting the father from the womb. I made a silent vow to be the protector, the provider, from that day forward. My child would never want. They'd know their father from birth. I'd give them what I never had myself growing up.

As if sensing my distress Talisa stroked my hair and rested her hand upon my head.

"Be at peace, my husband."

I took her words and the beat of my child's heart and slowly fell asleep.

The next morning I stood outside blessing the home with wolfs bane when a rider came from the distance. Instinctively I went for my crossbow and found my hip empty. I had not held my weapons close to me for well over a year.

As the rider approached I watched him with suspicious eyes. My life may have become a lot tamer than before but I still walked with the instincts of a hunter.

When he came close enough I knew he wasn't a threat. In fact he looked as though he had been riding for days. Dryness crusted his lips. Sweat matted his hair and shirt. He looked to be no more than sixteen or seventeen years in age. And suddenly I recognized something of my younger self in him.

The thin, wiry frame, the unkempt hair, completely unsure of himself. It was amazing how the years could've forged me into the man I was now.

"Ho rider," I called.

The boy nearly fell off his horse in the dismount. He hurried over to me with a piece of parchment extended in his hands. I took it from him and looked it over. The words were written in a language I didn't understand. I would have to get Talisa to translate for me.

"What is this about?" I asked.

"The elf sent me."

"Elf?" I thought for a moment and then my recognition brought a mix of joy and concern. "Paralay? Paralay sent you?"

The boy nodded. "He said to ride swiftly. Not to stop until I reached you. He paid me handsomely."

"What does he want?"

"He's in trouble. He asked for the demon hunter."

Talisa looked over the parchment by candlelight. Her eyes had been growing much worse over the years. I feared the affliction of blindness that had overtaken her father would soon become her fate and she would be robbed of the ability to see our child grow up.

At the moment she deciphered Paralay's message from one piece of parchment to another.

"He says he's in trouble."

"I'm not surprised. What else does it say?"

"He's been caught stealing something of great value and he needs you to come right away."

"What does he expect me to do?"

"Bail him out...as usual." Talisa paused. She read on in silence and then brought her hand to her mouth in shock.

"What is it?" I said rushing to her side.

"Oh Costa, he's really done it this time. He's stolen from a king!"

"Are you certain you translated it properly?" I asked looking over words I couldn't even begin to scratch out.

"Yes. The blame idiot tried to steal an artifact from the King of Trent and he's been thrown in prison for it."

I collapsed down into the seat next to her. With Paralay it felt as though I already had a child to watch after. He was always getting into trouble. Ever since the three of us went our separate ways he'd started pushing more and more boundaries. I feared a part of him was lacking the stability that being with Talisa and I had afforded him.

"Trent is two days ride from here," I said.

"You can make it in a day."

"That's still a day there and a day back. I'd be away from you."

"Whatever your decision you know I'll support you."

Talisa sealed her statement with a kiss. It filled my heart. I felt very fortunate to have earned the love of a good woman.

"Then there's no more debate." I wrapped her in my arms and held her close to me. "I'm staying. Let the elf fend for himself this time. Maybe a night's worth in prison will do him some good."

During the night the dreams would haunt me again and prove to change my mind. Paralay called to me from a dark cell. He seemed to have aged more than twenty years. The once proud elven sensation had become a withered old man. His sentence for thwarting the great King of Trent had been to rot out the rest of his days as a trapped man.

It had been the second night in a row I awoke with a start. This time Talisa woke with me.

"What is it? What's troubling you?"

"It's Paralay," I said through gasps. "He's going to die."

"Die?"

Even in the dark I could make out the concern on Talisa's face. I tried to calm her as best as I could.

"It doesn't have to be that way," I said. "He can still be saved. But I must go to him."

"You must do what you think is right."

"I don't want to leave you wife but Paralay needs me. I will only be gone for a few days' time."

"I'll be alright, Costa. You need not worry. But...."

"What is it? Please tell me."

"If you must leave me tomorrow then be with me tonight."

Without hesitation I took Talisa in my arms and kissed her our sweetest kiss. We made love through the night. By the next morning I was gone.

It pained me to leave her, especially in her fragile condition. But I trusted Talisa to take care of her own. She came from good stock. My mentor Talos, the famed weapons master, had instructed Talisa in the arts of war. She'd been exposed to nothing but the best...and why not? It was Talos' own daughter.

With my fears somewhat at ease I suited up in my heavy boots, hunter's cloak, and leathers for the first time in over a year. My crossbow once again hung at my side like a trusted friend.

It felt like old times. As I rode out a hint of the old spark started to return to me. A part of me had been longing for a reason to travel again. My intent had always been to move on to bigger and better as soon as I was capable. Somehow every time I tried to move forward I inevitably found myself back in this accursed place.

My soul had always cried out for more. Even when I was a young boy I sought adventure. Lately I'd been torn between my sense of duty and choosing the path less taken. Today I chose a new path.

Chapter Two

Sins of the Father

Dreams of a scourged land, my home destroyed. A terrible past I had no control over. The laughing face of The Devil himself staring back at me in the tavern I used to slave away at as a boy.

Suddenly I woke. The distance to Trent had proved greater than I first anticipated and I'd taken lodgings at a local town to rest. As they say there is no rest for the wicked. The nightmares robbed me of my sleep. I was finding it increasingly difficult to slow my breathing upon waking. It felt as though I were living the moments as they appeared in my mind.

Unable to sleep I took to the local tavern. It wasn't much to look at with its sagging roof and sticky floors but as long as they had some ale and something edible I didn't mind the décor.

The clientele on the other hand left a lot to be desired.

As I washed down a fine jug of ale a fool, apparently eager for an early death, bumped me and sent my drink spilling across the table.

The disrespect angered me.

Slow and steady I rose from my seat, tapped the man on the shoulder, and spoke in a calm, quiet tone.

"Excuse me, I believe you owe me a new mug of ale."

The man didn't bother giving me a second glance. "Go die you dog!"

I could've dropped the stranger in an instant but I hadn't traveled this far from home just to end up in a fight. My lust for violence hadn't grown so large that I could not contain it. I decided to give the man one last chance.

"That was mistake number two," I told him. "Don't let there be a third. Simply apologize, buy me another jug of ale and you can walk out of here in one piece."

Now the stranger turned to confront me. He was adorned in a chainmail coif, leather braise and a breastplate that were all as black as the midnight sea. But it was the image on his sur coat that caught my attention: a crimson scythe, the mark of death worn by Trent City's royal guard.

Fate had dealt me a rather good hand to play. I could speak with this soldier about Paralay's capture and impending release right here and now. By the time I got to Trent negotiations would already be halfway over.

This soldier had other ideas. Half drunk and itching for a fight he came at me. I was certain I would best the fool within seconds even with my years away from the chase of hunting demons.

What I did not realize until it was too late was that he had help. Six against one were too strong of odds for anybody. Luckily I wasn't just *anybody.*

They moved on me one at a time. As each one stepped forward I dispatched him quickly without even drawing my weapons. Their skills were good but I'd been taught by the best. It wasn't until they gathered ranks and came at me in a cohesive unit that I began to face trouble.

I hefted a stool and sent it into two of them, knocking them to the tavern floor. The other four leapt on me like dogs. Before I knew it I took a stab to the body. I felt the cold steel enter into my torso just underneath the rib cage. I staggered backward into the side of the table as the blade slid from my body.

The soldiers advanced, eyes of rage peering from beneath their coifs. All at once I felt a flail crack into the side of my head which quickly turned my surroundings to nothing but darkness.

I awoke some time later to a throbbing headache and a fire ripping across the wound at my side. Iron gauntlets imprisoned my hands and ankles with a long length of chain fastened to the wall. It smelled of putrid waste and I could hardly make out anything in the dark.

Disgruntled I tried to sit upright to better view my surroundings. Only a small stream of light came in through a window of bars high above. From what I could make out I was in a prison, chained like an animal. Did they not know who I was? My name had grown legendary in my years of hunting demons. These fools owed me a debt of gratitude for saving their rotten hides from the devil's plague.

The light outside told me I had been unconscious for the better part of the morning. I couldn't risk wasting any more time. Wrapping the chain firmly around my arms I shifted to pull the blasted thing from the wall itself. As I moved I felt the pain at my side flare like the scorching breath of a dragon. At this rate I wouldn't be able to find my way free with simple strength alone.

In a fit of anger I slumped against the back wall and cursed aloud. A familiar voice called to me from out of the darkness.

"Come now, it's not all bad."

From the adjacent wall a man rose to his feet and took a few steps closer to me. He stopped just under the cell window where the light crossed his face like a scar. His eyes were dark. His dark hair hung loosely just below his ears and a smile crossed his lips as he greeted me with so much optimism. It was Paralay.

"A person who dwells on the negative aspects of life really isn't living," he said. "If I'd focused on all the horrible things that had happened to me along the way I'd be scared witless right now. But I'm not. I knew you'd come."

"A fat lot of good it's done, Paralay. Now I'm their prisoner as well."

I looked him up and down as he stood before me with that cocky grin on his face.

"How is it you're not in your bonds?"

"I've picked greater locks than these," he told me. "No chains shall ever hold The Elven Sensation...or his friends."

Paralay knelt down before me and began extracting the locks from my wrists and ankles. It took him a moment but it was done. The relief couldn't have come sooner but once free I grabbed Paralay by the collar and pulled him face-to-face.

"If you could get out of your bonds why did you summon me to come for you?"

"Picking a lock is one thing, Costa. As you can see we are hardly out of our predicament just yet. Had I known you were going to wind up in the cell here with me I would've figured things out on my own."

I released him. He wasn't worth the trouble of pounding on.

"That's exactly what you should've done," I said. "You realize Talisa is pregnant? I left my pregnant wife to come and help you."

"I've always known Talisa to manage taking care of herself. You should've brought her along. It would be nice to see her again."

"How long have you been in here anyway?"

"Longer than I care to remember."

I shook my head astonished at Paralay's lack of judgment. "What would possess you to try and steal from one of the most well-guarded kingdoms in all the land?"

"I grew bored. Needed to stretch my legs. Ever since the three of us went our separate ways life just hasn't had that needed spark to keep me going. You know what I mean?"

I grew silent pondering his words. The wound at my side ached but strangely made me feel alive.

"Yes," I nodded. "The same plague has been eating away at me as well. We waged so much war there is nothing left but peace. I suppose I journeyed all the way out here to fetch you because it felt nice to be needed again."

Paralay's eyes lit up. I knew that twinkle well. He had a plan forming in his head.

"So let's travel the world together and find out what we trouble we can get into. It will be like old times."

I shook my head. "We're in enough trouble as it is. Besides, you're forgetting I have a wife and child awaiting my return as we speak."

He scratched the tuft of his beard as he mulled over my words.

"Sounds like you're making excuses to me, Costa."

I lost my chance to answer as the guards made themselves present inside our cell. As swiftly as he had freed himself Paralay was once again in his bonds, back to the wall, head slumped and pretending to be oblivious to all around him.

The guards approached in haste their sandaled feet scraping upon the dusty floor. They made their way over to both Paralay and myself, two on each of us, dressed in leather tunics with long swords at their sides.

"Come you dogs," one of the soldiers spoke.

He stood in front, the apparent leader, he was dressed differently from the others wearing chainmail fashioned tunic-style from his shoulders to his hips. His long sword was withdrawn and ready in his gloved hand.

"Your presence is requested."

They took us before King Omadon himself. I'd never had much use for royalty. Their lot was all but extinguished except for a few provinces. Getting into Trent at all took a great deal of effort. Paralay must've had a strong urging to piss off royalty that day.

Our hands and feet remained bound with a length of chain in between us. This lack of respect began to anger me and I made sure to let them know about it.

"Do you know who I am, soldier?"

The king raised his hand and the soldier stepped back.

"Silence Captain Borg," King Omadon said. Then he turned to us. "Do you have any idea what you've done? You turned a once peaceful town into a warzone tearing apart a Milo's tavern within minutes of your arrival."

I addressed his concerns with my own. "I was being watched then?"

"Trent is well guarded. We're well aware when a famed hunter is within our midst. But you'll find no demons here."

So they did know me.

"I came on behalf of my companion. His act of thievery, though questionable, is hardly worth imprisonment. After all nobody got hurt."

"The audacity of it alone should cost him his thieving hands...unless."

King Omadon had something else in mind for both of us. He read like an open book. It started me thinking about my father's journals and how he'd traveled the land seeking and destroying menaces to society. I thirsted for that same adventure and grew melancholy at the thought. What would my father say if he knew I'd abandoned his way of life and no longer walked in his footsteps?

"I could use a duo such as yourselves," King Omadon informed us.

Paralay had the nerve to question him. "For what?"

I threw him a look that told him to be silenced. Whatever the king had in store for us it would be better than spending a lifetime rotting in a dirty cell.

"As we speak my only daughter, Nadia, travels north to the ogre Fen. She was attending matters at the

Creole Ranch when she was abducted. She is to be his sacrifice."

The details of his daughter's abduction brought to mind memories that had been long dormant. I saw Rhone through the eyes of a child. When I was but a young boy the village had been raided, burned, and destroyed.

As the memories returned to me now I smelled the smoke choking my throat and felt the fire close to my skin. Such memories should remain sleeping at the recesses of the mind.

I implored the king to answer though I already knew what he wanted us to do.

"What is it you ask of us?"

"Steal my daughter back and I shall release you both of your charges," he said.

"Surely the king's guards would be better suited for such a task."

"My soldiers are very brave, very honorable men. They would do anything for king and country. But the two of you are expendable to say the least."

"The attack in the bar," I said, "you set that up so you could blackmail me now is that correct?"

He gnawed on his lip and had trouble answering. Surely he wasn't expecting me to see through his little plan. But for all my secrets that had been scattered across the four winds for people to pick up and dissect my gift of insight wasn't one of them.

"I'm well aware of what you can do, demon hunter. I know what kind of skills you possess. You're the only one who can save her. Don't make this king beg."

"King Omadon, we'll rescue your daughter."

"You will?" he sounded very surprised.

I lifted my chained arms signifying our release.

"All you had to do was ask."

Chapter Three

Beauty and the Beast

At first light we traveled far north into the foothills of Ogre Mountain. The wind grew strong blowing steady streams of sand that encircled us. As we reached the foot of the cave Paralay, who had not said one word since our departure, finally spoke up.

"I don't like this. Why are we risking our lives for this fool king?"

"Not for the king for your freedom in case you've forgotten."

"No man owns me," he said drawing his short swords. "I say we make our way free at this moment."

I glanced over my shoulder at the steady stream of soldiers who had followed us out on the trail. It was a firm reminder of our bind.

"Better to do what we're told," I said.

"Have you forgotten about Talisa?"

"Of course not. I want to get back to her as swiftly as I can but I can't sit by and leave a young girl to die either. Talisa would want me to go."

"We leave you now," the captain of the guards Borg said. "But take head, we shall not go far. If you accomplish your mission and rescue the princess we will be waiting here to take her safely home to the castle."

As I nodded in compliance Paralay had other ideas and began to antagonize the captain.

"Why is it that you do not step foot inside and battle the ogre Fen for your princess? Is it because you are cowards?"

"You do not know of what you speak. I would give my very life for the princess but my orders are to remain here. Go now, time is precious."

Water poured hard from the top of Ogre Mountain leaving vapor mists rising from the veil of water that cascaded over what should've been the entrance.

"I see no way to get in," Paralay said. "I'm going to get closer."

He shifted closer to the falls and stepped slowly onto wet rocks with the utmost concern for losing his footing and being swept down Snake River to his doom.

As Paralay disappeared under the wall of water I suddenly grew concerned for him. Our last incident with water demons had almost left both of us to face Death himself.

A figure emerged from under the falls but it was not Paralay. A woman, slender and beautiful, approached me. She wore nothing but seaweed laced throughout her hair. Her pale skin shone brightly under the morning sun. She stood before me and reached a milky hand out to caress my cheek.

"You seek help," she said, her voice echoing the soft sound of a gentle sea.

"Yes," I replied.

My mind grew fuzzy. The stranger before me seemed to shift into a watery silhouette.

"Come with me," she said grasping my hand and leading me forward. I complied immediately. Something in her presence soothed and calmed me. I rejoiced at her appearance, my savior from the sea.

"Stop! Do not go!"

A voice was calling in the distance. Was it my own?

The stranger hastened our departure and I suddenly felt a sense of danger around me. As we reached the shoreline that ended into the river I was pulled free of the woman's grasp.

My mind instantly cleared and I saw the guard captain Borg battling back the stranger. Before I could question Borg's motives the stranger shrieked a merciless pitch and transformed from the beautiful maiden into a formless mass of water.

"Back demon," Borg shouted as the water form returned to the river.

"What by all the gods was that?" I asked joining Borg at his side.

"That was a Kelpie, a particularly nasty one at that. In their own way they are more dangerous than anything we will encounter in Ogre Mountain's caves. They use their hypnotic charm taking the form of something appealing only to lead unwary travelers to their deaths in the water."

"I should've known. My senses must be out of practice. Why are you here?"

"I feel you are a man of compassion so I hope you can understand when I tell you that I am in love with Princess Nadia. Every day that she has been gone has been like a dagger in my heart. I would have gladly traded my life for hers but I did not dare defy my king. Only now as we are so close that I must put my loyalty aside to see that she is returned to safety."

"I understand. Often we are moved to do things we normally wouldn't because of someone we love."

My thoughts turned to Talisa. A strong tugging grew in my heart and told me that I needed to hurry back to her side.

As Borg and I spoke Paralay returned from behind the waterfall.

"Come," he said. "I have found the entrance to the cave."

Paralay didn't bother to regard why the captain of the guards was accompanying us. He'd grown more interested in the high adventure and the prospect that great treasure might await us as well. I too felt the adrenaline rise in my body. The thrill of the chase excited me.

"Just like old times," Paralay told me. I couldn't help but agree.

The three of us moved deeper into the cave with nothing to guide us but a small torch struck up after the water was at our backs.

"Be wary," Borg said. "We've not yet traveled to the core. Not long ago the caves were inhabited by the hoop snake."

"What's that?" I asked.

"A myth," Paralay said assuredly.

"No, it is very real," Borg contradicted.

"With all we've seen on our travels thus far I tend to agree with the captain," I said. "How do we defeat it should it cross our paths?"

"I don't know. When my king was at his best he fought and destroyed a hoop snake."

Paralay grasped Borg's shoulder and halted him.

"Your king has met this ogre before then?"

Borg didn't answer.

"Because your king angered this ogre his daughter was taken for revenge, not sacrifice. That's why we must risk our lives now."

"You have only yourself to blame for your predicament, thief."

"That's enough out of both of you."

Silence had always been one of my best allies when tracking and hunting. I didn't need the continuing argument of Paralay and Borg to announce our arrival. I wedged myself between both of them and we pressed on without another word.

As we moved higher within Ogre Mountain I began feeling lightheaded. The caves were poorly ventilated as well. Winded I kept my pace as best I could. As we made our way into a particularly deep and dark section of the cave Borg stopped in his tracks. I stopped too short and Paralay wound up bumping me from behind.

"Why have we stopped?" he barked.

"Quiet," Borg said. "I hear a rumbling."

The three of us stood silently with only the flicker of the torch flame to illuminate our vision.

"What is it?" I asked as I heard the rumbling in the distance for myself.

"It can't be," Borg exclaimed.

A python of gigantic proportion slithered its way into our direct path.

"Looks like your king's snake had kin," Paralay mocked.

We withdrew our respective weapons and the giant serpent recoiled from the glint of steel in the light of the flame.

I felt the hair on my neck stand up. My crossbow shook in my hand. I was in battle mode. It had been a long time but I was ready. It did not matter who or what stood in my way I was ready to kill.

"Fan out," Borg ordered.

We surrounded the snake on all sides.

"Let us cut the demon," Paralay shouted.

"No!" Borg told him. "It moves swifter than you can blink."

As Paralay and Borg argued once again I watched the giant serpent as it arched backwards taking its tail in its mouth and began a simple rocking motion. The movement caught Borg's attention.

"Move!" he shouted.

But it was too late.

The snake came hard and fast at Paralay rolling like a boulder as it threatened to crush him. He threw his body out of its path and landed hard on the graveled floor. I strained my eyes to follow the serpent's route in the darkness. It seemed to be tracking us as it went at Borg and then back to Paralay making an even circle around the floor.

"Follow the path!" I shouted. "We map its route and we can cut it off."

I watched with baited breath as the snake came closer and closer, faster and faster. Before it could completely pass I dove through its open middle. As I tumbled through on the other side the snake became disoriented and ran itself into the wall just next to me. Dazed but not defeated the snake shook off the blow and began to recollect itself.

Without hesitation I pulled my dagger, leapt upon its back, and began hacking away on its torso. Paralay joined me in the attack and Borg as well. Within seconds we had cut the monstrosity into chunks.

"Amazing," Borg said breathlessly.

"You haven't seen anything yet," I told him. "Let's keep moving."

We had walked quite a distance since destroying the hoop snake. Borg had filled a bag with pieces of the snake. When questioned he replied: "Monstrous wolves."

"Monstrous?"

I'd had my fair share of encounters with wolves before but I'd yet to run across anything that could count as *monstrous*.

"You'll see," was all Borg would answer.

And we did. Turning around what seemed to be the last corner we were met by three very large, very ravenous looking wolves. Strands of spit laced through their fangs as they snarled readying for an attack.

"You two make haste towards the exit. I'll hold them off," Borg said.

"Don't be a fool. We've tangled with these types of creatures before," I told him. "You'll be torn to shreds. Now give me the bag and go."

As Paralay pulled Borg clear I followed close behind keeping watch on the wolves at our back. They came swiftly with death on their minds. I was confidant in my ability to take on the wolves but what we lacked was time. The princess' life was hanging in the balance. What we needed was a distraction.

I took the bag of snake fodder and tossed it towards the wolves. They stopped short of their pursuit and attacked the bag with fury. I joined Borg and Paralay in their escape. The three of us collapsed just outside the exit. The tension had been great, the perils intense, but we made it to the top of Ogre Mountain unscathed.

I had to readjust my eyes from the darkness of the caves to the sunlight that shone on top of the mountain. It made me think of Talisa and the impending blindness that plagued her during the night. My heart longed for her I missed her so. But the mission at hand held great importance for many reasons. We could not go home until it was complete.

After a moment of heavy squinting I came to realize that the three of us were not alone. We were surrounded by several powerful looking men, each one with dove-like wings spanning three feet from their backs.

I quickly made it to my feet and went for my crossbow. Before the arrow could be loaded the birdmen swooped in and disarmed me. At any other time I would've been eager to do battle but I knew the odds were not in my favor. These creatures were foreign to me. Any attempt to engage without fully knowing the enemy would be futile.

After a brief standoff one of them spoke.

"Surrender your weapons."

With myself already disarmed Paralay and Borg reluctantly relinquished their own weapons as well.

"You are the scoundrels who took the princess!" Borg shouted.

"We are the Tengu. Your princess is safe, for the moment."

"Take us to her," I was insistent.

"We cannot. Just up that rise is Fen's resting place," the Tengu said pointing to a small hill just behind him. "Your princess is with him."

"Then you get her and bring her to us," Paralay told them. "We didn't come all this way to be stopped now."

"Calm yourself, Paralay," I said. Then turning to the birdman asked: "You Tengu serve this ogre then?"

"We have no choice," the Tengu responded. "Upon this mountain grows the Corvo Bush, it is all we Tengu can eat. If we do not do Fen's bidding he destroys the bushes."

"The way you bested me was impressive," I said. "It proves you are very skilled warriors. Why not fight to take back your food source?"

"We have tried but with the battle grounds atop the mountain Fen merely pulls our wings from our bodies and lets us plummet to our deaths.

"Better to die than be a slave."

"Your courage is great. We have been waiting for a warrior of your prestige for a long time. With our powers combined we can defeat Fen."

"What exactly do you mean?"

"Allow me to possess you. With your ground attack and the Tengu's superlative strength we will surely be victorious to regain our food supply and your princess. We will help each other."

"I don't like it," Paralay said. "It sounds like a trick."

I thought about the situation. What choice did we really have? The Tengus did seem to possess an unnatural strength and their familiarity of the ogre would help out. As I began to accept the offer Borg beat me to it.

"Use me instead."

"Don't be a fool," I told him.

Borg turned on me with raw emotion exposed on his face. "That's the woman I love up there."

I put up a hand to quiet him. "Trust me. I will not fail."

Borg could not argue. He knew I was right. He merely bowed his head and nodded.

"It is settled then," the Tengu said.

I nodded in compliance and readied myself for battle. With a sudden fear that this would be the end I looked over to Paralay.

"Tell Talisa I love her."

"You'll tell her yourself."

All at once I felt another presence in my body. The Tengu had taken over just like that.

"Relax," I heard the voice as clear as if it were my own. "Let me guide you."

I left my group and the remaining Tengus behind as I advanced on the last peak of the mountain where Fen and the princess Nadia waited.

As I made it over the last hill I saw him there lying in a field of what could only be the Corvo Bush and he was toying with the princess.

The girl ran in different directions towards the edge of the cliff only to have Fen's giant hand block her at every turn. The ogre bellowed out thunderous laughter and the princess finally collapsed in despair.

"Now is when we attack," the Tengu told me.

Whether or not I wanted to now I had no choice. The Tengu was guiding my body through every move. I leapt down in front of Fen hollering a cry of battle. Fen, angered by the intrusion, moved to swat me with the back of his hand. I tucked and rolled out of harm's way and came up with one of my short blades exposed.

Fend charged at me with slow lunging steps that covered half the ground. Sidestepping quickly I slashed the ogre just below the knee sending him off balance and spilling over the ledge.

It was over just like that. I returned my blade to its sheath and went to aid the princess who had fainted from the strain. As I hefted her in my arms the foundation shook beneath me.

"What by all the Gods was that?" I asked of the Tengu.

"The ogre Fen he still lives."

I looked towards the cliff's edge where I had just dropped the ogre and sure enough Fen was there. One large hand held firm against the side as he pulled his gruesome face into view.

"I thank you for your service to my people," the Tengu said softly.

All at once he emerged from my body. Wings amply spread the Tengu soared straight into Fen's face clawing and pecking at his eyes like a bird with a worm. Fen reached his hands up to defend the attack and dropped out of sight for the second time taking the Tengu soldier with him.

That left me alone with the princess. It took me a moment to regain my bearings but as soon as I did I took control. With Nadia in my arms I hurried back down to my awaiting party.

Borg met me halfway and relieved Nadia from my grasp. Tears filling their eyes they both rejoiced in their reuniting. The Tengu, on the other hand, each bowed their heads as they instinctively knew their leader had fallen.

"I don't know how to thank you," Borg said. "You of course have earned your freedom, I'll see to that."

"We both will," Nadia added. "And you will be rewarded handsomely."

Before Paralay could salivate over the mention of a reward I put up my hand to dismiss it.

"That won't be necessary. All we ask for is a bed for the night," I said. "Having another body sharing space with mine is an exhausting process."

"Of course," Nadia said. "And please join us for dinner. I'm sure my father will have a grand feast in your honor."

I let Paralay have that one.

My dreams that night were invasive and disturbing. I saw things through eyes that weren't my own. Troubling things. Deadly things. My hometown of Rhone flashed before me...burning.

At first I thought I was flashing back to my past when raiders had left my birthplace destroyed. But when I saw Talisa, my beautiful wife aglow with her first pregnancy cowering in terror I knew it was the here and now. I tried to tell myself it was all a dream but it didn't feel like a dream. It felt like reality that I was forced to watch but could do nothing to stop.

Talisa screamed out. It burned my ears. I tried to will myself awake but the visions continued. The air grew cold. I felt the very real presence of death wash down over the scene and all at once Talisa vanished.

I heard myself calling out her name. She didn't answer. I called again and again and finally I came awake. Paralay stood over me shaking me by the shoulders.

"You're dreaming," he said. "Just a dream. It's over now."

Somewhere in the deep recesses of my soul I knew that it wasn't over. A new horror was just beginning.

"I need to get home."

On the breaking dawn of the next morning Paralay and I set out for home. Nadia was kind enough to lend us means of travel from the kingdom's Creole Ranch. A great white steed with the wings of angels upon its back became our transport.

We moved swiftly upon the Pegasus. I'd never felt so marvelously free before. The wind pulled at my cloak and tussled my hair and I felt alive for the first time in years. But in my gut a familiar terror gripped me.

With Pegasus' help we made it back to Rhone in half a day's travel. The mighty steed touched down with the lightest of landings. I wasted no time dismounting.

"The place looks fine," Paralay said slipping off the mount and taking Pegasus by his reigns. "Maybe your visions were wrong."

"Have you ever known my visions to be wrong?" I asked.

Still when I looked around the village it surprised me. Everything flourished. The streets bustled with life and Rhone was thriving just as it had been when I'd left to fetch Paralay. It brought a smile to my face. I couldn't wait to see my wife.

"Come, I'm sure Talisa would love to see your ugly mug again."

We hurried through the streets like school kids. I could hardly wait to sweep Talisa up in my arms. She was my light, the best thing that ever happened to me. I'd been foolish to think that I needed high adventure to feed my soul. That restlessness had been sated and now I knew that with my wife and child, our family, I would never want for more.

My father had left me when I'd been just a boy. Even though I walked in his footsteps to carry on the demon hunter legacy I would be a better father. I'd never leave my family again.

When we reached the Calabrese home my happiness soured. From the outside everything looked picturesque but I'd learned long ago never to judge on looks alone. Multiple run-ins with shape shifters will do that to you.

I trusted my intuition and my inner alarm system was going ballistic. Something felt cold, odd, out of place, and we hadn't even crossed the threshold yet.

Paralay tied up the Pegasus and bounded past me.

"What're we waiting for?"

He hurried inside calling out after Talisa. I was tempted to hold him back but instead I followed him inside. The house was just as I'd left it. No altercation had taken place, nothing was out of the ordinary. But still I felt uneasy. Trouble weighed down on me like a heavy cloak.

After going through each room of the house and even through the backyard the reason for my discontent surfaced. Talisa was gone.

"Where'd she go?" Paralay asked.

I tried to piece together an agreeable answer. I had none.

"I don't know."

"Maybe she came to her senses and left you," he joked.

I shook my head. "It's not funny. Something isn't right."

"Relax Costa, she probably just went to the market or something."

A thousand possibilities ran through my mind. I tried to persuade myself that he was right. Talisa would come back and everything would be as it was before. Deep in my heart I knew the truth.

And then I saw it, the marking on the wall just as in my visions. It read:

"I am sent here by the chosen one. So shall it be written. So shall it be done. Child of light, be it daughter or son, is to be destroyed."

She was gone just like that. Vanished without a trace or an explanation. The only thing that made any sense to me were the visions. Something dark and sinister had invaded our home and swept Talisa off into the night.

How could I have let this happen? I speak all the time of not having regret and now I had to live with another. I would never, ever forgive myself for leaving her that that day.

I had tried to make peace within myself, saying it would only be for a little while and then I'd return to her and we'd live out our lives together until we were old and gray. But suddenly my perfect world had been turned upside down and I'd somehow lost the love of my life.

I fell to my knees shattered with despair. Paralay tried to comfort me to no avail. Nothing he could say would make me feel any better. The only person I wanted to talk to was the one person I couldn't find.

My breath caught in my chest and I started to shudder. I couldn't speak. Pain hollowed out my insides like a searing hot knife and I felt as though my heart might literally shatter. I couldn't catch my breath and when I did I only managed to utter one word.

"Destroyer."

Chapter Four
The Prophecy

In an act of desperation I tried to find Talisa. Even though in my heart deep down I knew she was gone still the fighter in me refused to let go. I tore through town seeking answers. When I returned I was even more confused.

Paralay greeted me at the door. For a moment I thought Talisa stood before me instead. Blind love can mess with your head sometimes.

"Costa, you need to calm down."

Sweat poured over my body; my breathing had grown labored and more than that I heard my heart and soul screaming out in anguish. I wouldn't be able to calm down until I made things right again.

If I believed in a merciful God I would've prayed for my sweetheart's safe return. I would've asked for things to return to the happy bliss I'd felt since the day I met Talisa. But my requests had never been answered before. In order to bring structure back to my life I would have to take matters into my own hands, just the way I liked it.

"I have to find her."

"Come inside," Paralay told me. "There's something you need to know."

"I don't have time, Paralay. You heard the prophecy. The Destroyer is after the first born. Talisa is in danger because of my lineage. Every second I waste could be her peril.

I moved past him into the house and prepared myself. Where I was going I didn't yet know but my skills as a demon hunter and tracker were insurmountable. I could rely solely on instinct. My bloodline had proven that in the past.

My pack had already been prepared from my last journey to save Paralay. All I needed to do was fill it with perishables. There would be no telling how far or how long I'd be gone.

"You don't need to go, Costa," Paralay told me. "Talisa won't be harmed."

"Are you insane? The creatures we've run across over the past few years are anything but merciful."

"The Destroyer is only after the child of light, the first born of the demon hunter."

"Right, just like when they came after me to try and get to my father," I reminded him. "The cycle continues now."

"But it won't," he explained. "Because your child is not the chosen one."

I stopped in my tracks. A hollow pit opened up in my stomach and I began to grow flush as possible scenarios built in my mind.

"What are you saying, Paralay? Did you sleep with my wife?"

He seemed genuinely shocked by the accusation. "What? No!"

"Because I remember you were always quite fond of Talisa."

"The child is yours."

"Then how could it not be the child of light, the next chosen one?"

"Because you are not Cain Coleridge's son. You're not the demon hunter."

At first I felt like laughing. The statement, after all, was absurd. It hadn't been that long ago that I'd traveled the world proving that I was next in the line of Coleridge children chosen to hunt and destroy the spawn of the devil. I hadn't wanted to believe it. The responsibility was too great. But since that time I'd come to embrace my heritage. For Paralay to speak those words felt like a slap to the face.

"What nonsense are you speaking now?" I asked.

"It's not nonsense, I speak the truth."

"And you came across such knowledge how?"

"Talos."

In spite of everything I laughed. "Now I know you're lying. Talos is the one who told me about Coleridge in the first place. He showed me the letter from my father, remember?"

"It was a fake. He made up the story. Coleridge was dying. He had never married, had no heir. They needed someone to fill the role left behind when Cain passed on. They chose someone without a real past. A boy who lived his life in servitude. They chose you but you are not of Coleridge's blood."

I shook my head in disbelief. He was lying, I knew he was. But then why did the pain in my gut begin to grow so fierce?

"You've always been jealous, Paralay," I began trying to defend my thoughts. "When we first met you didn't believe I was Coleridge's son. I thought we were past that but I don't know what game you're playing now."

"There's no game, no lies. Talos confided in me on his death bed. He didn't want to carry the lie to the grave with him."

I don't know what came over me then. Rage, despair, a combination of both maybe. Whatever the case I let loose and struck Paralay high upon the cheek. He toppled to the ground almost hitting his head against the dining table in the process.

When I realized what I'd done I reached out to help him up. Then something made me step back. A darkness I'd not felt in years began sweeping over me. I felt a great flood of sorrow unfolding within me and my first instinct became running away from it.

I took my bag and ran from the house. Pegasus remained tied to an outside post grazing. I quickly relinquished his binds, mounted, and took to the skies. Below me I saw Paralay come out after me. He waved his hands frantically calling me to come back. There was no going back. And without my identity there was no going forward either. Costa Calabrese, the once great demon hunter, was now a lost soul caught in limbo.

I let Pegasus lead the way. My thoughts betrayed me. I no longer trusted my judgment on anything, even something as simple as direction. I had no real destination in mind anyway. My intent had only been to get away from the scene as fast and far as possible. The problem was I couldn't run from what was in my head.

Who the hell was I now? I'd built half my life on the premise of being Cain Coleridge's son. The original chosen one, the demon hunter. Without that who was I? Without Talisa I had lost everything. She was my one and only, my light. I'd never find another woman to compare to her no matter how hard I searched.

It had never been easy for me to meet people. In my youth I'd been a loner save for my good friend Tuck. Somewhere along the way I lost everyone I ever cared about - including now Talisa, my soul mate.

Something or someone had stolen her from me - the Destroyer, entity unknown. And although I wanted to fight for her, to win her back, I knew deep down that I couldn't. I could no longer protect her. I couldn't save her. I'd been a blind fool to ever believe I had that power and control to begin with.

Accepting that fact dropped me deeper into despair. I could only deny it for so long. It felt like I had finally gained ground in my life only to have someone kick me in the teeth and send me spilling back into the dark pit of hell I'd fought so hard to climb out of. Now I lacked the strength, will, or want to even try.

My energy was spent. The armor of my spirit destroyed. I had no one to turn to. Talos was gone. My father was gone. I didn't even have the words in his journal to comfort me anymore, not that they would. I'd been lied to, deceived. How could I believe in anything anymore?

My eyes began to well up with tears and I let my head drop into Pegasus' soft mane. It blew back against my cheeks as the wind tugged at it. I allowed myself to weep. Way up in the sky no one would hear me. My pain warranted an unrelenting flow of tears and the anguish I felt in my heart brought out sobs from me that sounded like a wounded animal.

Pegasus cried out along with me. For a moment I thought the magnificent beast felt my pain and drew sympathy for me until I realized he had been struck. The shaft of an arrow stuck out from the rear flank.

Before I could pull myself together and register the attack another arrow found its way to Pegasus, this time clipping his wing. He could no longer keep us in the air and the descent came fast. I held tight so I wouldn't get dropped off his back. The vertical drop grew intense as the speed picked up and I couldn't believe this would be the end of me.

Before impact with the ground became imminent both Pegasus and I found ourselves caught up in a large net. It saved us from certain death but we remained in peril. Whoever attacked us undoubtedly snared us in the net as well. What they intended to do with us remained to be seen.

The net was sticky like webbing. It clung tight to the body making it very difficult to move or even catch a breath. On any other day I would've struggled and fought and found my freedom. On this particular day I lacked the strength and the desire.

Pegasus had gone completely still. I could only hope I hadn't been responsible for yet another loss. We were lowered to the ground. The minute we touched down a group surrounded us. I couldn't see past the weaponry at first. Dozens of spears pointed down on me. They were all hand carved of wood with sharpened stones fastened to the tips and their masters were women. A troupe of women dressed in fur and skins each standing almost six feet tall. War paint covered their faces but nothing could conceal the hatred in their eyes.

I wondered, having never crossed paths with them before, what I could've done to have pissed them off so fiercely. Then one of them spoke with equal fierceness and told me all I needed to know with one sentence.

"You're trespassing here...man!"

From the infliction in her voice I could sense this tribe of women held quite a bit of disdain for the male species. She stood out from the rest of them with fiery red hair and an almost regal crest of jewels dripping off her neck. I could only assume this was their leader.

"These are Amazon lands," she continued. "And you're not permitted here."

"I was flying overhead, how could I be trespassing on your lands?" I told her.

I got a poke for mismanaging my tongue.

"Silence, dog! Take him away."

They needed to separate me from Pegasus in order to move me. In that moment I could've dispatched them all but I hesitated. I was their prisoner. Back into servitude like the life I'd known before.

The Pegasus they revered. The man they beat, pushed, poked, and dragged until I fully complied. They stripped my weapons, my cloak, my boots, everything down to my under clothing. They bound my wrists in some of the hardest twine I'd ever come across and then blindfolded me.

We marched on a dirt path to a destination unknown. All their safety precautions were to keep their location a secret. I counted our steps, smelled cedar on the air, and felt the wind change from warm to cool as we went into higher ground. If I wanted to I could make it back to this location with ease. But I let them have control. I had no desire to fight back.

When they finally removed the cover from my eyes I found myself within a village that had been set up more like a military compound than a simple town. More Amazons came to greet me with spitting and shouts of anger.

They took me to my new home which was a small cage fashioned from solid bamboo shoots sized for someone much shorter than me. I had to fold into a small ball just to get inside.

"You'll remain here until the council decides what to do with you," Red Hair told me.

"What have you done with Pegasus?" I asked.

Red turned around and came close enough to the bars that I could smell the sweet scent of jasmine coming off her skin.

"You dare speak?" Her green eyes glinted as she spoke like diamonds in a midnight sky.

"I dare," I replied.

"Very well. The Pegasus shall be treated of his wounds and released. We have no grudge against such a fine animal."

"But you have one with me? I don't even know you."

"Not just you, your kind. All liars and betrayers. You don't deserve a beauty like Pegasus."

"Pegasus was a gift," I told her, "from a woman."

Red scoffed and then left me. I remained there in that cage unattended for quite a while. It grew very uncomfortable. My legs cramped and ached but the pain in my heart all but silenced my physical discomfort.

I had somehow thought that my heart had grown numb, maybe even stopped. I no longer held any use for it so it just shut down. But every now and then when I least expected it a memory of Talisa or my father would spring to mind and I'd feel the wash of hurt crash over me.

I tucked my legs in and held them close to me. Huddled in a ball hard sobs racked my body until I jerked and spasmed. I never expected to experience such loss again. I was a grown man, those troubles and tragedies of my childhood were in the past where they couldn't hurt me anymore. Never did I expect to have the love of my life taken from me as well.

Talisa and I were meant to be together...always. Now I knew why my father had warned me about falling in love. My father, another lie, another betrayal, another loss. Losing Talisa hurt enough. Losing my identity on top of that was too much too bare.

As I drifted to sleep in the small cage I hoped that whatever the Amazons had planned for me would include the sweet release of death.

Chapter Five

Amazons

I woke from the uncomfortable weight of eyes staring at me. My own eyes felt grainy and raw and I was very thirsty. I tried to stretch out and bumped hard against the unforgivable bamboo. Realizing my mistake I had to readjust my position. When I did I found someone staring at me.

One of the Amazons sat outside my cage watching me. She sat with her legs beneath her, chin resting atop her fisted hands just staring. Her green eyes penetrated my very soul. I felt more naked than if I'd had my loin cloth ripped from my body at that moment.

"What're you looking at?" I asked.

She didn't answer, just shifted her position slightly and continued to stare quietly.

"What're you looking at?" I repeated raising my voice into a fit of anger. "If you're waiting for your caged animal to do a trick for you then you can just forget about it."

Finally she spoke up. Her voice held a calm to it I hadn't been expecting. She spoke slow, measured, and it instantly put me at ease like a mother's hand stroking her child's hair.

"You were crying."

I shook my head. "I wasn't. Just resting."

"You were crying as you slept. Very painful weeping full of anguish. Are you uncomfortable?"

I shifted in my cage as best I could.

"Yes."

"But that's not why you are in pain."

It wasn't a question. This time the Amazon woman told me what she saw. Even though my heart had grown quiet for a time the ache still harbored there raw and waiting to burst open at its seams once again.

I grew silent reflecting inward and brooding. The Amazon sensed my reluctance to talk. She stood and began to walk away. Something in me suddenly shouted out.

"What's your name?"

She turned slowly, her eyes glinting something of a smile.

"They call me Raina. What is your given name?"

It was a simple question but one I couldn't answer easily. I was born a Coleridge and raised with the surname Calabrese. But who was I now? I gave Raina the only answer I could.

"I'm your prisoner. Nothing more."

She hesitated to speak and within those few seconds members of her tribe confronted her.

"Raina, what are you doing speaking to that man?"

"Nothing sister. Just keeping watch."

"Don't stand too close. There's no telling what that brute may try."

They pulled her by the arm and forced her away. I kept my watch on them all but mostly Raina with her copper hair and sun kissed body. She turned to look back at me several times and something in the weight of her stare told me she didn't hold the same disdain in her heart that her sister Amazons shared. Raina was different.

When night fell Red came for me. They called her Shamanee and as I assumed she was the current leader of the Amazons. A pack of the tribe followed close behind her. I looked for Raina but didn't see her amongst the crowd.

"The tribal council has discussed your fate," Shamanee told me. I simply waited for her to finish. Nothing could be worse than my current predicament.

"Our punishment for trespassers usually amounts to death. But you look as though you can be useful to us."

Useful how? I wondered. No matter. Whatever it was it couldn't be as extreme as death. Even though I cared little for myself and my fate before something had renewed my vigor for life...or maybe it was *someone.*

The "use" Shamanee spoke of came in the form of hard labor. I was strong and able bodied, a workhorse used to help fortify their compounds by building new structures around the perimeter. Any and all heavy lifting went to me.

Under the heat of the midday sun the strain became almost unbearable. But I didn't mind much. It kept me busy, kept my mind off of my troubles. Doing menial labor brought back memories of being a slave boy. Though I hated it then, and often longed for the days of high adventure, I couldn't help reminisce with fondness now.

Things were simpler then. I knew who I was - I was nobody and that is who I had returned to. A nobody. A slave.

For the most part the day's work went by just fine. But if I dared to rest, or didn't move fast enough, I'd taste the end of a stick across my back. More often than not they struck me for fun. I'd tolerate it. Physical pain didn't compare to the emotional wounds that scarred my heart and soul.

As I hefted a large grouping of bamboo I lost my balance and turned an ankle under the weight. The bamboo shoots came down around my head. The commotion brought several of the Amazons over. They began a tirade first of verbal assaults and then with kicks and strikes to my head and naked torso as I tried to get back to my feet.

The amount of blows kept rocking me and brought me back to a time where my house lord Mace Benton had beaten me in the middle of town for returning late.

Finally, thankfully, someone cried out and put a stop to the beating. At first I thought Shamanee might be taking charge of her tribe until I heard the soft voice of Raina sound out. She halted her sisters and then came in to protect my body by covering it with her own.

The softness of her breasts caressed my shoulder and her scent grew intoxicating. Suddenly I no longer felt my wounds.

"He's had enough," she said shooing them back.

"Very well," one of them responded. "Take him away."

They scooped me up away from Raina and dragged me back to my cell where I spent the rest of the morning. When night fell the other part of my usefulness came into play. They took me to one of the tents and instructed me to wait.

Before long Shamanee made an appearance. She had stripped down wearing nothing but a small deerskin across her hips. I looked over her dark skin and toned body with her nipples standing erect on firm breasts and I felt no arousal.

My sense were dead, useless now. Shamanee didn't seem to notice or care. She had business on her mind.

"To keep our lineage going we Amazons must breed. Only the finest stock will do."

She moved forward and kissed me full on the lips. Her hands moved over my pectorals, stomach, arms, and groin.

"Yes, you'll be just fine."

I performed for her out of obligation. Nothing ever felt quite so wrong. Even though I knew Talisa was gone I still felt her there in my heart and bedding down with another woman felt like an act of betrayal.

When we were done they sent me back to my cage. I felt filthy, disgusted with myself, and more forlorn than ever.

My life had drastically turned. One minute I'd been the happiest I'd ever known in all my days, the next I moved through life day-to-day carrying out meaningless work. I may as well have been one of the undead that I used to battle back when I carried the demon hunter name.

The days had become routine. Working all day and at night satisfying Shamanee's needs. I'd lost all my privileges of freedom and with each act I lost a little more of my dignity as well.

She wanted an heir, a successor to her title as Queen of the Amazons. I dared not ask what would happen if she gave birth to a male child. It made me think of the impending birth of my child with Talisa.

The first born male son, the chosen one, swept away by some phantom mover to be seen again. But according to Paralay my son, or daughter, was not the chosen one. The Destroyer would have no need for them. What would become of them then?

I had no way of knowing stuck as slave labor in an Amazon camp. Even if I had the freedom to find out I couldn't save them. That part of my life was over.

As I built walls and reinforced gates and watch towers I'd hear rumblings amongst the Amazons of an impending attack and upcoming war. I didn't know whom they spoke of, in fact I had it in my head that the entire tribe had grown paranoid following Shamanee's lead.

But on the morning of my third day danger struck. An alarm sounded out overhead and though I recognized no signs of intruders the Amazons began to gather in defense. Then it happened, lighting bore down from an otherwise clear sky and struck the watchtower.

The guard on duty fell to her death taking chunks of the tower down with her. Raina stood just below. As a sizable piece of brick came down towards her head my instincts took over. I made a mad dash across the gap of distance that separated us and tackled her just before the brick struck and killed her.

We landed with my body atop hers and I continued to shield her from harm while the rest of the Amazons ran around in panic. The lightning attack subsided moments later. I wondered if the Gods in their anger had thrown down thunderbolts. Nothing else made sense in such an attack save one - magic.

When the panic ended the Amazons misinterpreted my actions.

"Look, the prisoner is attacking Raina!"

Another beating commenced. I shielded my head as best I could as I rolled off of Raina. Her protests went unanswered this time and once again they forced me once back to my cage. It had become something of a home away from home. I'd even grown accustomed to the cramping of my legs.

I watched through the bars as the Amazons tried to regroup. Their fallen comrades were covered and taken away. No tears were shed just shouts of revenge. I grew more curious about the invisible attacker.

Once when Paralay, Talisa, and I had scaled the Peak of the Gods we'd thought an ice wizard lived on top controlling the elements to freeze out intruders. My mentor Talos had told us it had only been the weather itself that we'd been so afraid of. No wizard ever existed. I wondered if the Amazons had fallen prey to such thoughts as well.

Later, when the sun had been replaced by the moon they called on me to amuse Shamanee. As they marched me to her tent in the dead of the night I felt even less interested in the occasion than ever before.

Death had just touched their village yet they carried on as if nothing had ever happened. My Amazon guards undid my binds and then left me to my business. I knew they wouldn't be far, they never were. Each night they took their place just outside the door and returned only when Shamanee summoned them directly after.

I sat and waited for Shamanee to make her appearance and I grew anxious, not aroused, but anxious to get this dirty little deed done with and return to my holding cell.

Finally my mistress came but to my surprise it was not Shamanee. Slipping in through the back of the tent, wearing a veil across her delicate features, Raina revealed herself to me.

"What're you doing here?" I asked in surprise and confusion.

She silenced me and then began in a whisper.

"You saved my life. I wish to repay you."

With no more words she kissed me. The warmth and sweetness of her enveloped me. I drew her in and for the moment I was lost in an expression of affection I never thought I'd feel again. Raina had reawakened those feelings inside me that I thought had grown cold. But I pulled away trying hard to keep my wits about me.

"What about Shamanee," I asked.

"My sister is leading the high council deciding on what to do about our attackers. She'll be gone for the duration of the night."

"Then it was you who called for me?"

"Yes. I sent the guards word by parchment. They are none the wiser."

Raina returned to the kiss and this time I found I no longer held any more concerns. Tonight I made good use of Shamanee's bed. Raina and I joined together in passion and ecstasy but also through gentle emotion, not the raw animal instinct that took over when Shamanee rode me. As Raina sat atop me, gently thrusting her hips back and forth, I looked over her finely sculpted body and deep into her eyes.

She looked like a goddess and our connection grew electric. After my release came I held her close and it was all in that moment that my thoughts turned to Talisa. My memory of her had become just that...nothing more than just pictures in my mind of a lifelong since forgotten.

I held Raina close to me running my fingers through her hair.

"Who are these attackers," I asked. "What are the Amazons so afraid of?"

The answer did not come as a surprise.

"Witches," she told me. "They are powerful witches intent on taking our most sacred lands. Each holds more power than the next but it is when they come together as a whole combining the elements of earth, fire, wind, and water that they are most destructive. We don't know how to combat them."

"I do."

Before I could explain my past history with the witches we were interrupted by a group of Amazon guards. They pulled Raina and I apart and struck me across the knees so that I couldn't stand on my own. Then Shamanee entered.

She brandished a dagger and set it against my throat. I felt the steel bite into my skin.

"How dare you corrupt my sister. Such an act shall bring you your death!"

"He saved my life," Raina cried. "Please spare his."

"He's outlived his usefulness, Raina," Shamanee told her. "It's time to die."

Amidst the chaos I found my voice and my strength once more.

"I can help you defeat the witches," I said.

"Impossible," Shamanee told me but still she hesitated.

"I've dealt with them before," I continued. "I can help you."

Shamanee lowered her dagger. "How?"

Chapter Six
Four Elements

It took a little more doing but I finally convinced Shamanee that I could be an asset to the tribe in this battle. I explained how the witches had once tricked me in a quest sending me directly to Hell. In short I owed them.

The only way I knew how to battle such evil would be to divide and conquer. We set out at first light heading to the last known whereabouts of the witches. The mighty Amazons feared. I could feel the earth tremble with each of their shaky steps.

They'd returned me my clothing and weapons and I made good use of my trusted crossbow the moment we located the fearsome foursome Bliss, Hope, Charity and Faith. They had called themselves good witches who practiced white magic. Angelic names aside I could still remember their words to me that fateful day, something of a curse as they spoke in their evil tongue revealing their true dark identity.

> *"You will not find love. Every day will be the same.*
> *You may as well not have even been born."*

Now that I had lost Talisa those words stung and plagued my memory. I felt no remorse as I let my arrow bolt pierce the chest of the one called Charity. Water had been leveled. That left Earth, Fire, and Air to be dealt with and we no longer held the advantage of surprise.

The Amazons did their best to forge a formidable attack but they were no match against the cunning and powers of the witches.

Bodies fell all around me. Something in my heart lit up. I could not lose anyone more. They had trusted me to lead them to victory. I had to honor that promise or die trying.

I set my sights on Faith, the dark-haired one, but not through direct attack alone. Her lightning bolts pulled from the air had already taken down most of the tribe. So I came at her as a distraction. When she saw me she remembered.

"You!" the word almost hissed out from her lips.

A blast came quickly and knocked me to the ground. As she stood over me, mocking, I let the second half of my plan come into play.

"Why the Amazon lands, Faith? Rhone wasn't good enough for you?"

"Amazon lands are sacred. The powers here are endless," she told me. Her confidence would be her downfall.

"One witch down. You certain you have enough to finish this?"

"Silly boy, haven't you learned by now? I'm the one you should fear, I am the all-powerful and soon I'll have even more at my disposal. Let me show you."

With that she struck me with another bolt of lightning. It ripped through my body like a runaway fire. It hurt more than any physical pain I'd ever known but I drew satisfaction knowing that she had played right into my hands and I continued to rope her in.

Faith spoke with enough cocky glee to draw the attention of both Hope and Bliss. They pulled away from their individual battles to confront Faith. Egos unchecked always proved to be a downfall.

"What're you saying, that you don't need us?" Hope asked.

"Worse," Bliss added. "She wants the powers for herself."

"What makes you think you're so damn strong?"

Hope's fire grew with her anger and she lashed out on Faith. Air and Fire battled each other for the right to reign supreme. Not one to stand on the sidelines Earth joined the fray as Bliss tore up the ground beneath Faith and Hope sending them into a pit from which they would never return.

Bliss wouldn't stand victorious for long. As she celebrated her victory the Amazons, headed up by Shamanee, took her apart piece-by-piece. They were a savage lot when there was no longer concern of being torn down by magic powers.

Now it was the Amazons turn to celebrate. They shrieked and cheered and danced over the fallen witches. Then, to my surprise, they heralded me. Each one took a knee and bowed before me.

"We are in your debt," Shamanee told me.

I dusted the dirt from my shoulders. My body still ached from Faith's attack but I was able to stand on my own two feet. The show of respect from the Amazon nation moved me but I did not need any special treatment. As they themselves had said I was just a man, no more - no less, and they owed me nothing.

"What I want you cannot give me," I told them.

"I can grant you your freedom," Shamanee told me.

Raina pushed through the crowd and set her hand upon mine.

"Though I wish you would stay," she said.

Her offer was one that I could not turn down. Where else would I go if I left the village? Back home? It was no longer any home that I'd come to know. The Amazon village had become my new home, my new life.

I stayed with them, with Raina, for many weeks. The terms were different now, I was no longer a prisoner. I helped them rebuild their structure while they helped me rebuild myself. Through training and meditative prayer I slowly found peace with my new life.

Then life stepped in once again to shake things up.

In the middle of the night while Raina and I enjoyed each other a commotion broke out in the village. The alarm sounded out indicating an intruder had crossed into the territory.

I threw a skin around my waist and hurried out to see the significance of the disturbance. The Amazon's had another prisoner in their grasp, not a man this time but an elf. My elf, my friend, Paralay.

"What's happening here?" I asked.

"We caught him sneaking onto the grounds."

"Paralay what are you doing here?"

"I've come for you," he said. "I'm here for the demon hunter."

Chapter Seven

Answering the Call

I convinced the Amazons to release Paralay. Now it was his turn to convince me.

"I'm not the demon hunter anymore. You told me that."

Paralay shook his head. "I'm sorry. I lied."

"You lied then or you're lying now?" I was very confused.

"I never expected that you'd run off like that," he began. "I never thought you'd disappear for so long. It took all of my resources to find you but now that I have I'm not leaving without you."

"My life is here now, Paralay. These are good people. There's nothing left for me back there."

We sat alone inside my tent but I knew Raina wasn't far. She filled me up and made me feel whole again. I recognized that and I wasn't about to let that go. But Paralay's next words would challenge that thought.

"Talisa is alive."

I sat silently digesting this new information as he continued.

"I've located her at the base of the Mountain of Power. The Destroyer is keeping her alive to witness the birth of the child of light. Rather than kill the child they plan to corrupt him for evil. We have to save her."

I came to my feet and had to resist the urge to cover my ears. Just the thought of having Talisa back in my life again lifted my heart. But I had moved past that life, I'd moved on. The pain had finally subsided to a degree that I could live with it and that is what I planned on doing.

"No, this is your mission alone," I told him. "I cannot help you. I'm not the man I once was. I'm not the demon hunter."

Now Paralay rose as well. "Don't you understand I lied before? You were in such pain and so fearful of what would happen to Talisa. You blamed yourself. I was just trying to help ease some of that weight from your shoulders so I told you that you weren't Cain's son...but it was a lie."

I shook my head. "No, you were right. I'm just a man. I can't defeat The Destroyer any better than anyone else. You're better off going back to Borg and King Omadon. Maybe they can help you."

"Only someone with your special gifts could combat The Destroyer. Don't you even care about Talisa?"

"Of course I do but I can't save her."

"And I can't do it without you." His voice had grown quiet and solemn. I'd never heard Paralay so forlorn.

My head hurt, my heart hurt. I didn't know what to believe anymore. I had never needed guidance more than I did at that moment. But with both Talos and my father gone I had nowhere to turn. My mentors were no more.

Then, as if she were an angel sent to support me, Raina came to me with the answer.

"I'm sorry to have overheard," she said entering the tent. "But your troubles are my troubles and I want to assist you with solving them."

"How?"

"With the Vision Quest."

Raina explained that a vision quest is a sacred, spiritual journey intended to purify the mind, body, and spirit. Each of the Amazons had gone on their own vision quest when they came of age.

I would have to go out into the wilderness alone without food, water, or clothing and remain there until I could communicate with my guiding spirit.

"Only then will you learn your great personal truth."

"So be it."

Raina kissed me goodbye, Paralay wished me well, and I was on my way. I set out alone as always. It seemed no matter how close I got to anyone I inevitably ended up taking my challenges on by myself. Unfortunately now I didn't know if I could count on myself either.

I made my way deep into the woods naked on all levels. If anything came my way other than this so called "guiding spirit" I'd be in a world of trouble.

I'd had visions before and I always trusted them to guide me in times of need. But an actual spirit guide would be something entirely new. I didn't even know how to channel it.

When I grew tired of walking I staked my claim on a dirty path sitting cross legged on a pile of leaves. Raina hadn't imparted much more than a general description of events. She said that all the Amazons had walked their own path on the vision quest and that each found their guiding spirit in different ways. All I could do now was wait.

My thoughts had overtaken me. I couldn't quiet my mind while images of Talisa, and Paralay, and Raina all swirled through my memory. Everything that I had been and everything that I was now came together.

After a while I slept.

I walked in nothingness searching for something unknown. Soon I was back in the woods amongst the trees. All around me images of my life both prior and present were represented in the branches.

Many of them made me pause to take stock but none more than when I stood before the images of my father. As I looked upon his dark eyes and battle scarred face all around me all the images became nothing but Cain Coleridge.

His life, his legacy, his death. All of it splashed out across the trees in bold color. I became privy to parts of his history that I had only ever heard about through a second-hand source. Now I saw with my own eyes.

One moment in time drew me to it. I saw a young woman in labor. She screamed and strained until finally relief came with the birth of her infant son. Soon I came to recognize the woman as my own mother. She was younger than I remembered but I didn't have many memories of my mother.

The scene shifted before me and I saw a man on horseback watching my mother's home from a distance. He watched the birth and stayed to keep watch as the child grew into a toddler.

Suddenly it all became clear. This child was me in my first years and the man watching from the distance was my father...Cain Coleridge. He had always been there for me even if only from a distance.

Then Cain turned and faced me and somehow I knew this was no dream. I was walking my path. This was my vision quest and my own father was my guide.

"You are of my blood, Costa," he told me. "But you have always been your own man. Wake now and know your truth."

As my head cleared and I slowly came awake within the middle of the forest I remembered with clarity words that brought me renewed strength.

I recognize the difference between the worlds of
fantasy and truth.
I acknowledge that survival is the highest law.
I view death as the destroyer of life.
Therefore I will make the most of life, here and now.
I am the demon hunter.

I found my way back to the Amazon village. There Paralay, Raina, and the rest of the Amazons awaited me. Raina wrapped a bearskin about my shoulders and I drank from a water skin before I gave them all the answer they waited for with baited breath.

"I know who I am now." Then to Paralay I said: "Let's go get Talisa."

Chapter Eight
The Destroyer

We wasted no more time than it took for us to gather supplies and mark a trail towards the Mountain of Power. It seemed like an eternity. I spent the entire time reconciling the man I was with the man I'd become.

It had taken so much of myself to leave behind my former life...all of it down to my childhood and my dreams of having a family with Talisa. The Amazons and Raina had become my new family. I couldn't help feel as though I was abandoning them.

But I couldn't abandon Talisa either.

Even if our time together had ended I still couldn't cower like a mongrel dog and allow her to be tortured and killed by a beast like The Destroyer. No matter what happened between us she deserved better than that and I was going to do my very best to ensure she lived the life she was meant to live.

As I stepped outside my tent I stopped in shock at the sight. The Amazons had rallied. Many of the best soldiers of the village including Shamanee herself had armed themselves and readied to go into battle with me. The sight almost moved me to tears especially when Raina approached.

"Our village is very grateful to you for all you have done for us. It would give us great honor to fight alongside you once more."

I took her hand in mine and I could feel her trembling.

"You don't have to do this," I told her.

"Would you like to know what my spirit guide told me in my vision quest?"

I nodded.

"She said I would meet a great man who would show me and all of my sisters that our indifference to the opposite sex was without merit. He would come into my life for a season, teach me of love and then of loss for his heart belonged to another. Your quest is to return to her. You owe me nothing. It would be my privilege to accompany you."

I held her and kissed her our last kiss then it was time to move.

The dawn rose from dusk as the sun touched the morning sky. We set out upon the forbidden trail where corpses stained the road blood red. The living did not walk here without meeting a horrible fate.

We drew our weapons and moved as swift as we could in order to reach the Mountain of Power before the next sun set. Heat beamed down across my back making the journey even more intolerable. Still we trudged on with determination in our hearts and in our minds.

My inner resolve remained shaky. I felt uncertainty lingering at the back of my mind. Even though I'd accepted my heritage once again, and I knew what I wanted to build for my life, I didn't really know where to begin. For the first time I was lost, very lost.

We had no plan for The Destroyer. It felt good to have my friends at my back but I knew deep down that the battle would be decided one-on-one just as it always had. And sure enough when we reached the entrance to the Mountain of Power my comrades and I got split apart immediately.

A sheet of what looked to be glass or ice blocked the entrance just as I stepped inside locking them all out. No amount of blunt force or pressure caused even a crack no matter how hard we tried.

This fight would be mine alone.

Accepting this I set my palm against the glass with Paralay and Raina each doing the same in turn. In that moment we said our goodbyes and I turned and left them behind. At least I knew they were safe. I had no idea what was in store for me.

The Destroyer awaited.

"Are you afraid to face me?" I called. My voice echoed off the cavern walls deep down into darkness and returned to me.

"It is you who fear me."

The words were not my own. This was The Destroyer and he played a dangerous game, a game of the mind.

"I'm standing here waiting for you," I said.

Just to show him I meant business I removed my crossbow and dagger and threw them to the floor.

"Come claim me. My life for Talisa. If you want the chosen one then take the original."

Soon he appeared before me, the vision from my nightmares. I saw a dark hooded figure in the distance ahead and welcomed the beast with open arms. The Destroyer, an entity of death itself, come to claim my one and only and almost got away with it.

I'd battled all manner of monster, both man and beast. I bested vampire lords and eviscerated a coven of witches. Why I'd walked through hell itself and faced death in the eye on more than one occasion.

To rescue my beloved Talisa I would happily face death one more time. There would be no more running. I wasn't a runner. I'm a hunter…the demon hunter.

This battle could prove to be my last but if Talisa made it out safely that's all that mattered.

"Come Destroyer," I called. "Come face me."

"You couldn't just stay away like a good little boy," the Destroyer mocked me from behind its shroud of death.

"Nothing in this world could keep me from my wife…now where is she?"

"Where I've always been, right in front of you."

With those chilling words The Destroyer pulled back the dark hood to reveal my beautiful Talisa, only she wasn't beautiful any longer. Her illuminating blue-green eyes had been replaced by pupils of blood red. Sharp fangs pulled down from her teeth and long nails stretched from her fingers.

"Talisa…no."

"You should've left me, Costa," she told me. "I did everything I could to make you forget about me. I even tricked Paralay into making up that lie about your father. But still you came…why?"

I shook my head. "Do you really have to ask? I love you! I meant it when I said nothing could keep me from you."

She gave me a laugh shrill enough to make me cover my ears.

"It's too late, I'm already turning."

"Let me help you," I said moving closer.

Talisa put up her hand to warn me off. "I don't want to kill you, Costa, but by the gods if you come any closer…"

"I won't lose you like this, Talisa," I pleaded.

"Then you shouldn't have left me with LeCarde so many moons ago. I still remember the pinch of his teeth passing into my flesh. My body growing colder as he drank from me."

"But we killed him, he can't hurt you anymore."

The warmth of tears filled my eyes as I remembered hearing Talisa's screams as LeCarde bit her. I'd tried to reach her in time but it was too late. He'd already put his mark on her beautiful cinnamon skin.

"Then your brother fed me from him," Talisa said then. "Remember that? His vampire blood has run in my veins since that time. The only way I've been able to keep it under control was with medicine from my father. A powerful magic elixir that kept the vampire urgings at bay. But I can't take that anymore."

"That has to be the answer. We can get help from the other mages and learn how to make more of it."

My claim was a bold one. Her father, Talos, had been a powerful practitioner of magic. None could match the strength of his power. But we had to try. I couldn't just give up Talisa to the dark side.

"You're not listening," she said. "It will endanger our baby if I keep taking it."

My knees buckled beneath me as I was overcome with a mix of emotion. So long Talisa and I wanted a family. Now here it was, all our hopes and dreams, tainted by a vampire curse. I was in danger of losing everything. My visions, the taking of the first born, it was all the specter of death haunting me. If Talisa kept taking the medicine we could lose the baby. But if she didn't, would the child be normal or would it turn to a creature of the night the way my wife was turning before my very eyes. Now more than ever I needed to save Talisa. She could not succumb to this. I would not let my family die.

"I know you, Talisa," I said. "I know you could never feed on another human. That's why you ran away. But you don't have to run anymore. There's no need to worry. You're not a full vampire as long as you resist your urge to feed on human flesh."

Something in my statement brought a smile to her lips. She lapped her tongue up over her teeth and said: "I can't resist anymore."

Then she leapt upon me. I'd faced many vampires in my days as demon hunter. Talisa's maker, Lord LeCarde had been my most formidable opponent...until now. Talisa was unrelenting in her attack. She clawed at my face and snapped her teeth at my neck as I tried my best to hold her off.

She was my wife, my love, I could not bring myself to hurt her. And if I dared there was my unborn child to think of. Harming Talisa harmed the baby. With my options limited I did the only thing that I could and offered my neck to her.

"Do it," I said. "I won't live without you."

Her teeth came inches from my jugular and then she halted. Howling in pain as she clutched at her belly, she fell off of me.

"The baby!" she shrieked.

My child had saved me but now I needed to save him and his mother. I rushed to Talisa's side and she took a swipe at me with her long nails, catching me across the arm. With fresh blood to entice her, Talisa came at me again.

This time I slipped in behind her and captured her arms behind her back. Using a strength I'd never known her to have before she ran me backwards into the wall of the cave not once, but twice. On the second run my head caught a sharp blow and I lost my grip on her.

Talisa turned and clawed at my face over and over again until I fell to my knees and covered up in defense. Undaunted she continued to pummel me. I waited for my opening and took her down from the legs.

As she hit the ground I mounted atop her and pinned her arms to the ground. She thrashed and bucked with wild abandon in an effort to dislodge me. We struggled for a time but her strength overpowered my own and she pitched me overhead.

My body took a jolt as I landed, knocking the wind out of me. As I recovered I found Talisa standing over me, teeth bared and ready to commit me to death. As she bent down towards me she winced in pain. She clutched at her stomach as though trying to claw the baby out of her.

"It's coming," she gasped.

For a moment I saw the light of life return to her eyes and I knew this would be my only chance.

"Talisa, you have to let me help your deliver our child."

I felt a rush of relief as she nodded approval. The pain proved too much for her and she collapsed against the wall. I took her gnarled hand in mine and for a moment she tried to pull me in to finish me off. But I steadied myself and she finally accepted my help.

"Breathe through it," I told her.

"No," she said, tears streaming down her face. "I don't want this child. What if it's evil…like me?"

"You're the most precious, caring person I've ever known," I told her. "And you're strong, Talisa. You can fight off the vampire blood infecting you."

I kissed her forehead and dried her tears. She looked up at me and her eyes slowly started to return to their normal state, the fangs withdrew and as she focused more and more on our baby, Talisa came back to me.

The birth was arduous. A trial for each of us as Talisa fought back and forth with her inner demons. I remained steadfast even as the blood ran down my face and congealed in my arm.

Soon we had a beautiful little girl. I took her and wrapped her in my cloak then returned to Talisa to hand her our little miracle.

"No," she said. "I can't take her."

"It's alright," I told her. "She's just fine. In fact she's beautiful like her mother."

"I can't her…not yet. The other one is coming!"

"Other one?" I asked gently setting our daughter down and tending to the birth of what turned out to be our son.

Twins. A boy and a girl. The next in the demon hunter line. Conceived of love it was that same love that saved their mother and ultimately me.

Talisa successfully warded off the vampire change. Though not permanent by any means it still was enough for us to sit in the moment in peace. Each of us held a swaddling babe in our arms.

Our moment of bliss was short-lived. Footsteps, loud and moving with urgent intention, came towards us. In the chaos of my fight with Talisa I'd lost track of my weapons.

Handing our baby boy to Talisa, I stood ready to fight with my bare hands in order to defend my family. Fortune shined on us in that hour as friends, not enemies, approached.

Despite my wishes to the contrary, Raina and Paralay found their way past the glass wall and came to aide me in my battle.

"We heard horrible screaming," Paralay said.

"It's alright," I reassured them. "Everything is fine now."

As they saw the babies both stone-faced warriors melted. Raina dropped to her knees and began cooing and cuddling the little ones while Paralay kept patting my back in congratulations.

"So that's it then?" he asked. "It's over."

I looked down at Talisa. Her eyes had cleared, her fangs gone, but both of us knew it wasn't truly over. The vampire inside slept now. In order to keep it at bay we would need to stay vigilant. Now that the babies had been born Talos' magic elixir would be our salvation.

It wasn't long after that day that I decided my life as the demon hunter needed to end. I would not raise my children with the threat of violence all around them. Talisa and I agreed to live a quiet life and raise our children in peace.

My father had tried to shield me from the life but he did it by abandoning me why I needed him the most. I would never leave my children. They would always have me as a protector, a teacher, and a father.

But the hunter was no more.

Until the day the demons came calling then there would be a hero to answer.

Authors note:

The premise of Demon Hunter, though riddled with bloodshed; horrors from Hell; and demonic plagues, is ultimately a story about growth and change. Costa states it himself when confronted by Talos. It's a lesson that corresponds with time as I'm sure it resonates with you too dear reader.

Costa's tale bordered on my own and though I never had to face down demons in the physical sense I had to stand up to the demons that plagued my own sense of self: doubt, fear, anger, depression, isolation, all of which ate away at me for many, many years.

It was a challenge to reach down inside myself and discover the courage, serenity, and wisdom to make the needed changes to repair my soul. But I could not have done it alone.

I'd had role models over the years, nothing really solid and tangible, and I never once asked for help from anyone else with my suffering. I hadn't even realized my own plight until someone on the outside looking in pointed it out to me. And that is when I embraced the fact that I needed help along the way.

My help came from varied sources. I became a student of the game and began to piece together the missing facets of my life to develop my balance.

What it comes down to is developing that sense of spirit within yourself to face the inner demons, whatever they may be, and live a life worthy of who you truly are.

Follow your path. Live your dreams!

- Cyn

Cynthia Vespia, "The Original Cyn," is an author, screenwriter, and freelance journalist. Her creative work is adventure-based, designed to keep pages turning and hearts pounding. Writing mainly supernatural suspense and adventure fantasy, Vespia weaves varied genres into her work that deliver cross-over appeal for readers. She has been nominated for a "Best in Series" award for her trilogy DEMON HUNTER and has won a "Most Artistic Trailer" award for her work on DEMON HUNTER: SEEK & DESTROY. She has also turned her creative energy into ORIGINAL CYN CREATIVE SERVICES, an award-winning copy, design, and video source specializing in promotional media. During her downtime she enjoys getting lost in a good book or movie and keeping active through martial arts and weight lifting.Visit the official website at: www.CynthiaVespia.com

Other book/e-books by Cynthia Vespia:

- Demon Huntress: Destiny Unleashed
- Resurrection
- Lucky Sevens
- Sins and Virtues
- The Crescent
- Theater of Pain

Available through Amazon.com; Barnesandnoble.com; or request through your local bookstores and libraries.

www.ingramcontent.com/pod-product-compliance
Lightning Source LLC
Chambersburg PA
CBHW030820310726
48980CB00006B/573/J

* 9 7 8 0 5 7 8 1 2 8 4 1 2 *